HER *Knight* IN SHINING FOOTBALL PADS

KAITY NORRISS

Published by K and T Press

Page edges by Painted Wings Publishing

Paperback ISBN: 978-1-966907-00-8

To Granny,
thank you for believing in me and for your continual love and support.

CHAPTER 1
KAYLEE

I know this situation is getting dire
But I just want to play with fire
You left me out in the cold
My heart you steamrolled
Who knew you were such a good liar
I'm finally done playing with fire

The new lyrics ring out through the audience, and I soak up their attention. Being on stage gives me a rush like nothing I've ever experienced. The rest of the world fades away and it's just me and the music. The last cord vibrates through the room, and I'm brought back to earth, where our guitarist, James, looks annoyed by the change in the last stanza of "Playing With Fire."

I ignore his indignant look and say to the crowd, "Thank you for coming out! We're Outnumbered by Hysteria and we hope we rocked your night!"

I focus on the cheer of the crowd as the lights dim. It's one of the biggest crowds we've had at Black Circle, the record and coffee shop hybrid we play every couple of months. I'd like to think it means we're starting to have real fans, but know it probably has more to do with the coffee special they have running today. Regardless of why they're here, they seemed to enjoy our music. That's the important part especially since tonight we didn't play any covers, just our originals.

The lights are off of us and the crowd's attention is drawn to the poet set up on the smaller stage on the other side of the room. I soak in the atmosphere for another moment before starting to pack up our equipment. James is focused on his guitar, and I take the opportunity to take a load to the van without his interference.

James is my...well I'm not sure exactly what to call what we were. We were never officially together; he's made that more than clear. Can someone really be your ex if you weren't truly together in the first place? I mean we weren't completely not together either. We have too much history to just be nothing to each other.

I guess now he's like that old song and he's someone that I used to know. Although now, I'm wondering if I actually ever knew the real James. I wouldn't have thought the guitarist who joined our band had it in him to be such a cruel person.

I try to focus on the feelings I get performing and lose myself in the tasks of getting the van loaded up. Connor, our bass guitarist carries our equipment out as I arrange it all so it'll fit. One advantage of being in marching band and on the loading crew is I know how to make everything fit in a space that doesn't look big enough.

"That ought to be all of it, but you should take another look around the stage to make sure Sara didn't miss anything," Connor says after helping me lift the last load into the back.

Sara is our band's drummer and my younger sister. I head inside to make a final lap before we head out. Sara's nowhere to be found when I get back inside, but I'll worry about that after I'm sure we're ready to go. Knowing her she could've found a record or a cute boy she's interested in. Either way it can wait until I'm sure the stage is clear.

The front of the stage is clear of our stuff. I step backstage and am immediately engulfed in James's presence.

He towers over me and leans into my space. "It's cute how you think changing some song lyrics is going to convince me you're done with things between us."

The last stanza of "Playing With Fire" was supposed to repeat:

It felt like sweet bliss
I burned up with your kiss
I know this situation is getting dire
But I just want to play with fire

However, I think my new lyrics end the song much better. And if playing with fire is synonymous with whatever it is James and I have been doing, then I'm definitely done with it.

James flicks his platinum-blond hair before leaning in and whispering in my ear. "You've said you're done before, but you always end up crawling back to me. Maybe you shouldn't try so hard to convince me you mean it, when you don't even believe it."

His words send shivers down my spine in a way that isn't entirely unpleasant. I mentally scold myself. I'm not falling back under his spell. He doesn't care about me, and I need to remember that.

It wasn't so bad in the beginning, we'd occasionally make out after band practice and he'd send me flirty texts. He was there for me when things started to get strained with my parents. At the time I thought that'd be a turning point in our relationship. I was right, but it didn't go the direction I'd hoped. James was colder when we weren't together and not even always that nice when we were together.

This last time together was different, though. He had made it sound like he was going to actually commit, so I took him back and let him burrow into my heart. Then he shredded it like he always did, except this was way worse. This time I'm entirely done with the back and forth.

I take a step away from James to help clear my head. "You've made it clear there's nothing for me to come back to. We're just bandmates now, nothing else. Don't bother texting me unless it's about the band. I won't be answering otherwise."

"We'll see about that." James grabs my wrist before I can get too far away from him. "Act like you aren't completely hung up on me if you want. It'll just make it that much sweeter when you come begging for scraps of attention." James walks off leaving me flustered.

Even when I'm standing my ground it feels like he still wins which is so unfair.

Sara startles me with her presence. "I thought y'all were currently in your off-again phase?"

"We aren't off again; we're done for good. I deserve to be treated better and I'm not putting up with James's nonsense anymore." I hate that I sound so unsure. I want to be done with him, but he still has the broken pieces of my heart he stole.

"You always say y'all are done for good. It hasn't been true yet." Sara rolls her eyes.

"This time is different." I ignore Sara's look of disbelief. It is different even if I won't tell her why.

"Whatever you say. Are you ready to head out?"

"More than ready." We head out the backstage door and almost walk into a couple making out in the hallway. I'm not even surprised to see that it's James and some random girl. He seems to always have someone willing to kiss him wherever we go.

Refusing to let him get to me, I roll my eyes and step around them. Grabbing a hold of Sara as I go so she doesn't decide to make a scene. I love that her instinct would be to stand up for me, but the last thing I want to do is feed James's ego.

Dave, one of the baristas, catches us right before we make it back outside. "Hey, you have a fan asking if they can meet you."

Ugh. It's probably just another groupie hoping for some of the attention James has no issue with spreading around. I don't have the time or energy to deal with that.

"I'm sure James would be happy to meet her when he's done with his current groupie. I have no desire to be the middleman for that." I'm already stepping around Dave when he halts me with a gentle touch to my arm.

"It's a he and he specifically asked for *you*. I can tell him you're already gone if you want, but he seems genuinely interested in your music. He's got on an Our Last Night shirt and doesn't give off any creeper vibes. Not that I'd leave y'all alone with him or anything, but he appears to be a stand-up guy."

"A good guy with good taste in music. Seems like just what you need to make this break from you-know-who stick," Sara says from next to me.

Am I mildly intrigued by who this guy is? Absolutely. Am I in the mood to talk to people right now? Absolutely not. I may be interested in meeting a fellow Our Last Night fan that likes our music but not tonight. Our Last Night is my favorite band and Outnumbered by Hysteria started as an Our Last Night cover band. However, none of that is a good enough reason for me to interact with some guy I don't know when I'm already not in a good mood.

"I don't need or want another guy in my life," I say to Sara, trying to communicate with my eyes that she needs to drop the topic especially with James just up the hallway from us.

I turn back to Dave. "Tell him he missed us and to try again at our next gig. Our card with all our social media stuff on it should be at the counter."

Dave nods. "Have a good night."

We step around him and head to the van. I'm more than ready to get out of here and get away from everyone else.

CHAPTER 2
OLIVER

"Sorry man. You just missed them." The barista returns from backstage. "Maybe try at their next gig." He grabs a card from behind the counter. "I don't know when that is, but this has all their social media info. They post their performances there."

I nod, taking the card he offers to be polite. I don't need it; I already follow them everywhere I can. I head out to my SUV feeling disappointed. I didn't want a card of information I already have; I wanted a chance to talk to Kaylee. I figured talking to her at a gig would give me the best chance of showing her that we have things in common.

I don't want to wait for their next gig. They're taking a break due to marching season. That's part of why I wanted to talk to her tonight. I made myself get up the nerve because it could be my last chance for a while. Not that it matters now. It clearly took me too long to gather my courage.

I drive home wishing I had the confidence that radiates off of Kaylee on stage. Maybe then she'd notice me like I can't stop noticing her.

At the Fourth of July Celebration festival this past summer, my friends had paired off, so I wandered around by myself. I was near one of the smaller stages when a new band came on stage.

The lead singer had shoulder-length purple hair and wore a hot-pink crop top, black leather skirt, and black combat boots. She announced their band as Outnumbered by Hysteria. Then they started playing a cover of Our Last Night's "Losing Sleep".

I grew up listening to Our Last Night and they're one of my favorite bands. I walked to the front of the crowd and sang along.

That close, I could see she had blue eyes and wore bright red lipstick. She looked and sang like a rock goddess and made me want to believe in love at first sight.

I stood at the front watching the entire set. They played a few more covers and some original music. Afterwards I tried to find her but couldn't.

The next day, I found their band on Instagram. The lead singer was Kaylee Cobb, and she went to our school. Two-a-days (our summer conditioning for fall sports) started a few weeks later. We had to be at the school super early every morning to run and lift weights and then practiced plays in the evening.

I was going to try to talk to her since she was up at the school for marching band. I came up behind her while she talked with another girl in band. The girl said something about boys in football pants.

Kaylee shrugged and said, "Guys who can play music are better. No one can serenade you with a football."

I retreated and came up with a plan to woo her. So far, I've not succeeded in trying to talk to her much less woo her.

I've tried multiple times, but she doesn't notice me, and I'm not as outgoing as the rest of my friends. We have three classes together. In trying to talk to her, I've inadvertently memorized the rest of her schedule and might be toeing the line when it comes to stalking.

I've listened to all of Outnumbered by Hysteria's songs enough to know all the words. I'm planning on asking her to Homecoming but am running out of time.

When I get home my house is quiet. My parents went out to a work dinner and Grayson, my brother, must still be at Lynn's house. Lynn lives across the street from us. Her mom was our nanny, and we practically grew up at her house with Lynn's next-door neighbor, Daniel.

I consider heading over there and hanging out with everyone but rule it out. I'm not in the mood to talk about tonight, and someone's bound to ask me where I've been. I haven't told anyone about Kaylee yet, and tonight is not the night for that conversation. Besides, I'm exhausted, so I just head to bed.

"Dude, did you manage to fall asleep eating?" Tristan's voice pulls me out of my daze. Tristan has been my best friend since he moved here in sixth grade.

I shake my head and take another bite of food. I didn't fall asleep, but I am pretty tired. I spent half the night anxious about trying to talk to Kaylee this week. If I'm going to ask her to Homecoming, I need to get on it since the dance is this coming Saturday.

"Yeah, what's up with you? You were asleep before I got home." Grayson says from across the table. We're eating dinner at Lynn's house before going to our small group for church.

I shrug. I don't feel like trying to explain without telling them about Kaylee.

"Leave Ollie alone, you know he needs his sleep." Lynn elbows my brother.

"You could say he needs a good Knight's rest," Daniel says from her other side.

My friend group is referred to as the Knights. It started with our little dribblers team being the Silver Knights. Grayson and my last name, Ridire, is Irish for knight and Daniel's last name, Caballero, is Spanish for knight. We always used to jokingly call ourselves the Knights, especially since Lynn's family's last name is Kingston. It caught on and became something we got called around school. It spread until that was just how we were known.

Jet Vaughn, who was on our little dribblers team, is also one of the Knights. Tristan rounded out our friend group. We joke that he was always meant to move here and become friends with us because his last name is Knight.

Lynn rolls her eyes at her best friend. "You just think you're so clever, don't you?"

"Well, since you mentioned it, yes, I do."

They continue to joke around, and the topic of my sleepiness is long forgotten.

Theo, Lynn's dad, pops his head into the guest house. "Time to clean up, people should start arriving soon."

We quickly do what he says before dragging the chairs from the kitchen into the living room, so we have enough seating for everyone. For this quarter, Lynn's parents are hosting our small group and that's easier to do out here because all of Lynn's siblings are running around in the main house.

We've got everything set up when Mark Slater arrives. He's our football captain, but more importantly for tonight he's Lynn's boyfriend. He's been coming to church and small group with her for the last couple of weeks that they've been dating. He quickly glances around the room before zeroing in on where Lynn is joking around with Daniel.

Slater walks over to her and pulls her in for a kiss that's a little too long and a little too involved for my comfort, especially since Lynn's family could walk in at any moment. Lynn pulls away first, blushing and looking embarrassed now that most of the attention in the room has gone to their display. She plasters a smile on her face and starts a conversation with Daniel and Mark about the football team.

Mark slings his arm around Lynn in an overly possessive manner and I see her shrink in on herself at the action. Lynn isn't big on PDA, especially with her family near. I want to walk over there and say something, but I know Lynn would get mad at me. She's told us many times to stay out of her relationships and that she can take care of herself. I know she can handle it. It just bothers me to see a guy clearly making a girl uncomfortable.

The other Knights seem to be on edge as well and I can feel the tension in the room that doesn't quite dissipate with Lynn's attempts to lighten the mood.

Soon the rest of our small group arrives, and the atmosphere is lighter. Theo teaches a short lesson about gossip followed by a discussion. Most people weigh in and the conversation flows until the hour is up. Theo closes us out in prayer.

"Who's up for a game of Knockout?" Jet asks, already having a basketball in his hand. I have no idea where he's been hiding that this whole time, but he lives and breathes basketball so it's not surprising.

Most of the guys agree and head to the basketball goal outside. Daniel and I hang back to put the chairs back where they go. Lynn talks to Mark briefly before helping us. Mark just hovers waiting for us to be finished.

"See y'all tomorrow," Lynn says as we walk outside.

"You're not staying to play?" Daniel asks, nodding to the court.

Mark pulls Lynn into him as he cuts off whatever Lynn was about to say. "We've got plans."

"Um, yeah." Lynn tucks some hair behind her ear. "So, see you later." Lynn and Mark walk off toward his car.

It's weird that Lynn isn't playing basketball when that's her favorite pastime, but it's even weirder that she's leaving her house when there's other people here.

I look to Daniel since he knows Lynn best. "Should we do something?"

"Lynn's a big girl. She'll be fine for tonight. I'll find out tomorrow what's going on."

I don't know what else to say, but I have a bad feeling about whatever is going on with Mark.

"Don't worry about it," Daniel says when I glance back in the direction they went. "Let's go play ball. Lynn doesn't need our help. I'll check in on her when she's back to make sure everything is okay, but there's nothing for us to do right now."

I nod and follow him to the court.

CHAPTER 3
KAYLEE

"Kaylee! Get up!" Sara barges into my room rudely waking me up from the precious sleep I was finally able to get. "We need to get a move on or we're going to be late for band." She yanks the covers off of me increasing my irritation.

"I'm up," I say, swinging my feet off the bed and sitting up. "Go finish getting ready and I'll meet you downstairs."

"Okay, just hurry." Sara, thankfully, storms back out of my room.

I take a quick shower trying not to think about why I was up half the night. Once I'm dressed, I check my phone to see how much time I have left. Unfortunately, that just reminds me of the text I got last night. James texted saying he needed to move practice this Thursday to Tuesday because he has a date on Thursday. As in a real date where both parties are calling it a date.

I can easily tell you how many dates James and I have been on in the two years we've been on-again and off-again: zero. We make-out, he says he doesn't want a relationship and pulls away. I go on a date with someone else, and he throws a tantrum. He apologizes and is super flirty, and the cycle starts over again. It may fuel our song-writing, but I know it's unhealthy.

So when he wanted to hangout Saturday before our gig, which was his way of saying make-out, I told him no because we were over.

Yesterday he texted me and Connor saying we needed to reschedule band practice for his big date.

It's nothing new for him to flaunt other girls in front of me. But he's never dated any of them. Him actually committing to a date with some other girl, when we've never been on one, hurts even more than the numerous times I've seen him stick his tongue down some other chick's throat.

I try to shake those thoughts away as I hurry through applying my makeup. I'm running late enough that I should probably just skip it, but my eyes are puffy from crying last night and I look like crap. The last thing I want is for anyone to know something's wrong with me. I make a perfect smokey eye look complete with bold red lipstick. I grab my leather half-jacket before running downstairs. My makeup feels like warpaint and the jacket is my shield to help me get through today. Hopefully I can make it through without anyone seeing the cracks in my armor.

Sara's waiting by the front door for me. "Finally, let's go."

We load up in my van and I'm pulling out of the driveway before Sara even has her seatbelt clicked into place.

"Why'd you oversleep? We're never this late," Sara says, after she gets buckled in.

"I didn't sleep well last night. It's nothing to be concerned about. I'm sorry we're running behind." I really don't want to talk about it, and especially not with my younger sister.

"What's wrong? Mom didn't even go out last night."

Sara sees more than I want her to about what happens in our house, knowing I stay up until everyone is asleep. It keeps me from potentially being woken up in the middle of the night if something happens because of my parents' poor decisions. But Sara knows that wasn't an issue last night since our mother was passed out in her room well before we even thought about going to sleep.

"I had an idea for a song. I wanted to write it all down on paper so I wouldn't lose it." It's not a lie per say. I did write a song last night, an outpouring of all the emotions I was feeling. But writing it was more to soothe myself and put a stop to the tears. If anything, songwriting was what made it possible to go to sleep when I did, instead of something that kept me awake.

Sara seems to take my reason at face value and starts filling me in on freshman gossip I couldn't care less about. I try to be a good big sister and follow along as she tells me about who's dating who and what friends aren't speaking to each other anymore.

It seems like a waste of time, keeping up with other people's lives. But it makes Sara happy, and she has so few things at home that do these days. I would never want to take away her happiness.

I throw the van in park at school and we both jump out, hurrying to get inside. At least today starts off with watching Friday night's performance so we just need to be in the band hall on time instead of on the practice field with our instruments.

Mr. Gregory, the band director, is getting the TV set up as we breeze through the door. He gives us his trademark unimpressed look before glancing at his watch. I ignore it, since there's nothing I can do about the time anyhow, and head to my cubby to get my trombone. I grab the three pieces out of my case and sit next to our section leader and my best friend, Drew.

"You're late again," Drew says. "If you keep this up we're going to be stuck staying after Monday night practice running laps to make up for Mr. Gregory's time you're wasting."

Drew and I have been friends since we met in band class in junior high. He's usually soft-spoken, so getting on to me is abnormal for him. I'm guessing that means Mr. Gregory has already talked to him about my struggles with punctuality.

"I'm sorry," I say. "I overslept. I'll set more alarms for tomorrow, so it isn't a problem again."

Drew takes in my appearance and must see something on my face because his disapproval softens. "Okay. Just be on time tomorrow."

I nod as Mr. Gregory turns the light off to start the video. I assemble my horn quietly while we watch the video from Friday. Mr. Gregory pauses frequently, pointing out areas of the marching show we need to work on.

I'm glad to be focused on band and know school should keep me distracted enough I won't have time to think about James, much less get upset about it again.

CHAPTER 4
LYNN

"Lynn Kingston!" shrieks a voice I'd love to avoid.

Great, just what I need. I'm already running late.

My first period is a free period. Usually, I sleep in or work on homework, but after the whole debacle with Mark Slater the night before, I was antsy.

He said, "I love you" and I said, "No, that's not possible." He told me he loved me after dating for only two weeks.

Two weeks!

I was taken off guard and spoke before my brain had time to connect to my mouth.

He pushed the issue, and I broke up with him. He confessed his love, and I *broke up* with him. I wasn't even planning to break up with him, it just sort of happened.

With the impending awkwardness of today looming over me, I was at school before seven and ran drills for the last couple of hours. I should've been able to shower and change before second period, but after hearing the announcements, I might have shot hoops longer than I should have. When I no longer felt antsy, I barely had time to take a quick shower and run across the school to second period.

"Whitney, I don't have time for whatever this is. I need to get to class." I turn to face the cheer captain who seems to be the bane of my existence these last few weeks. Blonde, blue-eyed and completely annoying, Whitney is the last person I want to see right now.

"You stole my boyfriend and my crown! I don't care about your class. It was bad enough that you took Mark from me, he should have been mine. I don't even understand why he'd want you. You look like a drowned rat. But now you've taken my crown for Homecoming, too!" Whitney screeches.

I learned from our last few exchanges that ignoring her only made her worse and I definitely didn't have time for that level of a hissy fit. Mark's the quarterback and senior captain of the football team. Whitney didn't take it well when he decided to ask someone to be his girlfriend and it wasn't her. Me being a junior and a tomboy added even more insult to injury. I might be one of the most popular juniors, but I'm still a junior and therefore, in her head, beneath her.

She isn't exactly wrong about the drowned-rat comment. I barely had time to shower, which meant no time to do anything with my hair as I rushed out of the locker room. At least it's pajama day, so I have an excuse to dress like a slob. Not that I need one.

"I didn't steal anything from you. You and Mark were never together, and he asked me out. Homecoming Court is voted on by the students. Maybe no one voted for you because you're a raging hag. Besides, I was voted Junior Princess not a Homecoming Queen nominee. In no way did I steal your crown. Plus, Mark and I aren't together anymore, so maybe instead of yelling at me you can go bug him and see if he wants to date you." Her eyes light up and her anger fades at my last statement.

"He broke up with you? He must've realized we'd be so much better together." Whitney turns to go back to whatever witch trial she escaped from.

I might've been the one to break up with Mark, and I know Mark wants nothing to do with her, but I'm definitely done dealing with her brand of crazy. It's bad enough that I'll have to deal with the rest of the cheerleaders for all of the Homecoming nonsense for the rest of the week. I start back toward my class as the late bell rings.

I definitely didn't try to steal her crown. Not only did I not have a say in who the senior class nominated, but I didn't even care, anyway.

Being Junior Homecoming Princess isn't exactly the crowning achievement for me that Whitney seems to think it is.

It means more obligations this week on top of my already packed schedule. Not only with the actual Homecoming activities, but because I'm sure I'll now have to go dress shopping *again*. It's more responsibilities to juggle and more people not to let down. Also, Mark was nominated for Homecoming King, and I don't exactly relish the thought of having to spend a lot of time with *him* this week.

On the upside, the Junior Homecoming Prince is Grayson. He's the first-string wide receiver and one of my closest friends. Getting to have him by my side ought to make the entire Homecoming Court nonsense bearable. Colten, my younger brother, is nominated as Freshman Homecoming Prince, but he doesn't like for me to acknowledge him at school.

I finally make it to Mrs. Green's class and catch the door as it's closing behind someone else.

"Miss Kingston, Mister Prince, how nice of you to join us. Since you're both late, you can be partnered together for this project," Mrs. Green says.

One look at the room told me that in the few minutes I was late, everyone else had already been paired up. I catch Xander's eyes as he shakes his head. Which tells me there's no use fighting it and Xander probably already tried to argue the decision.

Xander's my twin and only friend in AP English. He's shorter than me at five feet, eight inches, and has blue eyes and brown hair. We don't have much in common, but since our parents insist on us taking all advanced classes, we've always had mostly the same schedule since sixth grade and we always partner together for projects. Living in the same house makes it easier to coordinate the work outside of school. That won't work for this project, though.

Being on the basketball varsity team since freshman year and being close friends with the best-looking and most-athletic guys in our school may make me fairly popular with most of the students at Carson Valley High, but the other kids in my advanced classes have never talked to me.

I walk to Mrs. Green's desk to get the packet she's holding out for us before sitting at one of the two empty desks. As Mrs. Green talks at the front about our project, I read over the packet she gave me.

This project will be thirty percent of our grade and we'll be working on it for the rest of this semester. We're supposed to choose a classic novel or play from the list Mrs. Green gave us, read through it, and watch its movie adaptation. Then we need to write a five-page paper on the differences between the book and the movie, discuss how well the story has aged and whether it's still relevant in our modern day, do a presentation to the class about what'd be different if a similar story took place now, and have some sort of visual aid—either a PowerPoint, diorama, or trifold.

This seems like it'll be a lot of work. The packet includes a grading rubric, which states that twenty percent of the total grade will be based on the presentation being original and creative.

Not only will I be partnered with someone other than Xander, but it'll be a long and in-depth project. First, I'm voted Homecoming Princess, then the run-in with Whitney, and now this. I hope my morning won't keep with this trend of less-than-stellar news.

Mrs. Green finishes her spiel at the front of the classroom then gives us the rest of the class to get started on our project. I turn to look at who my partner is.

Mrs. Green said Price, right? That at least gives me something to go on. The boy next to me has his eyes glued to his desk.

When I finally give up on him looking up of his own accord, I speak.

"Hey, I'm Lynn."

He finally turns to look at me.

He has brown hair that hangs over his face, covering one of his eyes. The eye I can see is light brown and still not looking at me. He has black thick-rimmed glasses that look like Harry Potter's but are square instead of round. He's wearing a white shirt, and I can't tell what's supposed to be on it because there's a brown stain all over its front.

He still doesn't say anything.

"I guess first we should figure out what days would work for us to get together to work on our project, then we can decide what we want to do the project over. Sound good?"

He still doesn't respond, but he does finally make eye contact.

He looks like a deer caught in headlights, which might be funny if I didn't need him to participate in this project. Maybe I can do the project by myself and put his name on it? Of course, I'd at least need to know his name for that. Guessing that it's Price probably isn't good enough to put on a project.

"Does that plan sound okay to you?" I repeat.

CHAPTER 5
ANDREW

I'm staring at Lynn like a moron, and the whole "not speaking" thing isn't helping. In my defense, Lynn is gorgeous.

She has long, wavy brown hair that's down today. Her light-brown eyes are hypnotizing, and being this close to her, I can see that there are flecks of gold in them. Her beaming smile is slightly crooked, which is better because it isn't perfect.

I'm not brave enough to even think about looking anywhere other than her face, not that it would have mattered much today since she's wearing plaid pajama pants and a hoodie. Unfortunately, I still know she has a killer body, which is not helping my higher brain function at the moment.

Come on, mouth, say something.

It should be easier to talk to her since we're sitting down and therefore about the same height. However, she's no less intimidating just because our foot height difference isn't a factor right now. Lynn is beautiful, smart, and kind. I've had a crush on her since junior high.

I was bullied in elementary school. On the first day of sixth grade, a boy who bullied me for a few years knocked my books from my arms and shoved me to the ground. Lynn was there and told him to play nice.

She was already taller than all the guys in our grade and she was flanked by four guys who I know now are Grayson, Oliver, Daniel, and

Jet. The bully realized he was outnumbered and walked away. He eventually moved away, and I haven't had an issue with bullies since.

Lynn had helped me up and picked up all my books. She introduced herself while I just stared at her. Then Jet called out to her, and she walked off. I haven't spoken to her since.

Lynn was my knight in shining armor that day. A bit ironic when I found out later that she and her friends were called the Knights. I'm still not exactly sure why. I figure it has something to do with them standing up for kids that get bullied.

It's a title reserved for Lynn Kingston, Daniel Caballero, Jet Vaughn, Grayson Ridire, Oliver Ridire, and Tristan Knight. I used to hope being in Pre-AP and AP classes with her would possibly make her notice me. But she sits next to her brother Xander and the other Knights. Lynn always partners with Xander even if some of the Knights are in the class.

I realize I've been staring at Lynn for way too long without saying anything.

So I say, "I know who you are."

Okay, so definitely not what I would've wanted to say.

Apparently, over five years of crushing on her didn't prepare me for actually trying to talk to her. Lynn blinks at me like she wonders how a dope like me is in AP English. I might be in the running for valedictorian, but my mouth sure isn't supporting that now.

I glance down, hoping breaking eye contact will help connect my mouth to my brain. Instead, I get a reminder of the reason I was late and therefore in this situation. I'd run into some guy on my way out of the band hall and his coffee had gone all over me. Not only do I sound like a dork the first time I talk to Lynn, but I'm also covered in coffee.

"Um, okay. That's cool, I guess. Do you know when you could maybe get together to work on our project?" She sounds like she's worried about spooking me.

I take a deep breath and make myself look back up.

"Oh yeah, sorry. I'm free tomorrow after five and Saturday after about two. Would... would either of those times work for you?" Complete sentences and none of them sounded weird; I count that as a win.

"Both times work for me. Why don't we plan on both, so we can really get a jump on this project? Where do you want to work on it?" Lynn writes in her planner.

"Both is good. We could meet at the public library…?" It's supposed to be a statement but came out as more of a question.

"I was thinking more of meeting at my house or yours. If that's okay? We can meet at my house if that's good with you." As she's speaking, she pulls out a sheet of notebook paper and starts writing on it.

"Uh, yeah. Your…your house is fine," I stutter back. I've never been cool, but I seem to have reached a whole new low while trying to talk with Lynn.

"Cool. So, here's my address and number. After class you can text me, so I'll have yours." She holds out the notebook paper to me.

After a pause, I finally pull my head out and take the paper from her. Lynn keeps talking about the project, and I'm vaguely aware of agreeing with her ideas before she writes them down.

The bell finally rings. I pack up my stuff in record time, hightailing it out of class before I have to endure anymore of my incessant awkwardness.

Kaylee is waiting at my locker for me with a cupcake. She has shoulder-length hair that's currently dyed dark blue, contrasting her constantly amused blue eyes. She's five feet, seven and therefore taller than my five feet, two inches, but she doesn't scare the thoughts away from my mind like a certain basketball player.

I open my locker, switch out my books, then take the cupcake from her. I'm about to open my mouth to say something, well anything other than how my day has been so far, when I get flicked on the ear.

"Ow. What was that for?" I turn to my other best friend, Carter Diez, who has just walked up behind me.

He runs his hand through his messy jet black hair somehow making it more disheveled. He's in band with Kaylee and me, only he plays trumpet. He's five feet, nine, and I feel like a little kid whenever I'm standing between him and Kaylee.

Carter completely ignores my question. Instead, he says, "Have you told Kaylee about all of your dreams coming true in AP English?"

"What? What dreams could possibly come true in English?" Kaylee has a look of horror on her face.

English is her least favorite subject.

Before I can open my mouth, though, Carter's answering for me.

"Our boy here spoke to the girl of his dreams *and* gets to work with her on a project for the rest of the semester. I *even* saw her give him her number."

"Drew, how could you not have led with that? That's so exciting that you're partnered with Lynn! Now she'll notice you, sweep you off your feet, and you can live happily ever after." Kaylee has a wistful look in her eyes.

"You've been watching too many rom-coms. I didn't tell you because Carter beat me to it, and it's not as grand as you guys are making it out to be." I shut my locker

"In case you forgot, being partnered for a project does not change me from being the socially awkward band nerd that I am. Not to mention I have coffee all over my shirt and couldn't get through a single sentence without stuttering awkwardly. After this project she might know who I am, but she'll know me as an awkward loser. Not exactly a step up in my book."

And it's not like I'm constantly down on myself or anything. I have two great friends, and I like who I am. I just know I'm not popular or smooth, and I look nothing like any of the guys Lynn has ever dated. Her type is tall, athletic, and sociable. Basically, the opposite of me; pretending she's remotely in my league is just laughable.

"I got so awkward today I basically zoned out when Mrs. Green gave us the parameters of the project and when Lynn brainstormed ideas for our project. This project is worth thirty percent of our grade, and I've no idea what I'm supposed to do for it or the topic we chose for our project. At this rate she'll think I'm stupid, and I'll knock myself out of the running for valedictorian." I peel the wrapper off my cupcake and try not to beat myself up over my awkwardness.

"Aren't girls supposed to be the ones swept off their feet?" I eat the cupcake hoping to make this conversation more bearable.

"With your current assessment of the situation, it doesn't sound like you'll be *figuratively* sweeping her off her feet anytime soon,"

Carter says. "And to be honest, you weigh, what, ninety pounds soaking wet? I don't see you *physically* sweeping her six feet, two inches of womanly perfection off her feet. I don't see how you march the trombone with your puny arms." He punctuates his statement by pinching my 'puny' arm.

"Look on the bright side: if your first impression was that bad, it can only go up from here," Kaylee says, "Now, will you let me give you the makeover I've been dying to give you since we hit high school?" She starts to walk down the hall.

"Again, way too many rom-coms. I'm not letting you give me a makeover. I don't even want to know what thoughts that would conjure in your twisted head. Why are you casting me as the lead female in your rom-com scenes?" I ask.

"You ought to just give in with the whole makeover thing and get it over with," Carter answers for Kaylee. "You know she won't give up until you agree. You'd be better off trying to rein in her ideas than to stop them altogether. And hate to break it to you, but if we're casting you in a rom-com and you're one of the leads, you're way more female lead than male lead."

I pinch the bridge of my nose and groan, wishing I was *anywhere* else. "It's way too early for all of this, and I'm already having a bad day. Can we focus on being on time to Pre-Cal?"

"If you prefer calculus to this conversation, then I guess we can drop it." I almost feel relieved that Kaylee is letting it go before she adds, "For now."

CHAPTER 6
OLIVER

After second period, Lynn texted the group chat saying her mom made lasagna. It meant something was up, and I'd need to cancel my plans. I type out a quick text to Noah to let him know I couldn't come to my guitar lesson.

The Knights and I don't always go off campus together during lunch, but when we do, we go to a restaurant or fast-food place. Lynn says she doesn't want to inconvenience her mom, and that way guys from the team or the girls the other guys are hanging out with can come too. I usually only go with them on Fridays, telling them I'm busy if they ask any other day.

Tristan keeps asking if I have a secret girlfriend. In reality, I hired Noah Clark to teach me to play guitar, specifically on how to play "White Tiger" by Our Last Night.

I'm hoping to get up the courage to play for Kaylee someday, but I'm not sure that's ever going to happen.

In the hallway, I see her heading in my direction with two of her guy friends. I walk quickly to intercept them, determined to finally talk to her. They stop in front of me.

I've never been this close to Kaylee before. Her hair's dyed blue now, which brings out her eyes. She's stunning.

"Can we help you?" It sounds like she means "what's wrong with you?"

"Hey, I'm Oliver." I give a wave that I immediately regret.

"Okay. I'm Kaylee. Do you need something?"

"No?"

"Well, we need to get to class." Kaylee and her friends step around me.

"Bye." I turn and watch her walk away. I finally get my act together and head towards Pre-Cal.

Daniel Caballero comes up next to me.

"Hey." I nod at him, hoping he didn't witness what just happened.

"Hey. You want to tell me what that was all about?" Daniel gestures to where Kaylee walked away.

So much for hoping.

"What…what was all about?" I ask innocently while increasing my pace. Maybe we can get to class before he can figure out exactly what happened.

"Your awkward conversation with the Queen of Punk." Or he already knows what happened. *Great.*

"I was being friendly…?"

"I might believe that if you were your friendly, outgoing brother, but you don't even talk to the guys on the team if you don't have to."

I shrug. "Maybe I'm trying to be more social."

"I'm not buying that, but if you don't want to talk about it, I won't make you."

"Are you ready for our Pre-Cal test today?" I say, diverting his attention. Daniel shudders at the reminder and the subject of Kaylee is dropped. *Whew.*

I haven't talked to any of the guys about Kaylee yet. In part because they don't have committed relationships. I'm the only one who has even had serious girlfriends. The rest of the Knights do good to have a relationship that lasts for a few weeks. Whereas mine last for a few months at least. A couple of them have even made it past the year mark.

The other girls I've dated either played sports or were on the cheer or drill teams. Meaning, they hung out in the same crowd as us and I'd talked to them before developing feelings for them. We had some common ground and topics I knew I could bring up safely.

The only thing I know Kaylee and I have in common is a love for Our Last Night. I don't know how to bring that up without sounding like a creeper. I'm not great at talking to new people to begin with.

For the most part with the girlfriends I've had in the past, the girl made the first move, so trying to initiate something with a girl I'm not even friends with is *way* out of my comfort zone.

The other reason I haven't mentioned Kaylee to anyone is because I know they'll tease me about it. Especially if they find out I learned guitar to impress someone I've barely even talked to. I mean, it took me over two months to speak to her, and our exchange in the hallway wasn't exactly a conversation. I do feel like it's progress, though.

After we turn in our test, we're allowed to have our phone back and sit at the tables in the back of the classroom. Mrs. Barnes, our Pre-Cal teacher, is quite relaxed on the whole no-phones-in-class rule.

Kaylee is already finished and sitting with her friend while writing furiously in her notebook. I sit next to Lynn at the table she and Xander have claimed. They're both wrapped up in working on another assignment.

I text Tristan Knight hoping he can help with the whole Kaylee debacle. He's my best friend so if I'm going to talk to someone, I'd rather it be him.

O. Ridire: I've been learning guitar during lunch breaks

Knight: Why?

O. Ridire: To impress a girl

Knight: Who?

Knight: Any luck?

O. Ridire: Kaylee Cobb

O. Ridire: I'll tell you more about her later

O. Ridire: Haven't talked to her yet

O. Ridire: I need help

Knight: You learned guitar for her and haven't even talked to her?

O. Ridire: I know

O. Ridire: I did say hi to her today

Knight: You've been learning guitar for at least the last 3 weeks of school

O. Ridire: I know

O. Ridire: Why do you think I'm asking for help

Knight: Does anyone else know?

O. Ridire: Caballero saw me talk to her but doesn't know anything yet

Knight: Are you telling anyone else?

O. Ridire: Until now I wasn't planning on telling you

O. Ridire: And Caballero just kind of found out

Knight: I won't bring it up at lunch then

Daniel finishes his test and comes to sit with me at the table in the back of the class.

Caballero: Queen of Punk?

When I look at him, he nods at my phone.

O. Ridire: Knight

Caballero: Bo-ring

Daniel rolls his eyes when I look up.

Caballero: About the Queen of Punk?

O. Ridire: Nonya

O. Ridire: Her name is Kaylee. She's in class with us, you have to know her actual name

Caballero: Wanna talk about it?

O. Ridire: Not really

Caballero: Why do you think Lynn's mom is making lunch?

O. Ridire: If I had to guess...

O. Ridire: Lynn broke up with Slater

Caballero: Good guess

Caballero: She hasn't said anything yet

O. Ridire: Maybe something else

Daniel shrugs his shoulders.

O. Ridire: With Frost we just got a text

Ethan Frost is one of our offensive linemen. Lynn dated him during two-a-days. They broke up the weekend before school started. He appeared to move on at the back-to-school bash. A week later Lynn and Mark were together.

Caballero: I hope it isn't HOCO

O. Ridire: Why would it be?

O. Ridire: Her and Grayson are the only ones on the Court

Daniel shrugs and sends me a finger-crossed emoji. The bell rings and we head to Physics together. Tristan joins us in the hallway. He's smirking and looks up to no good. Thankfully, Lynn takes off as soon as the bell rings and Grayson and Jet head the other way to go to their next class.

"Don't. We aren't talking about it. Especially not here," I say to

Tristan before he can start.

"Okay. I'll behave and won't ask about your guitar lessons. Any idea why we're having lunch at Lynn's?" Tristan's body is practically vibrating with energy.

"No idea," I say at the same time Daniel asks, "Guitar lessons?"

"I already said we aren't talking about this," I insist.

"Hold up, you're learning guitar for the Queen of Punk?" Daniel puts together what Tristan's inferring and stops in the middle of the hallway.

"Why do you keep calling her that?" I ignore his question but stop with him.

"Because it fits and no one else knows who I'm talking about. More importantly, you're learning guitar?" Daniel asks.

"Not talking about it," I say to Daniel, then turn to Tristan. "No idea. If she wanted us to know ahead of time, she'd have put it in the text." Translation: there isn't a way to get the information out of Lynn.

"So, what you're saying is we can't talk about the Queen of Punk and there's no point in trying to figure out what's going on with lunch?" Tristan asks as we start back toward our next class.

"There has to be a hundred other topics to discuss. How are things with your new neighbor?" I ask.

"I'm pretty sure the perfect princess has a stick so far up her butt, it'll never see the light of day again. But that's no different than things have been all summer. I'd rather talk about the Queen of Punk." Tristan wiggles his eyebrows.

"I'd rather listen to you complain for hours about your neighbor's distaste of basketball. Are you joining in on the Queen of Punk nonsense as well?" I ask.

"I don't know who she is, so it seems as good a name as any. If you'd prefer, I could yell her name up and down the hallway until someone answers." Tristan cups his hands around his mouth like he's going to do just that.

I knock them away from his face and mutter, "Why am I friends with you?"

"Because we make your life interesting." Tristan walks into his next class.

"You couldn't get rid of us if you tried." Thankfully, Daniel lets the subject drop on the way to Physics.

CHAPTER 7
KAYLEE

I spend the time after our test in Pre-Cal coming up with a plan to help Drew get the girl. Drew is the sweetest guy I've ever met. He deserves to be happy, and he's been head-over-heels for Lynn since I've known him. It was love at first sight, and I'm determined to get Lynn to really *see* him. Hopefully, when she realizes there's a smart, caring, adorable guy that's in love with her, she'll grab him up and they can live happily ever after.

I ignore most of my text messages, there's no reason to pay attention to the messages I'm getting from Connor or James, opening a new text to Carter instead to enlist his help in making sure we get Drew in the van after fourth period. I'm planning a mall excursion that Drew won't be on board with. I don't want him running away from his first real chance with Lynn.

It couldn't be more perfect. Lynn is newly single, and they're partnered up together for a semester-long project. That should be plenty of time for them to spend together and get Lynn to fall in love with him.

I stay right next to Drew as we leave Physics. Carter is waiting at the door for us. Once we're in the hallway, we each latch onto one of Drew's arms and lead him toward the parking lot.

"Why do I have the feeling we aren't just going off campus for lunch and that I won't like where we're going?" Drew begrudgingly gets into the passenger seat of my van.

Carter makes sure Drew gets his seatbelt on and can't go anywhere while I climb into the driver's seat.

"We're going to the mall," I say to Drew as soon as Carter is in the backseat and the doors are locked. "We can get you a new shirt for the rest of today so you aren't covered in coffee, and we can get food at the food court. We can make a plan of attack for how you're going to steal Lynn's heart." I deftly avoid the other vehicles leaving for lunch.

Drew crosses his arms. "I don't remember agreeing to any of this. And the mall is twenty minutes away. Do you really want to spend forty minutes of our lunch break driving?"

We all have a free fifth period, so we don't have to be back for an hour and a half.

"Oh honey, it's cute that you think you have a say in this. You're getting a makeover, and you *will* love it. Then we'll move on to phase two of wooing Lynn." I pat his hand.

And with a wink, I add, "And it's only a twenty-minute trip if you drive the speed limit."

"I don't want to woo Lynn. I want to get through this project without looking like too much of a dork. Hopefully getting an 'A' so my GPA stays competitive. Can we go get lunch and talk about literally anything else?" Drew leans his head back, looking at the ceiling.

"Drew, just go with it for today, please?" I put my hands together in a begging motion. I need this, even if I don't want to have to explain why. After the crappy weekend I just had, I need someone to get their happily-ever-after. And who better than my lovable and kind best friend?

Drew's head snaps toward me. "Will you keep your hands on the wheel and your eyes on the road?"

I place my hands at ten and two to appease him. "We can do some clothes shopping now and after school. We can leave all the tags on everything, and if you still hate it tomorrow, we can return everything. It's just clothes. It's not like we're planning on coloring your hair or anything drastic or permanent.

"Besides, you have coffee on your shirt. You can't tell me you want to keep wearing your faded 'I found x' T-shirt for the rest of the day when it's stained with coffee. My dad gave me his credit card for whatever I want—within reason—so it'll only cost you time."

"And my dignity," Drew mutters under his breath.

Carter and I choose to ignore that statement. A makeover will only help Drew's image.

Once we're at the mall, we head straight to the food court. Carter goes to get us food while we grab a table. I immediately pull out my planning notebook.

"How do you already have two pages full of notes?" Drew leans toward me to try to see what I've written.

"Oh, I have a lot more than two pages of notes, and it's because I've had two hours to work on this plan." Sure, some of these pages are old song ideas, but he doesn't need to know that.

"Shouldn't you have been listening to our teachers? AP classes are not fluff classes. What if you missed something important today?" Drew falls back into his chair, looking defeated.

"It's math and science; I only pay attention half the time, anyway. We didn't even have a lecture in Pre-Cal. It's not like it's Government or English where I have to somewhat apply myself to appease my dad and maintain an 'A' average.

"As long as I have an 'A,' my dad doesn't care what I do or how much money I spend. So, unlike you who wants to be valedictorian, I'm perfectly content with a ninety. Besides, you know I'm going to the community college so I can be there for Sara until she graduates. I don't need a whole bunch of scholarships to pay for school."

I brandish my notebook at Drew. "All of that to say you snagging the girl of your dreams is more important than one class period of lectures. If you're that worried about it, then use my plans, so the time isn't wasted."

"I want to say I can't believe you're trying to guilt-trip me because you decided to not listen during class, but I've known you too long to be surprised. I guess there's no getting out of this. Let's get started, then. The sooner we start, the sooner this idiocy can be over." Drew runs his hands through his hair looking like he'd like to pull it out.

But then he adds, "Although, I'm not sure how I'm supposed to win her over, especially since she's dating the senior captain of the football team. I don't see how you could have anything in your notebook that'd make it where I could compete with *that*." Drew levels me with a look that seems to indicate he's beaten my plan.

I smile. "It's not idiocy, and she and Mark broke up. Which means, now is the perfect time to capture her attention."

"How do you know they broke up?" Drew leans toward me.

"I have Government with Whitney, remember? Anyway, she talked to Brooke about it this morning. According to Whitney, Mark broke up with Lynn to go out with Whitney. So, not only is your girl single, but it sounds like she may need a shoulder to cry on. If she's heartbroken, it'd explain her outfit this morning."

"Wrong." Carter sets our food on the table and sits next to me.

"Whitney's running her mouth. I have Mark and Kevin in my Algebra class. I overheard Mark tell Kevin that Lynn friendzoned him and he's trying to avoid Whitney. He doesn't want it to be known that Lynn broke up with him, but he wants nothing to do with Whitney. I think Lynn agreed to say it was mutual when asked, but he's worried about what she might say if Whitney confronts her."

"Do either of you pay attention in our classes or do you just plot my demise and eavesdrop on other people's conversations?" Drew sounds exasperated. "Also, it's pajama day. You know, the school-spirit days we don't participate in? That's why Lynn was in pajama pants and a hoodie." He puts his head on the table.

"An upside to being invisible is people talk like you aren't even there. I might as well take advantage of that and listen." I shrug.

"I agree, but check your sources. Whitney's only a reliable source of information on the Kardashians and how to not take a hint when the guy you've been throwing yourself at is not interested." Carter pops a fry into his mouth. "Now onto this plan of yours. Please tell me it doesn't hinge on the bad info you got from Whitney."

"It's less of a single plan and more of I have multiple plans. I figured that way, there should be at least one Drew is onboard with. The shoulder-to-cry-on aspect won't work." I mark out an entire page of notes from reworking an old song. Drew can't see what I'm doing, so as far as he's aware they're notes on how to win over Lynn.

I flip to another page where there's actually some notes written at the top. "You could offer to tutor her and put all that work on your grades to good use. Or propose the idea of having a fake relationship to keep Whitney from giving her problems."

Drew looks up from the table. "First off, Lynn's in all AP classes, and as far as I know, has never struggled with any of them. I mean, she outlined our entire project while I zoned out like a dork during English. I highly doubt she needs a tutor, and even if she did, Xander has mentioned in class before about aiming for valedictorian. I'm sure she'd ask him. All my work for school already has a use, such as getting good grades, and hopefully, being valedictorian."

Drew scoots his food closer to him and starts opening the containers. "And second, Lynn would have no problem getting anyone to date her, so I don't see why she'd want or need a fake relationship. We've all seen the different altercations between Lynn and Whitney in the last two weeks that Lynn and Mark have been official. I'm confident Lynn can handle Whitney on her own and would find the idea that I could help laughable."

Drew scoops up a forkful of food. "Are all the ideas you wrote down that bad?" he asks before he starts eating.

So most of these ideas are just slightly tweaked story plots of some of my favorite rom-coms, but Drew doesn't need to know that. I just need to wear him down until the makeover seems to be in his best interest.

As we eat lunch, Drew vetoes all my "ideas," getting more agitated with each one. When I suggest he ask Lynn to be his kissing tutor, he finally loses it.

"Give it a rest, Kaylee. All of your ideas are outlandish. They're not plausible or believable. Frankly, I feel like this whole conversation is grounds for a rom-com intervention. This is not some movie. This is my life. Just because I may like Lynn doesn't mean I want to do anything about it, and especially none of the ridiculous suggestions you have. Can we go to Carter's house and play video games for the rest of lunch?" Drew gives me puppy dog eyes that almost have me caving into video games.

CHAPTER 8
ANDREW

Just when I think Kaylee is going to cave in, Carter intervenes.

"Kaylee's ideas are completely ridiculous. But you've had a crush on Lynn for how long?" Carter raises his eyebrows goading me into responding.

"Five years…" I mumble, knowing my answer won't help my case.

"Which is longer than I've known you, and quite honestly way too long. This is your chance to make something happen. I mean, even if she rejects you, we know she'll be nice about it. Why don't you ask her out? Then you'll know one way or the other what she'll say, and Kaylee will leave you alone." Carter shrugs.

"I think you're forgetting that I couldn't carry on a conversation about English with Lynn, which is schoolwork and one of my favorite subjects. The only girl I've ever been able to hold a conversation with is Kaylee, and she hardly counts since she carried all of our conversations for at least the first six months of our friendship."

I run my hand through my hair. "I'm already nervous about being partnered with Lynn for this project. I need to be able to talk to her to get our work done. I don't need to be more awkward because I asked her out and she said no. Which we all know she'd do. Lynn dates tall, popular athletes; not scrawny, short mathletes."

I throw my hands in the air, hoping they'll listen to reason. "I mean, she's a Homecoming Princess for crying out loud."

"It sounds like she carried the conversation pretty well earlier, and we have the whole semester to get her to fall for you. If you're against all of my plans that'd get us fast results, how about we start smaller and give you a makeover?" Kaylee looks a little too innocent.

"I don't know about *you* giving me a makeover. I don't even want to know what the guy version of your style is, much less wear it." I pointedly look at Kaylee's outfit.

She's wearing a ripped vintage band tee over a bright blue tank top, a black and white plaid skirt with ripped black leggings underneath, Doc Martens, and a leather half-jacket regardless of the fact it's ninety degrees outside.

"No offense, but you couldn't pull off any outfit that's my style." Kaylee rolls her eyes. "Besides, if we're giving you a makeover, we need you to look like someone Lynn would date, not someone I'd date."

"Good, because most of the guys you like wear guyliner and tighter jeans than you do." Carter raises one eyebrow at Kaylee.

"Oh, shut it. How about you make yourself useful and take everything to the trash?" Kaylee shoves the tray in his direction.

"You're just upset because it's true." Carter gets up and takes our tray, wiggling his eyebrows as he goes.

Kaylee turns her attention back to me. "I was thinking more of getting you pants that don't come from the kids' section, buying new T-shirts instead of wearing your older brothers' hand-me-downs, and wearing your contacts instead of your bulky glasses. Maybe new shoes. I'd love for you to get a haircut and maybe have it styled."

"Look, I'll agree to go look at clothes, but I'm not getting a haircut. And you know I hate wearing my contacts. Plus, don't all your rom-coms talk about how if someone cares about you it doesn't matter what you look like?" I stand as Carter gets back to the table.

"Yes, but we need to get her attention. Once she realizes how awesome you are and is completely enamored by your personality, you can go back to dressing yourself. Let's get started on clothes so we can get as much done during lunch as possible." Kaylee links her arm through mine, preventing any escape.

We spend the next half hour buying me an entirely new wardrobe.

Kaylee always complains about how women's clothing sizes are different when men's are universal. That's working for her and against me right now. I'm already done with their new project, and I have a feeling they're only getting started.

Once I try on a style of something and she approves, she gets multiple in my size. Carter has been relegated to pack mule. Although it's way too much, I'm impressed with how efficient Kaylee has been even if she's been somewhat of a dictator. Other than the coffee, I don't see what's wrong with what I'm wearing, but arguing with Kaylee will only make her more determined.

"Okay, so that has clothes covered and now we only need to come back after school to get shoes." Kaylee grabs the last of the bags of clothes from the store clerk.

"Finally." Carter's shoulders sag with relief as he temporarily sets down his armload of bags.

"We can stop by your house on the way back to school so we can drop everything off and you can change," Kaylee says as we load up in the car.

"Why do I have to change? I've already been wearing these clothes today. If we're aiming for subtle, which I hope we still are, isn't changing in the middle of the day pretty obvious?" I ask.

"While you normally might have an argument, you have coffee on your shirt. If you're changing your shirt, you may as well change your jeans too," Kaylee explains.

"Fine." I resign myself to her machinations.

When we get to my house, Carter and Kaylee help carry everything inside. Kaylee picks out the shirt and jeans I'm supposed to change into and then excuses herself to go to the bathroom. I get changed quickly, not wanting to risk being late getting back to class. Carter calls shotgun and I get in the backseat. On the drive back, we talk about nothing in particular.

Once we get to the school, Kaylee turns around in her seat. "So, I know you said no to the contacts, but I think you should at least give it a try for today."

"I hate my contacts and I don't even have them with me." I try to open the door, but it's locked.

"That's why I went to the bathroom and grabbed them and your contact solution while we were at your house. I engaged the child locks, so you aren't getting out of the van without giving me your glasses." Kaylee smiles evilly.

"That's insane." I turn to my hopefully sane friend. "Carter, will you let me out, please?"

"Look, I talked her out of staging an accident to break your glasses. This is the least crazy compromise I could get her to agree to. You may as well go along with it so you can get to class, and hope she doesn't change her mind and decide to break your glasses anyway." Carter gets out of the van and leaves me to fend for myself.

Kaylee reaches out her hand in a give-me gesture. I relinquish my glasses and take the contacts from her.

"Only for the rest of the day. Tomorrow I'm going back to wearing my glasses." I start putting my contacts in.

Once they're in, I look at Kaylee and she hands me my glasses case. At least she's thought to bring the case too. I don't have another class with Kaylee until Jazz Band, so I figure once she heads to her class I'll switch back.

I stop in the bathroom on the way to class. When I open my glasses case, I realize my glasses are in three separate pieces. I pull my phone out to text Kaylee.

Andrew: What did you do?

KK is the best 😊: I made sure you wouldn't switch back early. Don't worry all I did was take the screws out. I have them and can put them back in easily 😛

Andrew: Why do I put up with you?

KK is the best 😊: Because I was the first extrovert to adopt your introverted butt. Plus, you know you love me

I head to Government, resigned to wearing my contacts for the rest of the day.

CHAPTER 9
LYNN

After AP Physics, I corner Xander, hoping to discreetly ask him why Mrs. Green insisted on splitting us up for our project.

"Hey, want to ride home with me for lunch? I asked Mom if we could all come to the house for lunch. She said she'd make lasagna, both kinds." Lasagna is our favorite food. My favorite is traditional lasagna and Xander's is chicken alfredo.

"I assume by 'all' you mean the neanderthals you call friends are coming, too?" Xander looks like he's already irritated with my answer.

"Well, yes, but chicken alfredo lasagna." I wiggle my eyebrows.

"Fine, but I get shotgun. I don't care how tall your neanderthal friends are."

"Deal." I link my arm with his to keep him from changing his mind and running away.

"Aren't you worried someone will see you with your nerdy brother?"

"You might be a theater nerd, but you're my little brother and I love you," I say as we head out of the classroom.

"I'm six minutes younger than you."

"And six inches shorter."

"Whatever, weirdo."

"Love you too, dork."

Xander's question wasn't entirely unwarranted. I usually am only around him at school when we sit next to each other in our Pre-AP and AP classes. However, it's not because I don't want to be seen with him. More because I try to avoid tension and awkward situations, and he does not get along with Jet and some of my other friends.

Oliver and Daniel are waiting in the hall for us. I waved them on earlier when they looked like they were waiting for me at the end of class.

"I hear we're going to Casa de Kingston for lunch." Daniel falls into step on Xander's other side.

Daniel Caballero is our next-door neighbor and my best friend. He has dark brown skin with blue eyes and brown hair that's spiked up. He's the only one of the Knights who is shorter than me at six feet.

"And that we'll have the honor of both Kingston twins today," Oliver says from my other side.

Oliver Ridire is six feet, five and built bigger than the rest of the Knights. He has green eyes and light brown hair that he keeps short. He looks pretty intimidating but is a gentle giant and probably the sweetest of the Knights. He and his brother Grayson live in the house across the street from ours. They, along with Daniel, practically grew up at our house.

"Yeah, and I get a whole escort of Knights. Yippee." Xander's voice is dripping with sarcasm as he does unenthusiastic jazz hands.

"You're a king." Daniel playfully elbows Xander. "Aren't they supposed to be escorted by knights?"

"I'd rather be the court mummer, and you already have a king." Xander nudges me to punctuate the word "king."

"Mummer. Really dude?" Oliver holds the door to the parking lot open for us.

"Y'all are the ones the whole school calls Knights, but I'm weird for knowing what a medieval actor would've been called?" Xander asks.

"You can be a mummer all you like, but I am not a king," I say emphatically.

"But it's right in y'all's name *King*ston," Daniel argues as we get to my SUV where Grayson, Jet, and Tristan are already waiting for us.

"'Sup, Shrimp?" Jet sweeps his black hair out of his piercing blue eyes while looking down on Xander's much shorter frame.

Jet Vaughn is tan and my height. He's muscular but lean from all the running we do for basketball. He played on the same little dribblers team with us. He quickly became friends with the rest of us but has always fought with Xander.

"Shut it, Jet, you know he doesn't like that nickname. Xander already called shotgun." I wait until Xander is next to the passenger door to hit the unlock button.

"Yeah, shut it, Jet," Grayson shoves Jet into the vehicle.

Grayson Ridire has all-American good looks, his twinkling blue eyes flash under his ash blond hair. He rolls his eyes before hauling his six-foot-three frame into the SUV. Despite Oliver being almost a year younger, they're both in our grade because of how their birthdays fall.

"Can y'all behave and get in the car?" Tristan asks as they continue to jostle each other.

Tristan Knight is a commanding six-foot-four with dark skin, brown eyes, and dark brown almost not there hair, it's cut so close to his scalp.

When we were little, Xander was on the team with us and therefore a Knight. But as we got older, he quit playing. In sixth grade, when Tristan moved here, he sort of took Xander's place in our friend group and became one of the Knights. We joked that he was meant to be part of our group because of his last name.

Xander had already started doing more things on his own by then and pretty much stopped hanging out with us as a group. It made more sense for Tristan to round out the Knights, and Xander has always seemed pleased not to be grouped together with us. He used to be a Knight, but as he likes to say that was another lifetime.

"So, what is up with Mrs. Green?" I put the key in the ignition.

"For one, she isn't pleased with how frequently you're late to class. She hinted that she thinks you only partner with me so that I'll do all the work without ratting you out. She thinks you're a dumb jock who coasts through life on your athleticism. Which she wouldn't be completely wrong if she was talking about anything other than schoolwork." Xander's smirk says he's joking.

"I'm not *that* late to class, and what about all of my papers? Those are individual assignments. Does she think you're the one who writes them and then puts my name on it? I don't coast through anything." I pull out of the parking lot.

"Even if it's only a few minutes late, you're still constantly late to class, and if she looks at your schedule, she'd know you have a free first period. Today, you were at school before I got here. I don't even know how you were late to class. I know you do all your work, but I guess she wants to be sure." Xander squeezes my knee. "Look, I'd partner with you if I could. You know I hate having to talk to people I don't know very well and none of my friends are in AP English. You don't coast through any of the important stuff. I know you work hard for your grades and your spot on the team."

"I was in the gym this morning. I was already running behind when Whitney spotted me, and I had to deal with her nonsense about Homecoming." I explain. "Sorry if I seemed upset with you. I know it isn't your fault. Price will barely talk to me, though, so I'm not sure how we're going to get through this project. I feel like I'll end up doing all the work. And what is it you think I coast through?"

"Why were you in the gym that early?" Grayson asks from the back.

"Who is Price?" Oliver chimes in.

"What's for lunch?" Tristan asks.

"You only work out that early if you're anxious." Daniel points out. "What's up, Lynn? Did Mark do something? Do we need to have a *talk* with him?" He says the word "talk" like he means something more aggressive.

I pull the car to the side of the house in front of the garage. "Mark didn't do anything wrong. He...he told me last night that he loves me." I'm grateful this didn't come up until the car was in park because I'm already starting to feel anxiety creep in.

The boys sit in stunned silence which doesn't help my nerves.

"I handled it poorly and broke up with him. That's why I was at the gym so early. Also, Price is my partner for our AP English project we started today. And we're having lasagna." I'm hoping we can focus on the English project or lasagna instead of the whole thing with Mark.

"Mark said he loved you?" Grayson asks.

"And you responded by breaking up with him?" Oliver asks.

"That's cold, L," Tristan adds.

"But you were only together for two weeks," Jet says.

"Your partner's name isn't Price," Xander says.

"Wait, what? I thought that was what Mrs. Green called him...?" I ask Xander, ignoring all the guys' questions.

"She said Mister *Prince* like she called you Miss Kingston. *Prince* is his last name. His first name is Andrew. How do you *not* know that? He's in all AP and Pre AP classes; we've had basically all the same classes since sixth grade." Xander takes off his seat belt.

"We've never talked before today. You know the only people in our AP classes who ever talk to me are in this car. How am I supposed to know their names? How do *you* know his name?" I ask.

"You could pay attention to those who don't know how to handle a ball and you might be surprised by how many other students go to our school. Being a 'Knight' doesn't have to mean ignoring everyone else at school," Xander sasses.

"They don't talk to me, either," I point out.

"They don't talk to you because you're popular," Xander explains. "Not to mention that while you may be nice most of the time, you can be vicious when putting someone in their place. I know you only do it to stand up for yourself and others, but it doesn't always look that way from the outside."

"Are you going to ignore all of our questions about your love life?" Tristan asks.

"Yes, I am. If my *dating life*," I refuse to call it my 'love life,' "was any of your business I'd be sure to give you all the details. And I'm not vicious."

"Dude, as much as I don't want to agree with Shrimp, he's right. Just look at the whole Whitney thing," Jet says.

"Stop calling him Shrimp." I'm more annoyed by the topic but Jet gets most of my annoyance since he knows I hate it when he picks on Xander. "What Whitney thing? You mean how she's been annoying about me dating Mark? Because none of that conflict is my fault."

"Two weeks ago, when Mark called you his girlfriend in front of Whitney, she got angry and called you a slut." Daniel reminds me. "You told her only ignorant people use slurs to tear others down and maybe, if she wasn't so hateful, someone might consider being in a relationship with her. She stormed out, and now Brooke is the only one still talking to her. Why do you think she didn't get nominated for Homecoming Queen?"

"Whitney was being hateful," I say in my defense. "I didn't want to deal with it. Why isn't anyone talking to her? I can *not* be the reason she didn't get nominated for Homecoming Queen."

Oliver is the one to explain. "Because most of the guys at school think they're in love with you and don't want to talk to someone who's mean to you. Everyone knows these morons"—Oliver gestures to the rest of the guys in the car—"won't hook up with anyone who talks bad about you, so the girls who want a chance with them don't want to be seen taking Whitney's side. Why do you think she has continued to be so nasty to you since you and Mark started dating? You took her spot, and now she's a leper."

"Hey, we're not morons!" Daniel, Grayson, Jet, and Tristan say indignantly.

"Y'all are definitely morons. I didn't take her spot, and I never told anyone to stop talking to her. Why can't she move on and bug someone else?" I lean my head back against the headrest.

"You knocked the queen bee out of her spot without even trying or realizing it, and now she's been ostracized," Tristan says. "I think it's clear why the less popular kids are afraid to talk to you. Now that you've dumped Mark, I'm sure she'll move on in time. Although not until after the sting from Homecoming fades. Now can we go eat? I'm starving."

I turn off the car and unlock the doors so the guys can head into the house. I stare at the steering wheel for a minute. *Did I do that to Whitney?*

I thought she was only being hateful because of the whole Mark thing when she accused me of taking her crown.

I jump when there's a knock on the window. Xander's standing there, looking at me. I open the door and get out.

"Hey, anyone who knows you knows you're a good person," he says. "You defend yourself and others. You don't let the unpopular kids get bullied, either. You're intense about everything: basketball, grades, protecting your friends. That intensity makes you intimidating. Don't worry about it too much. Your Knight title is a bit of a double-edged sword. It gives you more influence and people listen to you. On the other hand, it can make some people afraid to approach you."

I note that he doesn't say *Knight* sarcastically like he usually does.

"Is that why you traded your Knight title away?" I bump his shoulder.

"I think we both know the title never fit me, anyway. Tristan fits more of what it means now. I prefer my obscure theater-nerd status."

"Obscure until you get your big break?" I smile.

"Of course." Xander smiles back.

"Do other people think I'm some stuck-up popular chick?"

"It's possible, but since when do you care about what other people think?" Xander shrugs. "If you're worried about how people perceive your rule over your kingdom, you could rule differently."

"What do you mean? I don't rule over anything."

"I think you unintentionally exiling Whitney would suggest you do. If you want to change things, you could try talking to the people in our classes. Maybe this project will be good for you. Now let's get inside before the neanderthals eat all my lasagna." I follow him into the house with a plan to try to be more sociable for the rest of the day.

In the kitchen the guys are helping my mother with getting everything to the table. Xander and I wash our hands, then join everyone else at the table. My twin blesses the food, and we all get started on lunch.

"How has y'all's day been so far?" Mom looks at me, since me asking to come home for lunch is abnormal.

"Well, we plebs are just lucky enough to be in the presence of royalty." Xander shoots me a wink.

I roll my eyes but silently thank him. If mom is distracted with Homecoming, she'll be less likely to interrogate me about Mark. Our parents are high-school sweethearts, and she's always disappointed when my relationships end.

"What?" Mom asks.

"Grayson and I are Junior Homecoming Prince and Princess." I quickly take a bite, hoping to head off further questions.

"Oh, congratulations!" Mom squeals. "That means we get to go dress shopping this week!"

"Do we have to?" I ask.

"Yes, you can't wear the same dress for the parade, the halftime show, and the dance. We already have your dress for the dance, so we need to get two more. Although, the parade is Wednesday, so we'll have to go shopping today or tomorrow," Mom insists.

"Okay, I have a fall league game tonight, but we could go tomorrow after school. I'm meeting with my partner for a project at five, but we should be done by then if I go straight from the school to the mall." I act slightly annoyed, but really, I don't mind dress shopping with Mom. It's one of the only mother-daughter things we do, just the two of us.

"Tomorrow after school it is. And since you aren't putting up a fight, we can get you some new shoes, too. I was thinking maybe a new pair of Converse?" Mom asks

"Yes! Mom, you're the best!" I wrap her up in a big hug.

CHAPTER 10
DANIEL

I'm equal parts relieved and worried about Lynn breaking up with Mark. On the one hand, they weren't good together. He's way too jealous and not at all understanding of her having close guy friends. I'm confident Lynn will be much happier now that they aren't together.

I don't think Mark will handle it well, especially since he told her he loves her. For a guy who's never had a girlfriend before, he sure had some strong opinions on how Lynn should act as his girlfriend and jumped to the "love" word pretty quick. Lynn's been off all day, and it worries me, especially since we don't know what exactly happened with Mark.

Lynn seems to be more upset about not being partnered with Xander for her project than she is about her relationship with Mark ending, though. Lynn's serious about school and prioritizes it over relationships, but something still seems off to me.

Xander already told her Andrew is a good student, so she shouldn't be worried about being paired with him. I'm sure they'll still ace their project. Having a different partner than Xander shouldn't be that big of a deal.

Unless she's more anxious about Mark than she's been letting on and it's more about Xander being her security blanket. As we grew up, they had less and less in common. They support each other's interest, but their schoolwork is about the only thing they do together.

Lynn has always been quite independent, but she still gets separation anxiety. It's especially bad during the summer when they go to different camps. I think it'd be worse if she didn't have all of the Knights around her.

"So, are any of my kids going to tell me what's going on today?" Mama Kingston asks.

She looks at each of us, then stares down Oliver. He tends to be the weak link when she gives us her "mom look." Oliver looks like he's about to crack when Lynn starts talking.

"I'm a little stressed about my English project. It's a big portion of our grade and Xander can't be my partner." I think Lynn only said that to keep Oliver from possibly spilling the beans about Mark.

"Oh, honey. I'm sorry you have to be partnered with someone else. But you're in AP English. There shouldn't be any slackers in your class."

"Andrew's smart and hard-working," Xander says. "He's my main competition for valedictorian."

"See? I'm sure it'll be fine," their mom assures Lynn. "It'll be good for you to get used to not having Xander as a partner. College isn't too far off, and you might not go to the same school."

"I know, Mom. It'll be fine. I'm a little stressed, is all." Lynn looks down at her plate and toys with her food. "Especially with the added stuff for Homecoming Court. We have a meeting after school to go over everything."

"It'll most likely be information for the float, the parade, and setting up when y'all will practice for the halftime show," Jet says. "That's all it was last year. You should be glad you're partnered with Grayson this year. Last year I had to be next to Tara the whole time. All she talked about was dieting, shopping, and makeup." He sticks his tongue out.

"You're the one who dated her, so you brought that on yourself," Grayson says.

Jet opens his mouth then closes it after glancing toward Mama Kingston. He was probably going to say something about it being a stretch to call whatever he had with Tara dating or that his reasons were shallow, but thought better of it.

"The point is, it won't be that bad. Jet survived last year, and I survived Freshman year." Tristan takes a bite of his lasagna. "It won't kill you, and you have one of your best friends with you instead of someone you might not get along with." He shoves another forkful in his mouth like someone might try to take his plate away from him.

Xander rolls his eyes. "Oh, the woes of being popular."

"Heavy is the head that wears the crown." Jet smirks.

"*Uneasy* is the head that wears *a* crown," Xander corrects.

"Whatever, Shrimp." Jet waves off Xander's statement.

"Don't call him Shrimp," Lynn reprimands Jet before adding, "Xander wants to major in theater. He ought to know what Shakespeare actually wrote."

Jet winces as she says it, and I think it's because she's kicked him under the table.

"Not everyone is uncultured swine living in the dark ages." Xander has a haughty expression.

"Boys. That's enough." Mama Kingston gives pointed looks to Xander and Jet.

"Yes, ma'am," they say in unison before looking down.

Her phone rings and she excuses herself to answer the call.

"Can't y'all get along for one lunch?" Lynn asks.

"Xander started it." Jet points across the table.

"Really? Did I miss the time jump where we went back to being five-year-olds?" Lynn says, exasperated. "It's one lunch; enjoy your lasagna and shut up. Daydream about girls or whatever will keep you quiet and happy."

Lynn seems super stressed. I place my hand on her arm.

"Ignore them. What's going on with you?" I ask.

"Nothing. It's just a lot in one day."

"The Mark thing is majorly getting to you. You don't normally get so short with us after a breakup," Oliver says.

"It's nothing. Like I said, it's just a lot in one day."

Xander squeezes her shoulder but doesn't say anything. After we finish eating, the other Knights head out back to shoot hoops for the rest of the time before we have to return to school. I hang back with Lynn and Xander.

"So…you gonna tell us what's up?" I ask Lynn.

Lynn glances to where her mom is cleaning the kitchen, then nods upstairs. Xander and I follow her to the upstairs den.

"Mark was upset when I broke up with him," she says.

"That's not entirely unexpected. That tends to happen when people get dumped." Xander shrugs.

"No, I know. It's just… He said some things." Lynn starts pacing.

"Like what?" I ask.

"Um, I don't want to repeat what he said." Lynn starts chewing on her bottom lip.

"If you're this upset about it, we need to know." Xander wraps an arm around her. Lynn briefly embraces him before going back to pacing.

"He made some derogatory comments about me having only male friends. Especially since most of you don't have serious relationships. He implied that the nature of our relationship is why I was breaking up with him."

"Basically, he called you a slut and implied you're sleeping with all of the guys?" Xander raises his eyebrows.

"He used different words, but yeah." Lynn shrugs, looking defeated.

"Anyone who knows you or us knows that's not true. He lashed out because he was angry." I reach out to stop her pacing and pull her into a bone crushing hug.

Lynn speaks into my chest without looking up. "Yeah, but he still said it. He has been weird about my guy friends the entire time we were together. What if…what if other people at school think it's true? What if no one says anything to us, but it's what everyone says behind our back?"

Her breath starts coming in shorter spurts, and I'm worried she's working herself into a panic attack. I squeeze her closer to me and rub a hand up and down her back hoping to soothe her.

"No one who knows you would seriously think that. Mark was angry. What's up with suddenly caring about what other people think?

First, you're worried people will think you're stuck-up, and now this. What changed?" Xander looks puzzled. I'm wondering what I missed about people thinking Lynn's stuck-up.

"What changed is they're saying that I have a harem." Lynn pulls her head back out of my chest to look at Xander. "Usually, when people talk crap it's about me acting like one of the guys and playing sports instead of doing girly things. Being called basically a boy isn't the major insult they seem to think it is. I take pride in the ability to do anything the boys can do. I can ignore that, but this? This is different."

Xander wraps his arms around Lynn from behind.

"It's high school." I say. "People spread ridiculous rumors and utter nonsense comes out of people's mouths all the time. It might be a different kind of nonsense than what you're used to, but you should handle it the same way. Ignore it and don't let people who don't know you get to you." I squeeze Lynn tight before letting go of her.

"Daniel's right. Besides, anyone who knows y'all knows none of you are sleeping with anyone. Anyone who knows our mother knows she'd castrate the boys for even thinking about it." Xander pulls Lynn away from me and into a proper hug.

"Are you sure?" she asks.

Xander and I both nod.

"Okay." Lynn takes a deep breath. "I feel better now. I'd rather the other guys not know about this. I don't want them turning it into a whole thing with Mark."

"Afraid they'd go all medieval on his butt and we'd lose our star quarterback?" Xander smirks.

"Something like that."

"My lips are sealed. We can always tell them you're feeling off because it's that time of the month?" I wiggle my eyebrows.

Lynn has used that as a way to explain away her moods before because it makes the other guys uncomfortable.

"That'd definitely keep them from asking questions." Lynn finally smiles.

"Is that why you've been off all day or is something else going on?" I ask.

"Just the stuff with Mark," Lynn says.

There's something off when she says it, but if she doesn't want to talk about it, I'm not going to make her. Lynn takes a deep breath, and we head out back to shoot hoops with the guys.

Xander even comes and joins us, much to Lynn's delight. It has been years since he played on a team with us.

Since I live next door and can see their basketball goal from my bedroom window, I sometimes find the twins shooting hoops together. It's usually something they do together when Lynn's avoiding whomever she most recently broke up with. However, it has been a long time since Xander has come to play when the Knights were here.

Xander and Lynn's relationship sometimes makes me wish I had a sibling. My house is usually empty.

Other times I feel like I have way too many brothers. Growing up, Mama Kingston always kept me when my parents were working. Now I'm old enough to stay on my own but am at Lynn's house more often than not.

I'm used to the controlled chaos of her house. I prefer dealing with all her younger brothers to the solitude at my house. I don't know what I'd do without them.

CHAPTER 11
OLIVER

"All kinds of royalty today." Tristan smirks at me as he grabs a basketball from the outdoor shed and passes it to me.

I glare at him and hope he drops it before Jet and Grayson catch on and start asking questions.

"It's just Homecoming nonsense. I don't see what the big deal is." Jet rolls his eyes. "More importantly, do y'all want to play Knock Out? We can start at half-court to make it interesting." Jet wiggles his eyebrows.

"Yeah. No. I don't want to go back to school all sweaty and gross." Grayson runs his hand through his hair, fixing it the way he likes.

"You're such a prima donna." Jet rolls his eyes again. "How about Horse? Then you won't have to worry about messing up your precious hair, just getting your butt kicked."

Grayson shoves Jet. "Stop acting like you're all that. We can keep up with you."

"Oh, yeah? That's why we were all on varsity together freshman year. Oh, wait, that was just me."

I pass the ball to Jet. "Just start the game. And you weren't the only one on varsity freshman year."

Jet dribbles the ball to half-court. "Yeah, but Lynn isn't out here so that doesn't count right now."

He, of course, sinks the ball in the basket even from half-court. I'm sure that only further inflates his ego.

"You're up, Grayson. Let's see if you can actually keep up."

Grayson grabs the ball and attempts to copy Jet's shot. It sails through the air before bouncing off the backboard.

"H!" Jet hollers as he rebounds the ball, passing it to Tristan.

"You must have really strong neck muscles to hold up that big head of yours." Tristan dribbles to the top of the key before sinking a three-pointer.

"If it gets any bigger, you won't be able to fit through doors." I grab the ball and copy Tristan's shot.

We continue shooting. Jet keeps making ridiculous shots every chance he gets and Grayson is out of the game before Lynn, Daniel, and Xander come outside.

I'm worried about Lynn and whatever they needed to talk about without us there. But I also get needing space and not wanting to discuss issues with a whole audience. It must be really bothering her if Xander is willing to come hang out with Jet just to keep Lynn company.

"New players. We're starting over." Grayson gets up from where he's been sitting at the patio table.

"But now we don't have time for a full game." Jet sinks another three while he's talking.

"We can always do teams, that makes it go by quicker. The three of us," Lynn gestures to Xander and Daniel, "against the four of y'all."

"Four is a handicap if everyone has to make the same shot." Grayson points out.

"I'll sit out. I don't really want to play right now, anyway." I walk over to one of the lounger lawn chairs and plop down.

"Ladies first." Jet passes the ball to Lynn with a wink.

Lynn rolls her eyes before lining up at the left elbow and sinking the ball in the basket. It's an easy shot for all of the Knights to make, but I'm sure she chooses that spot for Xander. He's left-handed and that's one of the shots he can make reliably, even without playing sports.

I pull my phone out as Xander lines up the shot. I take a picture just as the ball leaves his hand. I capture Lynn and Daniel in the background smiling at him. I don't see the ball go in, but I hear the swish that indicates it does. I get another picture as Lynn and Daniel high-five Xander.

I take a handful of pictures of everybody as they continue to play. Jet and Lynn trash-talking. Daniel encouraging Xander. Tristan goofing off for everyone's amusement. Grayson teasing Lynn.

I take a few pictures of the rest of the backyard: the discarded toys from Lynn's youngest brothers, the sporting equipment strewn about despite how often Mama Kingston reminds everyone to clean up after themselves, the various seating options for hanging out, and finally, the castle.

The castle is what we call the tree house that her parents built for us when we were little. There's a ladder going up the tree to the main part of the structure. A tunnel slide comes out of the right side of the castle and wraps around the tree, coming out near the base of the ladder. There're four small towers at each of the corners that go all the way to the ground.

The four towers are made of steel so the tree didn't have to bear the weight of us and the tree house. It also made the space bigger to fit all of us. Lynn's dad works with builders and had it built along with the shed, so the "castle" is made as up to code as a tree house can be. They even ran electricity to it, which powers the twinkle lights that Xander had strung up in second grade.

The small porch on the front still has a small broom for the rare occasion we played house. The towers each have a door at the bottom that opens to a small storage space. Inside are wooden swords and shields from when we would play at being real knights.

Even though my brother and I live across the street, we spend most of our time at Lynn's house. Her mom was our nanny and she practically raised us. I've always loved being over here because the house and yard are made for kids. And growing up, we always had a grand assortment of toys and space to play. Adults who were watching us, but who would also join in with whatever game we might've made up for that day.

My house across the street doesn't have warmth or laughter. My parents are rarely home and are preoccupied when they're there. All of our stuff was to be in our rooms neat and tidy and put away. Messes were an annoyance and never allowed. If Grayson and I wanted someone to play with us, we were sent across the street. I might live next door, but the Kingston's house will always be my home.

I shake the more melancholic thoughts away and refocus on the game. They're tied at H-O-R-S so the next team to miss a shot will get the final letter E and lose. Jet and Lynn are messing with each other as they take turns shooting. Daniel makes eye contact before rolling his eyes at the ridiculous antics.

Lynn makes her shot despite Jet trying to block her. Before anyone else can take their turn, Xander's alarm goes off, telling us it's time to head back to school.

CHAPTER 12
LYNN

We get back to school a bit early because I want to be early for AP Government. We're the first ones in class. As soon as Andrew walks in, I get up to go talk to him, realizing his glasses from earlier are gone.

He's wearing a different T-shirt with a graffiti design on it. Since we aren't sitting, I can tell how short he is. I know I'm taller than average at six feet, two, but I tower over him. I wonder if he's smart enough that he skipped a couple of grades or if he's just that short.

"What happened to your glasses?" So maybe not the approachable and social statement I was going for.

"Oh, um, they broke during lunch." He's not quite looking at me.

"Will you be able to see for class?" I ask.

"Yeah, I got my, um, my contacts from home during my free period."

"Oh cool. So, I just wanted to check in with you. I hadn't gotten a text from you, and I wanted to make sure you hadn't lost my number or anything."

"Oh, I didn't think. I mean, yeah, I should, um, have it somewhere." He starts rummaging around in his backpack.

"Since class hasn't started yet, why don't you give me your phone and I can input it so you can't lose it?"

"S-sure." He pulls his phone out of his pocket and hands it to me. I put my number in and then text myself so I'll have his number in case he forgets again.

"There you go." I hand him his phone back.

Our hands touch as he takes his phone, and he practically bolts away from me. I go to my seat between Xander and Daniel. Advanced Government is the only class all of the guys are in, and we pretty much take up the back corner of the room. They're giving me a quizzical look and I mouth 'English partner' as an explanation before sitting down. Xander passes me a note when I pull my notebook out.

Maybe try to dial back the intensity

I look at him, and he shrugs like it doesn't make a difference to him either way. I make a mental note to dial back my intensity the next time I try talking to Andrew.

Toward the end of class I get my stuff together early. That way I should be able to catch Andrew before he leaves class. The bell rings, and I'm at his desk before he has organized himself to get up. He keeps his head down as he gets up and doesn't seem to notice me, so I clear my throat. He jumps and looks up.

"Sorry, I didn't mean to scare you."

"Um. No…it's my bad…I…I should have been looking where…" He trails off as he looks down again.

"Still, I didn't mean to scare you and I did. Sorry. I've been told I can be intense."

"No, it's…it's not you. You're perfect. I mean, uh, you're fine. I was…uh, just in my own head." Andrew seems nervous as he scratches the back of his head.

I guess Xander had a point about me intimidating people. I need to remember to be friendlier.

"Okay. So, I was thinking during lunch about how we were partnered together for the English project. And how it was kind of random. I mean, we've never even talked before today."

"Oh, uh, yeah? Do you want me to, um, ask Mrs. Green if we could, uh, switch, so you can be partnered with Xander?" Andrew looks down at the ground.

"What?" Did he think I came over here to ask him to get the teacher to change our partners? I guess he does think I'm a stuck-up popular chick.

"I can talk to her." Andrew quickly glances up at me before returning his gaze to the floor. "I mean, I…uh…I get it if you'd rather be partnered with your brother."

"No, no, that's not what I meant at all. What I was trying to say was we've had mostly the same schedule for years and have never gotten to know each other. This project gives us the opportunity to finally get to know each other. Isn't it crazy that we've had so many classes together and have never talked before?"

"Uh, yeah, crazy."

"Anyway, I'm looking forward to getting to know you." I hope my smile looks friendly and not forced.

I feel like a giant next to Andrew and he seems to be cowering from me. I don't want to scare or intimidate him but am not sure what's making him so skittish in the first place. It's not like I have a reputation for being a mean girl.

"Um, yeah, it should be, uh, nice to get to know you better too." He's still looking down at his shoes.

"Well, I better get going to Spanish or I'll be late." It sounds lame even before the words are out of my mouth, but what else am I supposed to say? I don't know what to talk to Andrew about.

"Uh, yeah." Andrew shoulders his bag and heads out of the classroom.

"So, are you going to the game Friday?"

Andrew jumps as if he'd forgotten I was next to him.

"Uh, yeah. I, uh, have to be at every game."

"What? Why?" I know he's not in athletics or one of the trainers. If he was, I'd have known who he was before today.

"I'm in band."

"Oh. Uh, cool. What instrument do you play?"

"Trombone."

I nod. "Low brass. I'm told that's the best section. Of course, that's by my younger brother who plays euphonium in the junior high band. He might be biased. Although you seem pretty cool, so maybe he's right."

I bump my shoulder into Andrew, and he makes a squeaking noise I don't have time to interpret before Mark appears in front of us. Mark is about my height with blond hair, stormy blue eyes, and a very athletic body. He has an amazing smile that reeled me in a few weeks ago.

Now it seems to have no effect on me. I may not have planned it, but it feels like breaking up with him was the exact right thing to do. There're no butterflies in my stomach now, just anxiety.

There's so much more to my breakup with Mark than I told the guys about. I didn't want to get into it earlier, and if I decide to tell Daniel or anyone else, I figure that'd be a conversation better handled when we don't have to go back to school afterwards.

I may date around a lot, and I've kissed my fair share of guys, but that's it. I've never done more than make out with someone. Mark wanted more. We spent most of our brief relationship arguing over me having close guy friends yet not being willing to have more of a physical relationship with *him*.

Mark seemed to think with as many guys as I've kissed that it wasn't a big deal. He kept trying to put his hands where they absolutely shouldn't go. He didn't believe me when I told him I hadn't had a physically intimate relationship with anyone and didn't plan to change that anytime soon.

Honestly, I think that's a big part of why he said he loved me, jerk. Maybe if I thought he was in love with me, then it wouldn't be a big deal for him to be touching my butt or to do other things to me. Even if he *was* in love with me, it wouldn't change what I was and was *not* okay with.

Him saying he loved me was the final straw. I don't want to feel constantly pressured to do anything or to ditch my friends. Any guy acting that way isn't the guy for me. Even so, I still feel bad for hurting Mark's feelings. How crazy is that? He was more concerned with pushing my boundaries than getting to know me, but I can't help but worry about his feelings. All of that makes it where I don't want to talk to him right now.

"Hey, Lynn." Mark steps a little *too* close for comfort.

"Uh, hey."

"I wanted to know if I could talk to you. You know, about everything this weekend?"

"Um, maybe later." I don't want to have this conversation at all, and definitely don't want to have it at school in the hallway during a passing period.

I link my arm with Andrew's, hoping it doesn't make him uncomfortable and that he will play along. "I'm walking with Andrew to class. We need to discuss our project for English."

Mark looks down, seeming to notice Andrew for the first time. Mark seems to be at a loss for words. I speak before he can get his wits about him and try to come up with a reason why I need to talk to him.

"We better be off, so we aren't late for class." I drag Andrew toward Spanish as fast as I can.

Mark, thankfully, doesn't follow. When we walk into Spanish, Xander gives me a quizzical look, glancing between me, Andrew, and where our arms are linked. I release Andrew's arm.

"Sit with me?" I ask him.

Andrew gives a slight nod before following me to my desk at the far side of the room. I'm sure he now thinks I am a weirdo. Possibly a heartless witch.

After I sit down, I take a deep breath and turn to Andrew. His eyes are glued to his desk. *Crap.* He looks even more scared of me now than before.

"Um, I'm sorry about that. Sorry you had to see that exchange with Mark, and sorry I basically commandeered your arm and dragged you to class."

"It…it is, uh, fine."

"I still shouldn't have done it. I know running away from Mark is cowardly, but I just, I just couldn't handle it today. You know?"

"Uh, o…okay."

"Thank you for saving me and giving me a reason to not have to have that conversation in the middle of school. I owe you one." I reach out and touch his arm.

He looks down at the contact but doesn't say anything or move away. I pull my hand back.

"Sorry, I forget some people don't like to be touched. I'm a touchy person. Sorry."

"It's, uh, fine. I, uh, didn't…you didn't…um…no need…to um… owe me...?"

"I still feel bad about dragging you through the hallway. If you change your mind or if you need something, let me know. I'm sorry. I'm pretty sure you might want to ask Mrs. Green for a new partner now on account of me being so weird."

"It's not. You're not. I mean it's…"

The bell rings and Ms. Yaya starts class. She lectures the entire class period, so I never find out what Andrew was trying to say. When class is dismissed, Andrew bolts out of class like the room has caught fire.

Xander stops at my desk and gives me that same quizzical look again, but I shrug. We head in different directions to our last class of the day. I'm more than ready for athletics and for a chance to run off this anxious energy. I'm glad that Daniel missed seventh period today and isn't here to speculate with Xander.

CHAPTER 13
KAYLEE

When I get to English after lunch, I'm determined to help get Lynn and Drew together. I don't think he has ever looked at another girl since Lynn's knight-in-shining-armor moment in sixth grade. I honestly didn't think he'd go along with the idea of a makeover, and him not fighting it tells me how much he really is into Lynn.

Oliver Ridire walks into the class, and I have another idea. Oliver is friends with Lynn, and he seems nice. He's in AP Pre-Cal and Physics with me, but so is Lynn and some of their other friends. None of them are in English. When he sits down, I move to the desk next to him.

"Hey."

"Hi...?" Oliver has a look on his face like he's not sure if I mean to be talking to him.

"How's your day going?"

"Fine. Yours?"

"Great. So, I wanted to ask about your friend." I don't know why, but he looks pained at that statement.

Maybe earlier was a fluke and he regretted having a band nerd who thought they could just walk up and talk to him. Oliver's a popular jock like the rest of the Knights. None of them have spoken to me or my friends before today.

"They don't do relationships, so don't waste your time."

Yeah, he doesn't need to tell me that.

I know all of them have a reputation for being players on and off the field. I've had enough of that sort of nonsense already.

"Oh, no, not the guys. Lynn."

"Lynn?" Oliver's voice goes up an octave.

His cheeks turn pink like he's embarrassed for me. By how hot my face feels, I'm sure I'm blushing.

"That's not what I meant. I like guys," I insist.

Before I can come up with a better response, Mrs. Green starts class. As soon as class is over, Oliver leaves. I'm pretty sure he's running away from me. If I'm going to get information on Lynn for Drew, I'm going to need to be more discrete. That is if I can even get the Knight to talk to me.

I meet up with Drew in the hallway on the way to Jazz Band.

"Will you fix my glasses now?" he asks.

"Will you give the makeover a try for a week?"

"You said for one day, not a week." Drew dramatically throws his head back.

"If you give it at least a week, I'll put the screws back in your glasses Wednesday."

"Are you holding my glasses hostage now?"

"When you put it that way…yes." I nod.

"Why? I hate my contacts, and Lynn has already seen me without my glasses. Can I please have them back?" Drew put his hands together like he's literally begging for me to put his glasses back together.

"Because it's for your own good. Just because she was in the same room doesn't mean she saw you. If that was true, we wouldn't have to make a plan to get her attention."

"She saw, so *please* give me my glasses back."

"How do you know she saw you without your glasses?"

"She asked in AP Government where my glasses were. I told her they broke during lunch."

"Lynn talked to you?!? See, it's already working. And she noticed you didn't have glasses. That's great news!"

Then I add, "You told her your glasses broke, so now you can't wear them for the next couple of days until a reasonable amount of time has passed for you to get them fixed."

"Fine, but I'm going back to my clothes tomorrow." Drew pouts and looks like an adorable puppy.

"Please give it a week? If she's already noticing you and talking to you, then you should stick with it for a week. That way you can really give this experiment a try."

"You're going to annoy me relentlessly until I agree, aren't you?" Drew walks into the band hall.

"Of course. It's in your best interest to agree sooner rather than later."

"I don't know why I'm friends with you. I guess I'll wear your new clothes for the rest of this week. But I refuse to wear the bedazzled jeans you bought."

"Yay! And after school we can get you shoes that aren't so ragged!" I clap my hands in excitement.

Behind us, Carter walks into the band hall and says, "I want to ask why Kaylee is squealing, but I feel like I don't want to know."

"Drew is sticking with the makeover." I clap my hands some more.

"Correction, under duress I agreed to wear the new clothes for the rest of the week. I'd appreciate it if you'd stop saying makeover." Drew goes to assemble his horn for class. Mr. Gregory calls the class to attention and Drew doesn't have any more time to argue against the makeover.

"Remember when your sectionals are this week, and you need to be on the field ready to play at six tonight. We're marching the entire show Friday, so it needs to be ready," Mr. Gregory calls as the final bell rings.

"All right we have two and a half hours to get your makeover finished. Are you ready?" I ask Drew as we put our horns back in our cubby.

"Stop saying that. I thought we're only getting shoes; how long will that take?"

"Shoe shopping with Kaylee? That can take an eternity." Sara, my younger sister, walks over to us. Since she's a freshman this year she's in band with us. "Are you taking me home first?"

Sara would be a mini me if we didn't dress and do our make-up so differently. She's five foot, two and has bleached-blonde hair. Unlike me, she doesn't dye it. We have the same blue eyes and button nose. She wears minimum makeup in neutral tones.

I, on the other hand, love bold make-up that really pops. Sometimes I wear faux nose and lip rings. My wardrobe screams punk rock while hers is softer and more girly.

Today she's wearing black skinny jeans, sparkly sandals, and a pink halter top. She had a black cardigan on earlier so she'd be in dress code.

"We don't have time." I say to my sister. "And we're getting new shoes for Drew, not me. Plus, we need to have eaten dinner before we get back."

"I have homework I need to do," Sara whines, starting to pout.

"You can work on it in the van or in the food court. We don't need your help with finding shoes." I holler at Carter as he makes his way to us. "Hey Carter! Are you coming with us to the mall?"

Drew turns to look at him. "Please don't leave me alone with Kaylee when she's on a mission."

"Of course, I'm coming. This has been highly entertaining. Is Cornlet coming, too?" Carter ruffles Sara's hair.

She hates him ruffling her hair and calling her Cornlet. The first time they met, he called her baby corn since she's my younger sister and our last name is Cobb. She threw a fit and said she wasn't a baby. The next week Carter found out baby corn is called cornlet and has called her that since. When we were younger, she didn't mind the nickname. For the last couple of years, it has really annoyed her.

"Like I have a choice." Sara glares at Carter.

"Let's go. Time's a-wasting and we don't have much to begin with." I walk out of the band hall.

For all of Sara's complaints on the way to the mall about homework, she doesn't even bring her backpack with her.

"We're trying to get you to look like someone Lynn dates. She dates exclusively jocks, so I think Jordans," I say to Drew as we walk into the Shoe Dept.

"Wait. All of this is to get Lynn's attention? Lynn *Kingston*?" Sara sounds incredulous. "You realize changing his clothes won't turn him into a tall, hot jock. Which, as you said, is Lynn's type and she doesn't stray from it. She just broke up with the captain of the football team who is way hot. No offense or anything Drew, but that's not you," she chimes in unhelpfully.

"See, even Sara knows this is a dumb idea." Drew throws his hands in the air. "I just want to survive this project with my dignity and GPA intact."

"But it's already working—she came up to talk to you today. You have twelve weeks of working on this project to make her realize why band nerds are better than jocks," I point out.

"Lynn talked to him in a class where they were partnered together. I don't think that counts, Kaylee," Carter says.

"No, not then. She talked to him during AP Government. She even noticed he wasn't wearing his glasses," I counter.

"How did I not know Lynn came to talk to you? That's a huge step, man." Carter claps Drew on the back.

"She wanted to make sure I hadn't lost her number for our project since I forgot to text her after second period was over. Since class hadn't started, she put her number in, so I couldn't lose it."

"What? You didn't tell me that! What did she save her number as?" I reach for his phone.

"Lynn Kingston. What else would she save it as? And why does that matter?"

"Because if she saved it as something cute, it'd mean it's not only about the project. I need to see it," I say. Drew reluctantly hands me his phone. "She put a basketball emoji followed by the number twelve. Not just about the project."

"Pretty sure that's because she lives and breathes basketball and twelve is her jersey number," Drew says with zero enthusiasm. "Can we get this trip over with so we can eat before Monday-night practice?"

"Fine."

After an hour, we all finally agree on getting him low-top Converse and Nike tennis shoes.

CHAPTER 14
GRAYSON

When I first heard the announcements this morning, I was not at all excited to be named Junior Homecoming Prince. Normally, it's not something I'd care about either way. But watching Lynn be all loved up with Mark is usually annoying, which I'd assume would be worse with them being on Homecoming Court together.

I started looking at Lynn differently this summer, but then she started dating Ethan Frost. By the time they broke up, she was already enamored with Mark. Hearing that she dumped him yesterday made me much happier than it should have.

Now she's fair game, and we'll be doing all of the Homecoming activities together. I'm hoping to use it as an opportunity to show her I could be her Prince Charming, not just her Homecoming Prince. Okay, that sounded stupid even in *my* head.

I look at the text she sent earlier in the day. She texted the group chat after second period to let us know her mom made lasagna for lunch. Right after she sent a text just to me.

> Kingston: I'm glad we're on Homecoming Court together! You might be the only thing that makes dealing with the cheerleaders bearable 😊

When I first got it, I assumed she'd just be happy to have a friend with her, but with the news about Mark, I was hoping maybe she was glad it was me specifically and not because we're friends.

I want to ask her out, but that'd blow up in my face. Not only did she just break up with my teammate and captain, but we had a Creed within the Knights that I had to follow.

We've lived on the same block all of our lives. Since Lynn's mom, Stella, wanted to be a stay-at-home parent, she ended up being a nanny to Oliver, Daniel, and me growing up. Stella, who has always been big into sports, played catch with us, taught us to dribble, and would take us to watch at least one game a week. None of our parents were ever around much because they were workaholics.

When we were old enough to play, Stella was our coach. Our town didn't have a girls' league for any sports starting that young at the time, so Lynn played on our team. We played at least one season of every sport available because Stella wanted us to be able to try everything.

When we were four, Jet was put on our team and the five of us have been inseparable since then. Lynn's uncle, Logan, lived with them growing up. He played sports and even went on to play college basketball. He'd coach us when he was home, and Stella would take us to his games when she could. This sparked our love for basketball, which was the glue that held us together for a long time.

When we realized Lynn wasn't actually one of the guys, we started fighting over her. Never trying to be obvious when we're around her, but we'd try to sit next to her or guard her whenever we played sports. After a few weeks of this, we realized we needed to do something since we were always fighting and Lynn had started to notice.

We made our own Creed and decided the fairest way to handle it was that none of us could have her. That was the beginning of fourth grade. In fifth grade, more of our friends started dating and Lynn asked Daniel to be her boyfriend. Due to our Creed, he said no.

Lynn wouldn't hang out with any of us after that. After the first day that she wouldn't come out of her house, Daniel told us what happened. Jet then got mad and stopped talking to Daniel. At the time

I didn't care about Lynn wanting to date Daniel. The cheerleaders were pretty and flirty, and my tomboy of a best friend was already off limits.

So, three days later when Lynn still wasn't talking to us, Oliver and I invited Daniel and Jet to our house without telling them the other was coming. I told Daniel he should say yes to Lynn. The Creed was to keep dating from coming between the Knights and that was happening because he said no. Jet got mad, saying it wasn't fair because he wanted to date Lynn. We all argued for a while before we came up with a new Creed.

None of us were allowed to ask Lynn out or try to kiss her, but if she asked, we could say yes. When we were hanging out with the Knights, the flirting and relationship-y behavior would be kept to a minimum. The other guys couldn't stop coming over because they were jealous. They'd have to suck it up and deal.

Once we came to an agreement, Daniel ran over to Lynn's house to tell her he did want to be her boyfriend. Jet, Oliver, and I went to the park to play basketball. Jet said he wanted to go so Daniel could be with Lynn without the rest of us around. Oliver and I knew better but didn't call him on it. Jet was moody the next few weeks until Lynn and Daniel broke up, but he got over it.

Which meant I'd need to get Lynn to ask me out. I had a feeling Mark dropping the L bomb on her was not going to make her want to get back into another relationship. Nothing scares Lynn off faster than romantic love.

Every time a boyfriend says he loves her, it's always the beginning of the end of their relationship. Normally, it's not as sudden as it was with Mark, but it's only a matter of time. It doesn't come up that often because Lynn doesn't usually stay in relationships very long.

Lynn typically stays single longer if her most recent ex said they loved her. Daniel called her on it once after she and Josh Wicks, the pitcher of the baseball team, broke up. She said it was because she didn't want to hurt him any more than she already had.

I think it's more that it makes her gun shy with dating, especially since those are the only times she ever kisses guys without being in a relationship first. I'm pretty sure making out with the first baseman under the bleachers would hurt Josh just as much as her dating someone else. I guess she thinks as long as it's not officially a relationship, then no one will know about it.

I spend the afternoon trying to work out a plan for how to get Lynn to ask me out. I'm still in my head about it in the locker room when we're getting changed for athletics.

"Yo, Slater, I heard you dumped Kingston for Whitney over the weekend." This came from Dane Watkins, our other first-string wide receiver and team pot-stirrer. "What's up with that?"

"I don't have any interest in Whitney. That chick is nuts. Things with Lynn had run its course, so we decided to end it." Mark looks confident as he says this, but I catch him glancing toward where the Knights and I are changing.

He's probably worried about us contradicting him.

"So, is it cool if I ask her to the dance on Saturday?" Watkins asks.

"Dude, they just broke up. Not cool." Josh Wicks hits Watkins on the back of the head.

"What? Lynn's hot and she never stays single for long. The dance would be a perfect rebound date. Give her a shoulder to cry on, then bam! I have a hot date to the dance with a potential for making out afterwards." Watkins wiggles his eyebrows on his last remark.

Colten slams his locker and storms out of the locker room. This isn't the first time the guys have brought up Lynn. It upsets Colten, but being a freshman, the seniors don't listen to him. He has learned it's easier to walk away. It tends to egg them on when he tries to get them to shut up.

"Drop it, Watkins. You're being a jerk," Tristan says. "Besides, Lynn doesn't need a date to the dance."

The words have an instant effect on Mark. He deflates for a moment before looking pissed. No one else has noticed because all eyes are on Tristan.

"What? Did you get back out of the friendzone?" Mark scoffs.

During his relationship with Lynn, he was never comfortable with all of her close friends being guys, especially since three are her exes.

Tristan seems to pick up on the mood shift in the room. "We. Are.

Friends. That's it. We're all going in a group as friends. You can all calm down."

I'm done with this conversation and head out to the field. Tristan is close behind me, and I hope that means they dropped it after I left.

CHAPTER 15
OLIVER

Practice was brutal today. Apparently, Mark is joining the ranks of team captains who take their heartbreak from Lynn out on the team.

At least with football in full swing, all he can really do is make us run longer and do more reps of exercises during warm-ups. It'd be so much worse if it was still two-a-days and we were having captain's practices.

On the upside, Lynn has the later fall league game tonight, so we have time to come home and shower before heading back up to the school. I'm looking forward to having some peace and quiet before we leave, especially since Grayson talked nonstop about Homecoming on the way home.

I didn't think he'd be the type to care about Homecoming Court or another dance, but you'd think he was talking about making it to the playoffs when he was going on about being Homecoming Prince. Maybe being popular is more important to him than I'd have thought.

"I told you about this dinner months ago, Hugh. The firm partners will all be there." My mother's voice carries from the kitchen.

"And I told you about this dinner two weeks ago, Regina. It's with our biggest client. I can't miss it. You should've said something if you wanted me to try to reschedule," my father responds.

I can tell by what they're saying that they're arguing, but you can't tell from the tone of their voices. They could be discussing the weather for all of the emotion they're showing. I don't think I've ever seen my parents fight, and that's not because they have a stellar relationship. They both seem rather indifferent to each other and are more married to their careers than to each other.

It makes me very thankful they hired Mama Kingston as our nanny. You can see Lynn's parents' love for each other shining through all of their actions, even when they're balancing everything with all of their kids. They've always treated the Knights like they treat the rest of their kids and that didn't stop when we aged out of needing a nanny.

Even when we were little, Stella went above and beyond any other nanny. She'd come get us, even when our parents were home, to take us with them to church or the park. They even took us with them on their family vacations. I never missed having my parents be involved in my life because Stella and Theo were already there loving and supporting us.

"Don't worry about it now. We'll just each go to our own work dinner." My mother's statement brings me back to the present.

"Sounds good to me." They both walk past Grayson and me on their way to the garage with barely a nod to acknowledge our presence.

It's probably a good thing they set up an auto-draft to our account for food and gas each month. Otherwise, they'd forget to do that, like how they seem to forget we exist most of the time.

The closest either of them has come to parenting was when they decided we were old enough to not have a nanny and therefore be responsible for ourselves. My father gave Grayson and I each a book on money management and went to the bank with us to open our own accounts.

When we got home, our mother told us the monthly amount they had allotted for each of us, and if we thought that wasn't fair or enough, we could set up a time to discuss it. They both went to their home offices. Grayson dumped his budgeting book in my room before going to Lynn's to play ball.

I tried to read it but didn't understand most of it. I took it across the road to Stella. She and Theo helped us with budgeting and reassured us that it didn't matter how old we were, they were there for us and that was for always.

When I get out of the shower, I see a text from Lynn in the Knight's group chat.

Kingston: Dinner in ten

It was sent almost ten minutes ago and everyone else has responded with some sort of acknowledgement. I send a *thumbs up* before quickly getting dressed and heading next door. I'm not surprised to find the rest of the Knights already there. Even Grayson beat me here.

I sit down, and Theo thanks God for the food and all of our many blessings. He says, "Amen," and then thanks his wife for preparing the pot roast.

Theo asks everyone about their day and Stella keeps the chaos to a minimum. The threat of an early bedtime keeps Lynn's three youngest brothers from causing too much mischief.

It's hard to really listen to anyone because everyone talks over one another. I'd take the hectic noise of this home to the silence and emptiness of my house any day.

Lynn and Jet are sitting at the table, but they're only eating peanut butter crackers since they're about to go play a game. Stella reminds them she already set aside roast for each of them in the fridge, for after they play.

Jet's mom shows up still in her scrubs from work and gratefully accepts a to-go container and a hug from Stella before taking Jet and Lynn up to the school for warm-ups.

They could drive themselves, but since Julia works all the time, she tries to squeeze out as much time with Jet as she can. Lynn adores her and tends to crash their mother-son time—not that either of them seem to mind.

After we finish eating, I put away the leftovers. Tristan helps Stella clean the kitchen, and Daniel and Xander help Theo wrangle all of Lynn's brothers into the car.

It's only when we're loading up with Xander in his SUV that I notice Grayson already left with our SUV, presumably back to the school. I don't know what's up with him today.

"Is now a good time to talk about the Queen of Punk?" Tristan asks once all of the car doors are shut.

I close my eyes and lean my head against the headrest like that might somehow make him drop it.

"Who's the Queen of Punk?" Xander glances at us in the rearview mirror.

"No one," I say at the same time Daniel says, "Kaylee Cobb."

Xander nods. "Fitting. Why does Oliver not want to talk about her?"

"Because he learned to play guitar to impress her despite becoming an awkward dork whenever he tries to talk to her," Daniel, the traitor, says from the front seat.

"In other words: he *lurves* her." Tristan is being equally unhelpful.

"I don't love her. I've barely talked to her." I know my protest will fall on deaf ears.

"But you want to talk to her." Daniel turns around to look at me like that makes his point hold more weight.

"He learned guitar. He wants to serenade her." Tristan leans toward me, batting his eyes while using his annoying sing-song voice.

Tristan and Daniel go on about me having a crush on Kaylee and how I should just go talk to her and ask her out. Things like I'm a Knight and she'd definitely say yes.

Xander makes eye contact with me via the rearview mirror and raises a single eyebrow that manages to say more than the other two combined.

Xander gets how difficult it is for me to just talk to someone I don't know; he's the same way. He also conveys his thoughts on me learning the guitar, and he's right. I hate public speaking. In what world did I think I would be able to sing a song in front of people? Especially when that song exposes my feelings for someone who most likely doesn't feel the same way.

Xander finally takes pity on me and says, "Tristan, how are things with your neighbor? You know the one you said was cute?"

Tristan lets out a groan.

"I said that one time. Once! And that was before she'd ever opened her mouth. Now I know she's just an annoyance dressed like a frumpy librarian."

"I didn't know you actually listened to girls when they talked," Xander teases.

I catch Xander's slight smirk and know he's intentionally stirring Tristan up to distract him.

"I listen. It's not my fault they see all of this"—Tristan gestures to his face and chest in an over-the-top way— "and would rather be making out than talking."

"Yet, you wonder why your neighbor thinks you're arrogant." Daniel rolls his eyes.

"It's not arrogance if it's true. The perfect princess just hates that I have a social life and she clearly doesn't." Tristan spends the rest of the trip complaining about his neighbor.

CHAPTER 16
ANDREW

I'm getting my Government book out of my locker Tuesday afternoon when Kaylee elbows me in the ribs.

"Kaylee, I thought we talked about…" I trail off as I look over to see Lynn leaning on the locker next to mine. "Oh, Lynn. Uh, hi."

"Hey." She looks confident and cool, which doesn't do much for my speech capabilities.

"We're off to class. Have fun." Kaylee drags Carter away.

"I have something I have to do after school, so I might be late to our study session. Xander will be home, though, and can let you in if you get there before me." Lynn flicks her hair out of her eyes.

"Oh, uh, okay. Do we, um, do we need to reschedule?" I resist the urge to ask what she has to do after school. It's bad enough my voice comes out squeaky and unsure.

"No, it should be fine. I'm hoping to be back home by five but wanted to give you a heads up in case I'm running late. I'll try to text you if I'm running behind, but sometimes I forget." Lynn pushes off the bank of lockers.

"Uh, okay, um, I guess…I will, uh, see you then…?" I squeak. I wish being around Lynn didn't turn me into an even bigger dork than I already am.

"We're headed the same way and have the next two classes together." Lynn's face seems to say she's worried I've hit my head.

"Oh, well yeah." I turn to head down the hall.

"Government is this way." Lynn nods in the opposite direction.

I realize I was so flustered I went the wrong way. At this rate I'm sure I'll manage to make a complete fool of myself by the end of this semester.

"I knew that." I turn around, feeling like a dork.

Lynn doesn't say anything else but walks next to me the whole way to class. I notice some students looking at us, probably wondering if there's anything of interest going on. As much as the staring makes me uncomfortable, I can't blame them.

It's not every day that the queen that is Lynn Kingston walks down the hall with a band nerd. Not to mention, Lynn rocks the 80's look with her black off-the-shoulder shirt and neon tank top and leg warmers.

Yesterday, when she led me by the arm through the hallway, I was too distracted by the feel of her touching me to take in my surroundings. In hindsight, I'm sure there were people in the hallway who noticed. Although considering I'm a nobody at this school, they probably only took note of Lynn walking away from Mark.

That whole encounter was odd, and so was Lynn's chattiness. Maybe it was a result of her feeling flustered because of Mark. Regardless, I'm glad she seems to have chilled back to her usual self. Her touching me and talking with me was a dream come true. Except, it made me even more nervous and less capable of speech. Just another reason why things would never work out with us.

We walk to class in a comfortable silence. When we get there, she heads to the back to sit with her friends. I contemplate following her and sitting near her but decide against it.

She's only talking to me because we're doing a project together. I don't need to make more of a fool of myself than necessary. It's bad enough that I stutter every time we talk. I don't want her to think I'm following her around or expecting us to be friends.

Walking to the back where all the Knights are without even having Kaylee or Carter in this class as back-up feels like walking alone into the lion's den. I have no delusions about being an awkward, fumbling gazelle in that comparison and I'd rather not get eaten alive.

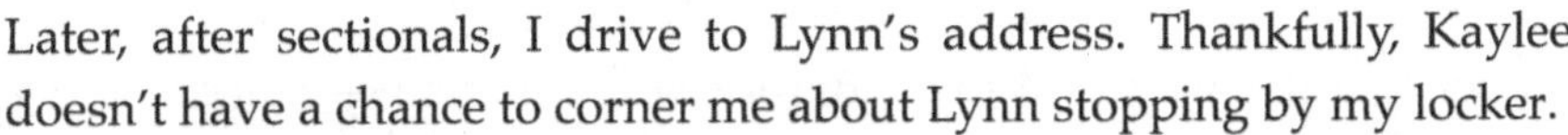

Later, after sectionals, I drive to Lynn's address. Thankfully, Kaylee doesn't have a chance to corner me about Lynn stopping by my locker.

I get to her house and I realize *house* isn't exactly accurate. It's more like a mini mansion. Which is a bit out of place since it's in the middle of a suburban neighborhood. And her house looks to be twice the size of the houses on either side. I passed a few other big houses while navigating here, but hers looks even bigger than those.

I pull into the circle drive. I wipe the sweat off my hands and onto my jeans. I take a deep breath, then get out of my car. A black Honda CRV pulls up next to me.

Lynn gets out of the passenger side, and I try to fight my instinct to look into the car, telling myself I don't want to see whatever popular jock is dropping her off. My eyes don't listen, and I look anyway. I'm relieved to see who I assume must be her mother in the driver's seat. Lynn looks like her mom. Brown hair, brown eyes, and a kind face.

"I'll bring your dresses and shoes into the house. You just worry about your project," I hear her mother say.

"Thanks, Mom." Lynn grabs her backpack and shuts the car door. Then she approaches me. "Hey, sorry I'm a bit late. Apparently, a Homecoming Princess needs three dresses for Homecoming instead of one. Anyway, I'm sure you don't want to hear about any of that. Ready to come in?"

"Sounds good." I grab my backpack and try to keep breathing. I follow Lynn through the front door.

"Mom doesn't let us wear shoes in the house," she explains as she takes her shoes off. I do the same and follow Lynn.

"I figured we could work in the dining room. It doesn't get used much since we have an eat-in kitchen." Lynn leads me through the gigantic living room and kitchen.

I try not to gape when we enter a formal dining room that's bigger than my dining room and kitchen combined. I obviously don't succeed in playing it cool.

"Oh, yeah, I forget that our house can be a bit much." Lynn blushes. She's even prettier when she blushes.

"My dad's a property developer and real estate agent. He worked with the contractor on this subdivision, so my dad built my mom the house of her dreams. At that point they already had three kids with another on the way, and my mom loves to entertain—hence, the big house and giant dining room. Although, if you were here for Thanksgiving when the whole family is here, it probably wouldn't look as big." Lynn looks embarrassed, which makes it easier for me to talk. Her blushing humanizes her.

"Your house is awesome. So, you have three siblings?" I ask.

I obviously know Xander is her brother and that she has another brother who's a freshman.

"We moved into this house when I was three and there were three of us then. Now I have six brothers," Lynn says.

"There's seven of you? I thought my house was full when both of my brothers were still at home. I can't imagine six brothers."

"You won't have to imagine for long since you'll most likely get to meet them all while you're here. I promise they aren't that bad."

"If they're like their sister, I'm sure they're awesome."

Crap, did those words actually come out of my mouth?

What do I do now?

I glance up to look at Lynn to gauge whether or not she's freaking out and putting distance between us. She tucks some of her hair behind her ear.

"Thanks. I don't know that I'd call them awesome, though—especially not where they'd hear it." She sets her backpack down and starts pulling things out.

It seems like the comment didn't register as weird. Which is good because she isn't looking at me funny and I didn't make her uncomfortable. But it's also a reminder that she has guys saying that kind of stuff to her all the time. Guys who are taller, more athletic, and more confident than me. Guys who know how to talk to girls and have a lot of experience with girls.

Unlike me who has never even been kissed much less gone on a date. Who knows, that might not have even registered as a compliment to her, much less any form of flirting. It's not like I've ever tried to flirt with anyone or had anyone flirt with me, so how would I know.

"So, I talked to Mrs. Green today and she approved of my idea. Now we just need to decide whether we want to go with *The Taming of the Shrew* or *Twelfth Night*. Which do you think we should do?" Lynn asks.

This must be a continuation of the outline she did yesterday that I completely didn't hear.

"What…what do you think would work better for your…I mean, our outline?" I ask, hopefully hiding that I don't know what her outline was. I'm hoping she doesn't realize I started daydreaming about her.

"I think they'd both work. If you don't care which, then I think we should go with *Twelfth Night* because I love *She's the Man* and I do better with sports analogies."

"What's *She's the Man*?" I completely give up on the pretense I know what's going on.

"The Amanda Bines movie with Channing Tatum. It's a soccer movie loosely based on *Twelfth Night*. Amanda's character Viola plays soccer. When her high school cuts the girls soccer team and her boyfriend breaks up with her, she goes to her brother's new boarding school pretending to be him and tries out for the boys' soccer team. The new team is her old school's rival." Lynn's clearly getting excited about the idea.

She starts bouncing in her seat and waving her hands around as she talks about what's obviously a movie she loves.

Lynn is adorable when she's excited. Which isn't great news for me. I already know she's gorgeous with killer curves. Her being adorable and sweet as well is almost too much.

"Sounds awesome," I say. "So, um, what's our game plan?"

"I did some more research, and there are eleven movie adaptations of *Twelfth Night* not including *She's the Man*. I figured we could both read the play on our own before this Saturday. Then each week we could watch a movie adaptation together and compare it to the play. We'd discuss it and then alternate each week writing a paper.

"When I talked to Mrs. Green, she said we could write one page comparing the play and the movie as long as we did at least five movies. I figured we could watch *She's the Man* during Thanksgiving break since we get the entire week off. We'd discuss the differences in how it compares to the play and the other movies. Then for our presentation, I thought I'd dress up as Xander. I could borrow some of his clothes and get a wig and blue contacts. I'd represent Viola when we do our presentation. What do you think?"

"Wow, you put a lot of thought into this already." I'm slightly taken aback by how much she already has planned out.

"Of course, it's thirty percent of our grade, and I'm not some dumb jock who coasts by in school." Lynn sounds offended.

"No, I didn't…I mean…I didn't think…I wasn't…trying to imply anything negative. It's just…I'm just…impressed. I'm not used to being the one less prepared for a project. I…I'm excited about this."

Lynn seems mollified by my enthusiasm. "Oh, okay. I thought when we got closer, I might ask Xander if he'd be part of our presentation if Mrs. Green is okay with it. He'd be a prop or actor in a skit. Just to be part of it for the whole twin aspect. Would that be okay with you?"

"That sounds great. I'm sure we'll have the best project in the class," I say.

We spend the next hour coordinating schedules and brainstorming ideas for our presentation. We're just putting the finishing touches on the layout of our plan when Lynn's mom comes into the dining room.

"Lynn, dinner's ready. You know you can't have the door shut if you're alone with a boy," she says in a stern tone.

"It's schoolwork, Mom, and I didn't want any of the heathens coming in here and interrupting us. This project is thirty percent of our overall grade for English," Lynn says defensively.

"It's still a house rule. If you want to keep the door shut, then invite Xander to study with you. I'm sure Mark wouldn't appreciate hearing you were alone with another boy."

Lynn blushes.

It's just as cute as it was earlier when she blushed. I'm surprised by what her mom said. I'm pretty sure the only question anyone would have about me being at Lynn's house would be "Why was there a dweeb at her house?" or "Who is Andrew?" The idea that Lynn would be doing anything with me that'd make someone else jealous is laughable.

"Mom, I've been meaning to tell you, but we broke up on Sunday." Lynn looks uncomfortable having this conversation in front of me.

"Okay, go wash your hands and you can work on your project more after dinner." Lynn's mother's smile grows tight as she talks.

"I...I should be heading out. I wouldn't want to, uh, impose on family dinner." I start packing up my stuff. I don't want to overstay my welcome.

"It's not an imposition. We'd love to have you. I assumed since you started your project so close to dinner that you'd be staying. Besides, it's not just family; Callie's here tonight since the varsity boys have team bonding." Mrs. Kingston gives Lynn a pointed look.

"We'd love to have you stay as long as that's okay with your parents. I meant to ask you earlier, but it slipped my mind," Lynn chimes in.

"Okay, I'll text and, um, let you know." I pull out my phone.

"Great! Lynn can show you where the bathroom and kitchen are." Lynn's mom's smile has turned beaming. She walks back out of the dining room, leaving the door as wide open as possible.

Lynn waits until she's out of earshot before speaking. "Honestly, she probably has enough food for an army, and she's a fantastic cook. You should stay. Had I thought about it, I'd have said something earlier. I'm used to the Knights staying for dinner anytime they're over in the evening. For them it's a given and not something I ask about."

"Are...are you sure? I don't want you to feel obligated or whatever because your mom invited me for dinner." I flip my phone around in my hands.

"I'm *absolutely* sure. For one, you're good company, and if we're going to be working on this project for the next few months, you may as well meet the rest of the family," she says. "To be completely honest, if you're there, it ought to keep my mom from interrogating me about Mark. And hopefully, distract her enough so she'll forget to ask later. But if you need to go, I understand. I don't want you to feel obligated to stay. I already owe you one for saving me from Mark in the hallway yesterday. I completely get it if you don't want to be more tied up in my boyfriend drama."

"Let me text my dad real quick, but I'm sure it'll be fine." I may not be excited to have dinner with a bunch of people I don't know, but apparently, I can't resist an opportunity to be Lynn's knight in shining armor.

Even if it's just to save her from an awkward conversation. Saving her from awkward conversations seems to be something I'm going to be doing regularly now. Which is ironic considering how awkward I am around her.

"Okay, great." Lynn beams at me, and I want to slay dragons for this girl.

I'm starting to think my focus for this project should be doing whatever I can to keep from falling completely in love with Lynn. I'll just end up getting my heart broken when this project is over, and she doesn't speak to me again.

"He said that's fine," I say a moment later after getting a reply from my dad.

I'm excited for a home-cooked meal.

My mom skipped town when I was born, so all I have ever had is my dad and older brothers. We eat a lot of take-out and freezer meals.

Lynn shows me where the kitchen is, then takes me to the bathroom so I can wash my hands, before she goes to help her mom finish setting the table.

When I come back to the kitchen, all of Lynn's family is there, and it's a little overwhelming.

"Andrew, we're so glad you could stay for dinner. Why don't you sit here?" Lynn's mom pulls out a chair that's between where Lynn and Xander are standing.

All three of us sit down. Everyone at the table puts their hands together and bows their head. I copy them, not sure what else to do. Lynn's dad blesses the food and thanks God for this day and all His blessings. It's not something I'm used to.

As Lynn starts serving the food, her mom begins introducing everyone. I'm glad they're different heights since most of Lynn's younger brothers have brown hair and brown eyes and an intense family resemblance. Xander's the one who looks least like Lynn, which is weird to me since they're twins. He and Dylan are the only ones with blue eyes.

"Colten's a freshman—he's a wide receiver on the JV team." She gestures to a boy with short hair.

Even though he's two years younger, he's much taller than me. I've heard of him before but hadn't met him until now.

"Callie's the football coach's daughter. She's a freshman and the quarterback for the JV team." Callie has brown hair and brown eyes and blends in with the rest of Lynn's family even though she's not related to them.

"Dylan's in eighth grade. He's first chair euphonium in the symphonic band and he plays guitar." Dylan is lanky and tall for his age with longish wavy hair.

"Leo's in sixth grade, and he shows heifers for 4-H." He's short and stout, his hair is unruly.

"And this is Parker and Sean. They're in first grade and play soccer." The twins are identical, and I have no idea which is which.

It looks like my main focus for dinner is going to be remembering who each of Lynn's siblings are. Hopefully it'll keep me from looking like too much of a love-struck idiot.

CHAPTER 17
LYNN

"Mom, I don't think Andrew needs to know all the boys' extracurriculars." I hope to distract her before she overshares any more than she already has.

I'm pretty sure Andrew's already regretting agreeing to stay for dinner. Callie meets my eyes from across the table before rolling hers. Because her dad's the football coach, she grew up playing football with Colten. She's sort of like a younger sister, except neither of us do anything girly. I guess it's more like having a younger brother who actually thinks I'm cool.

"Fine. How is your project going so far?" Mom asks.

"So far, so good. We're planning on getting together to work on it more this Saturday around two." I'm part letting her know and part asking for permission.

"That's great. You can get some work done, then go to the Homecoming dance. You're still going, right?" Mom asks.

"Yes, I'm still going. Me and the other Knights who don't have dates are all going together." I'm slightly irritated that she has brought it up again in front of Andrew. I've been hoping his presence would prevent all talk of my current single status.

"I'm sure you'll have fun." Mom turns to Andrew. "What about you, Andrew, who are you going with to the dance?" She's clearly decided everyone at the table should be uncomfortable.

"Um, well, I wasn't, uh, planning on going. I'm, um, only going to the game and parade because I'm, uh, I'm in the band." Andrew turns red.

"You're in band? What instrument do you play? What chair are you?" Dylan asks.

"Uh, trombone and first chair," Andrew answers.

"That's awesome. Low brass is the coolest!" Dylan beams. Even with the awkwardness in the room, it's good to see Dylan smiling and excited about something. He's been quieter and moodier since this summer.

"Do you not like dances?" Mom asks Andrew, apparently not done interrogating him.

Mom thinks you should enjoy being a teenager while you can and get the entire high-school experience before graduating and becoming a responsible adult. I guess that's extending past her children and the Knights now.

"Um, I guess I don't know for sure. I've never been to one, but, um, they don't seem like my thing." Andrew turns a brighter shade of red.

Mom shoots me a look. I'm hoping I can get her to drop it, so I cooperate with what she wants. Maybe that will even get me some leeway with the Mark situation.

"Would you want to come with me and my friends?" I turn to look at Andrew, who has his eyes trained on his plate like his pot pie is the most interesting thing he has ever seen.

When he doesn't answer right away, I look to Xander for help. After a brief silent exchange, Xander clears his throat.

"My best friend, Amelia, and I will be going with them, too, so it won't be all jocks." Xander's eyes are making it clear that I owe him.

"Okay, I…I guess." Andrew still isn't looking up from his plate.

"Great!" Mom's the only one happy about this situation.

"You can bring whatever you're wearing to the dance with you on Saturday when you come to work on your project—that way you won't have to go back home to change."

Translation: So that she can take way too many pictures before she lets us leave and make sure Andrew actually goes with us.

"If you and Xander are going in one group, can I go with y'all instead of having to be dropped off?" Colten asks.

"Can I come, too? I'd rather ride with you than my dad," Callie adds.

"Of course," I say, "my two favorite fishies can come with us."

Colten rolls his eyes, either irritated by being called a fish or my expressing any kind of affection for him. Knowing how he's been since starting high school, it's the latter. He'd have to prefer "fish" to "fresh meat," the other nickname for freshmen. He acts like he didn't just ask us to take him with us.

I mean, I'm the one going to Homecoming with not one but two of my brothers tagging along. I almost wish I was still going with Mark. Actually, I take that back; I'd rather go to Homecoming with *all* of my brothers in tow than go with Mark after what he said on Sunday.

Maybe Callie can take Dylan as her date, and Colten can have a younger sibling crashing his night and see how annoying he thinks I am then.

Thankfully, the subject of Homecoming is dropped and the rest of dinner is uneventful. After we eat, I offer to help Andrew pack up his school stuff and walk him out. It gets me out of doing dishes and we can have a talk about Homecoming without my entire family listening in. I wait until we're back in the formal dining room to say anything.

"I want to apologize for my mom with the whole Homecoming thing. She can be a bit much," I start, not sure what to say.

"It's…it's okay. I can, uh, come up with some excuse Saturday as to why, um, I…I can't go. That way your mom won't, uh, get upset with you." Andrew looks down at the ground.

"You don't have to do that. You're more than welcome to come with us, but I understand if you don't want to go. Dances aren't for everyone. I mean, Xander hates them," I say before remembering that Xander now has to go because of me.

"So, he goes to appease your mom?" Andrew asks.

"Basically." I don't want to correct him and make him think Xander is only going because of him. It's true, but I don't want to guilt him into coming with us.

"Mom's big on us enjoying high school before we enter the real world and have to be adults. If you want to go, you should come with us. Then at least you'll know one way or the other about dances. Plus, in my opinion, it's better to go with a group of friends instead of a date; it's less stressful and more fun. But I understand if you don't want to go with us."

"Don't you think your friends will, um, have a problem with someone like...someone like me coming with you?" Andrew asks. "I mean with your group, not with you."

"Nah, they'll be cool. They don't mind new people. You coming with us means either Xander or I will be driving, which they'll love."

"Are you sure? And are you sure you want *me* to come?" Andrew finally looks up at me.

He looks nervous, and suddenly, I'm worried he might see this as me asking him on a date.

"Yeah, it could help us get to know each other better, which would be good for working on the project together. Why wouldn't I want you there with us?"

"Because we aren't, um, exactly in the same social group. I'm more like a peasant that needs protecting than a Knight." Maybe Xander was right about how other people see the Knights.

"I mean, I know we haven't talked before this week, but we're in all the same classes. I'm sure we'll have plenty to talk about."

"Okay, if you're sure then, uh, I guess I'll go with you on Saturday." Andrew finishes packing up his stuff and I walk him to the door. We say goodbye and I head to my room to text the Knights.

Kingston: Xander, Amelia, and Andrew are coming with us to the Homecoming dance.

Vaughn: Why is Shrimp coming with us? And who r Amelia and Andrew?

O. Ridire: Amelia is Xander's best friend

Kingston: Andrew is my partner for my English project

Vaughn: 2 day turn around has got to be a new record for you

Kingston: 2 day turn around? What do you mean?

Knight: 2 days from dumping Slater to hooking up with Andrew

G. Ridire: Andrew must have some serious game

Caballero: Yeah that's not like you what's up?

Kingston: Woah we're NOT hooking up

Kingston: He's coming with us in the group. Mom found out he wasn't going and hasn't been to a dance before, so I invited him to come with us. Xander is coming that way Andrew will know someone besides me.

Caballero: That makes more sense

Vaughn: So it's a pity invite?

Kingston: It's not a pity invite

Vaughn: Sure it's not

O. Ridire: Dude be careful you aren't leading him on

Kingston: It's not!

Kingston: What do you mean?

Knight: You flirt with every guy you talk to

Caballero: And you asked him to a dance

Kingston: I do NOT flirt with every guy I talk to and we're going as friends not to mention all of you will be there too

Kingston: I almost forgot Colten and Callie are coming with us too

O. Ridire: You do flirt with every guy you talk to. It's just how you are

G. Ridire: How are we all supposed to ride in your SUV?

Kingston: Jet and Daniel have dates I assumed they'd be riding with them

Vaughn: You were supposed to get me and my date she doesn't have a car and I can't pick her up on my bike

Knight: Shotgun

Kingston: Have Daniel take you

Kingston: Xander is driving, so Amelia gets shotgun

Caballero: I don't have a date anymore

O. Ridire: What happened? I thought you were going with Courtney

That's when I get a FaceTime request from Daniel. I answer, then he connects all of the guys.

"Courtney saw me making out with Bailey during fifth period." Daniel explains. "She got mad, and I said something about how we weren't official, much less exclusive, and that got me slapped by both Courtney and Bailey."

"Wow, dude. You certainly have a way with girls," Tristan says.

"Yeah, yeah. More importantly, what's our plan for Homecoming?" Jet says.

"Let me go bug Xander, so he can weigh in." I knock on Xander's door.

"Come in."

"Hey, Xander, I have all the Knights on. We're trying to sort out plans for Homecoming."

"Fine. But keep in mind you already owe me for going."

"I know. I know. So, the problem is there are eleven of us and we can't all fit in one vehicle."

"Twelve, don't forget Kasey," Jet says. "Can't Shrimp take Colten and their girlfriends in his vehicle? Then the rest of us will fit."

Xander gives me a look that says it'd be a bad idea to have Andrew in a vehicle only with the guys. I know he offered to go because Andrew knows him and maybe Amelia.

"Can't y'all take whichever girl you made out with last to the dance? Then there won't be a problem because we'll easily fit in one car." Xander gestures between me and him.

"The last girl Daniel made out with slapped him." Grayson chuckles.

"Sounds smart," Xander says. "Why doesn't Tristan drive and he can take Jet and Kasey? Then Mom can take Colten and Callie. Problem solved."

"Sounds good to me," I say. Daniel, Grayson, and Oliver agree.

"But then I'm stuck being a third wheel," Tristan complains.

"Then ask someone to the dance; it isn't that hard," Grayson says.

"But then I have to get her a mum and whatnot," Tristan says.

"Why? I'm not getting Kasey a mum. That's why you ask the week of the game. They'll already have a mum ordered or it's too late to get one. You should ask a cheerleader, or someone on the dance team. They're busy during the game, so you don't even have to sit with them. Since you're playing in the game, you can ask whoever you want," Jet says.

"Jet, that's because you're a jerk," Xander says.

"Whatever, Shrimp. Not that it's any of your business, but Kasey told me not to worry about a mum when I told her Lynn's mom was making my garter," Jet says.

"A dense jerk," Xander says.

"Tristan, either be a third wheel or get a date. You live over by Jet, so it makes the most sense," I say.

"You could always ask your neighbor." Jet wiggles his eyebrows.

"Shut up. I'm pretty sure the stick Princess Merida has up her backside would prevent her from coming, much less having fun. Forget it, I'll sort it out on my own," Tristan says.

"Good night, losers." Daniel ends the call.

"Have I mentioned that you owe me for this?" Xander asks.

"Yes, you have. Thank you for coming. Andrew thinks you were already planning on going to appease Mom. If you could not correct him, that'd be great. I didn't want him to feel like he had to go since you said you were going."

"Of course, weirdo. How's your project going?"

"We finished our outline and planned out what we're doing. I think the academic part of the project will go well. I'm kind of worried about Saturday, though. Andrew seems super awkward around me and he's uneasy about being around the Knights. I don't see how they're scary, so I'm not sure what his deal is."

"He probably finds them and you intimidating," he points out. "For most people, talking to people they don't know is difficult. Not everyone is like you and never met a stranger in their life. Besides, knights are meant to protect and listen to their king, so of course they don't scare you."

"What? The guys never listen to me. I think you're mixing me up with Mom. And I'm not living in some castle needing protecting. I can take care of myself."

"I know most of them aren't a fan of the school-spirit days. They do it to make you happy and so you won't make that face."

"What face?"

"The one you're making right now. The one that says your way is correct and how could they *not* see that."

"I don't have a face like that."

"Whatever you say." Xander holds his hands up in surrender.

"Have you told Amelia that she's going to Homecoming?"

"Yeah, she's even letting Mom make her a garter."

"Will your name be on the garter?" I wiggle my eyebrows.

"No. We. Are. Just. Friends. She's two years younger than me, and I'm not the twin that dates all her friends."

"Two years is not that big of a deal, and I don't date all my friends. I've never dated Jet or Grayson."

"Oh, did I miss the memo that you're joining a convent and won't be dating anymore?"

"Shut up. I don't have to become a nun to not date them." I shove Xander's shoulder.

"You're pretty smart, which is a good case as to why you wouldn't want to date Jet."

"Yeah, yeah. You think you're so funny. Honestly, Jet doesn't date anymore, anyway."

"And that's different from before, how?"

"He has had a few girlfriends before even if they weren't serious or lengthy relationships. The last few months or so, not so much. I'm surprised he even has a date for the Homecoming dance."

"Maybe he finally perfected the art of zero commitment?"

"Maybe."

"What about Grayson?"

"With everything that went down with Oliver, I don't think it'd be a good idea to date Grayson."

"Worried he might become clingy?" Xander asks.

"It's irrelevant. I'm not planning on starting another relationship anytime soon. Grayson and I see each other as friends. If I did want to date someone else, it'd probably not be a football player. I don't want to have to deal with drama from Mark."

"You could just focus on school and basketball."

"Like how you just focus on school and theater?" I raise my eyebrow.

"Exactly. The only drama in my life takes place on stage." Xander strikes a dramatic pose.

"That sounds nice..."

"But...?"

"But I enjoy dating. Break-ups aren't exactly fun but flirting and dating are. Besides, I always have you and the guys to help deal with the fallout."

"Yeah, you couldn't get rid of me if you tried." Xander wraps me in a hug.

"I don't know. Uncle Zach is a trauma surgeon. I bet he knows how to make it look like an accident." Uncle Zach isn't our actual uncle, but he's Mom's best friend.

"Yeah, but he likes me better than you."

"Whatever, dork."

"Love you, weirdo."

"Love you, too." I head back to my room to get ready for bed.

CHAPTER 18
KAYLEE

Richard: Won't be there today. There's more money in your account.

I'm not in the least bit surprised Richard, my father, will be a no-show again. I could count the times he's come to see us since moving out on one finger. One I'd like to show him for abandoning Sara and me with Mary, our egg donor.

He was never around before the divorce, but then he was financing all of Mary's whims so she wasn't a problem. And now he's cut her off other than what he has to pay for child support. The only thing that money is supporting is Mary's alcohol habit, and it's apparently not enough to support her former social life.

She was kicked out of the country club after Richard stopped paying for her membership. She caused a scene and was asked to leave. That lost her the rest of her friends. Mary has replaced the void of her social life with dates from randos she meets online and alcohol. Lots and lots of alcohol.

She's always been self-absorbed and would make the occasional off-handed catty comment, but now she's a terror to live with. The alcohol makes her mean, and she's already catty and bitter to begin with. I try to minimize mine and Sara's time at home so we don't have to be around her.

This last year has shown me to be careful what you wish for. Before, our parents were never home and our house was always empty. Now, Mary's there all the time and it's awful. It makes me long for when she was never home.

I shake off thoughts of my absentee parents and focus on the present, where sectionals have ended. I guess I zoned out for longer than I thought because Drew has already put his instrument away and there's no sign of him. I'll have to wait until tomorrow to get all of the details on Lynn stopping by his locker and walking him to class.

He can complain all he wants about me casting him as a girl in my mental rom-com, but the popular jock leaning against a locker acting like they're God's gift to high school couldn't be more textbook main-male-character energy. If Drew wants to be cast across from Lynn, he's going to have to accept the part of leading lady.

"You ready to head out?" Sara appears next to me as I put my horn up.

"Yeah, just give me a minute. Where do you want to grab food from?"

"Can we go to the house?" Sara plays with the straps of her backpack to hide some of her anxiety.

"We don't have time. Remember, James moved band practice to today instead of Thursday. We only have about thirty minutes to get food and be at Connor's studio." I grab my bag and head toward the door.

I'm thankful I can skate over some of the stuff with our parents with a different reason we can't head straight home.

"Oh, yeah, I forgot about that. Why'd he have to move it again?" Sara follows me to the van and loads up while I try to calm the emotions raging inside me at the answer to her question.

"He has a personal thing on Thursday. Don't feed into his prima donna attitude by wondering about it." I put the van in drive as the real answer to her question cuts into my chest.

James has a date Thursday. A date supposedly so important that he needed to move our practice schedule around to accommodate it. It still hurts just to think about it and it makes me feel stupid that I gave James the power to hurt me. Nothing about his past behavior made him look like a good person to place my trust in. But he was there as my world started falling apart and I foolishly thought he'd realize I was more than a bit of fun to him.

"Wendy's?" Sara's suggestion pulls me out of my own head and the emo road it was headed down. She must be picking up on my mood because Wendy's is my favorite restaurant, not hers.

"Sounds good." I spend the rest of the ride asking her about her day and trying to pick up all the slack our parents have left with raising her.

After a quick stop by Wendy's, I pull into our driveway. Mary's car is here and I'm glad we aren't going inside right now.

"Leave your school stuff in here. We're late as it is." I spare a quick glance at the dash that confirms it's after five-thirty.

Oh well. It's more than fair for us to inconvenience James a little after everything he's done. I feel a little bad for potentially wasting Connor's time, but he's the one who's best friends with a jerk, so he can just get over it.

Connor's a junior like me. James, our lead guitarist and resident jerkwad, is a senior. We created our band, Outnumbered by Hysteria, a few years ago. We used to practice in my garage because it was always empty like the rest of the house.

Connor's our neighbor, and his parents built us a small studio to practice in a couple of years ago. I don't know if it's because they're that supportive or because they don't want to be able to hear us practice. Either way, I've been extra thankful for it since the divorce.

Connor is finishing setting everything up when we walk in. James is plastered to some groupie on the couch.

Great. Just great.

"I thought your date was Thursday and that's why we needed to practice today?" I ask loudly, startling the two lovebirds apart.

James shoots me a glare. There's no way he's more displeased with this situation than I am.

"Date? You told me you didn't date." The girl straightens her top as she gives James a confused look.

"I don't. Kaylee doesn't know what she's talking about." James leans back in like he's going to end this conversation by distracting this airhead with kisses.

"Oh, so this text saying you have an important date with a special girl is supposed to mean something else?" I take my phone out like I'm going to pull the text up.

The random girl slaps James and calls him a few colorful names before storming out. I'm still not sorry. If it were me, I would've decked him.

"Thanks for that." James stretches out his jaw as he slouches over to his guitar. "By the way, jealous doesn't look good on you."

I roll my eyes. "You moved our schedule around. I'm just here for band practice, not your drama."

James comes way too close to me.

"I seem to remember you liking my drama and all the perks that come with it," he whispers in my ear before finally going to his spot.

Thankfully, we focus on the music for the rest of practice. I'm able to get lost in singing and am reminded why I love this so much even if it means putting up with James's crap. James gets a call right at the end of practice, and I get to avoid any further scenes with him as he leaves to handle whatever.

"Hey, are you okay?" Connor asks after James has left.

"I'm fine. There's nothing to report to your bestie." I help him with putting everything away.

"You're my friend, too. That's why I tried to warn you about James."

"I don't need babying and I don't need help. I'm fine."

Connor raises his hands in surrender and lets the topic drop.

Sara and I stop by the van to get our school stuff before heading into our house. Sometime during practice, Mary left. I can only hope we have a quiet night, and she stays gone until bedtime.

"Do you want to talk about whatever that was with James earlier?" Sara asks once we're inside and upstairs where our rooms are.

"Nothing to talk about. We're over for good this time. He's still a womanizing jerk. I didn't want that interfering with band practice."

She opens her mouth, probably to push the topic, but I've had enough of James tonight, being around him thinking about him, and talking about him.

"I'm good. I promise. But I do have an English paper I need to work on."

Sara nods and heads to her room. I sit at my desk. I know I should start on my homework, but instead I pull my songwriting journal out.

CHAPTER 19
OLIVER

Mark takes the stool next to me in woodworking Wednesday morning. He's been avoiding me the last two days. I guess he's gotten over that now. I had hoped he'd surprise me by not coming to me about Lynn.

"Is what Tristan said Monday before practice true? Lynn is going with you to Homecoming as friends?"

"Yeah. We're going in a group."

"She hasn't started dating anyone new?" Mark leans in like he doesn't want to be overheard.

"Nope."

"Can you help me win her back? I mean, I don't know what she told you, but—"

"Lynn told me what you said Sunday," I cut him off. "I'd work on moving on, not trying to win her back."

"I know I jumped the gun on the whole L word thing, but I care about her. With the other stuff, she knows I didn't mean anything by it; I was upset. We're good together, and I don't want to lose her. Maybe I could do a romantic gesture at the dance or something. What do you think?"

"Lynn's not a fan of public displays of emotions. Lynn said she wanted to be friends. I think you should take her at her word and be friends. If she changes her mind, she's more than capable of asking you out. Trying to change her mind will only make her dig her heels in."

"So, I should be subtle in winning her back?" Mark looks confused.

"No, you shouldn't try to win her back at all. Lynn never dates anyone twice. She thinks you're better off friends and she'll stick to that. Trying to win her back will reinforce that to her."

"But we're perfect for each other. We can talk sports. She doesn't take forever getting ready. She doesn't play games. She's hot. She gets me."

His list is why Lynn's one of the coolest girls I know, not why they're perfect for each other. Not to mention, he seemed pushy when they were together, and it seems like he doesn't care what Lynn wants. This conversation makes me think he doesn't listen to what other people are saying. Mark hears what he wants to hear.

"Look, dude, you said Lynn doesn't play games and she doesn't. She says what she means and means what she says. The sooner you accept that and move on, the better off you'll be."

Mark opens his mouth, presumably to continue protesting, when Mr. Michaels thankfully starts his lesson. I had hoped that with Mark fueling the rumor that things had run their course and he was over Lynn, there was at least some truth to it.

The bit about the reason for their breakup was obviously rubbish, but I hoped maybe he realized he wasn't in love with Lynn. Apparently, he was saving face in front of the team. If anything, that makes it clear he's not right for Lynn. His interest in her seems skin deep and he's more concerned about appearances than anything else.

I've always gotten along with Mark and he's a good quarterback, but since he started dating Lynn, things have been different. Mark was known for being a player before they got together but became territorial with Lynn. He never liked that Lynn has all guy friends and was unhappy when Lynn had plans with us. It's like since he decided Lynn was the first girl he was going to date exclusively, he expected her to spend every second doing whatever he wanted and ignore all her friends.

Lynn hasn't said anything, but she has been more stressed the last couple of weeks. All of us are glad she finally broke up with Mark.

Now if only Mark could get through his thick skull that Lynn doesn't belong to him and doesn't want to be with him. I'm curious about what Mark said when he was upset that he didn't mean.

As soon as second period is over, I rush out of the classroom to avoid Mark trying to continue our conversation. In the hallway, I literally run into Kaylee. It's all I can do to keep our stuff from dropping to the ground.

"Hey," I say.

Her eyes light up when she realizes who is talking to her.

I'm hoping that's a good sign. I'm hoping we can pretend I didn't almost run her over.

"Hey, I actually want to talk to you. I wanted to apologize for Monday. I know I was being kind of weird."

"In all fairness, I was weird first." I just didn't know what to say when I was finally talking to her.

"Yeah, you kind of were."

"So, um, are you—" I start to try to ask her about Homecoming.

"Stop taking up the hallway," Brooke snarks from behind Kaylee. Kaylee steps out of the way. I see the look of disgust melt off Brooke's face as she sees me.

"Hey, Oliver. I didn't see you there. You can get in my way any day." She finishes with an over-the-top wink.

Brooke reaches out to touch my arm, and I take a step back. Brooke's one of my least favorite people. She's a jersey chaser and a shameless flirt. I don't date casually, and regardless, would never want to be with someone who is only with me because I play sports.

"Are you excited for the game Friday?" Brooke takes another step towards me. I take another step back.

"Uh sure, but I was in the middle of a conversation…" I trail off, noticing that while I've been trying to stay out of Brooke's reach, Kaylee has disappeared.

"It's so nice how you make time for the little people. I'm sure you made the band dweeb's day by talking to her." Another reason I don't like Brooke is that she doesn't have time for those she deems beneath her. That's anyone who isn't a cheerleader or doesn't play sports.

"Sure. I just remembered I have to go do something." I walk off. Brooke thankfully doesn't follow me.

"Hey, man," Daniel says as I take the desk next to his.

"Hey, can I ask you something?"

"Sure."

"Let's say you were about to ask someone to Homecoming and got interrupted. By the time you got rid of the interruption, they were gone. Would you take that as a sign you probably shouldn't try asking them again?"

"Are we talking about the Queen of Punk?"

"Does it matter?" I get my stuff out for class.

"We *are* talking about her... Hm, interesting. Maybe try talking to her again and see how it goes. Most girls will mention the dance if they want you to take them."

"She isn't like the girls we're usually around."

"We'll see."

Lynn walks into class with Andrew. Ever since they've been partnered together, they've been walking to class together more. Andrew heads to his desk next to Kaylee. He was in the hall with her the other day when I tried to talk to her.

Maybe I could use Lynn's project as a way to befriend Andrew and get on Kaylee's radar. If Andrew's coming with us to Homecoming, that might be the excuse I need to ask Kaylee to come with us. It definitely feels less scary to ask her to Homecoming if I have the option of backpedaling and saying I asked her to come with our group since she's friends with Andrew.

The biggest downside to that approach is that it might tip off the rest of the Knights to my crush, and I'm not sure I want them to know about it yet. Daniel and Tristan might tease me a little bit, but they get that I'm not as confident about asking girls out as they are.

I've never actually asked a girl out before. My exes were all more confident than me and asked me out before I got up the courage to say anything. As evidenced by me learning guitar, I'm pretty invested in trying to pursue Kaylee. I just don't know how to do that and I'm not ready to have all the Knights weigh in with their "advice."

CHAPTER 20
LYNN

Wednesday at school is uneventful. Thankfully, instead of having the entire Homecoming Court on one float like they did last year, each couple is in their own vehicle. Grayson's dad has a convertible that he let us borrow. My dad drives with Grayson and me sitting in the back.

It's a relief to only be with Grayson. Especially since we practiced for halftime after school today, and I felt super awkward around Mark. He keeps glancing over at me during the parade. I feel bad for him, but I did the right thing by ending things with him. He clearly was way more into me than I was into him.

In the long run, it's better not to have drawn out our relationship. Especially since he apparently wasn't okay with me having guy friends. He caught me in the hall earlier and apologized for what he said. Thankfully, the bell rang before he could get more out than that. The apology was appreciated, but I'm pretty sure he only said it because he wants to get back together.

Brooke spent half the practice glaring daggers at me and made a couple catty comments clearly directed at me. It'd be more convincing that she was standing up for Whitney, her so-called best friend, if Brooke hadn't spent the other half of practice flirting with Mark.

I'm glad Deitra and Brittney were nominated for Homecoming Queen. They're the only cheerleaders that are actually nice to me. Brittney also plays basketball with me, so I was able to talk to her about that. A much better conversation than what I overheard of Brooke and Nichole talking about how risqué they could make their Homecoming dresses without getting in trouble at the dance for them being out of the dress code.

The parade goes smoothly. Grayson and I joke with each other the entire time, and we smile and wave to the crowds as we go by. After the parade, there's a bonfire and carnival. The various booths are fundraising for different extracurriculars.

Normally, I'd have to help with the basketball booth where you try to shoot three-pointers, but since I'm on Homecoming Court, I don't have to and can walk around with Grayson. The other guys will join us when they finish their shift at the boys' basketball and football booths.

I'm so glad I wore Converse, because the rest of Homecoming Court looks like they're dying in their high heels. Yearbook takes a few pictures of the Homecoming Court before we're set free.

Grayson and I wander around, playing different games and goofing off. I get cold and he gives me his letterman. He wins me a stuffed koala at the ring toss...and then we run into Mark.

"Um...hi." I play with the koala's fur.

"I thought you said you just wanted to be friends and that there wasn't someone else?" Mark looks from me to my koala to Grayson and back to me again.

"I do want to be friends, and there isn't someone else. Grayson and I are just friends, which I've told you about a hundred times."

"Just friends? Then why does it look like you're on a date? I mean, you're wearing his letterman. You didn't even wear my letterman when we were together."

I almost never wear a boyfriend's letterman. To me, that's something you do in a serious, steady relationship. I figure if we've only been dating a few weeks, we aren't serious and definitely aren't steady.

My refusal to wear Mark's letterman because he was my boyfriend was a sore spot for him. I didn't want to wear it in the first place, but I hate being told what to do, especially by a boyfriend.

"Grayson is letting me wear his letterman because I got cold.

Friends do things like that, take care of each other. Stop trying to read more into it than there is."

"Which doesn't explain the bear or why you two are by yourselves."

Grayson steps up next to me. "Look man, when the guys finish their shift, they'll be walking around with us. This isn't a date, and you should lay off Lynn."

"Whatever." Mark shoulder-checks Grayson as he walks away.

I lay a hand on Grayson's arm.

"Don't. You don't need to get in a fight, especially not with your quarterback."

"Fine. Let's go get some cotton candy."

We get cotton candy, then go by where they're doing the cake walk. I love looking at the cakes, even if I don't need or want a whole cake.

When I see Andrew is the one selling tickets with his blue-haired friend from earlier, I decide maybe one round wouldn't be too bad. When I get to the front of the line, Andrew's face seems to lift and then fall a little, which is weird.

"Two tickets, please." I give him a huge grin, hoping to distract him from whatever made his face fall.

"Oh...um...yeah... Here...here you go." Andrew hands me the tickets and avoids eye contact.

Weird.

"Thank you, Andrew." We have to wait for the next round to start. Hoping to cheer him up and get him out of his weird mood, I ask, "Who is your friend?"

He looks up at me and almost seems confused. It's the friend who answers my question.

"Kaylee. Drew's best friend." She flicks her blue hair out of her face.

"Nice to meet you. Are you eating with us before the dance on Saturday?" I ask.

I get a look from Grayson I can't decipher. Kaylee looks confused while Andrew looks like he got caught sneaking out.

"Why would I eat with you before the dance?" she asks carefully.

"I figured Andrew would have invited you to eat with us before the dance since you're his best friend?" It was supposed to be a statement, but it came out as a question. Probably better that way so it didn't come out snarky.

"He must have forgotten to mention it. I'll have to get with my date and see if that works for him." A grin spreads across her face.

Andrew gives me a pained smile as the next round for the cake walk starts. Grayson and I take our places in the circle.

"Next up is a strawberry cake with chocolate filling and icing topped with chocolate-covered strawberries made by Kaylee Cobb, our resident baker and third chair trombone." Kaylee takes a bow.

The music starts to play and we walk around the circle. When it stops, I'm on number twelve, which is my jersey number. A little girl who looks to be about five pulls a number out of a hat and hands it to the announcer.

"This delicious masterpiece is going to lucky number twelve!" he announces.

"Oh, thank you." I take the cake from the man.

I planned on sticking around to try to talk to Andrew and Kaylee again, but he's acting weird and now I have a cake to deal with.

"You want me to take you home so you can drop off the cake?" Grayson asks.

"Sounds good. By the time we get back, the guys should be free and we can all hang out together. Plus, I can change while we're there."

When we get back to the carnival, I'm much more comfortable in my jeans and sweater. I dropped off my stuffed koala, so I wouldn't have to carry it around all night. We stop to get kettle corn before going to find the guys at the basketball booth.

We all walk around, playing different games. I can't quite put my finger on it, but something is up. The guys are acting weird. Jet seems super tense and Tristan keeps glancing at me. Whereas Oliver and Daniel seem like they're trying to avoid looking at me. Grayson seems to be the only one acting normally even if he's a bit more touchy-feely than normal.

When the carnival starts closing down and everyone's heading to the bonfire, I ask Daniel if he'll walk with me to the bathrooms. He hesitates before he agrees. Once we're away from everyone else, I turn on him.

"What's going on? Y'all are acting weird."

"We heard Mark was pissed you were dating Grayson."

"What?"

"We assumed the rumors we were hearing were only rumors, but Kasey said she saw him get you a teddy bear and that you left with him. We were going to ask when you got to the booth but figured the jacket was the answer."

"What?" I ask again, trying to keep up with what is going on.

"You're wearing his letterman."

"No, I'm not. I switched when..." I trail off as I look down and realize I'm in fact wearing Grayson's letterman, not mine. "It was an accident. I thought I grabbed mine at the house."

"Okay. What about the bear and the rumor you left to make-out?"

"He did win me a stuffed koala, but that doesn't mean anything. We did *not* go make-out. I won a cake at the cake walk, so we took it home. I changed clothes while we were there because I didn't want to wear a dress all night. Besides, you know you're the first person I'd tell if I was dating someone new."

"I believe you and that you didn't intend anything, but there's no way Grayson didn't realize 'Ridire' is emblazoned on your back. You may want to think about that and reframe the night in your mind."

"He might have missed it...?" I don't believe my words, so it's no surprise they don't sound convincing.

Daniel raises an eyebrow at me.

"You think Grayson is flirting with me?" I ask "But he told Mark it wasn't a date and to leave me alone."

"How about you give me your version of what has happened tonight and then I'll weigh in?"

I go back over everything from the parade until I pulled Daniel away from everyone.

"Sounds to me like he said it wasn't a date because *you* were adamant it wasn't a date," Daniel says. "Everything else you told me sounds like he hoped it could be a date. He probably didn't know how you felt and didn't want to say anything or push it. But by keeping the bear, wearing his letterman, and flirting back with him, you weren't exactly giving any signals that you're not interested. To be completely honest, it did look like y'all were on a date and like the rest of us were all the extra wheels. The real question is, do you want it to be a date?"

"It's only been three days since I broke up with Mark and he's clearly still upset and seems hung up on me." My head is spinning, and I feel my words coming out faster and faster. "We already decided to go to Homecoming as a group of friends. I even invited my English partner. I don't want to change any of our plans for Homecoming, and I don't want to hurt Mark any more than I already have. What do I do?"

I feel like the world is collapsing in on me and I can't take a full breath. I don't know how things got so complicated and convoluted. With all the drama with Mark I just wanted an evening of hanging out with my friends. And now that's caused even more drama.

I don't know what I'm doing wrong to keep causing so many problems. I can't even relax with the Knights without worrying about how everyone else will perceive it. Sometimes I wish I was invisible, and no one cared about what I was doing or who I was doing it with.

I feel hands on my shoulders. "Take a deep breath."

I hear Daniel's voice but I don't see anything.

"Breathe with me. In…Out… There you go."

I continue to take deep breaths following Daniel's voice. My vision slowly comes back into focus. I'm crouched down and Daniel is crouched directly in front of me. I focus on my breathing and that Daniel is here for me. My body slowly starts to relax, and my heart slows from its frantic pace.

"I've got you. You're okay." Daniel continues to say soothing things as I get my body back under my control.

When I feel more stable, I try to stand. It's a good thing Daniel stands with me because I'm wobbly. Daniel catches me before I can lose my balance.

"Thanks. I guess I'm not as stable as I thought." The other way my statement is true sinks in and I'm worried Daniel will see that. Who am I kidding? I just had an attack; it doesn't take a genius to figure out my anxiety has gotten worse. I thought I had it under control.

Daniel pulls me into his arms for a hug. "You're not alone. I'm here if you want to talk about it. Even if you aren't ready to talk, I'm still here."

His embrace grounds me and helps me to rein in my emotions.

"There's not much to talk about." I pull out of his arms and head to the parking lot. Walking should make me feel better and if not, maybe he can give me a ride home.

"It's been a busy week, and I haven't been sleeping much. The combination of everything just had me feeling overwhelmed. But I'm better now."

"Does your mom know you're having panic attacks again?" Daniel falls into step beside me.

"No. It's just one panic attack; it's not a big deal. She's got plenty going on and I don't want her jumping in to micromanage my life. It's been a hectic week; it's not like how things were in junior high."

Sixth grade was when we first realized I had issues with anxiety. Xander started doing his own thing and I wanted that for him. But it made my separation anxiety worse to the point I started having panic attacks. I was worried I was going to lose my brother.

I pushed the Knights away because I knew Xander didn't like hanging out with them, especially Jet. Daniel wouldn't let me push him away and stayed next to me throughout everything. The other Knights knew I was having a hard time, but they don't know any of the details of what was going on.

My mom took me to a psychologist who put me on meds for a while until I was able to talk about everything and get my anxiety under control on my own. They taught me grounding techniques to help bring myself down. Daniel and Xander both learned what they could do to help if I started having an attack.

My mom got freaked out by the whole thing and became a bit of a helicopter mom. She eventually calmed down the longer I went without an attack, but it took a long time to get my independence back. I wasn't even allowed to go for a run by myself because my mom was worried about something happening when no one else was around. Things are in a good place with us now and I don't want to ruin that because I had one slip up.

Daniel's voice brings me back into the present. "If you think it's just the week getting to you then I guess she doesn't have to know."

"I'm fine, really. I just got overwhelmed because I don't know what to do about Grayson."

"Why don't we walk through that one step at a time? Have you been having a good night?" Daniel asks.

"Yeah, but I wasn't thinking about it like a date. I always have a good time with the Knights. I didn't think there was anything else going on besides y'all all being a little weird."

"No one said you have to have it all figured out tonight. What if you treat the rest of tonight as if it was a group date and see how you feel at the end of it?"

"Okay, I guess that'd work." I shrug. "Wait, how would it be a group date? None of the rest of you have dates."

"Jet already texted Kasey to meet up with him. If it'll make you feel better, I could find a couple of cheerleaders for Tristan and me...?" Daniel wiggles his eyebrows when he mentions the cheerleaders.

"Not really. I don't want to be a part of your cheerleader drama. Besides, isn't getting slapped by two cheerleaders enough for one week?"

"Fair point."

I put my head in my hands feeling overwhelmed. "I don't know how I feel about Grayson. I don't think I want to get into another relationship so quickly, and I don't know that dating him is a good idea."

I pull my head out of my hands and look at Daniel. "I mean, look at what happened with Oliver, and that was when we were younger. I don't want to end up hurting Grayson, too."

"Hey, Grayson is a big boy. He can take care of himself. Besides, he isn't like Oliver. If anything, I'd be more worried about Grayson hurting you. His track record of dating and dumping girls is almost on par with Tristan's."

"You say that like you're any better."

"But *I* wouldn't be the one hurting you."

"I'm not a cheerleader, so I'm safe from your war path?"

"Something like that." He winks at me. "Do you feel better now?"

"Yeah." I reach out and pull him into a hug. "What about Grayson's letterman? I'm cold, and apparently, mine is at home. I don't want it to be a big deal either way."

"I could give you *my* letterman." Daniel smirks.

"Yeah, I'm not sure I want to know what the rumor mill would make of that. I've already heard enough nonsense about having only guy friends. Not to mention, Mark might have apologized for what he said Sunday, but I don't want to give him ammunition to be nasty."

"Ignore Mark. He'll get over it eventually, and you shouldn't be insensitive, but you don't have to plan all your actions around how it'll affect him. If he persists in being a jerk, we will handle it." Daniel bumps my shoulder with his. "You could always make some girl friends."

"But then you'd date them, dump them, and I'd be right back to only having you guys as friends," I tease.

"You're not wrong."

"Seriously, what are we going to do about the jacket?"

"We can get a hoodie from my car."

"Let's get one and get back to the group before they send out a search party."

CHAPTER 21
OLIVER

When Daniel walks off with Lynn, I turn on my brother.

"You want to explain why there are rumors you were with Lynn before she and Mark broke up, and that the two of you left to go hook up?" I ask.

"You know none of that's true." Grayson looks me in the eye.

"Of course not." Jet sounds irritated. "Lynn doesn't cheat or hook up. But the rumors had to come from somewhere. Lynn wearing your letterman three days after dumping Slater is out of character for her."

"I'm not sure what's going on since you normally tell me everything, but I found out from rumors that there *was* something going on." I raise an eyebrow at my brother.

"There wasn't anything to tell you." Grayson looks away. "Yeah, I may have realized I was into Lynn this summer. But she was with Frost, then Slater, so there wasn't a point in saying anything. I hoped something might come of us being on Homecoming Court together, but then she wanted to go in a big group of friends for the dance. Including her brothers and some other guy we don't even know. I figured she'd already moved on and found her next guy and was taking it slow not to upset Mark." Grayson kicks a couple of rocks down the parking lot.

"Okay. That explains why you haven't talked to me, but not why she's wearing your letterman or why everyone thinks you're together. I heard you got her a bear or something?" I step in front of Grayson, hoping he'll look up at me.

"Lynn was cold and I won her a stuffed animal at the ring toss. It might've looked like a date. I mean it felt like a date to start with." Grayson quickly glances up before looking off to the side.

"To start with?" Tristan asks.

Grayson tells us about running into Mark, who got upset, and how Lynn was very clear that she and Grayson were just friends. They went to the band cake walk where Lynn apparently got really excited to see Andrew, the guy who was selling tickets.

Grayson mentions how Lynn acted weird when she met Andrew's best friend, Kelly or something, and how Lynn invited her to eat with us before Homecoming, but the girl already has a date. Grayson seemed to think Lynn is into Andrew and hoping for something at Homecoming.

"I don't know. I mean after I recognized him, I realized it was the same guy Lynn has been walking into class with." Grayson is still not looking directly at any of us, but it feels a lot more like embarrassment instead of hiding something.

"And the rumors you left to hook up?" Jet asks a little too forcefully. Can't he see Grayson is already uncomfortable?

"Lynn won a cake at the cake walk, so we dropped it off at her house. Since we were already there, she changed clothes. She did come back wearing my letterman, which I hoped meant something, but I'm confused now."

"That's a lot of mixed signals," Tristan agrees, "but since we joined you, it has definitely seemed like a date. Maybe there's an explanation for the rest. Who is this Kelly that's now coming with us to Homecoming?"

"I don't know. She's in band and has blue hair."

"What?" I take an involuntary step back. "Do you mean *Kaylee*?"

I feel my stomach drop. I had hoped Kaylee might come to Homecoming with us, but that was with the hope that she'd be coming with me. Not that Kaylee and *her date* would be joining our group.

"Sure. That sounds right. Why? Do you know her?" Grayson finally looks at me to study my face.

"No," I say a little too quickly.

Tristan's eyes get big, and I can tell it's all he can do to keep his mouth shut. Grayson and Jet give me suspicious looks, but I'm saved having to explain when Kasey shows up with one of her friends, Jessica. While Jet and Tristan are distracted with the girls, I whisper to my brother.

"Be careful with the whole Lynn situation. You saw how Mark reacted in the locker room to other people talking about asking her to the dance. We have a solid chance for playoffs. Don't not date Lynn because of that, but don't rush things." Grayson nods.

When Daniel and Lynn come back, she's wearing a black hoodie. Grayson's face deflates as he notices it. I don't want to see him hurt, but at least he has a better idea of where Lynn's at. It seems she's not on the same date wavelength he is.

I ride home with Daniel to avoid potentially being a third wheel. I meant what I said to Grayson about not rushing things, but I hope it does work out for him.

"You're quiet tonight," Daniel says to me when we get in his truck.

"I'm always quiet."

"Fair, but tonight you may as well be mute. What's up?"

"The short version: I found out tonight Kaylee already has a date for Homecoming. I know that's my own fault since the dance is in three days and I've barely talked to her, much less asked her out, but it still sucks."

"The Queen of Punk has a date for Homecoming? How did you find that out? Please say it isn't because you asked her and got shot down." Daniel puts his hands together as he pleads for me to tell him I'm not that big of a dork.

"Kaylee is Andrew's best friend. Lynn's English partner who she invited to come with us. Grayson said she has now extended that invite to include Kaylee and her *date*." I lay back against the seat, losing the energy to stay upright.

"That sucks, man. At least I'll be there to keep you company. At this point, regardless of Lynn saying we're all going only as friends, I'm pretty sure you and I will be the only ones without dates."

"Yeah, Jessica and Tristan seemed to hit it off at the bonfire."

"Maybe you can steal the Queen of Punk's heart at the dance?" Daniel offers as he pulls out of the parking lot.

"If she has a date, that wouldn't be cool to even try."

"Yeah, that'd be more of something Jet would do. Maybe she and her date are going as friends?"

I sigh. "One can hope."

"Soooo…is now a good time to ask why you're learning guitar? Is it really just to impress Kaylee?"

"I also wanted to do something other than sports. If it made Kaylee take notice of me, then all the better. Although, it has been cool learning something that doesn't come easily to me."

I've also enjoyed doing something on my own. As much as I enjoy how close all of the Knights are, sometimes I feel like my identity is wrapped up in being part of a group. Most people at school just know me as one of the Knights, even the ones who know us better just know me as the quiet one. Breaking out of that and being Oliver, guitar student, is nice. Even if Noah Clark is the only one who sees me that way.

"How is it going?" Daniel's question brings me out of my musing.

"I finally have the song down and am trying to memorize it."

"What song, or am I not allowed to ask?"

"'White Tiger.'"

"Do you think she knows who Our Last Night is?" Daniel glances over to me.

"Yeah, she's in a band and they played a couple of their covers at the Fourth of July festival."

"You've been into her for that long? Also, if she loves Our Last Night, she'll get Mama Kingston's approval."

"Yeah. You should have seen her on stage. She's an amazing singer. And I don't know if her approval will matter. Need I remind you Kaylee already has a date to the dance?"

"With Tristan and me helping, we'll get something sorted out. If you've learned guitar, we need to figure out a different Our Last Night song you can learn."

"Why?"

"Because that'd be the best Christmas present for Mama Kingston.

Plus, if you learn the guitar part, the rest of us only need to sing the words."

"So I do all the work, then you take the credit because it was your idea?" I laugh.

"Exactly." Daniel shoots me a megawatt grin.

The next morning, I wake up to a text from the group chat.

Kingston: Is Bellissimo Feudo for dinner on Saturday good with everyone?

Bellissimo Feudo is the best Italian restaurant in town and Lynn and Xander's favorite place to eat. The group chat is filled with thumbs-up emojis.

Kingston: Cool, Xand and Amelia are on board. I'll check with Andrew during second

Daniel sends me a text in our private thread.

Caballero: I told Lynn I could let Kaylee know

O. Ridire: Why

Caballero: Cuz now you can do it without anyone else in the group knowing

O. Ridire: Again why

Caballero: You can have an excuse to talk to her and find out more about her date duh

O. Ridire: K

I spend the time it takes me to get ready for school going back and forth between being excited to talk to Kaylee and dreading finding out about her date. With my luck, he's her long-term boyfriend and dream guy.

I'm at school early and am waiting outside the band hall as first period ends. I'm trying not to be nervous as I lean against the wall opposite the doors. I'm hoping to look chill instead of dorky and eager like I feel.

Finally, when it seems the entire band has come out, she exits with the same two guys she's usually with. I push off the wall and walk up next to them.

"Hey, Kaylee."

She and her friends turn around. Andrew looks at me, then mutters something about heading to class and walks off.

"Yes?" Kaylee asks. She looks lethally good today. Her black ripped skinny jeans wrap her legs nicely with hints of her black tights peeking through the holes. Her formfitting *Nightmare Before Christmas* shirt clings to her slight curves emphasized by her black leather half-jacket. Her boots make her taller than normal and have all sorts of studs and buckles on them.

"Could I talk to you for a minute?" I straighten up and try to focus on my words instead of checking Kaylee out.

"Sure." Kaylee nods.

We walk to the side of the hall with the other guy following behind.

They walk together a lot, so maybe he's her date for Saturday? They're always together, so it'd make sense. I can't help comparing myself to him.

He's wearing a band shirt under a blue button-down that's open. I'm significantly taller than him, but don't know if that's a good thing in Kaylee's book. He's obviously in band with her, so he meets her preference for musicians. Is this the type of guy Kaylee goes for? Because we're nothing alike.

"Does Bellissimo Feudo work for you for dinner before the Homecoming dance?" I start, focusing on what I'm supposed to be doing here. "Lynn wanted to make sure that was good with you."

"Wait, you're going to the dance?" the guy says before Kaylee can say anything. He gestures at me. "And *with him*? What's Lynn got to do with it?"

Looks like he isn't her date, then. Although, he did say 'with him' with a level of incredulity, like he disapproves. His wild-hand gestures in my direction aren't exactly filling me with confidence, either.

"Shut up, Carter. Oliver and Lynn are friends. Don't you have a class you need to get to?" Kaylee punctuates her last statement with a glare.

"Uh huh." Carter has a huge grin on his face as he leaves.

Weird.

"So, does Bellissimo Feudo work for you and your date?" I ask.

Whoever that might be. I guess it could be one of the guys in her band. I can't remember their names, though.

"Bellissimo Feudo is great. Also, my younger sister is coming with us. I figured you might need to know for a head count or whatever."

"Yeah. I'll let Lynn know. I guess you should also let me know if your sister has a date. That way, we have a good head count."

"I don't have your number." Kaylee pulls her phone out.

I rattle off my number and try not to feel nervous. I'm giving her my number to figure out logistics for this weekend. It's not like she asked for my number because she has any interest in me. I finish as the warning bell rings.

"I better head to class," Kaylee says before we part ways.

I fire off a quick text to Daniel, updating him as I head to my class. I'm not sure if Kaylee bringing her sister is a good thing or not. You wouldn't typically want your little sister with you on a date. Unless you've been together so long your siblings are comfortable with your significant other.

I shake my head to clear my thoughts. I'm definitely overthinking this.

CHAPTER 22
KAYLEE

I don't say anything to Drew about Homecoming until lunch—that way I have all of lunch to find out what is going on instead of trying to squeeze everything in during passing periods. I think my overall plan is working since Lynn says hi or does that head nod jocks do when we pass her in the hallways. It definitely wasn't happening before this week. Not to mention, the few times she has walked him to class.

"What-A-Burger, then to Carter's for video games?" I ask as we head to the parking lot.

What-A-Burger is Carter and Drew's favorite fast-food place. I figure buttering them up will be the best way for the conversation to go the way I want.

"Okay…" Drew sounds suspicious but isn't going to pass up the opportunity to go. We talk about classes and band until we get to Carter's apartment. As soon as we set our food on the table, Carter speaks.

"So, what is going on with Homecoming?" He looks at me.

"It's not a big deal; I'm going to help Lynn appease her mother," Drew says, and Carter spins around to face him.

"Wait, what? I was asking about Kaylee going with Oliver. You're going with Lynn?"

"Not *with* Lynn. With Lynn. I'm going with her and her friends as a group of friends. Her brothers will even be there. Definitely not a date." Drew frowns. "What do you mean Kaylee is going with Oliver?" They both turn to look at me.

"I'm not going with Oliver. I do need a date, though," I say, looking at Carter.

Carter shakes his head. "No. You know I don't like you that way and there's no way I'm going to the Homecoming dance as your date."

"But I already told Lynn I had a date."

"That's a *you* problem."

"I can't go as Drew's friend," I protest. "Lynn might think I'm into him and that's counterproductive to getting the two of them together. I already said I was going and Drew could use the moral support if he's going to spend the night with popular jocks. It wouldn't be a real date. I don't like you that way, either. You're like an annoying brother."

Carter snorts. "Because calling me annoying is going to get you your way."

"Please?" I bat my eyelashes at Carter simply because I know it annoys him.

"Fine, but you have to tell me what's going on with Oliver."

"Nothing is going on with Oliver. I've been talking to him a little bit, but that's for Drew."

"Then why did he come talk to you about dinner before Homecoming?" Carter presses. "Lynn could've asked Drew and had him ask you."

"I honestly don't know what that was about. It definitely was weird. If Lynn and her friends didn't have a reputation for being the nicest jocks at the school, I'd be worried we're walking into a *Carrie* situation for Homecoming. Considering not even Lynn's exes have anything bad to say about her, I think we're safe."

"They're called the Knights for a reason," Drew adds. "Knights are the good guys and protect other people."

"Do we even know why they're the Knights?" Carter asks.

I wave my hands in front of them. "Do we need to go down this rabbit hole right now?"

Carter rolls his eyes as Drew says, "I guess not."

"Maybe Oliver has a thing for you," Carter says. "Oliver might find it suspicious that I'm your date when I obviously knew nothing about these plans when he came to talk to you earlier."

Kaylee waves a hand dismissively. "I highly doubt Oliver has a thing for me. I'm sure he'll forget about it by Saturday if he even noticed."

"Can we circle back to how you've been talking to Oliver for me?" Drew asks.

"Sure. I figured you could use all the help you could get in wooing Lynn. I planned on slowly befriending Oliver to have a potential avenue to get information about Lynn and possibly have someone on the inside who could nudge her in your direction. I even thought we could have Carter do something similar since he's partnered with Xander for the AP English project."

"You seriously think you could become good enough friends with Oliver that he'd tell you secrets about his best friend? Someone he's been friends with since birth?" Drew sounds incredulous.

"It's not like I want anything juicy or scandalous," I say. "Just tips on how to win her over, what she looks for in a guy, if you're on her radar, that kind of stuff. He wouldn't be betraying Lynn by helping me. Besides, it'd help Lynn. You're in an entirely different class than her usual beau."

"Yes, I'm well aware. I'm not tall, athletic, or popular. I look like a nerd, and I dress like one too."

"Hey, that wasn't a criticism. I meant that you're caring, smart, and thoughtful. Instead of a shallow, arrogant player. You're a way better person than anyone Lynn has ever dated. We need to get her to see that." I touch Drew's arm to reassure him.

"And if Lynn only cares about the surface-level stuff, then I don't think she's the girl you've made her out to be in your head. In which case, she wouldn't be worth your time," Carter says.

"I guess," Drew says.

"Unless you're only wanting to check off having your first kiss. With as much experience as Lynn has, she has to be a fantastic kisser. Plus, she's smoking hot," Carter adds.

Drew's face flames. He tries to stutter out a reply but can't get any real words to come out. I decide to save him with a topic change.

"Also, we're bringing Sara with us. I don't want her stuck at home with Mary if we're gone all evening."

Richard is ten years Mary's senior. He left her for someone half her age, upgrading his trophy wife, so to speak. Their divorce has been nasty, and Mary has been all over Sara and me about taking care of our skin to look young as long as possible and to enjoy our youth. Sara gets the worst of it because she has a fuller figure than me. My body shape is comparable to a stick whereas Sara has curves.

"Your mom might go out. It'll be a Saturday night," Drew points out.

"All the more reason for Sara to be with us. She shouldn't be home alone, and I don't want her dealing with Mary if her night doesn't go as planned."

Mary has been known to drink too much if her dates don't go well. She's an angry drunk. I try to shield Sara from her as much as possible.

A text pops up from Sara.

Sara: Hey no date for the dance. I don't have anyone I want to go with

Kaylee: Ok. We're eating at Bellissimo Feudo beforehand

Sara: Cool. Did you text the guys to cancel practice?

Kaylee: No I will now

Kaylee: Do you want to go dress shopping after school today?

Sara: Yes!!!

I open the text thread for Outnumbered by Hysteria.

Kaylee: Sara and I won't be able to meet up for us to practice on Saturday

James: Why not?

Sara: We're going to the dance

Connor: Since when do you go to dances?

Kaylee: Since now

Connor: Lame we can practice Sunday afternoon then

James sends an individual text.

James: Who are you going with?

Kaylee: None of your business

James: Tell me

Kaylee: No, if you want to know then come to the dance.

"Why are you frowning at your phone?" Drew asks.

"James is upset we aren't having practice Saturday and he's being annoying about the dance." I put my phone away.

"I thought you were done with James for good this time? Isn't that what you said last week?" Drew asks.

"I did and I am."

Carter and Drew clearly don't believe me. Not that I blame them. I don't even know how many times I've said I'm done with James just to fall back into the cycle. But this time is different, and I really mean it. I'm done with letting him treat me like crap. Drew's phone goes off, and I'm saved from having this conversation again.

"Lynn wants to know if we want to go to lunch with her tomorrow so we can finalize Homecoming plans." He looks up from his phone.

"Sure. Where are we going?" I ask.

Drew types out a response on his phone.

"Her house. Her mom is making meatloaf. She said to bring Sara too."

"Her house?" Carter asks.

"Apparently, her mom wants to meet us before the dance." Drew's still looking at his phone.

"What?" I ask.

"Her mom seems to be quite hands on. She's a great cook, though. The pot pie she made on Tuesday was the best meal I've ever had." He has a dopey smile on his face and is obviously head over heels for Lynn. I hope everything works out with the two of them.

"That's because your dad can barely cook a freezer meal. Come on, let's go kill zombies," I say before heading into the living room.

CHAPTER 23
OLIVER

Lynn texted us about lunch at her house tomorrow. I'm dreading it, but I'm also glad to meet Kaylee's date before the dance. Hopefully, it'll be less uncomfortable that way. I finish my lesson with Noah and head to English early. I'm hoping to talk to Kaylee before class starts.

"Hey, Oliver," Kaylee calls from behind me. I stay where I am until she catches up with me.

"Hey."

"Sara isn't bringing a date." Kaylee walks in step with me.

"Oh, okay. Are you coming to lunch tomorrow?"

"Uh, yeah. I wanted to ask you about that. Is there anything I ought to know? Like a dress code or house rules or anything?" Kaylee tucks a piece of hair behind her ear.

"Definitely no dress code. No house rules that you need to worry about."

"Why does that not feel like a no?"

"Oh, nothing. We're at Lynn's house so much that her mom treats us like we're her sons, too. She isn't hesitant about getting on to us."

I chuckle, thinking about when Tristan became a part of our group and had to adjust to her mother-henning all of us. There's a reason Lynn usually doesn't invite people to her house and has her mom meet them at sporting events instead. Well, multiple reasons.

I'm lost in my thoughts, and it takes a minute for me to realize that Kaylee is giving me a weird look.

"What's that face about?" I ask.

"Nothing. That just sounds like a lot, having a mom who is so involved with you and your friends." Kaylee twirls a lock of hair around her finger.

"I guess…" I shrug. "We grew up at Lynn's house and that's how it's always been. Both of my parents are workaholics, so it's nice to have an involved parent. She has always come to our games—even when we got older and Lynn wasn't playing on the same team anymore."

"That doesn't sound too bad."

"Yeah, we do have more rules than we would otherwise. Stella is way stricter than any of our parents are, and she's involved enough so there's no sneaking anything past her."

"But she's not your mom. It's not like she can ground you."

"She can't ground us or take away our phones or anything. But you've never seen her 'I'm very disappointed in you' face. Until last year when we got our licenses, she was the one who took us everywhere. And Lynn isn't allowed to hang out with anyone who would be considered a bad influence."

"It sounds like in a way she could ground you. That's not normal."

I let her go into the classroom first, so I can sit wherever she does.

"Eh, who wants to be normal?" I shrug again.

"I guess so. Is she involved with y'all because you're Lynn's friends?"

"She used to be our nanny, but her being involved has gone way past that and continued even as we got older."

"Are you sure I don't need to dress a certain way? It sounds like Lynn's mom could audition for *The Stepford Wives*. I feel like she'd disapprove of my usual attire." Kaylee looks down at her ripped skinny jeans and leather jacket before sitting at a desk.

"Trust me, she won't care. Lynn's mom supports the idea of wearing whatever makes you happy. She's seriously great and understanding." Besides, if anything, I'm sure Mama Kingston would love the way Kaylee dresses.

"If you're sure..."

"Sooo...is your date coming with you to lunch tomorrow?" I try to not sound too interested in her answer.

"Yeah." Kaylee looks uncomfortable with the topic change. "Carter will be there."

"Carter? Isn't he the guy who was with you this morning?"

"Him and Drew."

I was pretty sure Carter seemed confused this morning. Maybe she told Lynn she had a date, then asked Carter to cover for her? I'm not sure, but I'm hopeful. On the other hand, maybe she and Carter are more than friends, but not official. That'd explain him getting weird about thinking I was going to the dance with Kaylee. Maybe she only decided to come because Lynn invited her and hadn't had a chance to ask him to come with her?

"Cool."

Before I can come up with anything better to add, Mrs. Green starts class. When she turns to write on the whiteboard, I pull my phone out.

O. Ridire: Kaylee said Carter and Sara are coming to lunch tomorrow

Caballero: Why are you telling me?

O. Ridire: So you can tell Lynn

Caballero: K

Caballero: Any progress with Kaylee?

O. Ridire: Maybe

Caballero: Maybe?

O. Ridire: I'm not sure. I'll update you later

I put my phone away and it seems like I got away with texting during class. I notice Kaylee giving me a look and realize at least one person saw. I start taking notes on what Mrs. Green is saying. A piece of folded notebook paper slides onto my desk.

Texting during class? I never pegged you for a rebel 😜

I look over at Kaylee who is smirking at me.

There is a lot about me you don't know 😉

I wait until Mrs. Green's back is to us and then pass the note over to Kaylee. She reads it and nods before putting the note in her folder. The rest of English is uneventful, but overall leaves me more hopeful for lunch the next day.

"Anything new with the Queen of Punk?" Tristan asks when he walks up to me in the hallway on the way to athletics.

"She's coming to lunch tomorrow and dinner on Saturday."

"Did you find out who her date is?"

"Carter."

"Should I know who that is?" Tristan scrunches up his brow.

Xander has a point about most of the Knights not paying attention to anyone who doesn't play sports.

"It's the other guy she's with all the time."

"Hopefully, they're just friends." Maybe if enough of us say it, it'll make it true.

"Yeah, that's what Caballero thinks. Are you taking Jessica to Homecoming?" I ask.

The girl in question winks at Tristan as she passes us in the hall.

Tristan nods to Jessica briefly before turning back to me. "Yeah. She asked last night after the bonfire."

"Are she and Kasey coming to lunch tomorrow?"

Tristan glances behind him to make sure Jessica is long gone. "No. It's only a date to the dance. If they meet Stella, she could get the wrong idea."

"Are you worried about Mama Kingston getting the wrong idea, or Jessica?"

"Both. Definitely both."

I pause before saying, "Kaylee *did* come talk to me before English."

"Really?" Tristan raises his eyebrows.

I relay that conversation to him.

"Why would she care what Stella thinks?" he asks as we walk through the doors to the gym hallway.

"I don't know. She doesn't strike me as the kind to care what other people think about her."

"Am I allowed to bug you about your guitar lessons now?"

"No. I'd prefer if you never mentioned them. I'm not in the mood to talk about it until I know whether or not Saturday is a friend date or a real date." I look up like the ceiling tiles might rescue me from having this conversation.

"Fine. Are you going to the game today?"

"Yeah, Colten is playing." We get to the locker room and get ready for football practice.

I'm hoping to get a break from all of the Homecoming talk during football practice, but it seems the guys have nothing better to do than talk about who they're going with. At least no one mentions Lynn or who she's going with today.

Mark's already on edge with them discussing the dance. He'd probably lose his temper if they brought up Lynn again. I'm hoping nothing happens with Grayson and Lynn until after the dance. I'd rather not have to deal with their drama on top of dealing with Kaylee being with us and on a date. With how impatient Grayson tends to be, I'm not holding my breath.

Grayson thinks Mark will ask someone else to Homecoming. I think that's wishful thinking. It'd be the smart thing to do if he wants his nonsense about 'things running their course' to be believable. But Mark doesn't seem to be able to do the smart thing. The way he has been putting heat behind his passes, it looks like he's mad that Lynn dumped him.

On one hand, I feel for him. I remember what it's like to think you're in love with Lynn for her to say you're better off as friends. But they were barely together two weeks and from what Lynn has said about their dates, he was more interested in making out or talking about himself than getting to know Lynn or seeing if they are compatible.

The way he's been acting like he owns Lynn rubs me the wrong way too. As much as it'd be good for everyone for him to move on, I pity whichever girl he sets his sights on next. The way he's acting, it seems like he and Whitney are a match made in hell. They're both clingy, possessive, and annoying.

Maybe Whitney will get her wish and he'll ask her to Homecoming. That'd make Whitney happy and get Mark off everyone's backs. With the way Whitney has been behaving and treating Lynn, she'd probably deserve whatever fallout would come from being Mark's rebound.

CHAPTER 24
KAYLEE

After school, Sara and I go to the mall to go dress shopping. James has been blowing up my phone all afternoon. I haven't opened anything he has sent since lunch. It riles him up when I ignore him, but I don't have the energy to deal with him right now.

I'm happy for Drew that there seems to be some progress with Lynn. However, I'm not looking forward to going to the dance at all, especially not with a bunch of popular people I haven't talked to before this week.

"What about this?" Sara steps out of the dressing room in a floor-length pink number that looks like a pink version of Cinderella's dress.

"I think it's a bit much for a Homecoming dance. We can still get it if you want. It looks like it'd be perfect for a prom dress. You look like a princess." I play with my phone and resist the urge to look at the screen.

"Who knows if it'll even fit, then? I can't go to prom for, like, two more years. It's pretty, though."

I sigh. "When it gets closer to prom, if you want to go, I can take you this year. Underclassmen can come if they have an upperclassman as a date. If you don't want to officially be my date, I could probably talk Carter into taking you."

"You'd do that? Wouldn't you want to take your own date?" Sara is practically vibrating with excitement at the thought of getting to go to prom.

I think about it for a moment. "I probably won't go to prom unless you want to go. I highly doubt I'd have a date I'd want to take with me."

"What about Carter? You're going to the dance with him."

I roll my eyes. "That's more to make sure Lynn knows Drew is not interested in me and vice versa."

"What about the other guys who we're going with?" Sara swishes her skirt back and forth before twirling.

"The 'Knights' whom I'd never spoken to before this week? I don't plan on spending much time talking to them, much less dating them."

We continue trying on dresses, moving from store to store. Sara has found at least one she loves at each store. I've found nothing. We eventually end up in Hot Topic.

I find a black dress that's a V-neck with a lot of straps crisscrossing at the top. The skirt is overlapped with layers of black lace that hit me at mid shin. Sara grabs a buckle-strap pinafore dress and a puff-sleeve corset dress. I take all three into the changing room, saving the one I found for last.

I step out in the first dress to show Sara. But instead of my sister, James is standing outside the dressing room, clearly waiting for me. He stands up from where he's been leaning against the wall and flicks his platinum-blond hair out of his piercing blue eyes.

"So, is that what you're wearing for this dance you're going to?" He seems unimpressed as he looks me up and down.

"I don't see why it'd matter to you. I'm not going with you and you're not the type to go to a dance at all." I try to resist the urge to take in how good he looks in his skinny jeans and tight band shirt, but my eyes don't seem to have gotten the memo that we don't care about James or his appearance anymore.

"Neither are you," he says as he walks forward and crowds my space. "Who conned you into going to a dance?"

"I'm not telling you. You don't own me, and it isn't any of your business." I'm annoyed with his possessiveness and with my body for leaning into him.

Mentally, I'm done with James, but physically, I still like having him in my space. Toxic relationship or not, I'm comfortable around James. His closeness puts my nerves on edge and makes my body zing to life. Unfortunately, I'm not able to think myself out of responding to him.

"Why won't you tell me who it is? Or is this some sort of mind game?" James twirls a lock of my hair around his finger, and I tell myself I don't enjoy his touch. "You're probably going with Carter or Drew and are saying it's a date to trick me into going. You know I don't do dances, so you're doing all of this to try to get me to go."

"This isn't a mind game, James. I ended things last time, remember?" I cross my arms wishing my assertiveness didn't seem to desert me because James is here in person. "I don't want to be with you and definitely don't want to go to the dance with you. I've moved on from whatever we were. I've found someone better than you. We're done for good this time." I really mean it. This last heartbreak was almost more than I could handle. I'm never going back to him.

"You think you've found someone to replace me? It's only a matter of time before you come crawling back. You're mine whether you admit it to yourself or not." James releases my hair and gently brushes his hand down the side of my face.

"I'm not yours. You've definitely never been mine and I don't want you."

James leans even closer and whispers in my ear, "Say it again, and this time like you believe it."

His words push me over the edge and light a fire of indignation inside me.

"I. Am. Not. Yours." I punctuate each word with a shove to his chest to get some breathing room back.

"Whatever." He rolls his eyes but does move back.

My brain works a bit better when all of my senses aren't full of James. Then I remember. "Aren't you supposed to be on your own date? Isn't that why we couldn't have practice today?"

"Being obsessed with my dating life isn't making you seem all that over me. Sure you don't want to *hang out* more?" The amount of innuendo he puts on those two words is impressive even if it only ticks me off more.

Ugh. I can't believe his arrogance. How did I never see it before? I guess I did; I just took it as confidence. During a time when every part of my life was changing and I wasn't sure of myself, James filled that void with more than enough self-assurance. I don't need or want him anymore.

"I only know because it affects our band schedule. What either of us do outside of the band isn't the other's business, and quite frankly, I don't care what or who you do with your time," I say.

"I have better things to do with my afternoon than convince you of your delusions. I'll just wait for you to come knocking at my door. You will eventually." James walks away and out of the store.

"So, did I miss something?" Sara sidles up next to me, startling me with her presence. "Because last I checked, which was less than an hour ago, you're going with Carter and it's definitely not a real date."

I've been so absorbed with James that now I'm not sure if she's been there the entire time or if she walked up during our conversation.

"You didn't miss anything. I got mad and let my mouth run away."

"So you lied? I don't think that's going to end well."

"I didn't technically lie. I'm single—that means I have myself, which is way better for me than being with James. It's not like James would ever come to the Homecoming dance. He isn't going to know who I'm going with, or whether we're on a real date or going as friends. It isn't his business what I do, anyway."

My sister shrugs. "If you say so. I still think this will come back to bite you in the butt."

Sara drops it and we go back to dress shopping.

I end up getting the V-neck dress. Sara got the pink dress for prom and found a cute red dress for Homecoming. We decide to grab dinner at the food court before going home.

"I know you're adamant that this thing with the Knights is just you being a wingman for Drew. But that doesn't mean you don't have eyes." Sara wiggles her eyebrows.

"They might be nice to look at, but that doesn't mean I'm interested in any of them. Oliver's the only one I've even had a conversation with. I'm pretty sure the rest of them don't know I exist, which is fine by me."

"Maybe one of them will be the one to get you away from James for good."

"I'm not interested," I insist. "I'm not a damsel in distress and don't need a white Knight to ride in and save me."

Sara answers me with a smirk. "What about a Silver Knight?"

I toss a napkin at her. "I can handle James. I'm fine on my own."

"If you say so, but the way you were leaning into him earlier tells a different story." I hate that Sara was there to see that.

"I have it under control. That was a blip in my self-control. It won't happen again." I'm determined not to get pulled back under his spell. I just need to get my body onboard with that plan.

"I'm just saying a hot guy would be a good distraction and deterrent for James. Not to mention, the Knights that rule the school aren't going to be scared away by James like other guys have been before."

"It's good to know my sister has zero faith in me."

"It's not like you have the best track record with staying away from James," she points out. "If you aren't interested in any of the guys we're going to Homecoming with, then why don't you see if there's one that might play along to get James to steer clear? Especially if he ends up showing up at the dance to check in on your date."

"Are you suggesting I ask one of the most popular guys at school to fake-date me because you don't think I have enough self-control to stay away from James on my own?" Maybe Drew has a point about the number of rom-coms we watch.

"When you put it that way…yes, that's absolutely what I'm saying. Or you could commit to having a fling with one of them. From what I hear, Jet is all for anything that doesn't involve commitment. He's super-hot, and I bet he's an amazing kisser." Sara appears to be daydreaming about said kissing skills.

"Remind me never to come to you for advice. Especially about dating or morals. I'm not hooking up with Jet because he's hot or because of how James might react."

"You admit he's hot."

"That's *so* not the point. Everyone knows he's hot. Most importantly, he knows he's hot. They're no more virtuous because they call themselves Knights. They're still teenage boys."

"Fine, be boring. If you aren't interested in any of the guys we're going with, can we talk about Colten? And more specifically, do you know who his date is for Homecoming?"

Why does Sara have to be boy-crazy? I'm not ready to navigate her first heartbreak yet.

"Don't tell me you have a crush on Lynn junior. Drew crushing on Lynn is bad enough."

"What? Colten's hot, funny, and smart. What more could you want?" Sara sighs.

I can practically see the hearts in her eyes as she talks about Colten.

"Someone who has a notion of what commitment is?"

"As someone who has been on-again, off-again with James, I'm not sure you know what commitment is. Colten may have not had a girlfriend before, but it isn't like he's constantly making out with different girls in the hallway, either."

"James is the one with commitment issues, not me. Colten's younger than Lynn's crew. Maybe he hasn't grown into the level of player that her friends have achieved. That'd explain why he's called a Squire instead of a Knight." I'm still not sure what the whole Knight thing is about, though.

"Whatever. So, do you know who his date is?"

"No. All Oliver said was that he had one. I assume since all of Lynn's friends are going to lunch tomorrow whoever Colten is going with would be there, too."

"You're no help." She pouts.

"I'm not trying to be helpful. I'm trying to dissuade you from crushing on Colten."

We talk about other things as we finish our food and head home. I need to carry my trombone in, so Sara brings in all three dresses.

Mary's car is here. Hopefully, she's already in her room, messaging guys on her dating sites. If she's focused on being flirty and finding a new husband, she will leave us alone.

Of course, I'm not that lucky. Mary is in the living room with a half-drank bottle of wine.

No telling how long she has been drinking. She's always been a trophy wife, so she isn't taking to the idea that she needs to get a job well. Richard still pays for everything for me and Sara, which is a sore spot for her.

She thinks he should pay for everything she wants since he cheated. She wants to get everything in the divorce—that way she doesn't have to work.

"Oh, look, it's Daddy's little princesses back from a day of shopping. It must be nice to be able to go buy whatever you want." Mary gets off the couch and starts heading in our direction.

"Go upstairs. I'll be up there in a bit," I tell Sara.

Sara doesn't argue, heading straight upstairs with the dresses. Mary watches her go up the stairs.

"Those are fancy dresses. What are they for, Daddy's next wedding?"

"They're for the Homecoming dance Saturday."

"Someone asked *her* to Homecoming? She's not even pretty, not to mention she needs to lose weight."

Sara doesn't turn around, but I can see her flinch as Mary's words hit their mark.

"Sara is beautiful on the inside and the outside. Unlike you, who are ugly on the inside and outside."

SMACK!

My head whips to the side from the sheer force of Mary's slap. I should've known better than to talk back to her when she's been drinking, but it makes me angry when she talks about Sara that way.

"I'm your mother. You need to talk to me with respect."

"Maybe I would if I had any respect for you."

From there we fall into our usual pattern of arguing. She must not be too drunk because she doesn't hit me again. When she gets to the point of being fed up with me, she grabs her car keys.

"You're an ungrateful brat." She's slurring and I'm worried about her driving. "I wish I'd never had children. All you did was wreck my figure and take away my youth." She walks out the door.

I go upstairs to repair the damage she has inflicted on Sara with her words. Sara doesn't want to talk about it, so we work on homework and then get ready for bed. Sara goes to sleep, but I try to stay awake until Mary gets home.

I fall asleep sometime around three in the morning, and she still isn't here.

CHAPTER 25
ANDREW

Since it's Homecoming week, the JV and junior high teams have home games. The band helps run our side of the concession stands, so the parents get a break since the boosters have to run the one on Friday by themselves. As a section leader, I work each home game to set a good example. Carter's working with me today. The band concessions are on the visitor's side, meaning hardly anyone comes by.

Lynn 12: What are you up to?

Andrew: Working the band concessions. Why?

Lynn 12: At the JV game?

Andrew: Yeah. Why?

The three dots come up that say she's typing, but then they go away. Determined not to stare at my phone waiting for a reply, I slip it into my pocket and get back to work restocking the candy bars at the front.

"Hey."

I look up to see Lynn in front of me. She has changed out of the Batman costume she wore at school. The Batman costume was definitely proof I'd have it bad for Lynn regardless of her looks. Her looking hot in jeans and a fitted V-neck that hugs her curves is overkill.

"Uh, hey. What are you doing here?" I ask.

"My brother's the wide receiver for the JV team." Lynn points toward the field.

"Oh, uh, yeah. I remember your mom saying something about that."

"Speaking of my mom, she wanted to know if you did any extracurriculars other than band."

"Um, I'm on the math science team. Why…?"

"She wanted to know what all to put on your garter." Lynn types something out on her phone.

"My garter?" I hope Lynn didn't hear the squeak in my voice as it went up.

"Yeah, for Homecoming…? You don't already have one, do you? I completely forgot to ask before she started making it." Lynn looks up from her phone and I feel trapped in her gaze.

"Uh, no I don't…I don't already have one. Why is your mom, um, making me a garter?"

"She makes one for all of my friends. Since you're coming to the dance with us, that includes you."

"Oh, uh, okay. That's nice of her. I mean…she, um, she doesn't have to." Having all of Lynn's attention when we're basically alone is not great for the speaking part of my brain.

"Trust me, she loves making them. I think she wishes I was more of a girl and would let her make me a mum. Instead, she compensates by making a dozen garters. Oh crud." Lynn slaps her forehead with her hand. "I forgot that Kaylee and her sister are coming with us. Do they have mums?"

"I don't know, that doesn't seem like Kaylee's style. Wouldn't that be a lot for your mom to add?" I'm thankful for the reminder that Lynn wants everyone to feel included and that her being over here doesn't mean I'm special.

"Yeah, but if they show up to lunch without one, I'll get an earful about being thoughtless. Any chance her date is getting her one?"

"Hey Carter, are you getting Kaylee a mum?" I turn to face where he's at in the concession stands.

"No, why would I?"

"Because you're her date for Homecoming."

Carter shoots me a look that clearly says what he thinks about that statement.

"It'd be the thing to do as a good date," Lynn chimes in.

"The point is moot. I don't have the time or money to get one. Sara won't have one, either."

Lynn's eyes get big at his last statement.

"Wrong thing to say," I say, still looking at Carter. I turn back to Lynn. "They'll be fine without one."

"I'm sure they will, but my mother won't. She's all about making sure no one is left out. Can you text me their names so I can make sure they're spelled correctly? And whatever they participate in?"

"I guess so." I pull out my phone to do as she asked.

"Do you think they'd prefer a mum or a garter?"

"Probably a garter," I answer, "and wouldn't that be easier to make?"

Lynn nods.

"Sounds like that'd be a lot of garters for you to hand out tomorrow," Carter pipes up. "It might help if you had Oliver or someone deliver Kaylee's." His expression is a little too innocent.

Lynn nods again. "Yeah, that'd be a great idea. What about yours and Sara's?"

"Mine?" Carter sounds bewildered. "I don't need or want a garter. Maybe one of your other friends could deliver them. You can get my number from Drew and give it to whoever and I can coordinate with them." Someone walks up and Carter goes over to help them.

"Thank you for going with this," Lynn says to me with a grateful tone. "I know my mom can be a lot. And thank you for agreeing to lunch tomorrow. She's over the moon to be cooking for so many people."

"I'm glad to be there. It doesn't hurt that your mom is a great cook." This last week of talking with Lynn in class and her continuing to acknowledge my presence has made it easier to talk to her. At least when other people are around. Being the center of her attention is still a lot.

"Yeah, but I know most parents wouldn't require meeting everyone going to the dance with their child beforehand. I mean, Grayson and Oliver's parents probably don't even know they're going to a dance."

"I think it's cool your mom is so involved."

"Yeah?"

"Yeah." We share a smile.

"It looks like you finally got your glasses fixed." Lynn points to her own face.

"Yeah, I got them back this afternoon." Translation: I finally got Kaylee to put them back together for me.

"That's good. Your glasses suit you better than your contacts."

"Oh, um, thanks…I guess?" I have no idea what that's supposed to mean.

"I meant it as a compliment. You look more like you with them. Like you're more comfortable."

"Thanks, I definitely prefer them to contacts." I didn't think I was visibly uncomfortable with my contacts, but I guess I was.

"I better head back to the stands. See you in the morning."

"See you then." I watch as Lynn walks away.

"You've got a little drool there." Carter points to my face.

"Shut up. I do not."

He laughs.

I wipe my chin to be on the safe side.

"You're completely head over heels. It's adorable. And it definitely looks like it has the potential of going somewhere."

"Sure," I say sarcastically.

Carter begins ticking points off on his fingers.

"She asked you to Homecoming. She pays attention to you enough to notice when you're wearing your glasses. She's getting you a garter. She came over here to talk to you when she could've texted. She was definitely flirting with you."

I push each finger down as I state my counter argument.

"She asked me to the dance because her mom wanted her to. Because

I've never been to one. She has to look at my eyes to talk to me, so of course she'd notice my glasses. Her mom insists on making everyone a garter, including you. She probably came over here to get a break from her mom. And she most definitely is *not* flirting with me. At best I'm on her radar as a potential friend, and who knows if that will even last past this project." I don't need Carter getting my hopes up. Lynn is so far out of my league that I don't think she can see me from there.

"You've most certainly been adopted as her friend, and by all accounts, Lynn doesn't drop her friends ever, even after breaking up with them. So if you're right and she only sees you as a friend right now, in less than a week you went from her not knowing you existed to being friends. Give it some time and she'll fall for you, too."

"You. Are. Delusional." I shake my head and start restocking the chips.

"You're just scared to get your hopes up. You're her friend now. All her relationships started as friends first. You're one step closer than you've ever been before."

"So, what if I am scared? Lynn has a very specific type. A type I'm the exact opposite of. Not to mention, I can barely hold a conversation with her without stuttering. Even if we ignore all of the reasons Lynn would never see me as dating potential, I'm not sure dating her would be a good idea. I can't compare to any of her exes and none of them could keep Lynn for longer than a few weeks, if they even lasted that long. I think it'd be better to secretly admire her than to briefly be the center of her attention and then have her ultimately break my heart. She'd eventually move on, and I think that'd be worse than her not reciprocating. Friends is nice and friends isn't going to get my heart broken."

"First off, it hasn't even been a full week and your stuttering has already started to get better. Secondly, you aren't her usual type, that's kind of the point. Her usual type clearly isn't what she wants. That has to be why she has so many short-lived relationships. Since you aren't her usual type then you could be exactly what she's looking for. She just doesn't know it yet."

"Now it sounds like you've been forced to watch too many rom-coms with Kaylee." I can't let Carter know he's making good points or that I've thought those same things this week.

"Be the king of denial if you want, but I think there's potential there. I don't let Kaylee bully me into doing things I don't want to. I think you're mixing me up with you."

"Whatever." I busy myself with making sure everything is ready for tomorrow night.

Carter's words stick in my head, and I start to wonder if maybe he's right. Maybe it isn't fooling myself to believe that something might happen with Lynn. I feel hope start to bloom and try to stomp it out.

This project will be long enough without me deluding myself and setting myself up for heartbreak. Realistically, that's where my feelings for Lynn are headed—either because she still doesn't see me or because she notices me only to move on when she decides we'd be better off as friends.

No, it's better to focus on being friends. Less hurt that way.

CHAPTER 26
GRAYSON

Lynn seems to take forever at the concession stands, so it's surprising when she comes back empty-handed.

The guys and I accompany Lynn and Stella to as many of Colten's home games as we can. It's important to Stella, and it only seems fair since she comes to everything we do.

I've been sitting next to Lynn and trying to flirt with her, but she seems mentally checked out today. It doesn't help that she's been working on her homework whenever Colten isn't on the field.

"Were they out of everything?" Daniel asks as she sits back down.

"Huh?" Lynn asks.

"You went to the concession stands, were gone for a fair amount of time, and came back with nothing," Oliver points out.

"I went over to ask Andrew about stuff for Homecoming. By the way, Oliver, Grayson, and Daniel, can you come by the house on your way to school?"

We all nod.

"Why?" Daniel asks.

"Because my mom's making enough garters for an army, and it'd make my life easier if I didn't have to try to hand them out before school by myself. I figured I'd give Jet and Tristan's to Daniel. Grayson can do Carter and Sara's. And Oliver can give Kaylee hers. Plus your own, of course."

"Why…why would you give me Kaylee's?" Oliver shoots a look I don't understand to Daniel.

"Carter suggested it and it seemed like a good enough idea." Lynn says. "Why, is there a problem with that?"

"Not at all. He'd be happy to help you out. We all would." Daniel rescues Oliver from having to respond. I wonder why he needed to be rescued in the first place. I make a mental note to ask him about it later.

I raise my hand. "I'm all for helping, but how am I supposed to get Carter and Sara's to them? I don't know where they'll be in the morning." I'm not even sure who they are, but I don't think pointing that out will earn me any points with Lynn.

"Oh, Andrew sent me Carter's number and told me to give it to you." Lynn texts his contact info to me.

"I'm sure your mom's thrilled about making so many garters this year." Jet leans forward so he's right next to Lynn even though he, Oliver, and Tristan are in the row behind us.

"Yeah. She's especially glad about getting to make a mum for Amelia. Xander got major brownie points for talking Amelia into a mum instead of a garter. I'm pretty sure he's the favorite twin right now." Lynn nudges Jet back and leans back against his knees. Maybe I should've sat behind her instead of next to her.

For the rest of the game, we cheer for Colten and Callie and discuss tomorrow night's game. Even though this is Stillwaters' JV, there ought to be enough crossover for us to get an idea of how they play. While Lynn is focused on the field, I text Oliver to ask him if he can come up with a reason to ride home with Daniel and not have Lynn with them. He nods after looking at his phone. We beat Stillwater thirty-four to twenty. Hopefully, we have similar results against their varsity tomorrow night.

"Hey Daniel, could I catch a ride home with you? I wanted to talk to you about something," Oliver asks as the JV team heads toward the locker room.

"Sure." Daniel nods, then adds, "Lynn, do you mind riding home with Grayson?"

Lynn looks up from putting away her homework.

"I want to congratulate Colten on the win. I'll ride home with my mom and brothers."

"I want to talk to Colten, too," I say. "You know, wide receiver to wide receiver. You can decide who you want to ride with after we see him."

"Um, okay, I guess. I'll see the rest of you losers tomorrow," she says.

The guys all say bye and head out.

Lynn turns to me. "So…"

"So what?"

"I don't know. Are you sure you want to wait with me? You could talk to Colten tomorrow. He doesn't expect y'all to be at his games, much less to stay afterwards." Lynn slings her backpack over one of her shoulders.

"But he's glad to have us here, and it means the world to your mom."

"Even she doesn't expect you to stay until he gets out of the locker room." Lynn starts heading toward where her parents are sitting.

"I want to."

"Okay, I guess."

Stella and Theo are both at the top of the bleachers with all of Lynn's brothers. The boys are all getting their stuff together.

"Hey, mom."

"Hi, honey. Xander's taking the boys home, so they can get started on getting ready for bed. Can you go with and help him manage the twins?"

"Oh, I was going to stay to talk to Colten," Lynn says.

"You can congratulate him when we get back to the house." Lynn and her mom have some sort of silent exchange.

"Of course, Mom." Lynn hugs her parents and then follows Xander.

I catch up to Lynn. "If you want, I could give you a ride so you don't have to be stuck with all the boys until you get to the house."

"I thought you wanted to talk to Colten." She raises an eyebrow.

"I figured I could help with wrangling the little ones and then talk to him when he gets back to the house." Maybe somewhere in there, have some alone time with Lynn and sus out how she feels about dating.

"Oh, okay. That's probably for the best, anyway. I think my parents want some one-on-one time with him," Lynn says. Then calls out to her twin. "Hey, Xand. I'm going to ride home with Grayson."

"Cool." Xander nods.

"Can I please ride with y'all?" Dylan walks closer to us. "Having to sit through an entire football game with the heathens is my limit."

"As long as it's okay with Grayson." Lynn looks at me.

"Yeah, of course."

So much for having a one-on-one conversation with Lynn. Maybe it's for the best. Daniel told me to be patient and give Lynn time. I just don't want to miss my opportunity and have to deal with watching Lynn in another relationship.

On the way home, Lynn mostly talks to Dylan, asking him about school, band, and his guitar lessons. Lynn is the best older sibling I've ever met. She doesn't grumble about having to help out with her younger siblings. She actively takes an interest in their lives like their mom does with us as well as her own kids. I barely keep up with what Oliver is doing and we do most of the same things.

Arriving at the Kingston house is a flurry of motion. By the time Sean and Parker are bathed and in bed, Lynn's parents are home with Colten. Lynn hugs Colten and tells him how proud she is of him. Colten shrugs her off. He used to love Lynn being at his games and congratulating him afterwards. Since he hit puberty, he acts like he's too cool for his big sister.

"Grayson wanted to talk to you. I better go make sure Leo is actually getting in the shower." Lynn leaves us, and her parents follow behind her.

"You did great tonight. It looks like you might be gunning for my spot next year," I say holding my fist out to Colten.

Colten reluctantly gives me a fist bump. "Yeah, yeah, whatever."

"I mean it."

"I'm sure you do. However, I know I'm not the member of the Kingston family you want to be speaking to. Maybe try to be less transparent, especially if you're going to be around Mark." Colten looks behind him at the stairs where Lynn has just disappeared from.

"I don't know what you mean. Lynn and I are just friends."

"Sure." Colten rolls his eyes. Man, he's sure gotten an attitude lately.

"We are."

"Whatever, man. Maybe you should worry less about convincing me and more about convincing your face. You go all moony when she's around, giving her goo-goo eyes. It's gross and annoying. It's bad enough to have to listen to the guys on the team talk about her in the locker room. Watching you fawn over her is too much. If you're into her or whatever, do me a favor. Don't use me as an excuse to talk to her. You're friends. You shouldn't need to pretend to be interested in my life to be able to talk to her."

"Hey, regardless of my friendship with Lynn, I'm interested in your life. Or have you forgotten who practiced with you all summer when you were going for quarterback? You're like a kid brother to me."

"Whatever." Colten heads up the stairs.

Giving up on talking to Lynn, I head home. It almost feels like she's avoiding me, anyway. Not to mention after that talk with Colten, I'm feeling like I need to regroup. If Colten has noticed my feelings for Lynn, it wouldn't be that big of a stretch to assume Lynn knows, too.

Maybe she's still dealing with her breakup with Mark and not ready for a relationship. That's okay. I can wait if I need to. I just want her to be thinking about me that way. I want her next relationship to be with me.

Now I need to get her to see that. As I walk into my house, I start thinking of a plan to woo Lynn.

CHAPTER 27
OLIVER

Once we get in Daniel's truck, he turns to me.

"Are you wanting to talk about Kaylee, or are you trying to be Grayson's wingman?"

"Bit of both. He asked me to catch a ride with you, but also I'm worried Lynn knows something. Homecoming will be super awkward if everyone knows I have a thing for Kaylee and she's on a date with someone else." I lean my head back against the headrest.

"If Lynn suspected something, she'd say as much. Isn't Carter Kaylee's date?" Daniel starts the truck.

"Yeah, why?" I turn my head toward Daniel hoping he has a good reason for bringing her date up.

"Because I'm pretty sure they're going as friends. I mean, Lynn said Carter suggested you give Kaylee her garter. He wouldn't do that if it was a real date. It'd make the most sense to give them all their garters at the same time. Didn't you say they all have band first period? Lynn may not know that, but Carter does." Daniel gives me a meaningful look like this is concrete evidence.

"That sounds too good to be true. Why would Carter even want to help me out, anyway? I've never even spoken to him." I'm cautiously hopeful.

"Maybe that means Kaylee has a crush on you, too."

"Whatever." I roll my eyes. "On to a more interesting topic, you know Grayson is going after Lynn?"

"Yeah, he's not exactly subtle. I wish he'd be patient and stop pushing it."

"I don't think patience is a trait Grayson possesses. I just hope Mark doesn't catch wind of Grayson's crush."

"I thought I'd need to worry about drama from Courtney and Bailey at Homecoming."

Daniel kissing two cheerleaders in the same week has barely been a blip on the rumor radar with everyone wondering what happened with Lynn and Mark.

"And now odds are there'll be plenty of drama in our own group." I close my eyes for a moment.

"Yeah, this'll probably be the most entertaining dance of the year."

Which isn't great for people like us who don't like drama.

"When Mark talked to me on Wednesday, he said he didn't mean what he said when he was upset. Do you know what he was talking about? Or what he might have said to Lynn?"

Daniel hesitates for a moment. "He called her a few choice words. She didn't want us stepping in and doing anything. That's why she didn't want the rest of you to know about it. But Lynn's fine. She handled it on her own. Nothing to worry about."

I don't believe that's all there is to it, but I know better than to push Daniel. If Lynn doesn't want us to know, he won't be the one to tell me.

"Yeah, okay. Later, dude." I get out of the truck and head inside my house.

The house is silent. My parents must already be asleep. They both get up super early for work. Unless they have a work dinner to attend, they're usually in bed pretty early.

After the chaos of the game, I'm glad for the quiet. I'm secretly glad not too many people come to the JV games. I'm not a fan of crowds. I prefer it when it's just the Knights and Lynn's family. I don't have to worry about what I say or if I say anything at all.

On my days when I don't feel like talking, I can sit there and listen to them talk without feeling obligated to say something. It's nice to be a part of the conversation without having to contribute to it. None of them think I'm weird just because I don't always have something to add.

I love being so close to the Knights and growing up with them. I know I can always be myself, no matter who that might be in the moment. They love and accept me no matter what.

I used to wish my parents would be the same way, but I've come to terms with the fact that they don't really want to be very involved in our lives. They're proud of our achievements, like when I bring home straight A's again or we win a championship. But they're never going to be at a game or check to see if we need help with homework.

It's like they entirely gave the reins to Stella to raise us, instead of her just being our nanny. I'm glad her whole family welcomed us in, back before any of us knew it was weird to stay more overnights at your friend's house than your own. I'm pretty sure Theo, who has always worked full time, changed more of our diapers than my parents combined.

I shake off my thoughts and put my headphones on. I connect them to my phone and play Outnumbered by Hysteria's most recent song: "Remains."

When the façade fades, this is what remains.
If the deceit and lies continue, dust will be all that is left of you.
White wash tombs can't hide the decay, plastic smiles won't make it okay.
When the façade fades, this is what remains.
Corpses and broken hearts litter the past. How long do you think playing pretend will last?
A garden fertilized by the dead. Who else will you consume to be fed?

As the lyrics continue to play, I plug my phone into my computer. I upload my pictures from Colten's game tonight and start editing them. These will be a good new addition to the digital photo frame we got for Mama Kingston a few years back. Soon I lose myself in the music and in my work.

CHAPTER 28
DANIEL

I fire off a text to Lynn, suggesting Oliver ride to school with her so they can go first thing to deliver Kaylee and Andrew's garters and I can come over before they leave to get the ones Grayson and I are supposed to hand out.

Hopefully, that will keep Grayson from pushing things anymore. Grayson has made my dating life seem so much less problematic. At least none of the football team cares about who I kiss under the bleachers.

My parents are sitting in the living room when I walk in the door. My mom is reading a book while my dad watches some crime drama on TV.

"I'm home."

"Oh good, honey." My mom briefly glances away from her book.

"Yeah. Colten and the team won their game."

"Wonderful." She's focused back on her book as she turns to the next page.

"Tomorrow is Homecoming. Do you think you'll be there?"

"You know how busy I am at work right now. We're designing the new industrial park on the outside of town. I didn't get home today until after eight." My dad is an architect and usually works long hours.

"Yes, and I'm on call tomorrow." My mom is a neurosurgeon at the hospital in the next town.

"Dad, you could come late. And Mom, I thought you were switching with someone else so you could come?"

"I'm too tired to go to a football game after working for over twelve hours. We already came to one of your games." His eyes are still on the TV. It feels like I may as well not be here.

"That was last year. This year I'm on varsity. Lynn's mom is at all of our games."

"She doesn't work. I have to be at the hospital early in the morning. If Stella will be there, you don't need us there anyway." My mom gets up to hug me briefly before going to their room.

My dad turns the volume on his show up, signaling he's done with this conversation. I head upstairs to my room. I get my homework done and feel restless. I text Lynn.

Caballero: You up?

Kingston: Yeah helping mom finish garters

Caballero: Want an extra set of hands?

Kingston: Sure

I head next door without bothering to tell my parents even though I'm leaving the house after ten on a school night. It's not like they'd notice I was gone, anyway.

When I get there, Lynn's mom puts me to work. Since I'm not crafty, I mostly hold things in place for Lynn. We work for the next hour until all of the garters are finished. Lynn's mom goes to get hangers so we can hang them up and keep them from getting tangled.

"What's up? And don't say 'nothing.' You hate crafts." Lynn always knows when something's off with me.

"My parents won't be at the game tomorrow. They said they've been to one and that's enough."

"That was last year. You weren't even on varsity then."

"I know. I told them as much. It doesn't matter to them."

"I'm sorry."

"It is what it is. Mama Kingston will be there and that's all that matters." Lynn smiles at the name we came up with for her mom growing up. Her mom comes back and we finish up with the garters.

"Now we only have Amelia's mum. I'm so excited that Amelia is going to Homecoming and wanted a mum this year. I haven't got to make one since you were little and that one was so small it was more of a garter than a mum." Mama Kingston picks out the materials she wants.

"It was still annoying. I don't see how all of those girls walk around with those giant mums all day." Lynn shivers like the thought is abhorrent to her. "I'd much rather have a garter on my arm than a mum pulling at my shirt."

"Not everyone prioritizes comfort over absolutely everything else." I nudge her with my elbow.

"They should. The idea of a bigger mum making you more popular is ridiculous. Like wearing a dress you can't sit in because it makes you look good. There are plenty of dresses you can sit in." Lynn shrugs. "It's not like any male can tell the difference from one dress to another. You never pay attention to what girls wear."

"Well…" I start, then glance at Lynn's mom.

"Okay, you pay some attention to what they're wearing. But they could still find things to wear that look hot that aren't super uncomfortable. I mean, softball pants aren't uncomfortable." Lynn raises her eyebrows at the last statement.

She's referencing having to go with us to watch the softball team play last year. We might have spent a significant portion of the game focused on the benefits of softball pants instead of the score of the game.

"I'm sure they're as comfortable as baseball pants or football pants," I say.

She can say what she wants about our conversations during softball games, but she isn't any better during football or baseball games.

"At least I keep up with what is happening on the field as well." Lynn sticks her tongue out at me.

"What are you two talking about?" Mama Kingston asks. "And what does it have to do with mums?"

"Nothing important, and it has nothing to do with mums," Lynn says, and we go to work helping with the mum.

It's a little after midnight by the time we finish with everything. Mama Kingston hugs me and thanks me for my help. She tells Lynn to see me home and tells us both *good night*.

"So, do you want to talk about it? Or hang out and not talk about it?" Lynn asks after we hear her parents' bedroom door shut.

"Not really. There isn't anything more to tell you. And as much as I'd like to hang out, I'm pretty sure your parents wouldn't be happy about us staying up even later on a school night."

"I'm sure my mom knows something is up. They'd understand if you wanted to hang out for a bit and crash in y'all's room."

We don't technically have a room, but one of the guest rooms is full of our stuff and where we stay when we crash at Lynn's. It's the Knights' unofficial room, and it has two bunk beds in there from back when we all stayed over more frequently.

"Honestly, I feel better after being over here with y'all. I'm good now," I try to reassure her.

"You sure? We could always go stay in the castle. Or if you want heat and air, we could go to the guest house. We could always hang out in my room if you want to be quiet as a church mouse. I can pull the trundle bed out that Callie sleeps on when she stays over."

"It's sounding like you're the one wanting me to stay. Why do we have to be so quiet in the house?"

"Xander already went to bed and he needs his beauty sleep. You know what he's like when he gets woken up." Lynn can say what she wants about Xander being a bear when he gets woken up, but she's not exactly a morning person, either.

"Fair point. How about we head to your room? We can hang out for a bit, then go to bed. Tomorrow will be a long day and we don't need to be up all hours of the night."

I mostly agree because I think Lynn is offering because of my parents, but also because she doesn't want to be alone. With her panic attack yesterday I'm a bit worried about her. She seemed fine today, but she was fine yesterday until she wasn't.

I go to the Knights' room to get ready for bed then head upstairs to

Lynn's room. She's in her fuzzy pajamas and an oversized hoodie she stole from one of her uncles when they moved after college. I help her pull out the trundle bed for me to sleep on. I turn the light off and we get settled into our respective beds. We talk about nothing in particular for a little while making sure to keep our voices down, so we don't wake up any of her brothers.

CHAPTER 29
KAYLEE

Early morning practice is my least favorite part of marching band. Being at school almost an hour before everyone else isn't the way I'd schedule practice. This morning, we had to be there extra early because we're practicing on the football field instead of the parking lot, and it takes longer to walk there.

Drew and Carter are talking about something as we make our way to the field, but I'm not listening. I didn't sleep well last night, even when I did finally fall asleep. My sleep was fitful after the run-in with James and dealing with Mary.

Carter elbows me.

"Ow! What?" I glare at him.

"Look who's at the gate." Carter nods his head in the direction of the gate leading to the football field.

Lynn and Oliver are standing there. Lynn notices Drew and waves at him before they start heading our way.

"What are they doing here?" Drew asks.

"Let's go find out." Carter walks to meet them halfway.

"Good morning," Lynn practically sings. "I wanted to bring you your garter before school started, so you could wear it all day." Lynn holds up a garter for Drew. I'm impressed. It isn't generic but specific to him and his interests. That bodes well for his interest in Lynn.

"That's so sweet." I beam at them both.

Oliver clears his throat, and that's the first time I look over at him.

"I have one for you." Oliver gestures to the garter he's holding.

"Oh, okay. Um, thanks." I feel my face heat up and know Carter will be teasing me for this later.

I don't even like Oliver or know him that well. But no one has ever gotten me anything, much less a garter for Homecoming. I don't want him to think I think it's a big deal, because of what I said about Lynn getting one for Drew.

"Do you want me to put it on for you?"

"Sure." I extend my right arm to him.

"Your left arm would probably be best."

"Why? Is there some sort of Homecoming etiquette I'm unaware of?" My voice is sharper than I intended.

"No, I thought it'd be easier since you move your slide with your right."

"Oh, yeah. That'd be good." *Ugh!* Apparently, I can either be awkward or snarky this morning.

I need more sleep. I feel uncomfortable with this situation and feel embarrassed that I'm uncomfortable.

Oliver carefully pulls the garter up my arm just below my shoulder. His fingers lightly brush my skin, sending tingles in every direction. I feel goosebumps forming as my body reacts to his closeness and gentle touch. My face heats with a blush and I feel even more awkward.

"Did you come early to deliver these before our practice?" I attempt to have some sort of normal conversation.

"Yeah, that and Lynn wants to paint us blue and silver before school starts. If you haven't noticed, she gets really into the school-spirit days. According to her, wearing our jerseys isn't enough." Oliver rolls his eyes but has a soft smile playing at his lips.

"Is that why she has blue ribbons throughout her hair today?"

"Yep, and she's only getting started." Oliver shuffles his feet. "I better let you get to practice."

"See you at lunch." I give him a small wave and immediately feel stupid for doing so.

Oliver waves back, settling my nerves. "See you then." He smiles fully before walking off.

I can't help but enjoy the view as Oliver walks away from me. Once I fully process what I'm doing I shake my head to clear the thoughts about Oliver away. I don't need to be thinking about the way his jeans cling to him or how strong and muscular he looks in his football jersey. I need to be distancing myself from all boys right now. Especially ones whose touch brings my skin to life. That road will only lead to more heartache.

I turn around and see Carter at the gate. I hustle to catch up with him. Lynn is still talking to Drew, but I don't want to interrupt them.

"Are you still in denial about Oliver?" Carter asks as we walk through the gate.

"The garter doesn't have to mean anything. It's not like it has his name on it or anything."

"Keep telling yourself that."

"Kaylee! Carter! Quit yapping and get to your starting positions!" Mr. Gregory bellows from the stands.

We hustle to our spots. Drew must have heard because he catches up to me when I get where I'm supposed to be.

Practice seems to go on forever. Finally, when Mr. Gregory says *one more time* and actually means it, we're dismissed.

"Remember: Every rehearsal is a performance and every performance is a rehearsal," he calls after us as we head to the band hall.

"Soooo, Lynn made you a garter for Homecoming. Are you still confident that the dance isn't a date?" I ask Drew as we walk.

"Her mom insisted on making me one because we're *friends*. She makes garters for *all* of Lynn's friends; it's not a big deal. Her mom made one for all of the Knights and some of them have dates to Homecoming. I mean, she insisted on making one for you, Sara, and Carter."

"But Lynn didn't hand-deliver ours or flirt with us so long we were almost late to band practice," Carter says.

"You told Lynn to give yours to one of her friends. That doesn't count." Drew tries to cross his arms but can't quite pull it off since his trombone is nearly as big as him.

"Oh yes, because the pretty and popular always listen to what I have to say." Carter rolls his eyes.

"Lynn did about my garter and Kaylee's," Drew says.

"You told Lynn to have Oliver give me my garter, then tried to make it out to be something it isn't?" I look at Carter.

"I merely suggested it. Also, Oliver knows I have band with you first period. Yet, he didn't tell Lynn to bring mine and Sara's garter with them. If he's only helping her deliver, he'd have done that. But he didn't," Carter points out.

"That does not mean he likes me. He might not have remembered we're in band together. It most certainly does not change that he's a popular jock. We all know jocks are not my thing."

"Maybe he secretly plays piano and has a sweet side." Carter nudges me with his elbow.

Drew huffs. "Playing sports does not make him a jerk. Lynn's friends with him. I'm sure he's a nice guy. Of course, nice guys aren't your thing, either."

"Ooooh shots fired." Carter makes finger guns at me.

"Shut up, Carter." I hit him upside the head.

"Seriously though, if Oliver does like you, you should give him a chance. I mean, your usual type hasn't gotten you anywhere but hurt." Drew cringes a little as he says it, as if he's waiting for me to hit him next.

"Whatever." I snap. "I don't think I need dating advice from someone who has never been on a date."

The words have an instant effect on Drew. His face shuts down and he walks away.

I wince. "I'm sorry. That was mean. I'm tired. James has been irritating, and I didn't sleep well last night."

"That doesn't make what you said okay." Carter's joking demeanor is gone. "James is always irritating. You know Drew's sensitive about having no dating experience, and even more so now that he's actually talking to Lynn."

"He started it," I say halfheartedly.

"Drew's words were well meaning to encourage you to do something that'd be good for you. It wouldn't be the worst thing in the world for you to pursue something with Oliver. You insulted Drew and probably made him even more insecure about everything with Lynn."

"I know. I screwed up." And Carter's reinforcement of that isn't helping anything.

"I have to go meet Grayson to get my garter." Carter walks off.

I need to think of a way to make this up to Drew and quickly. Before lunch would be preferable. I'm sure that'll be awkward enough without him being upset with me. Especially since Carter is upset with me, too.

My phone dings, reminding me I need to put it on *silent.*

James: A Knight seriously?

James: Why is he taking you?

James: Are you a sellout now?

I'm still resolved to ignore James. I only need to talk to him about the band; anything else isn't his business.

Last night, while Sara and I got our stuff ready for bed, I promised her I was done with James. I promised her I wouldn't talk to him unless absolutely necessary. That means no texting, and especially no texting about Homecoming or dating.

I can't believe he has the audacity to be spying on me. When we were somewhat together, I never saw James at school. I was never sure if our paths just never crossed, or if he was that good at avoiding me in public.

James: What is next? Are you gonna join the pom squad?

James: I never thought you'd care about popularity

James: When he dumps you for a cheerleader you'll get what you deserve

James: Don't come crying to me when he gets bored

After the last text, I turn my phone off entirely. I don't want to know what else he might send. It sucks that he still has the power to hurt me even if I don't want to be in a relationship with him.

From what I know about most of the jocks at our school, they do mostly date cheerleaders or members of the dance team. But being told I'd be dumped for one of them still stings. It feels ridiculous.

Oliver and I are barely on speaking terms, much less dating. Therefore, he can't dump me for a cheerleader. It still hurts that James, to whom I've devoted so much of my time, looks at me and obviously finds me lacking.

CHAPTER 30
ANDREW

Andrew

$y=x^{2/3}-\sqrt{1-x^2}$

$y=x^{2/3}+\sqrt{1-x^2}$

I try to shove Kaylee's words out of my head as I walk to English, but it doesn't work. It's another reason Lynn would have no romantic interest in me. She's beautiful, outgoing, popular, *and* experienced. Everything I'm not.

The only thing I have in common with who she usually dates would be that I'm male. Even with that, I know I'm way less masculine than any of her exes. Maybe Kaylee's words are a good thing. I guess I needed to be brought back down to reality after everything with the garter this morning.

Carter's words during the game last night were still bouncing around my head this morning. I know Lynn only brought me a garter because her mom insisted.

But this morning felt like flirting. In hindsight, it was probably Lynn being her friendly self. I'm too inexperienced to know the difference between flirty and friendly.

Lynn is not, nor will she ever be, interested in me. We do seem to have become friends and that's nice. I'm hoping spending more time with her will help me see her as a friend only. I mean, it hasn't worked so far, but maybe that's because I'm still adjusting to her friendship.

When I get to English class, Lynn is talking to Xander. I decide to sit in my usual seat, but then Lynn waves me over.

Even though it has only been an hour and a half since I saw her, she has completely transformed. She has added silver ribbons to the blue ones in her hair. There are blue and silver designs on her skin, starting at her ankles and curling around her collarbone. She's changed clothes and is now wearing a silver skirt and a blue sparkly tank top. She has blue Converse with silver splatters on them. She's the embodiment of our school colors and looks distractingly good.

"Hey, do your friends want to meet us at the door to the athletic parking lot after fourth period?" she asks.

I've been so distracted from taking in Lynn's whole appearance that I didn't realize I've stopped walking nor register her coming over to me.

"Um, why? I know where your house is." *Brilliant.* I seriously need to learn to keep my mouth shut if I can't come up with anything intelligent to say.

"Everyone will fit in our vehicles. We figured instead of having a bunch of vehicles parked around the house, it'd make more sense to drive together."

"Oh, okay. I'll let them know." I send a group text before class starts.

"Awesome. You can ride with me. I'll even make sure you get shotgun." Lynn touches my arm and smiles at me.

I feel myself blush and try to remember we are just friends. This is friendly, not flirty.

"Oh, um, you don't have to do that. I know most of your friends are bigger than me. They need the space more than I do."

Xander walks up and joins our conversation.

"Trust me, you don't want to be stuck in the back with the neanderthals. Take Lynn up on her offer. Plus, it'll save us time if she has already designated you as shotgun."

"Why?"

"Because the guys will spend forever arguing about it. I love them, but they act like small children sometimes." Lynn rolls her eyes.

"Only sometimes?" Xander nudges Lynn with his elbow.

"Go sit down, dork." Lynn gently shoves Xander in the direction of his usual seat.

"Whatever, weirdo." Xander walks away.

Lynn sticks her tongue out at Xander. When she looks back at me, she blushes.

"So, athletic parking lot after fourth?" she says.

"Yeah, and if it makes things easier, I'll sit up front, but I don't mind sitting in the back." Seeing Lynn be silly with her brother makes her less intimidating.

"It would make my life easier. Besides, I'd rather you be up front." Lynn sits down.

That makes me tongue-tied. So much for my mouth working better. Before I can get my act together, Mrs. Green starts our class.

Mrs. Green gives us the last twenty minutes of class to get with our partner to work on our project. I turn to Lynn.

"Where are you at with reading *Twelfth Night*?" I figure homework is the safest topic to broach.

"I finished it yesterday. How much have you read?" Lynn pulls her planner out.

"I'm only halfway through. How have you read it all already?" I've never had a partner make me feel like I'm the slacker before.

"I had my mom get me the audiobook. I listened to it yesterday and Wednesday while I ran." Lynn blushes.

"I didn't think you'd be a slacker or anything, but I've never had a partner make me feel so underprepared for a project. You're like three steps ahead of me no matter what I do. That cannot bode well for my chances of being valedictorian." *Oops.* I didn't mean to say that last part out loud.

"My mom is constantly on us about not procrastinating." Lynn shrugs. "Both of my parents had their associate's degrees when they graduated high school. As far as valedictorian, you're worried about the wrong twin. My brother's the one aiming to follow in my mother's footsteps. At least as far as class rank goes."

"What do you mean by that?" I'm taking AP classes, but there's no way I'll be graduating with an associate's degree.

"My dad graduated two years before my mom. He'd already built their first house together before she graduated. That's now the guest house that's behind our house. Spring break of her senior year, they eloped and immediately got pregnant with Xander and me. She's probably the only married, pregnant valedictorian to ever graduate from here."

"Wow. I don't even know what to say to that." I didn't know couples who started dating that young could get their lives that together so quickly.

"Yeah, that's part of why I don't talk about my parents much. They're a little insane, and so is their story." Lynn is writing in her planner, and her not looking at me makes it so much easier to talk to her.

"It might be different, but that's cool. My parents were high-school sweethearts, too. A third kid that was ten years younger than the other two was too much for my mom, though. She took off before I was a year old."

"I'm so sorry." She pauses briefly. "So, your brothers are that much older than you?" I'm grateful that's the statement she focuses on.

"Yeah, they're twenty-six and twenty-eight. They live far off, so I don't see them often. I was so young when they were out of the house that it was like being an only child." I'm glad I didn't make the conversation more awkward with sharing about my parents, or more specifically, my mom.

"I have no idea what being an only child is like. Xander was born six minutes after me. By the time I started school, I had three siblings with another on the way. Not to mention Oliver, Grayson, and Daniel practically grew up at my house."

"You've been friends your whole lives?" I wonder what it would've been like to have a house full of siblings.

"Basically. Their parents hired my mom as a nanny. It worked out well for everyone. My mom wanted to stay at home with us. That made it where she could and still have an income. Daniel's mom went to med school, and Oliver and Grayson's mom went back to work."

"If you don't mind me asking, why aren't they friends with Xander? I mean, they grew up with him, too, right? And you seem so close to Xander."

"They are, to an extent. But Xander's always been more reserved. He doesn't like to get dirty or do things that are reckless. When we were outside playing in the mud, Xander would be inside drawing or reading. The older we got, the more he wanted to do his own thing. We're still super close. I mean, we're twins after all. But he's introverted and doesn't like being around a bunch of people. Xander and Daniel are closer than they seem—you just don't see it at school. The other two guys are on good terms with him, but they don't have a lot in common."

Through her smile, I see the affection she has for Xander and the Knights.

"But aren't there five Knights?" After I say it, I'm worried she might think I'm stalking her or something now.

"Six, if you include me. Tristan didn't move here until sixth grade, and by then, Xander had already stopped hanging out with us as a group. Jet and Xander have never gotten along. Even now, when they have to be around each other, they usually end up fighting."

"So why are y'all Knights? I've heard people call you that since junior high but didn't know why." I've heard different rumors, but no one was ever really sure.

"Caballero is Spanish for knight and Ridire is Irish for knight. My mom used to call them my knights because wherever I was, they were right there with me." Lynn puts her planner away.

Then she continues, "When we started playing basketball, Silver Knights was our team's name. Jet was on our team, and that's when we became friends and he became one of the Knights. It has been a running inside joke ever since." Lynn smiles directly at me, and I'm thankful the bell saves me from needing to respond.

We walk to Pre-Cal together. Since Tuesday, Lynn has been walking with me to class off and on. It feels weird, but at the same time, we mostly have the same schedule, so it's not like she's going out of her way or anything. I try not to make a big deal out of it because I don't think Lynn means anything by it. She may be walking with me, but at least one of the Knights or Xander is usually with us. It feels more like I've just been adopted into their group, which is still weird for me but less stressful than having Lynn's full attention.

We still get stares and looks when we walk down the hallway, but I don't think Lynn notices. That, or she's used to people looking at her and it's only a new development for me. For all I know people just watch the Knights wherever they go.

Lynn and I don't sit next to each other in any class other than English where we're partners. I've thought about sitting with them during AP Government or Spanish since Kaylee and Carter aren't in those classes, and I don't have anyone to sit with. But I'm not brave enough to invite myself over and Lynn hasn't asked.

In Pre-Cal, I sit next to Kaylee as usual but avoid looking over at her. I wish I had the courage to sit with Lynn, so I wouldn't have to sit next to Kaylee. Instead, I'm just settling for trying to ignore her. Mrs. Barnes lectures all the way through class today, which I'm thankful for. I don't want the option of speaking to Kaylee right now. I don't know that I'm necessarily mad at her, but I don't know what to say to her, either.

Kaylee has been leaving Pre-Cal quickly. It makes me think she's trying to make herself scarce, so Lynn will keep walking with me. Usually, it makes me feel slightly abandoned, but today I'm definitely grateful for the space. What Kaylee said was mean, even if she's right.

Lynn walks with me to Physics. The last couple of days, Daniel and Oliver have been hanging back talking about their own stuff. Today they're talking with Lynn about different stuff for Homecoming.

It's kind of nice to get to be near Lynn without having to actively try not to embarrass myself. I don't even have to try to come up with something to say that won't sound dorky or awkward. The main downside is it cements in my mind that she'd only ever see me as a friend. But becoming friends in a week is still a lot more progress than I've made in the last five years.

CHAPTER 31
LYNN

After Physics, I walk with Xander, Daniel, Oliver, Andrew, and Kaylee to the athletics parking lot. Colten, Callie, Sara, and Amelia are already there waiting for us.

"Andrew and the neanderthals are riding with you, so I assume I have everyone else?" Xander asks.

Before I can respond, Colten whines, "I want to ride with Lynn, especially if Jet and Tristan are going with her."

Xander rolls his eyes and looks like an exasperated parent.

Tristan, Jet, and Grayson arrive with Carter a little behind them.

They look awesome. Before school, I painted one arm blue and one silver on each of the guys. I did blue designs on their silver arm and silver designs on their blue arm. I painted their faces, too. It looks great with their jerseys.

Jet's the only one who doesn't play football. He's wearing a basketball jersey my mom special-ordered. It looks like the one he wears for regular season but has his last name across the back where it normally says "Mustangs." She got one for each of us at the beginning of the school year.

"Why don't you and Callie ride with Lynn? Oliver and I will ride with Xand," Daniel says, which is weird.

Like I told Andrew earlier, they get along with Xander, but it's out of character for him to offer to switch with my little brother. Before I can ask him about it, Daniel shoots me a "go with it" look. I decide to save my questions for later.

"Fine. Whatever. Load up so we can get this over with," Xander mutters as he gets in his SUV.

The guys and Callie talk football the whole way to my house. I keep trying to think of a way to include Andrew in the conversation but come up with nothing.

Today was the first time we talked about anything other than homework or Homecoming plans. I can't exactly segue from football to parents. He has talked about being in band, but I don't know much about marching band. Dylan is the first of us to play an instrument and he only does concert band.

"Sorry about them. They get carried away when talking about sports," I say, hanging back so I could walk with Andrew toward my house.

"It's fine. It's interesting to hear them talk about something they're excited about. Even if I don't understand what they're saying." He smiles, and it reassures me that he isn't feeling left out.

"You want to sit with me at the game tonight so I can explain what is going on?"

"I would, but I'm in marching band." Andrew looks down.

"But isn't that for the halftime show?"

"We only march during the halftime show, but we play in the stands for the rest of the game. We do get third quarter off to eat. I could come sit with you then, and you could teach me a little." Andrew looks up when he finishes speaking.

"Sounds like a plan." I open the side door of the house that leads to the mud room and take my shoes off. Carter comes up on the other side of Andrew.

"You downplayed the size of her house," Carter says to Andrew. "You said it was kind of big, not basically a mansion."

I blush, feeling slightly uncomfortable. This is part of why I don't usually invite people over to my house other than the guys.

"That's not polite to say." Andrew elbows Carter and shoots him a look.

"Hey, I live in an apartment. This is like culture shock. I mean, there's a wall of shoes. I'm allowed to react." Carter elbows Andrew back.

"Carter, shut up. You're the only one who thinks you're funny." Kaylee flicks his ear as she walks by.

"Mom, we're here," I call out as I head into the hallway.

My mom sticks her head out from the kitchen.

"Great. Can you go get extra cheese from the kitchenette?"

"Yes, ma'am." I head toward the kitchenette upstairs.

Xander follows me and turns to me at the top of the stairs.

"What's up? It's not like the meatheads to split up, want to ride with me, or give Colten what he wants."

"I don't know. I thought it was strange, too. I plan to interrogate Daniel about it later." I glance downstairs but don't see anyone close by.

"Okay. Be careful with Andrew."

"What do you mean?"

"I mean your friendliness can be a lot. Some might mistake it as flirting. I don't want you leading him on and hurting him. Unlike the jocks, he doesn't go through girls faster than Kleenex. I don't think he dates much, if at all."

"I'm not flirting with him. We're just friends. You're the one who told me I needed to make friends outside of sports."

"Friend*sss*." Xander puts a huge emphasis on the "s." "Maybe take that energy you've been devoting to befriending Andrew and spread it around a little. You'll have more friends, and Andrew won't get the wrong idea."

"I'm still adjusting to Andrew, Kaylee, and Carter. I don't know if I feel up to trying to befriend anyone else."

"I know new people are a lot but it's just something to think about. At least try dialing back the friendliness with Andrew."

I nod, not sure what else to say and Xander goes back downstairs.

Lately it feels like every move I make is the wrong one. If I hang out with the Knights, there must be something more between us. If I stick to the people I know, I'm stuck up. If I hang out with anyone else, I'm leading them on. I just want to be myself without having to think about all of my actions.

I'm nice and I try to be friendly, but it seems like my friendliness is being taken the wrong way. But I don't want to come off as mean or standoffish. I just don't know what the right level of friendliness is and wish it wasn't even an issue. Why can't I just be me without everyone feeling the need to judge all of my actions?

I grab the cheese from the fridge trying to push my racing thoughts out of my head.

Back downstairs, I help carry everything into the dining room. Mom's waiting for the apple pie to be done and then will bring it with her. In the dining room, there are two empty chairs. One at the head of the table for Mom and one that's between Grayson and Andrew.

I sit between them and try not to read too much into it. I hadn't given much thought to the weirdness on Wednesday. It had seemed like Grayson was back to being more friendly and less flirty, so I just assumed Daniel was wrong or Grayson had changed his mind.

Which is a relief since I'm not in a place to get into another relationship. It'd upset Mark, especially since he was always so jealous of the Knights. I may not be dating him anymore or like him that way, but I do care about him and don't want to hurt him more than I already have. I don't want to give Mark any reason to think there's any truth to the hateful things he said when we broke up.

Now I have the additional worry from what Xander said. I don't think I've been flirting with Andrew. I'm trying to be friendly. The better friends we are, the smoother Saturday will go, and it'll make our project easier if we get along.

I don't want him or anyone else to think I'm stuck-up. I tend to stick with my friends, but that's because I'm comfortable with them, not because I think I'm better than everyone else. I wish who I spent time with wasn't the big deal it feels like it's been lately.

I may not be looking for a relationship, but I've noticed Andrew is cute. His brown hair is constantly falling into his face. He fidgets a lot. I'm pretty sure he's always in motion. It's adorable how his face lights up when he talks about band.

I kind of liked that his glasses were broken because then you can see his eyes better. Up close, they remind me of milk chocolate. But he looks more comfortable in his glasses. His glasses add to his cute nerd look. Besides, you can still see his eyes through them.

On the other hand, Grayson is good-looking. His blue eyes are bright and remind me of the ocean. He's tall and muscular. He's my friend, which complicates things. But that means he knows me. I know we already have a lot in common and plenty of things to talk about. I know he doesn't have any issues with how close I am with the other Knights. Odds are, if he was intentionally flirting with me on Wednesday, he'd want a short-term fling.

He's never had a serious relationship before. Daniel is right—Grayson being Oliver's brother doesn't mean he's going to suddenly want to have a serious committed relationship with me.

I realize I've been staring at the tablecloth, zoned out for who knows how long. I look up and catch Oliver staring at Kaylee who seems oblivious. *Interesting.* Before I can ponder that too much, Sara speaks up.

"So, are we supposed to know any specific etiquette for this? I've never eaten in a formal dining room."

"I'm sure you have better table manners than the neanderthals. Don't worry about it." Xander smiles. I snort.

Jet and Tristan give out an indignant, "Hey!"

"We only have a dining room so we can have a bigger table. Besides, as a mostly male household, I'm pretty sure my mother gave up on anything more than basic table manners a long time ago." I ignore Jet and Tristan since Xander isn't wrong.

"Says the one who can out-burp all of us." Daniel rolls his eyes from the other side of the table.

"It's not my fault I can beat you in everything. And I always say, 'excuse me,' and that's what matters to Mom. At least I don't talk with food in my mouth." I shoot a look down the table at Colten.

"Oh, shut up. That was ages ago." Colten rolls his eyes.

"Didn't you get in trouble for talking with your mouth full last week when I was over with my dad?" Callie asks.

"But he thought he didn't have to count that because Lynn wasn't here." Xander chuckles.

"I hate you guys." Colten crosses his arms and pouts.

"Anyway, what they're all trying to say is they don't even know fancy etiquette. Mama Kingston will definitely not expect you to know any. Now could you all stop acting like children?" Oliver looks around the table at each of the Knights and my brothers.

"Daniel started it." I reach across the table to point at him.

"Picking on each other is how we show our love." Daniel flicks my finger away from him.

"Then maybe save this love fest for when we don't have guests." Oliver rolls his eyes.

"You say that like we're at your house," Sara says.

"That's because the Knights basically live here. They occasionally go to their houses to get clothes and sleep," Xander says.

His statement gets some looks I can't decipher from Andrew and his friends, but Mom walks in before anyone can say anything.

CHAPTER 32
KAYLEE

Lynn's mom enters the dining room and validates my comparison to a Stepford wife. She's wearing a gray quarter-sleeve, crew-cut top, black slacks, and a patterned apron. She has a string of pearls around her neck, for crying out loud. The apple pie she's holding pushes the look over the top. I want to ask if she's for real but considering how none of the guys or Callie are acting weird, I assume this is how she dresses.

Her house is giant and immaculate. I wonder how many maids they have to keep it so clean. It's all too much and has me feeling like I've stepped into a horror movie. One where everything looks perfect on the surface for you to find out later everyone is a serial killer, vampire, or something equally awful.

Xander says grace, and it makes me more uneasy. Everyone passes the food around the table, filling up their plates. I don't get much because I'm slightly nauseous and a touch concerned that the food is drugged. I'd quicker believe this is how we get initiated into a cult than that this is Lynn's family and completely normal. Sara kicks me under the table, and I realize my thoughts might be broadcast on my face. I try to wipe my face clean of emotions and focus on eating.

I'll give the Stepford wife one thing, she can cook. Everything on the table is delicious. I'm curious to know whether she does the cooking or if she has a cook none of us have seen.

"What are your plans for tomorrow?" Lynn's mom asks after everyone starts eating.

"We're going to Bellissimo Feudo for dinner beforehand." Lynn pauses, taking a deep breath. "Josh Wicks is having a party at his house after the dance I was hoping we could go to?"

"A party? Will there be any parents there?" A mom with a scary-mom look is new territory and all the freakier with her perfect demeanor.

"I don't know. If I had to guess, I'd say probably not."

It's weird watching Lynn ask permission to go to a party. My parents wouldn't know if Sara and I moved out.

"Xander, are you wanting to go?" Mrs. Kingston asks.

Lynn looks at Xander and they seem to have some kind of silent communication.

"If we're allowed to go." Xander keeps eye contact with Lynn.

I wonder if their mom is making them take their younger brother with them.

"Will there be alcohol there?"

"I don't know. I don't think so. Josh doesn't drink. Josh is a good guy. You love him, remember?" Lynn says.

"Be home at midnight. Take care of Colten and Callie. Don't make me regret letting you go. If there's alcohol there, I expect you to come home immediately." Lynn's mom eyes each of the guys in turn as well as Lynn and Callie.

Lynn gets up and hugs her mom. I had assumed they drank like most of the other popular kids who go to parties. I guess Lynn is too good to drink.

"Thank you," Lynn says. "I promise we'll behave, and I'll keep an eye on all of the boys."

"See that you do. Has everyone else already asked their parents?"

The boys all nod.

"I don't think we're invited." Sara looks uncomfortable. "I didn't even know there was a party."

I didn't know about the party, either. I'm impressed that Sara spoke up, though. It doesn't sound like our scene. I figured we'd head home after the dance.

Lynn's mom raises her eyebrows at her daughter. "Is that true, Lynn?"

"There's not a guest list or anything. Josh said I could bring whoever." Lynn shrugs.

"Of course, he did," Tristan says, before adding, "Ow!" I'm pretty sure Lynn kicked him under the table.

Lynn's mom looks confused and opens her mouth. Before she can say anything, Colten says, "Mom, can I talk to you in the kitchen for a minute? Please?"

"Sure, honey."

As soon as they leave the room, Lynn glares at Tristan. "Are you trying to get me in trouble?"

"No. I was just teasing you."

"You should know better than to say that kind of stuff in front of my mom." Lynn huffs.

"Hate to butt in and all, but what are you talking about?" Sara asks.

Daniel is the one to answer. "Lynn and Josh dated last spring. He's still somewhat hung up on her and therefore would do anything for her. Mama Kingston hates that Lynn doesn't seriously date. Lynn hates us talking about her love life in general, but especially in front of her mom."

Lynn doesn't seriously date? I mean, I know most of her relationships were pretty short-lived, but if she doesn't seriously date at all, then that does not bode well for Drew.

Lynn's cheeks turn bright pink. "He's not still hung up on me. We weren't even together for an entire month. And those are big words coming from someone who got slapped and dumped by two cheerleaders this week."

"I don't think it counts as being dumped if they weren't actually together." Tristan shoves more food into his mouth.

"All the more reason you should leave my *dating* life alone. I might not have found anyone to be long term with, but I can at least manage to be in a relationship." Lynn sticks her tongue out at Daniel.

"Tristan and I are the only ones who have dates for Homecoming, maybe you should listen to us." Jet smirks.

"I'd only ask you for advice on how to have a noncommittal make-out session," Lynn shoots back.

Jet leans across the table. "I could certainly teach you a thing or two."

"I highly doubt *you* could teach *me* anything I'd *want* to learn." Lynn leans toward Jet.

"Guys, I don't know if you remember or not, but there are other people at this table. Maybe save this spat for when we don't have an audience," Oliver says.

Lynn and Jet both settle back into their seats. I'm not sure if there's unresolved tension between Lynn and Jet, or if that's just how they are with each other. They sure leaned pretty close to one another while talking about kissing.

"Sorry about that." Lynn turns to our half of the table.

"If Tristan and Jet have dates, why aren't they here?" Sara asks. I'm wishing my sister was more introverted.

"Because Jet and Tristan's dates are only dates to the dance. They can either go along with what's planned or go to the dance by themselves. Jet and Tristan are jerks like that. Like, they didn't get a mum for either of their dates." Xander's face says he judges them immensely for that behavior.

"Shut it, Shrimp. At least we can get a date." Jet leans forward to look at Xander.

"I told you to stop calling him Shrimp." Lynn says. "Plus, he has a point." Jet jumps back a little at Lynn's statement and I think she kicked him.

"Not everyone wants to make out with every cheerleader. You're allergic to commitment and act like that's a good thing." Xander rolls his eyes.

"Whatever." Jet gets up and leaves the room. Daniel follows him.

"And I was worried going to dinner and a dance with popular jocks would be boring," Carter says.

There is a pause at the table as everyone freezes and looks at Carter. Before he can backpedal, Xander bursts into laughter. It breaks the tension and causes everyone else to laugh. Colten and his mom come back, and it seems she has been thoroughly distracted from Tristan's earlier comment.

"So, I thought since you're all going in a group it might be nice for the girls to all come over early and get ready together," Lynn's mom says. "Then the guys could come here, and I can take pictures of everyone together all dolled up."

Oh joy. More time in this mansion with Lynn and her perfect family. Hopefully, Drew counts this as my penitence for being mean earlier.

I mean, could Lynn's life get any more perfect? She's smart, beautiful, and athletic. She seems to be the perfect princess who lives in a perfect castle. Everyone adores her. Even the guys she has dumped will still do anything for her.

Other than commitment issues, I don't know what else is wrong with her. She's too perfect. It's nauseating.

"Mom," Lynn says, "Andrew and I have to work on our project Saturday. It's only going to take me ten minutes to get ready. It seems a bit much for them to come over for that."

Prioritizing schoolwork over getting ready for a dance as well as how quickly she can get ready because she's so naturally wonderful. *Ugh.* Either Lynn is as perfect as everyone else seems to think she is or she's a better actress than her twin.

I take a deep breath and remind myself how much Drew likes Lynn. It'd be good for him if she's everything he thinks she is. I need to focus on getting her to notice how wonderful Drew is.

Her mom frowns. "Lynn, you're being rude. And it wouldn't hurt you to have some girl time."

"Fine, but I have to have the paper written for this week's movie before I'll consent to whatever makeover idea you have in mind."

"That's reasonable," Lynn's mom agrees.

We finally all agree on coming to Lynn's house at five to get ready. While we're sorting out the details, Jet and Daniel come back into the room. Lynn seems tense and uncomfortable.

Maybe she dislikes us being in her house as much as we dislike being here. Maybe Drew is right and Lynn is only inviting us with them because her mother is practically making her. Maybe the perfect-daughter stuff is an act because her mom is here?

I notice Grayson's arm brush Lynn's as he reaches for the salt. She jerks her arm back. Lynn seems pretty focused on her food and has been quiet. I haven't been around her much before, but I've seen her around school. She's usually talking and laughing with her friends, so it's weird that she isn't talking, especially since this is her house and for the most part these are her family and friends.

"You're going as a group of friends? No one has a date for the dance?" Lynn's mom brings up the topic of Homecoming again.

"Nope," Lynn says, popping the 'p.' "I'm newly single and none of the guys are currently in a relationship."

"What about you, Callie?" Mrs. Kingston asks.

Colten snorts.

"Colten Jace Kingston! I know I've taught you better than that."

"Sorry Mom. But it's not like anyone would dare to date Callie."

"What? Why?" Callie says.

"You're Coach's daughter; that makes you off limits."

Callie glares at Colten.

If looks could kill, he'd be toast.

"I'm sure if Callie wanted to date, she could. Ignore Colten. It's not like he has a date to the dance, either." Oliver pacifies Mrs. Kingston and Callie.

"We're all going as friends, Mom. Please stop trying to play Cupid." Xander seems annoyed at his mother's antics.

Mrs. Kingston huffs. "Is it so wrong that I want to see you happy?"

"No, but not everyone finds their soulmate in high school. Can't you wait to worry about us dying alone until we're at least thirty?" Xander says.

"Why don't you focus your matchmaking on Uncle Tommy or Uncle Zach?" Lynn asks.

"Fine," Mrs. Kingston says.

Talk turns back to the game tonight and the various ways everyone is participating. From the football players that will be on the field, those of us in band that will be in the stands, and those who will be part of the halftime show for Homecoming.

Not only are Lynn and Grayson Junior Homecoming Prince and Princess, but Colten is also Freshman Homecoming Prince. Xander seems to be the odd man out since he's not school royalty. If I had to guess, I'd assume their parents were probably Homecoming King and Queen back when they were in high school.

Lunch is finally over, and it's time to head back to school. I'm glad we have the underclassmen with us since they have to be back for fifth period. I'm more than ready to be out of this house.

If we get Drew and Lynn together, I hope it doesn't mean I'll be stuck over here all the time. I'm not sure if we've made any progress on the plan to get Lynn to notice Drew. Lynn seems to flirt with him at school but has been reserved throughout lunch.

It could be because her mother is present or because her friends are around. Although, I'm pretty sure she flirted with Drew this morning and Oliver was there then.

CHAPTER 33
GRAYSON

Mrs. Kingston has her three kids stay behind so she can have a word alone with them before we go back to school. The twins hand their keys off to Daniel and Oliver so the rest of us can load up while we wait on them. I tell Oliver I'm going to the bathroom and will be out in a minute. He raises an eyebrow at me but nods anyway.

I sit in the mudroom, waiting for Lynn. I untie my shoes since I didn't bother when I took them off earlier. I fiddle with the laces while I wait for them. I send a text to Daniel and Oliver, letting them know what I'm planning.

Lynn is wearing high-top Converse today, which will take longer to tie up. The Kingston siblings enter the mudroom. Xander quickly slips on his Toms and heads out the door. Colten is right behind him.

"Hey, Lynn, I was wondering if after we drop off the others, if you'd want to go get ice cream or something. I have something I wanted to talk to you about."

"Oh, um, I guess. I'm full, though. We could go for a drive?" Lynn sits down to tie her shoes.

"Sounds good." I smile at her, but she's focused on her shoes.

I figure it's best not to push her. I quickly tie up my other shoe and head outside. There's only one SUV still in the driveway. I guess

Xander already headed back to the school. Jet is in the front seat, so I open the back door.

"Dude, what are you doing?" Daniel asks as soon as I'm in the vehicle.

"Getting in the car. What does it look like?"

"That's not what he meant and you know it." Oliver rolls his eyes.

"What are you doing with Lynn? Asking her to go hang out one-on-one sounds a lot like a date. Which it can't be since we all agreed we could never be the ones to ask her out." Jet turns around to face us from the front.

"You even made me agree to the Creed when I officially became a Knight in sixth grade." Tristan crosses his arms.

"I wanted to talk with her to try to gauge how she's feeling. I didn't ask her out. Besides, I don't see why that rule matters anymore. The three of you have already gone out with Lynn and Jet has no romantic interest in her." I don't get why they're making a big deal about this.

"It's still our Creed. We each had to wait for Lynn to ask us out. It's only fair that's the same across the board." Oliver looks apologetic.

"If y'all are fine with us dating, then why does it matter?" Sitting in the middle row is making me feel surrounded.

"For one thing, Mark will flip out and most likely take it out on Lynn. That will upset her and cause problems on the team." Tristan leans forward so he can look directly at me.

"For another, Lynn has said she's not ready for another relationship and is worried about hurting Mark again." Daniel turns his back to the car door to better face me.

"So, I need to wait until Mark moves on before I can be with Lynn? How is that fair?" I grumble.

"It's not fair, but it's for the best," Oliver says. "Besides, if you ask her out now, one of two things will happen. She'll say no because she thinks it's too soon. Or she'll say yes and Mark will blow up. She'll then break up with you because she doesn't want to hurt Mark."

"Do you want to be like Jason McCall? Where you and Lynn kiss a few times before she feels guilty about it and ends things?" Daniel asks.

Jason McCall is the first baseman for our baseball team. He and

Lynn had a fling last year after Lynn broke up with our pitcher, Josh Wicks.

"That was different. Jason didn't want a relationship, either," I point out.

"That's what he said to save face after he asked and Lynn said no because of Josh and ended whatever they did have," Oliver says.

"How would you know?" I ask.

"Lynn told me," Daniel says.

"And Jason came to me for advice afterwards." Oliver shrugs.

"You never mentioned this before," I reply.

"Because what Lynn talks to me about isn't any of your business. I'm only telling you now to convince you this is a bad idea," Daniel says.

"What about you?" I look at Oliver.

"Honestly, I assumed since I don't want to hear from each of Lynn's exes, none of y'all would want to hear it, either."

"What?" Tristan and I say at the same time.

"You mean all of her exes come and talk to you?" Jet asks.

Oliver nods. "Yeah, asking for advice, how to win her back, telling me how perfect they are together, and so on. It's annoying. I'd think since most of them have a reputation for being a player, they wouldn't be so clingy. Apparently, they're as clingy as the girls they usually lead on."

"Wow. Why do they come to you and not Daniel? He's Lynn's best friend," Jet asks.

"I've asked that before. Since I've had the longest relationship with Lynn, that makes them think I know some secret. I have a reputation for being more approachable. That's at least what I've heard when I've to deal with y'all's exes." Oliver rolls his eyes.

"Wait, does that mean Mark has come to talk to you about Lynn?" I read between the lines of what Oliver's saying.

"Yeah. Wednesday morning. Which is how I know it'll be bad if you start dating Lynn less than a week after they broke up. You need to wait until after Homecoming at least. Hopefully, Mark will move on with someone at the dance. It'll be better if he gets over Lynn before she dates someone new, especially anyone on the team," Oliver says.

"It wouldn't go over well if we've spent all week telling him we're going in a group as friends, then you show up as Lynn's date on Saturday."

"Fine. I'll wait and see how Saturday goes." I try not to pout.

"Are we not going to address Oliver having to deal with our exes?" Daniel types something out on his phone.

Jet shrugs. "I'd rather them bother him about why we should get back together than to bother me. Neither approach is going to get them anywhere, anyway. This way, they aren't bugging me."

"Which would be why I haven't brought it up before. You'd think by now the female population of Carson Valley would know none of you are relationship material. But they never learn and all seem to think they're going to be the one that gets you to change. When you move on, they come to me thinking because I know how to commit that I have the ability to make y'all do the same. If I had a dollar for every time a girl asks me to convince one of you that she's girlfriend material and you should seriously date her or every time a guy asks me how best to get back out of the friendzone with Lynn, I'd be able to pay for college."

"I'm glad not to be you and have to deal with all that." Tristan shivers in disgust.

"Now that we covered all that and cancelled Grayson's fifth-period plans, I'll let Lynn know the coast is clear." Daniel types more on his phone.

"Wait. What? What did you tell her?" Why do I need to keep my mouth shut if Daniel was going to tell her anyway?

"Don't get your panties in a twist. I told her we sent Xander back to the school with everyone else and that I needed her help for a project. She went to get a new notebook and her planning pens." Daniel shrugs, looking up from his phone.

"What project?" Tristan asks.

"Helping Oliver get the girl." Daniel smirks.

"What? No. You didn't tell her." Oliver looks horrified.

"I didn't tell her who…" Daniel pauses before adding, "She figured it out on her own. I told her to wait to come out so I had time to convince you. I already told her to come outside. Unless you want to tell Lynn we're discussing her love life, you're going to have to go along with this."

"You shouldn't blackmail your friends." Oliver crosses his arms and leans back in his seat.

"I prefer to think of it as helping y'all achieve your goals, and in this case, taking care of three problems at the same time."

Lynn opens the driver door then, ending our conversation.

"Are you going to tell us who we're helping you woo?" Jet asks.

"Kaylee!" Tristan says.

"Tristan," Oliver complains.

"What? I knew, Daniel knew, Lynn figured it out, and I assume Grayson knew. What does it hurt for Jet to know?" Tristan raises his hands in defense.

I had no idea Oliver liked anyone, much less that he liked Kaylee. I feel like I'm being a bad brother, especially if Daniel knew and I didn't. Tristan is one thing because he's Oliver's best friend. Finding out at the same time as Jet sucks. Definitely a bad brother, since Oliver and Kaylee were eating at the same table in front of me and I didn't notice anything when Lynn did. I guess I'm too focused on Lynn.

"Yeah, and I need to know who we're talking about if I'm going to help," Jet says.

"You wouldn't know a relationship if it bit you. Why would I need your help?" Oliver rolls his eyes. I tune them out as they start to bicker.

Lynn starts driving toward the school. I'm glad we're focusing on Oliver's love life now. I'm now feeling like all the positive signs I've noticed were in my head and Lynn still sees me as a friend. She pulled away from me when I brushed her arm during lunch. But I thought that was because her mom was there.

I thought she'd been keeping her distance because of Mark's words on Wednesday, but I hope that will blow over soon. I get what the guys are saying about waiting and being patient with Lynn. At the same time, I've been into her for longer than I think they realize and I don't want to keep waiting.

I was surprised that they weren't okay with me asking her out. I mean, it's not like any of them are interested in dating Lynn, so I don't see why it matters. Maybe they don't think Lynn and me going out is a good idea. I don't know.

Hopefully, the dance goes well and I have a better understanding of how Lynn feels about me. I'm hoping Mark finds someone new to obsess over at the dance. The sooner he moves on, the better for everyone.

CHAPTER 34
OLIVER

Just what I wanted: all of the guys not only aware that I have a crush on Kaylee, but appointing themselves as my wingmen to 'help me get the girl.' Once we're back at the school, Lynn leads us to the library because no one will be there right now. Lynn signs us in for a study room under the pretense of her English project. Lynn is clearly taking her new project seriously because she has brought her favorite set of pens with her and one of her nice notebooks.

"Why do we have to do this? I'm the only one of us to ever have a long-term relationship. Why do y'all feel the need to commandeer my love life?" I ask when we're all sitting with the door shut.

"Because you may be great at maintaining a relationship, but that experience and knowledge only applies if there's an actual relationship. You've been crushing on the Queen of Punk for months and didn't even talk to her before this week. Clearly, you need help," Daniel says.

"Come on, dude. You can't try to say this is no big deal. You learned guitar for this girl. As your best friends, we're obligated to help you capture her attention." Tristan taps his fingers on the table.

"You've liked her for that long?" Grayson looks a little hurt.

"And you learned guitar for her before you even tried talking to her?" Jet looks at me like I've lost my mind.

"That's so sweet!" Lynn squeals.

For as much as she's not a fan of romance or feelings in her own life, she loves reading about them and helping other people get their happily-ever-after.

"Yeah, yeah, very sweet." Jet waves away Lynn's enthusiasm. "What's your plan, dude?"

"Originally, I was going to ask her to Homecoming or maybe a different dance. I learned 'White Tiger' on the guitar and planned on serenading her and then asking her out. However, Lynn beat me to it by inviting her to Homecoming. Plus, she already has a date. Current plan would be to wait and see how tomorrow goes and go from there. If she and Carter are only going as friends, and there doesn't seem to be anything more between them, maybe try to feel out the possibility. Like maybe try to ask her to dance and see what happens."

"They're definitely going as friends. They didn't sit together on the ride over or at the table during lunch. If they were dating, they'd be sitting together." Daniel reaches out and stops Tristan's tapping.

"Personally, I don't bring my sister on dates with me and would never want to. Kaylee is bringing her *younger* sister." Tristan pulls a pen out of his bag and starts twirling it. At least he's being quiet now.

"Yeah, and Tristan's sister is older and actually cool." Jet rocks back in his chair.

"You only say that because you think she's hot," Grayson says.

Jet shrugs in response. Lynn hits him upside the head.

"Maybe they have been together long enough that her sister being there doesn't matter. Or maybe she's close with her sister. I mean, Lynn is going in the same group as two of her brothers. Sara could be like Colten and need a ride."

"They still didn't sit next to each other at lunch. Kaylee sat next to *you* during lunch, Ollie. I don't think there's anything between Carter and Kaylee. And there's definitely a potential between you two. But that's not why we're here." Lynn effectively commands our attention.

"Why are we here?" I ask.

"First, to get everyone caught up, so we're working with all the information. Second, we need to know more about her. That way we can better come up with ideas and so we know if she's good enough for you. Third, make a plan to woo her." Lynn says before asking me, "So, how did you meet Kaylee?"

Seeing no other option—Lynn's like a dog with a bone when she wants something—I tell them about the Fourth of July festival, the conversation I overheard during two-a-days, and what has happened this past week. Lynn's taking notes the whole time. I focus on her because I don't want to see what the guys' faces look like.

Jet leans forward. "So, you saw her perform in the festival nearly three months ago and have only had surface-level conversations with her this week? Are you sure this chick's worth all this time you've spent on her? I mean, she's kinda cute, but she dresses weird. Not to mention, she isn't exactly in our usual group."

I bristle. "Unlike you, I don't care about whether someone's considered popular at school."

"Jet has a point, though," Lynn says. "Not about her not being popular, but how well do you know her? It sounds like all you know about her is that she's a good singer with excellent taste in music. And I'm all for helping you, but I don't want you to change who you are for a girl. You're amazing. If someone can't see that because you play sports, then they aren't worth your time or energy."

"It might've been an offhanded comment. Don't burn her at the stake for preferring musicians to athletes. Kaylee seems to have no problem with talking with Oliver knowing he plays sports." Tristan accidently flicks his pen across the table to Grayson.

"Yeah, like when Jet says something stupid about preferring blondes to brunettes. He's joking around." Grayson tosses the pen back to Tristan. "We know he's being stupid, but someone else who overheard it may not."

"But she only recently started talking to him. After he learned to play guitar," Lynn argues.

"Unless she has been spying on Oliver or has some crazy radar that tells her who knows how to play an instrument, she wouldn't know that. We're his best friends and didn't know until this week," Daniel says. "It's not like there has been any physical or obvious change because he learned guitar."

"Fair point," Lynn concedes. "Do you know anything else about who she is as a person, or are we basically starting from scratch?"

"Considering this is the first week I've talked to her, and you already know about each interaction we've had, you should know the answer to that."

"The first priority is recon," Lynn says. "We need to know more about her. I told Andrew to find me for third quarter tonight so I could explain football to him. I could have him invite Kaylee and Carter and try to find out more about them."

"And you can invite them to fifth quarter after the game, too." Jet spins around in his chair.

"Fifth quarter" is something Mama Kingston started at their church when we hit junior high. It's an alternative to going to an afterparty after home games.

"That will make your mom happy and get her more on board with us going to Josh's party tomorrow," Tristan says.

"Sounds good. And since Mom insisted on all the girls getting ready together tomorrow, I'll be able to get to know her without her best friends around." Lynn reaches out and stops Jet's chair from spinning.

"Won't Andrew be at your house to work on your project?" Daniel asks.

"Oh yeah." Lynn nods. "Maybe he can hang out with Xand for a bit. I'm going to owe him so much by the time Homecoming is over."

"Are we finally done analyzing my love life?" I ask. I'm pretty sure Lynn's lost the attention of the table, anyway.

"For now. Assuming everything goes well, we'll have to figure something out for you to dance with Kaylee at the dance," Lynn says. She writes a few more notes down in her notebook.

I'm not worried about what she wrote down because Lynn uses some weird shorthand when she writes notes for personal things. Once we found her diary and were going to read it. It was a jumble of letters, numbers, and symbols, and complete gibberish. Jet confronted her about having a bunch of nonsense written in her diary. She said that if she wanted us to know what was in there, she'd have written it where we could read it.

We spend the rest of fifth period talking about nothing in particular, which is a relief. Especially since I'm already a bit nervous about seeing Kaylee in English. I'm glad that at least none of the Knights are in that class with us. I don't know how I feel about them being in the same class as Kaylee and me when they know I have a crush on her.

I leave the library a bit early to get to my class before the bell rings, enjoying the halls being empty. I see Kaylee and head in her direction. She's facing away from me and talking to some blond guy who looks vaguely familiar.

"What happens between Oliver and me isn't any of your business. What I do outside of the band isn't any of your business," Kaylee is saying.

The guy she's talking with notices me walking up to them and smirks. With the help of Kaylee's words, I recognize him as the guitarist in her band.

"Interesting that I've never seen you talk to Oliver before, but now you're talking, flirting, and going to Homecoming together," he says, still smirking.

His words surprise me. I want to say something to announce my presence but can't get words to come out of my mouth.

Kaylee crosses her arms. "None. Of. Your. Business. Leave me alone."

"Here comes your white Knight to scare off the big bad wolf." He makes eye contact with me. Kaylee spins around to see what he's talking about.

"Oh, um, hi, Oliver." She steps next to me, looking startled and unsure of what to do.

I wrap my arm around her shoulder, hoping I'm reading the situation somewhat correctly.

I look down at the guy enjoying that I'm a few inches taller than him. "Can I help you?"

"Not at all. You're already providing free entertainment." He tilts his lips in a somewhat condescending manner. Before he walks away, he says, "Kaylee, I'll see you when he gets bored."

I look at Kaylee. Her face is a mask. I have no idea what is going on or how she feels about it. I wish I wasn't so confused and could just enjoy being this close to her.

"What's his problem?" I ask her.

"That's James. He's a jerk." She pulls away from me and tucks her hair behind her ear. "Sorry about all of that."

"Has he been bothering you?" I loop a finger through my belt loop feeling awkward and unsure of what to do with my hands.

"I can handle James. He's being moody because he saw you give me the garter this morning. He jumped to other conclusions on his own. I haven't been telling people we're going to Homecoming together or anything."

"Okay…? Aren't you going with Carter?"

"But we're just friends. Everyone knows that, including James."

An idea occurs to me.

"Would it help you get James to leave you alone if we went to Homecoming together? I mean, if that'd be okay with Carter." I try to look nonchalant instead of nervous.

"You don't have to pretend to be my date to the dance to help me deal with James. Like I said, I can handle him on my own. I don't need your pity," Kaylee snaps.

I raise my hands up in surrender.

"I'm just trying to help. We're eating together and arriving together, anyway. It's not like it'd be a big deal if I sat next to you at dinner and danced with you at the dance." It'd be great to have the chance to be close to Kaylee and get to know her better without all the pressure of asking her out on a date.

"I don't need your help. I'm not one of the football team's groupies who's waiting for one of you to notice me. Hoping you will pay me a modicum of attention before discarding me and acting like I don't exist. Thanks, but no thanks."

"I didn't say you were. And I don't know what you've heard, but I'd never treat a girl that way. I was trying to help."

"Like I said, I don't need your help, I can handle James on my own." Kaylee storms off.

"Whatever," I say even though she can't hear me.

The bell ending fifth period rings as I walk away. Lynn might be right. I don't know Kaylee very well. What I just saw doesn't look like who I thought she was.

Some of what she said about how my teammates treat girls might be true. But I'm not like that and never have been. I've always been completely committed to any relationship I've been in.

How can she lump us all into one category just because we play sports?

CHAPTER 35
DANIEL

"Do we think this Kaylee is good enough for Oliver? Do any of you know more about her?" Lynn asks after Oliver leaves the library.

"If she hadn't been at lunch today, I wouldn't have even known who she was." Jet begins spinning in his chair again.

"I only know what he's told us. Like Jet said earlier, she's not exactly in our usual group. I haven't been around her." Tristan puts his pen back in his bag.

"What about you?" Grayson says to Lynn. "You've been talking to Andrew a lot this week."

It could just be me, but Grayson sounds irritated. It seems weird for him to be upset about Lynn working on a project, though. Maybe he's still upset about us interfering with his intentions with Lynn.

Lynn starts packing her stuff up. "We've mostly just talked about our project and a bit about Homecoming."

"You can get to know her tomorrow," I pipe up. "Although I'm sure Oliver would appreciate it if you didn't go all FBI interrogator on her." I know Lynn can get carried away when she's started on a project.

"What do you mean?" Lynn asks.

"He means you can be intense and go overboard. We don't need her social security number or a background check on her entire family." Tristan goes back to tapping his fingers on the table now that Oliver's gone.

"I don't do that." Lynn protests. "Besides her sister and Callie will be there. I'm going to have 'girl time.' There will be no interrogation." She makes a face when she says *girl time.*

Jet raises his eyebrows.

"Do you even know what 'girl time' entails?"

She shrugs. "Not really. I'm hoping with Callie there we can at least talk sports while we succumb to my mother's makeover ideas."

"Good luck with that." Tristan says, "It sounds like Kaylee hates sports, and I highly doubt her sister is a big fan. There's no way your mom will let you leave them out of a conversation."

"And talking sports won't help you get to know Kaylee, either," I say.

"Ugh." Lynn makes a face. "Why couldn't y'all let me live blissfully in ignorance until tomorrow?"

"Because we're your best friends. It's our job to torture you." Jet smirks.

"Whatever," Lynn says as the bell rings.

The guys get up to go to class. Lynn seems on edge so I hang back after the other Knights leave the library.

"What's up?"

"Nothing…" Lynn slings her bag over her shoulder.

"Worried about Oliver and Grayson?"

"Yeah, for different reasons."

"It seems like you're worried about both of them getting hurt, just by different people." I grab my backpack.

"You're not wrong."

"How are you feeling about everything with Grayson?"

She sighs. "I don't know. I'm not sure if I like him that way and even less sure it'd matter if I do. I don't want to even think about being in another relationship right now. This week has been stressful enough on its own."

"If you aren't sure about how you feel, then take things slow. Give yourself time to figure it out. Hopefully by the time you know what you want, things will have settled down."

"Hopefully." Lynn still looks unsure.

I wrap her in a bear hug. She hugs me back and I can feel the tension leave her body.

"It'll all work out," I tell her as she lets go.

Hearing Lynn's parents talk about love and falling in love makes it sound like something I'd want some day. Most of what they talk about, like being each other's best friend, always there for one another, being the first person you want to tell news to whether it be good or bad, or wanting to be next to them because existing is easier with them there… it all sounds great, but the only person who fits that description is Lynn.

But we don't see each other that way. We have no romantic feelings toward each other. When we dated, things were okay, until the first time we kissed. It was super awkward. At first, I thought it might be because it was each of our first kiss. We dated for about another week and tried kissing a few other times, but it felt off. After we broke up, I dated and kissed Devon Hankins. It didn't feel awkward or off. It wasn't particularly memorable either, but it did make me sure that kissing Lynn was weird because she's Lynn. Now, I know Lynn is just a friend and, honestly, more like a sister. Although, I treat her more like a brother than a sister.

As we're walking to class, I fire off a text to Oliver.

Caballero: Sorry about throwing you under the bus. TBH Lynn would have interfered soon enough on her own and we needed a cover for talking some sense into Grayson.

O. Ridire: Don't worry about it

O. Ridire: It might not matter anyway

Caballero: Why?

O. Ridire: Pretty sure Kaylee hates me

Caballero: What? What could've happened in the last ten minutes?

O. Ridire: I'll tell you later

Oliver leaves straight after Government so I don't have a chance to talk to him until after seventh period. Since it's Homecoming, instead of having a pep rally before lunch, we have a community-wide pep rally during our eighth period.

I catch Oliver in the hallway. On the way to the football field, he fills me and Tristan in on his most recent encounter with the Queen of Punk on our way to the football field.

"I was not expecting that," Tristan says. "Has she been burned by a jock before? Is that why she's so uptight about it?"

"I don't know. I feel like if any of our friends dated her before, we would've known about it," Oliver says.

"Maybe someone from another school?" I ask.

"Maybe," Tristan agrees. "You didn't know who she was before this summer. We've no idea who she might have dated before."

"Can we just keep this between us? I don't feel like everyone needs a front row seat to me trying to figure things out." Oliver's shoulders slump and he looks defeated.

"All right, but what are *you* going to do about it?" Tristan asks.

Oliver shrugs. "I don't know. I feel like confronting Kaylee would only make it worse. I guess wait and see what happens. Maybe try to show her I'm not who she thinks I am?"

"Being devil's advocate here, but what if that's what Kaylee is like and you haven't seen it before?" I ask.

Oliver sighs. "Then I should probably start learning a song for Mama Kingston's Christmas present so I can put all my work learning guitar to good use."

The conversation shifts to the game tonight as we join the rest of the team for the pep rally.

CHAPTER 36
KAYLEE

James has been getting on my last nerve, and I want to prove to everyone that I don't need him and I can end things on my own. Carter, Drew, and Sara don't believe that I can walk away from whatever James and I had in the past. I'm determined to prove them wrong and do it without help.

James is the least of my problems now, anyway. Drew's already not happy with me. He'd be upset if he knew I pissed off Oliver. I need to be nicer to Oliver and maybe try to get on his good side. I just don't know how to do that especially without him thinking I'm some damsel in distress that needs his saving.

I'm broken from my musings when Drew speaks.

"So, Lynn invited us to something called 'fifth quarter' after the game tonight. Do y'all want to go?"

"What's 'fifth quarter'?" Carter asks as we head back to the band hall after the pep rally.

"She said they play games and hang out at her church's rec center. It sounds like fun to me." Drew sounds so hopeful.

Carter nods. "I'm in. What about you, Kaylee?"

"I'm good. I have to be up early for the math-science meet tomorrow and it sounds like we'll be out late after the dance. I should probably be at home tonight."

Really, I need a break from all of this, but I can't say that to Drew. He thinks Lynn hung the moon. I don't want to fight with him and don't want him to know about my conversation with Oliver, either. Oliver puts me on edge which is the only explanation I have for going off on him earlier.

"Oh, well, maybe we shouldn't go then." Drew sounds dejected as he kicks a rock in the parking lot.

I shake my head. "No, y'all go and have fun. It'll give you a chance to get to know Lynn better when she's around her friends. It'll help you to be more comfortable around them on Saturday."

Sara walks up to us and asks, "Where are we going?"

"*We* aren't going anywhere," I say, gesturing to her and to myself with my free hand. "Drew and Carter are hanging out with Lynn and her friends after the game tonight."

"Are y'all going to fifth quarter?" Sara asks excitedly.

"How do you know about it?" I ask, frowning.

"I overheard Callie talking with Colten about it."

I swear I can see in her eyes her planning a future with Colten.

"I thought we already discussed how chasing after Colten is a bad idea."

"We discussed how *you* thought it was a bad idea and *I* decided not to take relationship advice from someone who thought at any point in time it was a good idea to get involved with James when he clearly said he didn't want to be in a relationship. I can handle the Colten situation on my own. Besides, it's not like he knows I exist."

"I'm done with James. And James is part of the reason I'm so protective of you. I don't want you to get hurt." I try to wrap my arm around Sara, but she sidesteps my attempt.

"I can take care of myself," she says. "Why don't you focus on keeping yourself from being hurt?"

"Whatever. You're going to do what you want, anyway."

"That's the pot calling the kettle black." Carter rolls his eyes. "How many times did we tell you James was bad news before you listened?"

"I get it, okay?" I throw my hands up and Carter has to dodge my trombone. "It was stupid to get involved with James. I know his behavior isn't going to change. I'm no longer with him and I'm not going back to him. My point is, I don't want Sara to be hurt the same way."

"It's not like our parents are going to say no, so I'm going. I can take care of myself." Sara storms off.

"That went well." Carter looks in the direction Sara went.

"Shut up."

"What has you in such a foul mood today?" Drew stops walking to look directly at me like he can read the answer on my face.

I shrug. "Nothing. I didn't sleep well. Mary never came home last night. We had a fight about how she treats Sara, then she left. When we left for school, she still hadn't made an appearance."

"That sucks." Carter tries to wrap his arms around me for a hug.

I step away from his attempt using my trombone as a shield. It'd be easier to avoid Carter if his trumpet wasn't so small. "It is what it is. I only have two years left of dealing with it."

"Are you still planning on getting Sara to move out with you after graduation?" Drew continues walking and kicking his rock.

"Yeah, I don't think our parents would notice, much less care, and it'd give her a more stable home environment."

"Have you talked to Sara about it yet?" Carter looks back to where my sister has disappeared.

"No. I figure there's no point until it's closer. I won't turn eighteen until next December. That'll give me six months to find somewhere for us to stay. I have a few thousand saved from what I can pull out of the account our father set up for us."

I've been taking money out of it in cash since he opened it freshman year. I have the cash all hidden in the lining of my guitar case, so Mary can't find it. I have to be careful not to pull too much out at a time.

Once I took five hundred out and my father had a lot of questions. I told him I liked shopping at this one boutique that doesn't take cards. He bought it, but I haven't taken that much out since.

That's why I spend so much money shopping. If he knows where most of the money's going, then he won't ask too many questions about the cash I pull out. He thinks I spend it all on meaningless things. It benefits me for him to think I'm like Mary.

"If you don't want to wait until graduation, I'm sure my mom wouldn't mind you moving in with us. She adores both of you and she's always wanted a daughter," Carter offers.

"Thanks for the offer, but if my dad found out, he'd flip. It'd look bad, and you know he values his reputation over his daughters. Besides, you, your mom, and grandma live in a two-bedroom apartment. You don't have room for us to move in. At least if Sara and I are on our own, our father can pretend no one else knows about it."

I hate having my friends pity me because of my parents. It makes me feel vulnerable and vulnerability makes my skin crawl. "Let's talk about something else."

"Well…Lynn asked me to sit with her during third quarter." Drew stares at the rock he's been kicking like that's who he's talking to.

"What? Why didn't you lead with that? That's great!" I lightly punch his arm.

"Kaylee, take a chill pill." Carter waves my hand away from Drew. "And Drew, details. How did this come about?"

"On the way to her house for lunch, everyone talked about the game. She apologized for them getting carried away talking about sports. I admitted I didn't understand what they were talking about. She asked me to sit with her during the game so she could explain everything to me."

"See, I told you my plan would work. You're finally on her radar!" I pump my fists in the air.

I'm happy for Drew, especially because with this new development, he seems to have forgotten my harsh words from this morning.

"I'm pretty sure she's only being friendly. I'm still excited, though. The friendzone is still a major step up from her not knowing I exist. Even if it's only as a friend, I get to spend time with her." Drew is still looking down, but now he's smiling.

"Is that when she invited you to the 'fifth quarter' thing?" Carter nudges Drew's shoulder.

"No, she asked about that during Government. She said y'all could come sit with us during third quarter to learn football and hang out."

I shake my head no. "We're definitely not sitting with you during third quarter. That'll only push you closer to the friendzone. The game should be a good opportunity to spend some time with her one-on-one other than working on your project. All of her friends are jocks, meaning they'll be on the football field, not in the stands with Lynn."

I'm hopeful that Drew will get comfortable enough being around Lynn without us there that I can avoid her and her friends. I especially want to avoid Oliver after this afternoon. If Lynn and Drew get together, then I don't have to worry about Oliver. Until then, I plan to try to be extra nice when I have to be around Oliver.

I didn't want to go to the Homecoming dance from the beginning. With everything that has happened with James and Oliver, I really don't want to go. But I feel like I need to, just so I can prove I can go out to a dance and have fun without James.

I've moved on from him and I wish everyone else could see it. I want them to see I don't need another boy to keep me from going back to James. It's not like Oliver would be interested in me anyway. I'm nothing like the cookie cutter girls that hang all over the football team. I don't have curves or school spirit. And James has made it painfully obvious there's nothing special enough about me to get a guy to break the mold.

The only possible reason Oliver offered to go to the dance with me earlier is because he pities me. He saw how James was treating me and felt bad for me. Oliver thought I was in need of saving and was offering to do that. I don't need saving, especially not from a guy my body unhelpfully reacts to.

We arrive back at the band hall without more discussion of the game or the dance. We put away our instruments before heading to Drew's house. Since we have a couple of hours to kill before the game I want to look over what he's wearing to the Homecoming dance and what he's wearing to Lynn's house that afternoon to work on their project.

The boys and Sara play video games while I go through Drew's closet. I already know what I want him to wear, but I take time going through everything. It gives me something to do with my hands and gives me some space from everyone else.

I don't want to hear about how perfect Lynn is, or how I need to stay away from James, and I'll lose it if they bring up Oliver.

After spending as long as I can justify going through Drew's closet, I hang the two outfits on his closet door and join them in playing *Call of Duty Zombies.* At least shooting zombies helps release some of my pent-up anxiety.

CHAPTER 37
ANDREW

The first half of the game goes well. We're winning, and we get somewhat of a break for halftime since they're doing the Homecoming crowning. We stand on the field playing the school song over and over again while they announce Homecoming Court and Band Beau and Sweetheart.

Carter and Kaylee are convinced Lynn is starting to see me as dating potential. As much as I want to believe them, looking at Lynn all dressed up and on the arm of a football player reminds me that Lynn is way out of my league.

She's wearing a floor-length silver dress that hugs her curves. Her hair's straight and the top part is pulled back, showing off the tiara she's wearing. I think she's got something on her arms, too, because they seem to sparkle under the lights.

Listening to Lynn's introduction cements it in my mind. She has so much going for her. She's beautiful, smart, athletic, and can date any guy she wants. The majority of the Homecoming Court are her exes and they're nothing like me.

The announcer introduces the nominees for Homecoming Queen and King, and I watch as Grayson whispers in Lynn's ear and makes her laugh. They're Junior Homecoming Prince and Princess and have been friends forever. They're perfect for each other. They look like they belong together. Her all dolled up and beautiful and him in his slightly dirty football uniform.

I try to let go of the disappointment as my hope of a relationship with Lynn is squashed. Instead, I try to focus on the fact that we're becoming friends and I enjoy her company.

When we leave the field after halftime, Kaylee takes my horn and jacket so I don't have to go up to the band bleachers to put them up. Lynn texts me, telling me to meet her at the top of the bleachers on the fifty-yard line.

"Andrew, it's good to see you." Lynn's mom waves when she sees me.

I look around but don't see Lynn.

"Lynn will be back up here in a minute. You can sit with me until she gets back," Xander says from a few rows below where the rest of his family is sitting.

"Uh, cool." I shuffle past the others on the bleachers to sit next to him.

"Lynn went to change, then she'll be up here."

We sit in silence until Lynn comes up the bleachers in denim shorts and a football jersey. She may not look as much like a goddess as she did on the field, but even dressed as a normal teen, she's obviously still out of my league.

Her tan legs go on forever and she looks hot even if her jersey obscures most of her curves. I don't realize I've been staring at her until Xander clears his throat next to me.

When I look over at him, it's apparent he caught me checking out his sister. I feel my cheeks heat with embarrassment. I try to think of something to say, but Xander speaks before I can come up with anything.

"Be careful with Lynn."

"I um, I don't know what you mean. I mean, I…I'd never do anything to hurt her. Not that I could because—"

"I'm not warning you off because I'm worried about *you* hurting *her*." Xander interrupts me, which is good because I don't think anything good could come out of my nervous rambling.

He continues, "She'd kill me for saying anything like that, and I know she can take care of herself. My warning is more like so you don't get yourself hurt. Lynn's very friendly. I don't want you to mistake her behavior for something it's not."

"Of course not. I mean I wouldn't..." I stammer. "...she wouldn't... I didn't think... I know she wouldn't have more than friendly interest in someone like me."

Xander nods as Lynn finally makes it to our row and sits down beside me. That's when I noticed Jet's with her and that they have brought all kinds of food.

"Hey, I figured if you only get third quarter off, then that's probably when you have time to eat, so I got you food," Lynn says. "I didn't think to ask what you'd want so I got one of everything."

"Oh, wow, umm thanks." That's so thoughtful of her.

"You should thank me, not Lynn." Jet grumbles from Lynn's other side. "I'm the one who had to go to the concession stand and get everything,"

Lynn turns to him. "Shut up, Jet. You don't have to always be a jerk."

Jet leans in until there's hardly a breath of space between them. He grumbles something I can't hear and they seem to be in some sort of silent standoff. Eventually, Lynn whispers something back that makes Jet's face soften slightly. He turns back to the game, cramming a pretzel into his mouth.

Third quarter seems to fly by as Lynn gives me a play-by-play of what's happening on the field. With Xander's reminder of Lynn only seeing me as a potential friend, and Jet being there a reminder that having male friends is nothing unusual for Lynn, I'm able to relax and enjoy spending time with her and learning about something that's obviously important to her.

When there's thirty seconds left on the clock, I head back to my spot in the band bleachers. Most of what Lynn said went over my head, but I did at least learn what a first down is and why they're important.

Later, after the game, Sara rides with Carter and me to fifth quarter. We get to the address Lynn gave me earlier and there're only a few cars here. I park and then realize how far out of my element I am.

I'm about to walk into a place I've never been and spend time with a bunch of people I don't know. There're people in band with me I haven't talked to, and they're way less intimidating than Lynn's friends.

"Drew, breathe." Carter shakes me from my freak-out, and I take a much-needed breath of air.

"What's wrong?" Sara asks from the backseat.

"I'm, um, starting to wonder if this is a good idea."

"Lynn invited you. That means you belong. It'll be more low-key and relaxed than Homecoming. This'll have most of the same people. Think of it like a test run with less people." Carter pats my arm before getting out of the car.

"Right." I take another deep breath and get out of the car.

We walk into a giant room with a kitchen running the length of one side and the wall across from the door is lined with windows. Through the windows, I can see a gym and Lynn's playing basketball in there. Without thinking about it, I start walking toward the gym.

She's completely in her element. I don't understand much about basketball, but I've always enjoyed watching Lynn play. My favorite part of being in pep band is getting to watch her in action while we play stand tunes.

Lynn and Callie are playing two-on-two against Jet and Colten. They seem pretty evenly matched, from what I can tell. Sara lets out a low whistle, reminding me there are other people here and I shouldn't be openly staring at Lynn.

"Other people are starting to arrive—wrap it up, kids. And boys, please go find your shirts," Lynn's mom calls from the door.

Sara lets out a disappointed sigh next to me. Carter starts to tease her about ogling Colten and Jet shirtless. Sara shoves him.

Taking my eyes off of Lynn, I look at Jet and Colten and can't help but compare myself to them. I may have some muscle tone from marching band, but overall, I'm scrawny and short.

Jet is way taller than me and basically the same height as Lynn. He has defined muscles that are apparent even from this far away. I'm pretty sure he has a six pack, though it's hard to be completely sure at this distance. Reinforcing why Lynn wouldn't ever think about dating me.

Why would she when she has guys who look like Jet willing to date her?

Friends. Focus on being friends.

Lynn pivots around Jet and makes another basket. Jet seems to be guarding her way too close for a pickup game of basketball, but that could be jealousy talking.

Of course it doesn't matter. I don't see there ever being a time when I'd be comfortable not wearing a shirt around Lynn, much less being that close to her even if it was for a game. She and Jet trash-talk as Callie goes to put the ball up.

"Hey, guys." Callie nods at us.

Lynn looks our way then and smiles. My heart skips a beat. She walks over to us, and my hands start feeling clammy with sweat.

"Andrew and Carter! I'm glad y'all were able to make it!" I freeze up and struggle to respond.

"We're glad you invited us." Carter elbows me. "So, what do you usually do at fifth quarter?"

"Whatever you want to do. There are board games and card games set up on the tables. Video games are set up over there. After more people get here, we sometimes play Knockout or Jungle Pong."

"Cool," Carter says.

Before I can get my mouth to work, someone calls out to Lynn from the other room. As she heads that way, I see that Josh Wicks is the guy who called out to her. Another reminder that Lynn is out of my league, no matter how nice she is to me.

"So have you found your voice yet, or do I need to wait until Lynn is farther away for you to say anything?" Carter asks.

Thankfully, everyone else has already walked away, so no one else hears him.

"Shut up."

"He speaks!" Carter grins. "Are we going to go hang out with Lynn or stand here awkwardly in the corner all night?"

"Let's go see what Lynn is doing." I shove his shoulder as I head in the direction Lynn went.

CHAPTER 38
GRAYSON

When the guys and I get to fifth quarter, everything's in full swing. Since we shower after the game, we're always the last ones here. Lynn's in the middle of a card game with Andrew and his friends and some of the guys from the baseball team.

There's an empty chair next to her so I start to head that way. Daniel stops me to talk about the plans for tomorrow and about the game we played. By the time I get him to walk with me to the table, Josh Wicks is sitting in the seat next to Lynn.

Daniel and I sit in the only two open seats that are on the other side of the table. For the next hour, I get a front-row seat to Lynn and Josh flirting.

I know if I said anything, Lynn would say she's only being friendly. She'd deny that Josh is still into her because he briefly dated a girl from the softball team this summer. In my opinion, he only did that to get over Lynn, and they broke up when the other girl realized he was still hung up on Lynn.

Now that he has 'moved on' in Lynn's eyes though, they're back to being overly friendly. She avoided him in the weeks after they broke up but has gone back to acting like she was before they dated since he had a different girlfriend after her.

Regardless of what Lynn might say, it definitely looks like Josh wants to get back together. This is the last thing I need. I already have the Mark issue to deal with, but having someone else fighting for Lynn's attention is a complication I don't want to deal with.

Lynn has never gone back out with someone after they broke up, so maybe that means Josh isn't a threat regardless of his intentions. But there's a first time for everything. I don't know, and I don't know how to get Lynn to notice me as more than a friend.

Oliver was dared to kiss Lynn during a Truth-or-Dare game, which is what led to them dating. Daniel has always been Lynn's best friend, so it makes sense he was her first crush. I'm not sure how Tristan got out of the friendzone. Maybe I should ask him.

Flirting with Lynn doesn't seem to be getting me anywhere. She flirts back, but we've always had a friendly, flirty relationship. I've definitely had enough girls complain about my relationship with Lynn to know we're closer and more physically affectionate than most friends.

I wonder if those girls would keep doing that if they realized that it always ends their relationship with me. Even before I had a thing for Lynn, I didn't want to be with anyone who's going to say anything negative about her or want me to stop hanging out with her.

I've leaned more into the flirty side of my relationship with Lynn, but I don't think she's even noticed. I feel like I need to do something bigger to get on her radar, but I don't know what. The whole "not being allowed to initiate anything" rule is a major pain.

When the group moves to go play video games, I'm hoping this is my chance to sit next to Lynn and get her to focus on me instead of Josh.

Oliver and Daniel have other plans, though. As soon as I get up, they steer me into one of the classrooms off to the side of the fellowship hall.

"What are you doing?" I'm seriously annoyed with them getting in my way with Lynn.

Daniel crosses his arms. "Better question is, what are *you* doing? You need to be patient and wait until after the dance to even try to get Lynn looking your way. You don't need to be mooning over her or glaring with hate at any guy who's next to her."

"I'm not mooning or hate-glaring." I roll my eyes.

"If you were glaring any harder, I'm pretty sure Josh would have caught fire." Daniel stares me down.

"You couldn't be more obvious if you were trying." Oliver's tone is less confrontational than Daniel's. "What's up with getting all jealous of Josh? You know they're just friends, and Lynn never goes back to someone she has broken up with already."

"I'm not jealous. I don't like him being all over Lynn."

"Josh isn't all over Lynn. He's flirting a little with her. We all know Lynn can take care of herself. If she had an issue with the flirting, she could and would take care of it." Daniel sounds as fed up with this conversation as I feel. "It seems more like you're upset she doesn't seem to have a problem with it."

I run my hand through my hair in frustration. They just don't get it. "Is it so wrong that I don't want to watch Lynn being cozied up with some other guy when I'm into her?"

Oliver steps between me and Daniel. "Lynn is just being friendly. You need to chill. There's no reason for you to get jealous. Besides, if Lynn notices that you're jealous, that's only going to make her less likely to want to start something with you. In case you forgot, this afternoon we already discussed why you need to be patient and take things slow. I'm pretty sure I remember you agreeing to wait until after the dance to even start trying to get her attention."

"I know, but I already watched her be with Frost and Slater. I don't want to wait too long and miss my chance again. I don't want to watch her with another guy."

"You've liked her for that long?" Oliver asks with surprise.

"Yeah, I mean we've always been friends. I've always known how awesome she is as a person, but now it's more than that. I want to be with her and not just to make out for a couple of weeks before moving on to someone else. I want to try to make it work long term."

Daniel leans back against the door frame. "If you're invested in it for the long haul, then waiting a couple of days should not be that big of a deal. Rushing things is only going to make it blow up in your face."

"That's why I waited after she dumped Frost, but then she moved on with Slater before I could even try to throw my hat in the ring," I argue.

"Yeah, and that relationship lasted for two weeks," Oliver says. "Two. Weeks. If you don't want a two-week fling, then you need to be patient. Pushing Lynn is not going to have a positive outcome." Then he adds quietly, "Worthwhile things are worth waiting for."

Oliver looks a bit wistful. That gives me an idea. I decide to change topics to get them off my back.

"How are things going with Kaylee?" I ask my brother.

Oliver shrugs. "The same, I guess. We talked about it at lunch. Other than Lynn inviting her to fifth quarter and her not coming, there isn't anything to tell."

Oliver looks a little uncomfortable. He has never been comfortable with being the center of attention. He's the least comfortable being around girls. For the most part, his past girlfriends were the ones pursuing him. Crushing on Kaylee and actively trying to get her attention is new territory for him.

"Did Lynn say why she didn't come?" I ask.

"No, I haven't talked with Lynn about it. I only know Lynn invited Kaylee and she obviously isn't here. It's probably for the best. I don't want Lynn giving her the third degree in front of so many people." Oliver starts pacing.

"Do you think she'd do that?" I ask.

"Stupid question. That's exactly what she'd do." Daniel rests his hand on Oliver's arm, stopping his pacing.

"Yeah, at least tomorrow there'll be less people there. When Lynn goes all overprotective mama bear during her FBI interrogation, only Callie and Sara will witness it and have any idea that I like Kaylee." Oliver sounds unhappy.

"Lynn said she wouldn't interrogate Kaylee and wouldn't go overboard during girl time," I say, defending Lynn.

"I'm sure she said that. I'm less confident that she'll be able to follow through with that statement." Oliver rocks back and forth from his heels to his toes. "Best case scenario Lynn and Kaylee hit it off and Lynn will go into match-maker mode. Either way, girl time is going to end with Kaylee knowing I like her."

"Maybe Mama Kingston will be so excited about Lynn having girl time that she'll commandeer the whole thing and Lynn won't have an opportunity to interrogate Kaylee or play match-maker." Daniel pats Oliver's arm to reassure him.

"I'm probably better off trying not to think about it and dealing with whatever the resulting fallout might be," Oliver says in a dejected tone.

"You act like Lynn is going to intentionally make things worse or cause problems." I'm starting to get mildly irritated with my brother.

Oliver rolls his eyes. "Lynn would never intentionally hurt me. I know that. I'm being real about how tomorrow is likely to go. Lynn's my friend, too. No reason to get all up in arms about things."

"Yeah, you need to majorly chill, man." Daniel recrosses his arms. "I get that you are into Lynn, but don't get mad at us because you can't have what you want right this second."

"Whatever. Let's go back out there and do something other than discuss our feelings." I push through the door without waiting for them to respond.

They may have a point, but I don't want to acknowledge it right now. So, avoidance it is.

Back in the fellowship hall, my eyes immediately find Lynn. She's sitting in between Andrew and Callie.

I decide the best way to avoid another intervention from the worry twins is to go somewhere Lynn isn't. Colten and some of the guys on the JV football team are playing Knockout in the gym, so I join them.

CHAPTER 39
LYNN

I wake up to giggling, which is never a good sign. Not wanting to give away that I'm awake, I try to keep my breathing even. I don't feel anything abnormal against my skin, so that's good.

I crack my eyes open to see Sean and Parker, my six-year-old twin brothers. They are trying to sneak into my room with water guns. I slowly move my arm to the other side of my bed.

When they aim and start counting down, I raise the water gun from the other side of my bed and spray them, catching them completely off guard.

"Retreat!" they yell as they run out of my room and down the hall.

I get up and start getting my stuff ready for a shower, waiting for my mom to come in my room. It takes less than three minutes.

"Your brothers are wet and they say it's your fault. Care to explain why that is?" She raises her eyebrows with her "I'm not amused" face in place.

"I woke up to them sneaking into my room with water guns. A preemptive strike was in order. On the upside, they have to change for their game anyway and no blankets got wet." I keep my face neutral.

"You're the older sibling and over a decade older than them. You should be setting an example, not launching preemptive strikes." Mom looks like she doesn't want to be getting on my case, but like, she still has to go through the motions.

"I set an example of always being prepared and showed them the consequences of not having situational awareness. Don't you and Dad always say we should be prepared for anything?" I ask a little too innocently.

"Uh huh. Maybe next time you could put all the water guns in the shed where they belong and make sure it's locked. That way there are no water guns in the house?"

"Yes, ma'am." There's no way I'm putting my water gun up, but I can make sure the rest are secured.

"Good. Since you're up, do you want to help me with breakfast?"

"Sure. I'll take a real quick shower first."

When I get downstairs, Mom is already frying bacon and sausage.

"Will you start on eggs?" she asks.

"On it." I pull two cartons out of our fridge.

"So…" she starts, "I noticed Mark was absent from fifth quarter last night."

"I already told you we broke up. He probably went to Watkins's house after the game. Tristan said they were having a victory party there." I begin cracking eggs into a pan.

"Watkins? Isn't that the boy who wrecked his car into a tree last year?"

"Uh, yeah." I was sort of hoping Mom might've forgotten about that.

"You weren't hanging out with him when you were dating Mark, were you?"

"No. Mark wasn't interested in hanging out with his friends or mine when we were dating."

"What's that supposed to mean?" Mom raises her eyebrows at me.

"Nothing." I shrug. "He'd rather go places by ourselves than with a group. Look, I broke up with Mark, but I don't want to talk about it. He isn't the guy for me and that's that." I put the empty cartons in the trash can with more force than is necessary. I'm tired of having to deal with questions about Mark. I wish I'd never agreed to go out with him.

"Okay. We don't have to talk about it, but I'm always here if you want to talk. Even if you haven't told me what is going on with you this week, I know something is up. I know Daniel stayed here Thursday, and he didn't stay in the guest bedroom like he's supposed to."

"Nothing happened. It's just Daniel." As annoying as it is to get lectured about Daniel staying in my room, it's familiar territory and far less uncomfortable than talking about Mark. It's not like it's the first time we've had this conversation since junior high. I get where my mom is coming from, but Daniel is like a brother to me. She doesn't care when I crash in Xander's room.

"I trust you and I trust Daniel, but trust is a lot easier to break than it is to build."

I figure I'm going to have to give her something even if I don't want to talk about it. My parents have strict rules and high expectations for our behavior and achievements, but my mom can be pretty laid back as long as we're honest with her. I'm sure she'd drop the issue entirely if I told her about my panic attack on Wednesday. But then she'd go into helicopter-mom-mode, and I don't want to deal with that again. Besides, it was just the one attack.

"Daniel's parents blew him off when he tried to see if they'd come to a game this year since he's on varsity. That's why he came over in the first place. I asked him to stay because I haven't been having a very good week." I focus on scrambling the eggs in front of me. "Mark keeps going back and forth between trying to talk me into getting back together and being mean and hateful. I told him I don't want to get back together, but it's like he can't hear me or doesn't want to listen. I want him to leave me alone but don't know how to get him to."

Mom pulls the bacon off the stove while she talks. "I'm sorry Daniel's parents don't make his games a priority. But if he's staying over, he doesn't need to be in your room. He needs to be in the guest room. You both know that. Otherwise, he can stay in the guest house. You might just be friends, but that doesn't mean you should be sharing a bed—"

"Gross, Mom! We didn't share a bed!" I interrupt her. "He slept on the trundle bed. We didn't do anything wrong." My face scrunches up at the thought of doing anything with Daniel.

"Even if nothing happened, you still broke the house rules." My mom turns to give me one of her scary-mom looks before refocusing on cooking the sausage.

"Yes, ma'am. I'm sorry." I'm glad that Jet stayed in the Knight room last night or I'd be in even more trouble. He stays with us when his mom has to work super late or super early. Or in the case of this weekend, when she has to do both.

"You should think about what kind of example you're setting for your younger brothers. And before you try to justify it by saying you got Daniel out of your room before any of them were up, that's definitely not the point. Even though he left your room before six, I still knew about it."

"I'll keep that in mind, especially the part about you apparently being all knowing." Seriously, how did my mom know what time Daniel snuck into the guest room?

"Now as far as Mark goes…are you sure it's over between you two? You were barely together before you broke up with him. Maybe he seems so hot and cold because he cares about you but is hurting."

I scoop the eggs out of the pan and into a bowl. "I'm sure it's over. I don't like him that way. He went to Watkins's party last night. He probably drank. Even if I was allowed to, I don't want to date someone who drinks or parties."

Which is true: I want to play basketball professionally someday. I don't need a bad decision or a high-school scandal affecting my future. But I know it'll help get my mom off my case about Mark.

"I hope he didn't. He seemed like such a nice boy. But if you say it's over, then I'll leave it alone." She hugs me.

"Thank you."

Just when I thought this interrogation was over, Mom asks, "How has Josh been?"

"He's fine. You should know that; you saw him yesterday."

"I did see him last night. He spent most of the night glued to your side. What's going on there?"

"Nothing's going on. We already dated last spring and decided we're better off as friends. We're good friends, but we're just friends. I'm not interested in anyone right now."

"Okay, I can take a hint." Mom lifts her hands in surrender. "Will you go get the boys while I get the food on the table?"

"Of course." I head upstairs and tell my brothers breakfast is ready.

I fire off a text to Daniel, Oliver, and Grayson to see if they're up and want to come over for breakfast. I hope my mom's true to her word and doesn't bring Mark or Josh back up.

By the time I get back to the kitchen, Daniel's already there talking with Xander. Jet looks like a zombie but is awake and sitting at the table. I check my phone but haven't heard back from Oliver or Grayson. They probably aren't up yet.

Breakfast goes by without any more awkward conversations. The twins have a soccer game today, so my parents and three youngest brothers will thankfully be out of the house when Andrew comes over to work on our project.

Jet leaves right after breakfast, saying he has laundry and stuff to do at the apartment before coming back over for the dance later. The rest of the morning passes relatively quickly as Xander, Daniel and I work on our homework.

"How are you feeling about *girl time* now?" Daniel asks after my parents leave for the soccer game.

We're sitting on the living room couch. Xander headed up to his room to practice for his upcoming play.

"Eh, I'm hoping since I didn't agree to it until yesterday that it won't be too much. Callie will be there and she's the little sister I never had, and from what I saw of Sara last night, she seems pretty cool. The jury's still out on Kaylee, but hopefully I can get to know her better and find out if she's a good match for Ollie."

"Try not to go overboard with asking her a thousand and one questions. Oliver really likes her. Please try not to scare her away." Daniel crosses his arms.

"I would never—" I protest, but Daniel shoots me a look. "I'll try hard not to…?"

"That seems more honest."

"I only scare girls away from Ollie who are no good for him. Is it so bad I don't want girls like Tara getting a hold of Ollie and taking advantage of him?"

Daniel raises an eyebrow at me. "I seem to recall your efforts to scare her away from Oliver ended up in her fling with Jet."

"That wasn't intentional," I protest. "But be real, Jet's more of a fling type of guy anyway. He isn't going to get invested in a girl who decides they only want a fling. Then get hurt when it ends. Ollie, on the other hand, is too nice for his own good."

"He's still a big boy who can take care of himself." Daniel says, "If he wants to pursue Kaylee and gets hurt, let him. We'll all be here to pick up the pieces and help him through it. Don't baby him. You know you wouldn't do the same thing if it was any of the rest of us." His face tells me he really means what he's saying so I make a mental note to try not to be overprotective of Oliver.

"I already said I'll play nice." I huff. "Can we go play Horse until Andrew gets here?"

Daniel gets up from the couch. "Sure. Also, Xander said he has to go pick Amelia up. I told him I could hang out with Andrew while you have girl time."

"I wish we could switch and you could deal with girl time," I complain.

"Yeah, yeah. The woes of having an involved mother." Daniel playfully shoves me before heading into the backyard.

"More like the woes of having a uterus." I follow him outside.

CHAPTER 40
ANDREW

"Am I so inept that I can't dress myself?" I ask Carter when we get back to my house.

Since he doesn't have a car, we decided it'd be easier for me to pick him up before heading to Lynn's house. He's already arranged to work on his project with Xander since he's going to be there, anyway. We're in my room and looking at the two outfits Kaylee picked out for today.

"I hear you, and I know that Kaylee can be controlling. But you're currently wearing a polo that says: 'Carson Valley Math Science Team,' and it's tucked into khakis that don't quite reach your shoes."

"This is what I have to wear for math science meets. It's not what I'd wear normally."

"I know I'm not on the math science team, but I'm pretty sure your pants flooding isn't a requirement." Carter flops down on my bed.

"No, but I don't wear khakis any other time, and it seemed like a waste of money my dad doesn't have, to get a new pair for TMSCA. It still doesn't mean Kaylee can insult me, then dictate what I wear."

"I agree. About Kaylee bossing you around, not about the khakis."

"But if I don't wear what she set out, I'll have to listen to an earful from Kaylee."

"You could learn to ignore her like I do." Carter puts his hands behind his head as he makes himself comfortable. Harder than it sounds since I still have a bunk bed and Carter's a lot bigger than me.

I give him a look.

"How about start small?" he suggests. "You could still wear the dress pants and button-up shirt she picked out for the dance but pick out your own clothes for studying at Lynn's."

I nod. "Good idea. She might even be so distracted with whatever girl time they're having that she won't notice what I wear to work on our project."

I go ahead and grab one of my favorite shirts out of the closet. It's not like Lynn is going to see me as more than friend potential, anyway. Going to fifth quarter last night pretty well solidified that she has way better offers romantically than me. There's no reason she'd ever be interested in me.

If anything, all I get are friend vibes from her. Even being friends with Lynn is a step up from where I was before. It was kind of cool to try to teach her how to play *Super Mario Bros.*

Lynn has always seemed so pretty, popular, and perfect. She's good at sports. She's smart. She's nice. She's outgoing and social. She seems to excel at everything she does.

So it was nice to see her be horrible at something as simple as trying to play video games. I didn't mind sitting right next to her while trying to show her what to do.

"So," Carter starts, "are you going to try to turn Homecoming into a date with Lynn? Do I need to try to make myself scarce while working on my project with Xander—that way you and Lynn can have some alone time?" He wiggles his eyebrows when he says *alone time.*

"No, please don't do that. I'm barely getting a little bit comfortable with being friends with her. I feel like alone time would make me more nervous and go back to stuttering. If you need space to work on your project or if Xander wants to go somewhere else, that's cool, but please don't abandon me."

"I promise not to abandon you. Now hurry up and get changed so we can get this show on the road."

Per Lynn's instructions, we come in the side entrance that we used yesterday. I start taking off my shoes when Lynn comes in through another door that I presume leads to the backyard.

Daniel is right behind her. They're both wearing workout clothes and appear to be drenched in sweat. The way Lynn looks is not fair to the rest of us mere mortals.

Instead of looking like a disgusting mess like I'm sure I do after exercising, she's glistening and her form-fitting tank top is clinging to her curves.

Carter elbows me, which pulls me out of my staring. Lynn is focused on taking her shoes off, so she hopefully didn't notice.

"Hey, sorry. I meant to be ready when y'all got here. We were playing a game of Horse and that turned into an intense game of one-on-one," Lynn says by way of explaining her and Daniel's current state.

"Yeah, and I'm sorry you have to smell Lynn." Daniel waves his hand in front of his nose.

"Hey!" Lynn shoves him with her shoulder. "It's not like you smell any better."

"I don't know what you mean. I smell wonderful. All the sweaty gross smell is coming from you." Daniel sticks out his tongue and avoids Lynn's next shove.

"Sure, you keep telling yourself that." Then Lynn seems to remember Carter and I are there.

"Um, anyway, I can show y'all to the living room. Xander should be in there and you can get your homework stuff set up while I take a real quick shower."

"S-s-sounds good," I stutter.

Lynn leads the way to the living room. Xander is in there with one of her other brothers. I think it's the one who plays euphonium, but I can't remember his name. Xander looks to be deep into his homework already.

"Xand, Andrew and Carter are here. I'm going to take a quick shower, then be back down here."

"Y'all reek," Lynn's younger brother says.

Lynn and Daniel look at each other before simultaneously running at him and enveloping him in a group hug.

"Ew. Get off of me. I'm telling Mom." Lynn and Daniel let him go.

Lynn laughs and says, "Good luck with that, Dylan. Mom and Dad are at the twins' soccer game, remember?"

"Whatever. Y'all are still gross." Dylan leaves the room.

"Are you sure you're the oldest?" Xander asks. "Because your behavior suggests I should be at least a couple of years older than you."

"This is why I'm the fun twin and you're the old soul." Lynn sticks her tongue out at Xander and disappears up the stairs.

"When are the rest of the neanderthals supposed to be here?" Xander asks Daniel.

"I think Mama Kingston told them to be here at five-thirty, so she could get pictures of all of the guys while the girls finish getting ready. Jet and Tristan will probably be barely on time, per usual. The Ridires will probably be late." With that last statement, Daniel gives Xander somewhat of a weighted look.

Xander nods like he understands. I have no idea what the exchange was supposed to have meant.

As if Daniel wants to change topics, he follows up with saying, "And you're stuck with me until then."

"Duh. You practically live here. I'd expect nothing less."

"If only your parents would adopt me and make it official." Daniel smirks before heading to one of the bedrooms off of the living room.

"I want to ask what you mean by Daniel practically living here, but I feel like it's none of our business," Carter says.

"His parents aren't home a lot." Xander explains. "Growing up, he stayed with us a lot. He's here more often than he's at home and is like a bonus brother. Even though none of us need another brother. He's probably the least annoying brother I have, so it's all right."

Having nothing more to say on the matter, Xander gets the movie set up for Lynn and me before he and Carter go to the dining room to work. Since they're doing a different play, they don't want to have to watch *The Twelfth Night*. I get my notebook out to take notes and arrange the rest of my stuff. I hear Lynn laughing and look up to find her smiling at me.

"I like pie, too."

"Huh?" I ask.

"Your shirt. I like it." She points at my shirt, which says,

$$\sqrt{-1}2^3\sum\pi$$

... and it was delicious

"Oh, um, thank you." This should help convince Kaylee to back off the whole makeover idea.

Lynn sits next to me and starts the movie. It's surprisingly comfortable to sit next to her. She's clearly engrossed in the movie and taking notes for our project. I don't have to worry about feeling or being awkward.

Accepting that we will only be friends has definitely helped with my awkwardness. I focus on the movie and taking notes. I barely even notice when her arm brushes mine or when she moves her hair and I can smell a faint strawberry scent.

Okay, I notice, but I don't get completely awkward and am still able to take some notes.

After we finish the movie and start working on our paper, Lynn's parents get home.

"Boys, hurry up and go get changed. Uncle Logan and Aunt Lily will be here soon to take you to the park," Lynn's mom says as the twins race up the stairs. To Lynn, she says, "How's the paper going, honey?"

"Fine. I think we're about halfway through."

"That's great. You ought to be done by the time Amber and the girls get here."

Lynn looks up with wide eyes. "You invited Amber?"

"Of course—" The doorbell rings, cutting off the rest of what she was saying.

"Who is Amber?" I ask after Lynn's mom steps back into the hallway.

"My mom's friend. She's great and everything, but she's a hairstylist. If Mom invited her, that means she's definitely planning to go overkill with the whole girl time thing and getting ready for the dance." Lynn cringes.

"I take it girl time isn't usual for you?"

"Nope." Lynn pops the 'p.' "Usually, the only girl I hang out with is Callie. She's as feminine as me, so I don't think she counts."

We finish our paper and get our school stuff put away. This afternoon has been productive and relaxing, and I'm a little disappointed when Xander gets back to the house with Amelia, signaling the start of girl time.

CHAPTER 41
KAYLEE

I'm glad to have Sara with me when I get to Lynn's house. Drew seemed back to normal this morning, so I'm hoping that means he has completely forgiven me for my harsh words yesterday. He told me fifth quarter went well, even if he thinks Lynn might be friend-zoning him.

Now I have to deal with having girl time with perfect Lynn and her perfect mother. I need to keep my tongue in check because I don't want to cause any problems for or with Drew.

On top of everything else, Mary wasn't home again last night. There were more dishes in the sink and evidence that she'd come home at some point during the day, so she hadn't entirely run off.

Sara leads the way into the Kingston's house like she's comfortable here despite only being here the day before. Xander is in the living room with Carter, Drew, and Daniel. He tells us Lynn and Amelia are upstairs in Lynn's room and Callie has just headed up.

When we walk in, Lynn's room is mostly what I'd have expected. NBA and WNBA posters on the royal-blue walls. A silver bookshelf full of books and topped with trophies. A queen-sized bed with a royal-blue comforter. It looks like school spirit threw up in her room. Everything seems to be neat, tidy, and in its place.

What I hadn't expected is the vanity full of makeup and hairstyling products. Maybe her natural 'I woke up looking this amazing' look isn't as natural as she makes it seem.

Amelia is here sitting in the blue plush chair in the corner of the room. She plays flute, so I have seen her at band. But I haven't ever talked to her before. Lynn is sitting in a chair in front of the vanity while a middle-aged woman wearing a hairstylist apron stands behind her, curls her hair.

"You're here. I'm saved!" Lynn says when Callie walks in before us.

Callie laughs.

"I might be here, but we both know that'll have no bearing on Mama Kingston and her makeover ideas."

"Yes, but now that attention will be spread out and maybe she'll leave me alone," Lynn points out.

Callie only shakes her head.

Then Lynn says to the rest of us, "Oh, by the way this is my mom's friend, Amber. Amber, this is Kaylee and Sara." We politely say hello.

"Whoa." Sara walks up to the wall that's behind the bookshelf. "Kaylee, do you see this?"

I follow her and look at the wall on the other side of the bookshelf. It's a signed band poster from Our Last Night. Above it is a framed picture of Lynn with Trevor, Tim, and Matt. I stare dumbly at the picture and poster as my brain tries to make sense of this information.

Lynn is a fan of my favorite band.

Lynn has gotten to meet them.

I'm shocked because I assumed Lynn would have crap taste in music and like the Top 40's music. I'm jealous because my parents would never take me to one of their concerts and I can't go on my own until I'm eighteen.

Around it are several other signed posters from bands like I Prevail, We Came as Romans, and Citizen Soldier.

"Oh, uh, that's Our Last Night. I went to their concert last year," Lynn says, as if that's why I'm staring at the photo.

"I know who they are. They're my favorite band. The band Sara and I play in started out as an Our Last Night cover band." I gesture to Sara as I talk.

Then I ask Lynn, "The only other people I know who've heard their music are the people I've made listen to their music. How do *you* know who they are?"

"My mom loves their music. I was raised on it. How did you discover them?"

"I heard their cover of 'Heavy' by Linkin Park on YouTube. I liked it and started listening to their music more and more. What's your favorite song?" I ask.

"'Invincible.' 'Barricades' is a close second, though. What about you?"

I hate that I'm impressed that she knows their music. A passing fan wouldn't know either of those songs.

"It's a tie between 'Outnumber' and 'Hysteria.' That's a big part of why our band is called Outnumbered by Hysteria."

"That's a cool name. The next time y'all have a gig, you'll have to let me know so the Knights and I can come."

We actually have something in common.

I didn't think me and Miss Perfect would have anything in common.

Plus, she wants to see my band play. Maybe having to be around her for Drew's sake won't be as bad as I thought it'd be.

Getting ready seems to pass by in a blur. We talk about Our Last Night and maybe start to bond a little bit. Amber leaves after helping each of us fix our hair. Lynn's mom has been in and out the entire time. We're all dressed and ready, putting final touches on our makeup.

"So, who's Colten taking to the dance?" Sara asks. Discretion has never been her strong suit.

"Officially, no one. But I'm sure he has a girl he's planning to meet up with at the dance." Lynn rolls her eyes.

"Why wouldn't he have an official date? Does he not date?" Sara asks. Callie snorts.

"Colten is secretive about who he dates. He doesn't want an interrogation from Mama Kingston or anyone else. I'm sure if he became serious about someone it'd be different." Callie subtly looks at Lynn when she says, *anyone else*. Lynn doesn't seem to have noticed.

"Yeah, if you tell my mom you're dating someone, she hears you're in love and a wedding is imminent. It can be kind of annoying," Lynn says.

"So then, why do you always tell your mom who you're dating?" Amelia asks. She has been so quiet this whole time I forgot she was here.

Lynn shrugs. "It's easier to deal with my mom being a little annoying than to try to keep my relationships from her. Besides, the more honest I am with her, the more freedom I have. The freedom is definitely worth listening to her opinion on my dating life."

"You still don't bring it up more than necessary," Callie says.

"I don't feel like my mom needs all the details. She knows when I start dating someone, when we go on dates, and when we break up. That covers the basics. Anything more than that lengthens the conversation when the relationship ends. I prefer for that conversation to last no longer than me explaining why we're better off as friends," Lynn explains.

"Have you friendzoned every guy you've ever dated?" I ask.

"I wouldn't say that…" Lynn starts to say.

"You might not, but everyone else would," Callie pipes up. "Some of the guys might agree with you and say it's mutual, but I'm pretty sure that's them trying to save face because it's bad enough that they're on the receiving end of a dumping."

"So, you've dumped every guy you've ever dated? You let them get invested and start falling before moving on to the next shiny thing?" I'm irritated with Lynn's history.

If she discards every guy who is interested in her, then she isn't the right girl for Drew. If only it'd be easy to convince him of that.

"Would it be better to continue dating them?" Lynn raises an eyebrow. "Especially when I know I'm not interested in them romantically? I don't lead anyone on, and I'm always upfront and honest about how I feel."

"Hey, we aren't saying you're doing anything wrong. Just that your relationships typically end with you friendzoning the guy you're dating." Callie says. "It's not like I have a real opinion anyway. I've never been asked out. What would I know about dating?"

"So, is what Colten said yesterday about you being off limits true?" Sara asks.

Callie shrugs. "It's not that. I've been playing football with the same guys since kindergarten. I'm pretty sure they don't know I'm a girl. Not that it matters. I'm not interested in any of them, and I don't think dating a teammate would be a good idea."

"What about you, Kaylee?" Lynn asks with sudden interest. "What do you think of the football boys?"

"Jocks aren't my type," I say bluntly.

"More into band nerds, like Carter?" Lynn asks.

Sara snorts. "Like Kaylee and Carter would ever go on a real date. They'd kill each other before the night was over."

I love my sister.

I really do.

But right now, I want to strangle her.

Sara adds, "They're best friends. But they're sort of like brother and sister. They definitely fight like siblings."

"We do not." I playfully shove Sara's shoulder.

"Oh really? So you're saying I only imagined you having a petty squabble over who got what controller yesterday playing video games at Drew's house?"

Okay, so she had me there.

"Fine. Maybe you have a point."

"I thought he was your date for tonight?" Lynn asks.

"We're going as friends. I'm not looking to date anyone right now." I don't want to talk about it.

"I hear that. After everything with Mark, I think I'm better off single for a while," Lynn says, and Callie snorts.

"What?" Lynn asks.

Callie shakes her head but there's a slight smirk on her lips. "Nothing. I've heard that before and know how long that usually lasts. But you know, more power to you if you actually manage to stay single for a bit."

Lynn sticks her tongue out at Callie but doesn't argue.

"Girls! The boys are here!" Lynn's mom says as she bursts into the room with as much cheer as a whole squad of cheerleaders.

It's hard to believe her mom who looks like an ex-pageant queen likes heavy metal, but maybe she isn't what she seems.

I mean, Lynn seems okay. Not that I want to be friends with her or anything, but after this afternoon, I feel like I could hang out with her for Drew's sake.

CHAPTER 42
OLIVER

Grayson has about had it with me when we're finally leaving the house. We're running late which is all my fault. I just got super nervous while trying to get ready. I mean, Kaylee is going to be next door. I'm spending the entire night with her. Okay, so not like *with* her. She's on a date with Carter and all of our friends will be there. But we'll still be around each other all evening.

I try to push my ridiculous nerves away. Kaylee probably won't even pay attention to me. I mean, she has a date. She's just here because she's Andrew's friend and because of that she got roped into everything. I take a deep breath before opening the door to Lynn's house.

Mama Kingston waves us in and puts us in line. She has us stand according to height because she's going to take pictures as the girls come down the steps. This puts me closest to the steps because I'm the tallest. Tristan is next to me, and he glances over as I try to discretely rub my sweaty palms on the side of my pants.

"Here," Tristan says, holding out a corsage to me. "Carter told me to give it to you. It's Kaylee's."

I take the corsage from him and want to ask him a dozen questions about what this means, but Amelia descends the stairs and Mama Kingston starts taking photos.

I fiddle with the corsage, not sure what else to do. The ribbon made to go around her wrist is made of black lace. There're white flowers with silver, blue, and black ribbons arranged around them. I wonder if this is a preview of what her dress will look like.

The girls are descending in order of height so that means Kaylee will be after Sara. I still have a lot of time because Mama Kingston is taking several photos of the girls as they descend the stairs and get their corsages.

I watch Xander put Amelia's corsage on as he dutifully smiles for the camera. I try to take note of everything before I realize how ridiculous I'm being. It's not like this is the first time I've put a corsage on a girl, and it just slips on over their wrist. I mean, I put Kaylee's garter on her arm yesterday without any problems and that's more difficult.

Kaylee just makes me so nervous. I've heard the expression of butterflies in your stomach, but whatever is flying around inside me isn't as peaceful as butterfly wings. It feels more like a nest of hornets getting ready to sting.

Carter jokes around with Sara as he puts her corsage on her wrist. She looks annoyed but is trying to smile for the camera. I wonder if Carter gave Kaylee's corsage away so he could have Sara's. Before I can wander too much down that rabbit trail, they finish up with pictures and Mama Kingston calls for Kaylee.

Kaylee rounds the corner at the top of the steps coming into view. Now, it doesn't matter what was in my stomach because it feels like it's dropped clear out of my body. Kaylee is gorgeous.

Her dress is black, which contrasts with her skin tone and makes her blue hair pop. The top has a bunch of straps that crisscross highlighting her figure while keeping her more than modestly covered up. The hem of the dress hits halfway between her knees and ankles. There's nothing revealing about her dress, but she takes my breath away all the same.

I can't help but stare as Kaylee makes her way down the stairs. She looks fierce with her smoky eyes and heeled combat boots. She's almost to the bottom when Tristan nudges my shoulder bringing me out of my trance.

I'm mildly annoyed when I look over at him, but he's nodding toward the base of the stairs. *Oh, right.* I'm supposed to be over there to give Kaylee her corsage. I was too busy taking in her appearance to remember anything else that was going on.

I wipe my palms on my pants again hoping to get any and all sweat off of them. My nerves build with every step I take toward Kaylee. She glances at Carter who gives his head a slight shake before looking my way. Kaylee takes in the corsage in my hands before making eye contact with me.

Surprise flashes in her eyes before she goes back to her neutral expression. I have no idea if me having her corsage is a good surprise or a bad one. Her eyes stay on me, and I want to get lost in their swirling blue depths. It feels like a gravitational pull is drawing me closer to her. I stop when I'm right next to her feeling unsure of myself.

"You look amazing," I breathe out. She's still on the stairs making us closer to the same height for once.

"Um, thanks." Kaylee has a slight blush on her cheeks. "I think now is when you're supposed to put that on my wrist."

Oh, yeah. I'm supposed to be doing something other than looking dopey-eyed at Kaylee.

I feel heat creep up my neck and look down at her wrist. My hands are slightly shaking as I slide the corsage on her. My fingers ghost along the inside of her wrist and it feels like electricity is coursing through our contact. Kaylee jumps slightly at my touch, and I wonder if she feels the connection, too. After the corsage is in place I look back to Kaylee's face, captivated by her beauty.

"Wonderful!" Mama Kingston's voice grounds me back in reality and reminds me of all of the eyes on us.

"I've got plenty of pictures." She says waving us to step out of the way before Callie comes down the stairs. I hadn't even been aware of the click of the camera.

Kaylee pulls her hand away from me. It looks like she might be blushing, but she's not looking at me so it's hard to be sure. She walks over to Sara and Carter and starts a conversation with them. Not sure what else to do, I walk back over to where Tristan is standing.

Callie and Lynn come down the stairs and have their pictures taken but I'm not really aware of anything other than Kaylee whom I keep stealing glances of. I'm sure I'm being beyond obvious, but her back is to me so it's not like *she's* going to notice.

When we line up for pictures, I realize my staring at Kaylee did not escape Mama Kingston's notice. She positions Kaylee directly in front of me and has me place my hand on Kaylee's waist. I feel the same zip of electricity at the contact and hope I'm not the only one affected.

Pictures pass by in a daze as I struggle to keep my focus off Kaylee. I'm sure most of the pictures will show me looking at her instead of the camera, but I just can't help it.

"Honey," Mr. Kingston says, gently placing his hand over his wife's phone. "I think you have enough photos, and I'm sure the kids are ready to go eat."

As if on cue, Lynn's stomach growls. Xander bursts into laughter, quickly joined by everyone else.

Stella puts her phone away. "I guess y'all should be on your way." She follows us to the front door. "Have fun. Take care of Colten and Callie. Make good choices. Curfew is at one and remember—"

"If we aren't up and ready on time in the morning, our curfew will get earlier," we finish.

"We'll be good. Love you." Lynn hugs her parents and heads out the door.

Carter climbs into the third row of Xander's SUV, claiming it's easier for him to get in the back than the girls. I'm bigger than him, so it makes sense for me to be in the second row. But it almost feels like Carter is avoiding being next to Kaylee and sending her in my direction.

I'm not sure how much I should read into his actions, but it definitely doesn't look like he's on a real date with Kaylee. It makes me more confident that they both see each other as friends only. I just don't know how Kaylee sees me.

She made it pretty clear she didn't need or want my help with James yesterday. Originally I thought that could be an aversion to my company, but maybe it was more about her being independent. She might not want to use me as a shield against James, but maybe she wouldn't be opposed to dating me in general.

At Bellissimo Feudo, Kaylee ends up seated across from me which gives me hope. But she spends all of dinner talking to her sister who's seated next to her. It's just a reminder that her not being interested in Carter doesn't mean she's interested in me.

CHAPTER 43
KAYLEE

Dinner was interesting to say the least. Carter was right yesterday, about being with a bunch of popular jocks not being as boring as I would've thought. Kasey, Jet's date, was whining all through dinner and threw a hissy fit about dessert. Lynn looked highly irritated by Kasey's behavior and sent as many of us as would fit in Xander's SUV on ahead while they dealt with everything.

I was glad to get away from the scene Kasey was causing but also relieved to get away from Oliver. I don't know if the universe, or someone else, is conspiring against me. But every time I turn around today we were being pushed together. There was the corsage, photos, the ride to the restaurant, and he even was seated across from me for dinner.

Oliver puts me on edge, and I don't like it. My body has been reacting to his when he's close by. I'm treating that like a warning bell telling me to stay away from him. The last time I reacted to someone's closeness was James. We all know what a disaster that has been over the last couple of years, and I don't need a repeat of that drama with Oliver.

We walk into the gym, and I try not to be impressed with its transformation. The floor is covered with some sort of mat that makes it look like a swirl of silver galaxies. There're royal blue curtains covering where the stands are pushed against the walls. Since the stands are against the walls instead of splitting the main gym from the back gym, the whole room looks much bigger.

There's a scattering of round tables around the room and a long table with punch and water against one wall. A stage is set up blocking the doors that lead to the locker rooms. If you look up you can still see the basketball nets that are tucked up in the ceiling. But they, along with the rafters, have twinkle lights strung from them. I try to tell myself the atmosphere doesn't have something magical to it, but it's hard to deny that the dance committee did a good job with decorating.

People are milling around the gym, sitting at tables and standing in clusters around the dance floor. Music is playing but no one is dancing; it makes me wonder how much dancing actually happens at dances.

Carter sees a few people we know from band sitting at a table and heads in their direction; Drew follows him. I glance Sara's way, not wanting to abandon her. She's looking at Colten and I watch her face fall as a girl saunters up to him. She grabs his hand and pulls him toward the group of popular underclassmen hanging out in the corner. Callie rolls her eyes at the girl before following Colten to their friends.

"Hey," I say to Sara hoping to distract her. "Do you want to go sit with Carter and Drew?"

Sara blinks away her disappointment. "Yeah, that, uh, sounds good."

When we get to the table most people are in the process of getting up.

"Do y'all want to come dance?" Helen asks. She plays clarinet and is dating Mal, in percussion, who is currently tugging her toward the dance floor.

"No one's dancing," Sara says, looking to the empty dance floor.

"If we don't start the dancing none of the sheeple will ever dance," Clare says, pulling Sara into a twirl.

Clare is one of our tuba players, which is impressive with how short she is. She's only slightly taller than Drew and he struggles with marching the trombone.

I wave Sara on as I take a seat at the table. I'm not sure I want to dance with a herd of band kids, I know how rowdy they can get. Besides, Drew is still sitting, and I don't want him to feel abandoned.

Carter stays seated as well, and pretty soon it's just the three of us at the table.

"So how was girl time?" Carter asks.

"Fine. Lynn said she plans on staying single for a while, so that gives us time to get her to see that Drew is the right guy for her." I turn toward Drew. "If that's still what you want?"

"I want to be friends with Lynn. Being more than friends with her..." Drew trails off before shaking his head. "I don't think she sees me that way."

"Maybe you need to do something to get her looking at you as more than just a friend," Carter says. "We're at a dance she invited you to. Maybe asking her to dance can show her you don't just want to be her friend."

Drew shakes his head. "I don't even know how to dance. I'd probably just embarrass myself."

"Fine, no dancing," Carter concedes. "Just go talk to her when she gets here, and not about homework or anything school related. Flirt with her and see where it goes."

"I can't do that. I don't think I have the nerve to just walk up to her and start a conversation. Even if I wanted to, I can't flirt with her. I can barely talk to her without stuttering, and I don't know how to flirt."

"Compliment her," I say, entering the conversation. "Laugh at her jokes and find reasons to brush against her. I'm sure she'll get the hint."

Drew shifts in his seat. "I don't think I can do that. Besides, Josh was blatantly flirting with her last night and that didn't get him anywhere. He even put his arm around her shoulder, and she just playfully shoved it off."

"That's because Josh is her ex," Carter says. "Besides, I seem to recall her leaning into you as you showed her how to play video games. Lynn doesn't seem to mind having you in her bubble."

I wonder what all I missed at fifth quarter last night. If Lynn was flirting with Drew even a little then maybe this is working and he's starting to get on her radar. I'm still not sure she's the best girl for Drew, and her lack of long-term commitment isn't exactly a good sign. But she's the one he wants, and I want him to be happy.

Drew shrugs. "I don't want to get my hopes up for something that's super unlikely to happen. I'm still working on being comfortable talking to her. I think I need to just focus on not embarrassing myself as her friend before worrying about anything else."

"You want to take things slow." Carter nods. "I can respect that."

Drew looks like he's about to contradict Carter, but Carter turns to me before Drew can speak. "So, how are things with you and a certain football player?"

"There isn't anything between me and anyone, much less me and anyone on the football team." I'm not talking about Oliver, not that there's anything to talk about anyway.

Maybe my heart speeds up when he's near. My nerve endings might stand at attention when he brushes against me. My nose may want to drown in his masculine scent. But my body isn't getting a say in things this time. It's proven it can't be trusted to lead my heart in a safe direction. It doesn't matter what could become of Oliver and me because I'm determined to keep my heart on lockdown.

"Me thinkest thou protesteth too much." Carter's voice brings my head out of thoughts of Oliver.

I roll my eyes at him. "Why don't we dissect your love life? How are things going with Hannah?"

Hannah is a sophomore who plays flute.

"There's no thing with Hannah." Carter shrugs. "My love life isn't nearly as interesting as either of yours."

"What do you call making-out with her at the back of the band bus last week?" If he's going to question me about Oliver then it's only fair to return the favor.

"I call it a bit of fun that's over for both of us. There might have been some chemistry there but that's it."

For a moment his words remind me of something James would say. There must be something on my face betraying my thoughts, because Carter starts shaking his head.

"Don't look at me like that. I didn't do anything wrong. If you must know, Hannah wanted to make her ex jealous. The only interest she had in me was because I'm first chair and Jeremy's section leader."

Jeremy is a sophomore like Hannah and plays trumpet with Carter. I've never paid much attention to him.

"I guess that explains why Jeremy has been glaring at you all week," Drew says.

Carter smirks. "Yeah, if only he'd channel that energy into learning the marching show, then I wouldn't have to be constantly adjusting him during practice."

Our conversation moves away from relationships, and I find I'm actually enjoying myself. They may be annoying at times, but I've got two of the best friends a girl could ask for.

I'm laughing at something Carter said when I feel something in the atmosphere change. I refuse to turn around to look at the doors. There's only one group that could cause that much attention by walking into a room and I don't want to be another gawking onlooker.

Drew looks to the door like he's got Lynn on radar, and I see his goofy smile as he takes her in. He's really got it bad, and I hope it works out for him. I just don't want to have to spend too much time around Oliver, while trying to get them together. He's a complication my life doesn't need.

CHAPTER 44
OLIVER

Because of Kasey's scene at dinner I ended up riding to the dance with Daniel, Grayson, and Lynn. Lynn filled us in on the highlights of girl time and that Kaylee said she had no interest in a relationship of any kind. It was sort of a letdown, but I'm hoping if I take things slow she may decide to take a chance on me. From what I've seen it sounds like James didn't treat her the best, and she's not interested in having a repeat of whatever happened with him.

I've been trying to get up the courage to ask Kaylee to dance since we got here. When we got here she was talking and laughing at a table with Carter. I didn't think she'd want to leave a fun conversation with her friend to come dance with me. I'm not sure she wants to dance with me at all which is only making me more nervous.

Kaylee is unlike any girl I've ever dated before, and it makes me feel like I've never done any of this before. I like that Kaylee is different. It's refreshing. She definitely doesn't fawn all over me and it's going to take some major work to get her to give me a chance. I just wish I had more confidence in how to pursue her.

I did dance with Lynn earlier, and she gave me a pep talk after giving me another warning not to get my hopes up too much. I see Daniel step in when Lynn and Grayson have been dancing together for a while. Grayson doesn't look happy as he spots me and heads my way.

"Is there a reason y'all seem determined to keep me away from Lynn?" Grayson asks when he gets to me.

"You have no patience, and we don't want there to be an issue with Mark. Besides, I don't think Lynn is ready to be in another relationship right now."

"She probably doesn't want to be in another relationship because you called her a player and upset her." Grayson gestures toward me as he speaks.

Lynn's dating history may have come up on the ride over here as part of why Kaylee might not want to talk boys with Lynn. I pointed out that Lynn was more likely to do the playing than get played. She argued that she has no issues with being in a relationship and that she's always completely focused on whomever she's in a relationship with.

Daniel said Lynn's relationships last about as long as the other Knights' flings; they just have a different label. He said she had a thing for players of both kinds. She seemed confused, so I explained she only dates athletes and guys who don't have a track record of not committing either.

"I was being honest. If you think it upset her, I'll talk to her about it tomorrow and make sure she knows I didn't mean anything bad by it."

I didn't think it hurt her feelings, and I definitely didn't mean to. I'll have to get things cleared up with her. That'd be a good time to find out what in the world Mark said when they broke up. Now that Daniel and Lynn have alluded to it as well as Mark, I'm curious. It seems like it's something that upset Lynn and is messing with her head.

"I don't know, man. I'm frustrated. Is this whole 'keep me and Lynn apart' plan only for the dance? Or is it going to be an ongoing problem?" Grayson growls, running his hands through his hair.

"Mark's giving every guy who dances with her a death glare. We're trying not to add fuel to the fire," I say, hoping my brother will see reason. "Hopefully, he gets the hint after the dance and leaves Lynn alone. But until he calms down, there's no need to cause unnecessary drama for Lynn to deal with. She hasn't danced for more than one song with anyone other than you." I fiddle with my phone, taking pictures of my friends around the room.

"Fine," Grayson says in defeat. Then he asks, "So, why haven't you asked Kaylee to dance yet?"

"I don't want her to tell me no." I try to focus more on getting a good picture of Lynn and Daniel dancing together and being goofy than on this conversation I don't want to have.

"She has only danced with her sister. Other than that, she's been sitting at the table with Carter and Andrew. If she was involved with either of them, she would've been dancing with them. No other guy has even gone near their table. It's not like Kaylee has a lot of options," he points out.

"Just because no one else is asking her doesn't mean she will say yes to me. She might not even want to dance. She could be humoring Sara by dancing with her." Not wanting to dance at all would at least be a reason for her to tell me no, that isn't just her saying no to me.

"She bought a dress and is at the dance. She wants to dance. Unless you're that worried about her hating jocks. She hung out with Lynn and Callie all afternoon and they're jocks."

"Lynn and Callie are girls, so that's different. Besides, I don't think Kaylee actually has a thing against jocks." At least I hope not. It'd suck for me to have no chance just because I play sports.

"If you're so sure about that, then go ask Kaylee to dance," Grayson says with a hint of challenge in his voice.

"Why do you care so much?" I snap a picture of Tristan and Jet joking together at the punch bowl with their dates plastered to their sides.

"Because you're my brother and I want you to be happy."

"Try again. The truth this time."

"All Lynn talks about with me is the two of you. If you pursue Kaylee, then it'll resolve the issue one way or the other."

"I need to figure things out with Kaylee so you can find out if you have a shot with Lynn? Sounds about right." I roll my eyes.

"What's that supposed to mean?" Grayson says carefully.

"Nothing. I'm on edge."

"Now's probably the best time to go ask her. Sara's dancing with someone else, Carter's dancing with some other girl, and I don't see

Andrew at their table. If she does shoot you down, you won't have an audience."

"Okay. I'm going," I huff.

I walk over to where Kaylee is sitting. With each step, I feel the ball of nerves in my stomach get bigger. It's a short walk, but I feel tongue-tied by the time I get there.

Okay.

Time to ask her to dance. Remember, the worst thing she can do is say no. If you don't ask, she can't say yes.

I continue to try to psych myself up, but it's not working.

"Can I help you?" Kaylee asks. I realize I've been standing in front of her zoned out while trying to get up the nerve to talk.

"Um, I was wondering if you might want to, uh, dance... with me?"

Well, I asked.

It wasn't smooth, or cool, or witty, but at least the words came out.

"Why?"

"Why what?" I might not have expected her to say yes, but I didn't expect her to respond with a question.

"Why do you want to dance with me? If this is some pity thing or Lynn is making you include me because she invited us, then don't worry about it. Tell Lynn I said no. I'm quite fine sitting and watching as my sister dances the night away." Kaylee's voice drips condescension, but underneath it there seems to be some vulnerability. Or maybe I'm imagining that because I want it to be there.

"I'm not asking because Lynn told me to. I want to dance with you. Is that so hard to believe?"

Kaylee scrutinizes me as she considers my words. It's nerve-wracking, wondering what she thinks. Wondering what she sees when she's looking at me. Kaylee's so obviously confident in who she is. I've never been that confident and it's intimidating.

"Fine. One dance." Kaylee stands and places her hand in mine.

I'm surprised she said yes. I'm not sure what to say. Thankfully, when we get to the dance floor, the song changes to something slow.

"So, how are you enjoying the dance so far?" I ask, and Kaylee snorts.

"Is that the best conversation starter you can come up with?"

"Yeah, sorry, that was lame. I'm nervous." I still can't believe she agreed, albeit reluctantly.

"You're nervous? Why?"

"Because—" Before I can try to come up with an answer that isn't embarrassing, I notice James dancing with Whitney.

I feel like I should say something to warn Kaylee, but no words come.

"Because what?"

"Huh?"

"You're nervous because…?"

"Oh, um, yeah," I say distractedly, still looking behind Kaylee at James and Whitney.

"What are you looking at?" Kaylee glances over her shoulder. "Oh."

"Yeah." I'm not sure what else to say.

"I can't believe he's here. He hates dances and anything school-spirit-y."

"He's probably here because of you. Do you want to play up that he thinks we're on a date? I mean, because if you do, I'm cool with that." I'd love to be able to help her, and if pretending this is a date helps her, I'm completely on board. Especially if it means getting to hold her close and spend the whole night with her.

"You're fine with me using you to show my…to show him I'm not interested in him?"

"Why not? He seems like a jerk. Besides, we're already dancing together."

I want to protect Kaylee from James. I'm hoping her wanting to show him she has moved on means she has. Maybe helping her deal with James will get her to notice me.

"But if you'd rather us be dancing as friends and ignore him, that's fine," I add quickly. "I don't know what went down between you two, so I don't know what you want."

"Let's dance and ignore him. I don't want to spend the night thinking about him."

When the song ends and Kaylee doesn't walk away, I'm glad. She may only be dancing with me to avoid James, but she's still dancing with me. I try to keep her back to James and Whitney; I don't want her to see them and have them possibly upset her.

James keeps glancing at Kaylee and his looks get longer each time his eyes wander over here. By the end of the second song, he's all out staring at Kaylee.

"Do you want to get some punch?" Kaylee asks.

"Sure."

I lead us over to the punch table and get us both a cup. When I turn back around, James is there with Whitney plastered to his side.

"Can I help you?" I ask.

James smirks. "Checking on my little bandmate and seeing how she's doing at her first dance."

"Oh, you've never been to a dance before. How *cute.*" Whitney gives Kaylee a condescending look.

"I'm doing wonderful. It's *soooo* sweet of your date to be concerned," Kaylee says to Whitney, not even acknowledging James.

"James is sweet, isn't he?" Whitney says. "But he has nothing on Oliver. How nice of him to take you to your first dance. It must have been such a surprise to you that someone as popular as him would ask you. I mean, who would've even thought he knew you existed? You must feel so lucky. I mean, one of the Knights of the school was willing to be seen in public with you."

I wrap my arm around Kaylee's shoulder. "I'm the lucky one. To have someone so beautiful and talented as my date."

I'm trying to keep from letting my anger get the best of me. I hate that Whitney is talking down to Kaylee and I want to protect her from it. I don't know what her deal is, as far as I know she's never spoken to Kaylee before. I wonder what James told Whitney to have her lashing out at Kaylee.

"But not nearly as lucky as Whitney is that you asked me. I mean, if James didn't feel like he needed to check on me, then Whitney wouldn't even be here. Unless of course she came by herself. That would've been so hard to not be nominated for Homecoming Queen, and to not even have a date to the dance. I can't imagine how difficult that'd be for someone like you."

"What's that supposed to mean?" Whitney spits out.

"Oh, just that I'm sure to an utterly fake, airheaded, popular cheerleader Homecoming Queen was going to be the crowning achievement of your life. But now you've lost that. Which must be super difficult to deal with after being shut down multiple times by the football captain. Status is obviously important to you and you've lost yours, but at least you have a date who cares about you." Kaylee fake frowns. "Oh, wait. I forgot who you were with."

"James, are you going to let her talk to me like that?" Whitney stomps her foot like a petulant child.

"I think you have James confused with someone else. He's no knight in shining armor. Besides, I don't think anyone believes you're a damsel in distress." Kaylee smiles.

Whitney's face turns red in rage, and she looks like she's about to come closer and claw at Kaylee. So I step between her and Kaylee. Whitney huffs and storms off.

"I'll see you tomorrow. This won't last long, so enjoy the ride while you can." James looks me up and down looking unimpressed before he saunters off in a different direction than Whitney.

Kaylee takes one of the cups of punch from my hand and downs it.

"Come on. Let's get back to dancing." She clamps down on my hand and starts toward the dance floor.

I set my punch down before getting completely dragged away from the table. Her shoulders are tense, she has a death grip on my hand, and she's forcing a smile like she's determined to make it look like she's having the time of her life despite how she actually feels. I decide instead of asking her about it to try to distract her with dancing until she's actually enjoying herself.

CHAPTER 45
ANDREW

I think it's safe to say I don't care for school dances. I've spent the whole evening watching Lynn as she dances with pretty much every single guy here. She's only left the dance floor a couple of times to get punch.

Kaylee and Carter have each encouraged me to go ask Lynn to dance, but I don't think she'd say yes when she has so many other guys to dance with. If she did say yes, it'd probably be out of pity, which seems worse than not dancing with her.

The other issue with asking her to dance is I don't know how to dance, and I'd rather not embarrass myself any more than necessary.

The night started well enough. Mrs. Kingston gave me Lynn's corsage to place on her wrist. Lynn looked radiant descending the stairs in her royal-blue dress. Her hair was curled with her tiara in place, and she looked beautiful. She wore royal-blue Chuck Taylors with her dress instead of fancy shoes.

I sorta love that she isn't wearing high heels like a lot of girls here are. She's already so much taller than me and I don't need to feel shorter.

I was so nervous putting her corsage on her wrist and I'm pretty sure my hand shook, but if she noticed she didn't say anything. Lynn even joked about not stabbing me when she put my boutonniere on my shirt.

Taking pictures before the dance was even kind of nice. I got to stand next to Lynn for a bit and watch as she took pictures with her friends. It was nice watching how they all interacted with each other outside of school. They seemed to take a bunch of silly photos together, especially Lynn, Daniel, and Xander. It was like getting a glimpse of a side of Lynn I haven't seen before.

We met Jet and Tristan's dates at the restaurant. I was seated next to Lynn, which was nice, but for the most part, her friends were on one side of the table and they mostly talked amongst themselves. It was a reminder that I might get to see Lynn more relaxed, but that doesn't mean she'll ever see me.

I may get to see Lynn when she's comfortable and in her own world, but that doesn't mean I'll ever be a part of that world.

I'm not looking forward to the after-party at Josh's, but Sara wants to go. None of us wants her going alone, so we're all going whether we want to or not.

Carter has danced with the other girls from band that are here, and he seems to be enjoying himself. I'm hoping that doesn't mean attending dances will be a regular thing.

Kaylee's been all over the place talking about Lynn. Either I'm too good for Lynn and shouldn't waste my time on someone who clearly doesn't understand commitment, or I should ask Lynn out. She'd probably say yes, and that'd take care of the issue of me crushing on her.

Back and forth between encouraging me to chase the girl of my dreams or find a new girl to crush on who isn't such a player.

Tired of sitting at the table and having Kaylee bug me about Lynn, I decide to get a cup of punch. I'm throwing my empty cup away when there's a tap on my shoulder.

"Hey, Andrew. Would you like to dance?"

I'm so surprised Lynn is behind me and asking me to dance that my brain shorts out and I end up staring at her.

"Would you like to dance?" Lynn asks louder, probably thinking I didn't hear her the first time.

"Um, I…I don't…don't know how…" I manage and then immediately regret it.

Lynn has just asked me to dance and I stuttered and told her I don't know how to. Can I get any lamer?

"If you want, I can show you…? Or if dancing isn't your thing, that's cool, too." Lynn tucks a piece of hair behind her ear.

"Uh, okay." I'm pretty sure Lynn's asking out of pity for how pathetic I am, but it's not like I could say no.

"Great!" Lynn grabs my hand and leads me to the dance floor.

A slow song starts and Lynn places my hand on her waist before putting hers on my shoulder. I'm glad my hand isn't supposed to be on her shoulder; it's already a stretch just holding her other hand.

Thankfully, she leads and all I have to do is follow. It's easier than I thought. I still feel awkward and am not sure where I'm supposed to look. Being this close to Lynn I have to crane my neck up to see her face, but it's not like looking straight ahead is an option. With our height difference, my eye level is not where I should be looking. Hurting my neck is much better than looking like a creep or a weirdo.

I accidentally step on her toes a couple of times.

"Sorry, I keep stepping on your toes." Maybe I just need to look at the ground so I can watch where my feet are going.

"Eh, don't worry about it." Lynn shrugs. "I wear a size twelve. I'm used to having people step on my feet." Lynn smiles.

You'd think with how small my feet are in comparison; I'd be able to keep from stepping on her. But even with looking at my feet I can't avoid missteps. At least I don't have to worry about hurting her, the small fragile one here is me.

We dance to a few songs together, and even though I feel awkward, especially with the faster songs, it's nice.

Finally, another slow song starts, and Lynn continues to teach me how to two-step. I'm so focused on not stepping on her feet again, I don't notice someone approaching.

"Hey, Lynn, can I cut in?"

I look up to see Mark standing next to us.

"No." Lynn doesn't even look at Mark. "I'm dancing with Andrew. And you and I aren't together anymore."

I feel Lynn tense, but I don't know what to do.

"You can't be serious. We're great together." Mark steps closer and reaches out to touch Lynn's arm.

"I'm serious. We broke up, and I don't want to be with you. Please leave me alone." Lynn continues to dance and tries to lead us away from Mark.

"You've danced with every available guy here. I get that I was a jerk, and I'm sorry. I've learned my lesson. You can stop all this, and we can get back together." Mark stays right at Lynn's side no matter which direction she goes.

"I'm enjoying the dance. I'm not trying to teach you anything. I don't want to be with you. I'd appreciate it if you would leave me alone and move on."

"You can't mean that. You couldn't have moved on already. We haven't even been apart for a week. I still lo—care about you." Mark steps in front of Lynn, forcing us to come to a stop.

Lynn finally looks at Mark. "I do mean it, that's why I said it. We were only together for two weeks. Stop acting like we were together for years. I've moved on, you need to, too."

Mark seems to look at me for the first time, then he glances down to where Lynn is still holding my hand in hers.

"You can't seriously want him over me. I mean, he doesn't even look old enough to be in high school. Is he a freshman or something?"

Lynn plants herself between us as Mark takes another step toward me.

"He's a junior, and unlike you, he's respectful. How about you go back to your evening, so I can enjoy mine?" Lynn's tone is civil, but she's full of tension.

"You're choosing this scrawny nerd over me?" Mark's voice continues to get louder, drawing the attention of those around us.

I'm uncomfortable being in the spotlight. I feel especially small when thinking about how everyone around us is probably wondering who I am and why Lynn's holding my hand. I feel small in more ways than one. Not only do Mark and Lynn tower over me, but they both have a large presence that draws others to them.

"What I do or who I do it with is none of your business. We aren't together. Leave me alone." Lynn tugs me farther behind her.

"So, you're saying no to me for him?" Mark gestures at me.

"I'm saying no to you because I don't want to be with you. If I spend my time with Andrew or anyone else, that's none of your business. I don't belong to you." Lynn squeezes my hand. I'm not sure if it's for her comfort or mine.

"You witch!" Mark backhands Lynn.

Before Lynn can react, Daniel and Xander are there between her and Mark. Daniel's telling Mark to back off and Xander's whispering something to Lynn I can't quite hear.

Lynn spins around and storms off, towing me with her by the hand she still holds.

She gets to the hallway outside the gym. As she storms away, the grip on my hand keeps getting tighter. Xander tries to keep up with us.

"You want to let go of Andrew's hand before he loses circulation?" Xander asks, having kept pace with Lynn.

"Huh?" Lynn asks before looking down and releasing the death grip she has on my hand. "Oh, sorry. And sorry about dragging you out of the gym."

"It's…it's okay," I say. "Um, do…do you want me to, uh, leave?"

"What? Why?" Lynn asks, confused.

"If y'all need to…to talk or whatever," I say as Josh comes out of the gym doors.

"You're welcome to stay. Although, I understand if you don't want to be swept up in any of my drama. *I* don't want to deal with it, so I totally get it if you don't." Lynn sags against the wall looking, exhausted.

"Some of the football team got involved and Mark is leaving the dance." Josh pats Lynn reassuringly on the arm. "Daniel was talking to Grayson, and I figured you'd want to know."

"Okay. Thanks, Josh." Lynn gives Josh a hug before he goes back inside.

"Do you want to talk about it?" Xander asks.

"I want to *not* talk about it." Lynn pinches the bridge of her nose.

"I'd guess you have maybe two minutes before all the guys come out here. What's your plan to avoid talking?" Xander glances at the closed gym doors.

"Dance the night away and don't give them a chance to corner me?" Lynn looks all kinds of anxious.

"With wh—no, that's not a good idea on so many levels." Xander shakes his head.

"But it makes it future Lynn's problem, not present Lynn's." She shrugs.

"What are y'all talking about?" I'm so lost in this conversation.

"Would you like to dance the night away with me and be my shield from questions I don't want to answer?" Lynn brings her hands together like she's begging me to say yes.

"Oh, uh, I…I guess so." As soon as the words are out of my mouth, Lynn grabs my hand again and drags me back into the gym and onto the dance floor.

The rest of the dance seems to pass in a blur of dancing, talking, and laughing.

I feel tense when we first reenter the gym. I can feel a lot of people staring at us. After a while, with no more drama happening, people lose interest and I start to relax.

Lynn talks about basketball, her brothers, and other random things. She asks me about band and math science. It's nice and eventually I figure out what to do with my feet without having to stare at them the whole time.

Daniel comes up to us once, but Lynn says something that sounds like 'Mau.' He nods then walks off.

It seems weird that neither Lynn's closest friends nor mine have come around us. We stop to get a drink of punch. I see Kaylee's dancing with Oliver. Jet and Tristan seem preoccupied with their dates. Daniel and Grayson seem to be in the middle of an intense conversation at a table by themselves. And Carter's nowhere to be seen.

"Thank you for not asking a bunch of questions," Lynn says when we're dancing to a slow song.

"I figured if you didn't want to talk to your brother or your friends about it, you wouldn't want to talk to someone you barely know about it."

"You'd be right about that. About not wanting to talk about it, not about barely knowing you. I mean, it's only been a week, but I think we're on our way to being friends." Lynn smiles at me before continuing, "I still appreciate not having to talk about it. I appreciate you letting me commandeer the rest of your evening."

"It's…it's not a big deal." I don't want her to know how much this night is a big deal to me.

Even if she's using me to avoid uncomfortable conversations, she's still spending the evening with me.

"It is. I didn't even think to ask earlier. Is there anyone here you were planning on dancing with? I took over your whole night. That was so rude of me."

"N…no. The only people I, uh, know that are here came with us. And I…I don't mind. I've, uh, enjoyed talking with you."

Gaw. If I was any more awkward, I wouldn't be able to talk. I was doing so well until she brought up who I came to the dance for. There's no way I could tell her she's the only one I've wanted to dance with.

"I've enjoyed spending time with you, too. Sorry it's because you got dragged into my drama. I definitely owe you one. On the upside, since it's Homecoming, it should blow over before Monday."

"What do you mean?" I don't see how Mark slapping her in the middle of the school gym could just blow over in less than two days.

"That a lot of people have after-parties after the dance, and they won't be as parent-approved as the one at Josh's. Odds are good there'll be some other scandal that'll make Mark's scene forgettable."

"Oh, okay. That's good, I guess."

The DJ announces that the next song will be the last one. This evening might be forgettable for everyone else, but it's been one of the best nights of my life. I guess school dances aren't as awful as I thought.

CHAPTER 46
KAYLEE

I can't believe James came to Homecoming and that he brought Whitney as his date.

Okay.

I can believe it.

Him doing something he hates to just try to control me isn't unexpected.

But who does he think he is?

Why does he put more effort into keeping me from getting in a relationship with someone else and making me feel like crap than he does into actually having a relationship with me?

The entire time we were hanging out or whatever, I never saw him at school, and he'd never been to a school dance. Now he thinks I'm with Oliver, and he's there every time I turn around.

It still sucks to think I gave him so much of my time and my heart when I don't mean anything to him. *Ugh!* And then he stood by as Whitney said all that stuff at the dance. He doesn't do any sort of commitment.

Where does he get off on bringing up that Oliver will get bored of dating me?

Not that Oliver even could since we aren't dating. But it's still hateful to keep talking about *when*, not *if*, he gets bored of me. It shows that if James and I ever did have a friendship, it's long gone now.

I continued to dance with Oliver since he didn't seem in a hurry to break away from me. I don't know if that was because he wanted to dance with me or because James thinks we're together, or because Lynn told him to include me.

It could definitely be the Lynn thing, though. It's like as soon as she realized Drew was sitting by himself and not dancing, she made it her mission to include him.

I don't think he sat back down after the first time she asked him to dance. At least I'm assuming she asked him. It'd be impressive if he asked, but highly unlikely.

Hopefully, since they spent the whole night together, it means Drew has a chance. He ought to be on her radar at the very least.

I'm hoping Drew will be fine with only Carter going with him to the after-party. I don't want to have to spend any more time with everyone. I'm exhausted after all the drama with James and the stress of trying to figure out Oliver's motivation.

I don't want to have to go and deal with anything else that could happen. Everything going on with Oliver is confusing, and I need a break from it. Dancing with him felt…well it felt amazing. Oliver is so big and strong, and I almost felt dainty in his arms.

Being held by him made me want to believe he'd protect me. He was my shield from James and his harsh words. Part of me wants to buy into him always protecting me, giving me someone to lean on so I don't have to always stand on my own.

I shake those thoughts away. The last time I thought a guy could save me from a situation, it got me more entrenched in things with James. I don't need to be considering going down that path again.

After the last dance, we all meet by the SUVs.

"Carter, will you and Drew be good on your own for the after-party? I have a headache." I rub my temples.

"Yeah, but do we need to drop Sara off afterwards, or is she going with you?"

I look at Sara.

"I wanted to ask you about that," my sister says. "Callie's staying the night with Lynn after the dance, and I wanted to know if I could go with her?"

"You can't invite yourself over to someone else's house." I start to feel an actual headache coming on.

"Callie invited me." Sara raises her eyebrows.

"It isn't Callie's house." I cover my face with my hands.

"It's cool," Lynn says, walking over to us. "My parents will be fine with it. Did Callie tell you the rule for staying over?"

Drew is still by her side. I look forward to debriefing him on that tomorrow.

"No?" Sara says.

"If you stay the night on a Saturday, my parents expect you to be at services with us in the morning."

"Services? Like church?" I ask.

Callie joins us.

"Yeah. We have to be ready to leave for Bible class at nine."

"Oh, I don't have any church clothes." Sara looks sheepishly down at her dress.

"If you want, you can borrow a shirt, and you can wear the jeans you were wearing earlier." Lynn shrugs.

"I don't need a dress or anything?" Sara asks.

"No. I mean, if you want to wear one you can. I never do." Callie shrugs.

Sara looks at me.

"If you want to go, you can go," I say. "Text me what you want to wear tomorrow, and I'll pack you a bag and drop it off at Lynn's house."

Sara squeals and hugs me.

"Thanks! You're the best!"

"Yeah, yeah." I roll my eyes, but I'm glad Sara and Callie have seemed to hit it off tonight.

The more Sara can be out of the house and away from our mother, the better. Even if I don't love the idea of her being at Lynn's house, especially with their weird rule about church. I hope I'm not letting my sister get initiated into some sort of cult.

"If you don't want to go to the party, I can take you back to your car after we drop everyone else off," Oliver says.

I've been so focused on everything with Sara, that I didn't notice him appear beside me. My body lights up at his proximity and I try to tamp down its reaction. We aren't interested in any boys right now, especially not boys whose mere presence makes my heart speed up.

"Uh, yeah, that'd be great. Thanks," I say when I remember I have to actually respond to Oliver because he can't read my mind. Honestly, it's probably a good thing he doesn't know what I'm thinking right now.

We load up in the SUVs. Callie and Sara chat excitedly with each other the whole way to Josh's house. Callie occasionally says something to Colten. Every time he replies, Sara blushes. Colten is on his phone, so I hope he doesn't notice.

When we get there, Sara asks if I'm sure I don't want to come. I tell her I'm tired and wanna go home and go to bed. With leaving for the math science meet at five this morning, I've had a long day.

"So, how are you doing with the whole James thing?" Oliver asks when we drive away from Josh's house.

"I'm fine. It's not like we're friends. He's my bandmate. If he wants to be a jerk, that's on him. If anything, he's Whitney's problem."

"Oooookaaay. What about all the stuff Whitney said?"

"I care even less what Whitney thinks of me. She doesn't know me and I don't know her. Her opinion is of little consequence to me."

"Okay…" Oliver trails off and drums his fingers on the steering wheel.

"Sorry, I'm not being very conversational." I've been biting out my answers and that's not fair to Oliver. He didn't do anything wrong. "I appreciate your concern. I don't want to let their nonsense take up any more space in my head or my life."

"That makes sense. How did your band start?"

So, I tell him. About teaching myself guitar and Sara learning drums. We were originally going to make our own band. We practiced a few times with the two of us.

James was over at Connor's house one day when we were practicing. Connor is our next-door neighbor. They heard us and came over. James already played guitar and had been trying to start a band of his own. Connor started out as our lead singer but learned to play bass because he doesn't like being up front.

I get so lost in talking about the band and our music that I don't realize how much time has passed. I glance down at the clock—over half an hour has passed. Which is especially suspicious since it only takes ten minutes to drive across our entire town.

"Does Josh live that far away from Lynn?"

"Um, well. I was enjoying listening to you talk." Oliver looks a bit embarrassed.

"It's okay. But I'm tired and do need to get home." Even if time slipped by while I was talking to him, I still want to go home.

"Okay. Do you want me to take you by your house first? That way you can grab the stuff for Sara and drop it off when you get your car?"

"Sure." I give him my address.

I wrack my brain trying to think of something he likes to ask him about, but all I know is he plays football and maybe basketball.

"So, how long have you played football?" I ask.

"Since I was five-ish, I think that's when Top of Texas starts."

"Oh, wow."

"Yeah. Stella, Lynn's mom, had us involved in every sport we could play growing up. Once we were old enough to try something, we did."

"Is football something you want to do long term?" I don't want to talk about Lynn or her mother.

"Not like professionally, no. I think it'd be cool to play college ball, but it's not something I'm set on or anything." Oliver glances at me. "What about you? Is music what you want to do?"

"That's the dream. My backup plan is to get a degree in music production or marketing. That way, I could still work in the industry if I never get a big break."

"Sounds like a solid plan." Oliver pulls into my driveway, which is thankfully empty.

I quickly go in and put an overnight bag together for Sara. When I get back in the car, Oliver starts a new round of questions.

"So, if you play guitar, why don't you play guitar for your band?" he asks. "It seems to me like you could be the lead singer and still play guitar."

"James plays guitar and having two guitarists seemed excessive."

He nods. "That makes sense… Maybe if two guitarists are excessive, then you don't need James?"

"Maybe not, but we need Connor, and they're friends."

"It was just a suggestion." Oliver pulls into Lynn's driveway.

"Thanks for the ride."

"Of course. Have a good night."

"You, too."

It's not until I'm in my car and heading back home that I realize I didn't tell Oliver I was the lead singer now.

How did he already know that?

Maybe he isn't just being nice because Lynn told him to be.

CHAPTER 47
OLIVER

I take my time driving back to the party. I feel on cloud nine after spending so much of the evening with Kaylee. Parties aren't really my thing anyway, too many people and too many expectations to interact with people I don't know as well.

Holding Kaylee in my arms while we danced was like magic. I hope she couldn't hear my heart pounding like it was trying to beat out of my chest. She makes me so nervous but in a good way. Tonight sealed my fate, I have well and truly fallen for this girl.

I'm glad to have the Carter issue cleared up. I don't know what I would've done if Kaylee was taken. I shake that thought away; the important thing is she's single. Now I just need to show her how special she is and hopefully get her to give me a chance. I still haven't quite worked out how to do that.

When I get to the party, everyone seems to be congregated in the living room. I enter in time to watch Kasey slap Jet before storming away. The crowd nearby disperses after whatever drama preceding the slap is over now.

I see Grayson and walk over to him. He looks upset, but I'm not sure I should dive into that right now. I nod to him in greeting.

"You missed the drama," Grayson says, returning my nod. "Kasey wanted to play Spin the Bottle then threw a fit when Jet kissed Lynn."

He's acting nonchalant, but it's clearly a front. He's clearly bothered by Jet and Lynn kissing, even if it was just for a game. But if he wants to pretend otherwise I'd rather not deal with his jealousy.

"Anyway, I guess we should go check on Lynn." Grayson starts across the room. I follow him, already feeling exhausted and ready to go home.

Only the Knights are in the hall when we get over there.

"Eh, it is what it is." Lynn shrugs. "He'll get over it eventually and leave me alone. Until then, I plan to keep ignoring him. If I react, it'll only encourage him."

"Do you want us to do something about Mark?" Grayson asks. I can see the aggression he's barely containing and hope he doesn't decide to do something about Mark on his own.

"Don't worry about it. He isn't worth the time or effort. It's not like his behavior's having a real effect on my life. Now can we please stop talking about mine and Jet's problematic dating lives and go back to the party?"

"Hey!" Jet protests. "I'm not problematic."

"Your Homecoming date slapped you for kissing another girl." Tristan chuckles, appearing behind me. "If that's not problematic, I don't want to know what your definition is. Maybe you and Daniel could start a club." Jessica's glued to Tristan's side.

"Shut up." Jet rolls his eyes.

"Anyway, the pool table is open. Jet and Grayson, are you up for a rematch?" Tristan points his thumb toward the pool table.

"Always. I enjoy kicking your butt." Jet bumps Tristan's shoulder as he walks by.

"Daniel and I play winner." Lynn glances around. "Maybe we should ask Andrew and Carter if they want to play."

"Y'all go set up and I'll find them." I walk off with Lynn following behind me. I mostly want some space from everything. This party already feels stifling.

Andrew comes to play pool with us. Carter declines clearly more interested in the girl he's talking to than hanging out with us. More proof that he and Kaylee aren't even remotely a thing. It's more of a relief than I'd like to admit.

Andrew hasn't played pool before so Lynn teams up with him to teach him. It gives her a severe handicap, but she seems fine with losing. She just cheers Andrew on as he tries to figure out what to do. Daniel and I beat them easily and Lynn challenges Tristan and Jessica to a game.

Jessica is just as bad as Andrew, but some of that seems to be because Tristan is very hands on about teaching her. They seem comfortable being in each other's space and they aren't even together. They've just been hanging out for a few days.

It makes me wish I had that same level of confidence. Tristan seems totally at ease pressed up against Jessica, flirting as he helps her line up a shot. My palms start to sweat just *thinking* about being that close to Kaylee.

We may have spent most of the dance together, but there was a respectable distance between us the whole time. Not that I want to rush things with Kaylee. She's worth waiting for and taking things slowly seems like the best course of action. I don't want to scare her off or bulldoze her. Our earlier interaction with James tells me she's had plenty of being pushed into what other people want.

Feeling like an awkward fifth wheel to the pool game I look around to see where the rest of the Knights have gone. Jet is nowhere in sight, but Daniel and Grayson appear to be having an intense conversation in the corner.

I walk across the room to join them. I have a feeling I know what they're talking about and Daniel looks like he's ready to pull his hair out from dealing with Grayson.

"Why would I be jealous?" Grayson asks as I walk up.

"If you mean, why should you be jealous, you shouldn't be," I say. "There's no reason to be jealous. Lynn's just being friendly with Andrew."

"Very friendly," Grayson mutters.

"Dude, chillax. Lynn isn't looking for another relationship right now. She needs her *friends* supporting her through this nonsense with Mark, not being jealous jerks." Daniel stares Grayson down.

"I'm not being a jerk." Grayson crosses his arms.

"Not to her directly, but right now, anger's coming off you in waves. Be patient. If it's meant to be, it'll work out." I gently pat his arm.

"Is it so wrong that I want her to think of me as more than a friend? Or that I want her to think of me when she's ready to date again? By the way this week's going, she's more likely to think of Jet or Andrew." Grayson throws his hands up in the air.

"Lynn and Jet are just friends. You know that. Kissing during a game doesn't mean anything. You being a jealous idiot because of that kiss will be a bigger deal to Lynn than the kiss was." Daniel leans back against the wall.

"It wasn't only *a* kiss. They full on made-out for seven minutes, and it didn't look like Lynn regretted it." Grayson pouts.

"Lynn is a good kisser—" Grayson turns his anger and jealousy my way. "Hey, don't give me that look." I raise my hands in defense.

"I might not care about her that way anymore, but it doesn't change the facts. From what the girls around school say, so is Jet. It'd stand to reason if they're both good kissers, they'd enjoy kissing each other. That doesn't mean it'll happen again or that it meant anything to either of them." I shrug. I may not get kissing with no feelings being involved, but it's something the other Knights seem to do. I don't see why it's a big deal now.

"But what if it did? What am I going to do if she starts dating my best friend?"

"Deal with it when it's an actual problem," Daniel says. "If they get together, avoid them until you're comfortable with it. Honestly, even if they got together, can you see that lasting very long? They're both so much alike and so hardheaded. It'd take one disagreement about anything, and it'd be over. Just being friends, they're like oil and water. They can only spend so much time together before they get into a fight and need space from each other." Daniel gestures to where Jet has joined the group at the pool table. It looks like he and Lynn are bickering over something.

"And Jet doesn't get along with Xander. I don't think you need to worry about Jet." I look at Grayson with compassion. I get liking someone who doesn't seem to return your feelings.

"But how do you know they won't start dating? Are you both forgetting her relationship with Oliver started from a kiss during a similar party game?" Grayson gestures towards me.

"But that was years ago, and Lynn has kissed multiple guys during party games she never dated. This isn't even the first time they've kissed during a party game," Daniel says.

"But she was practically dating someone else or fresh out of a relationship. This is different. They're both single. The one time before when she kissed one of her best friends in a party game and they were both single, they started dating."

I shake my head. "What happened in junior high is completely different from what just happened. Let this issue about Jet drop. It's in your head."

"Other than us being older, how is it different?" Grayson asks looking irritated.

"For one, we're older and supposed to be more mature. For two, Jet and Oliver are *sooo* not the same person. For three…" Daniel trails off, looking at me.

"For three?" Grayson asks looking between us.

I let out a sigh. So much for hoping Lynn could keep a secret from Daniel. "I should've known she'd tell you no matter what she promised. Sometimes I wish Lynn had a girl best friend. It'd at least save my pride a little."

"Hey, trust me, Lynn treating me like her girl best friend is no walk in the park for me either." Daniel says. "There may be a few tidbits of information you don't want me to know, but there's a whole mountain of information I wish she'd never told me. Some of which seems to be permanently branded on my brain no matter how much I wish I could forget it."

"I'm curious as to what you're talking about, but I think whatever it is would be mentally scarring," I say.

"Sorry to interrupt," Grayson waves his hands between us, "but do either of you want to clue me in on what you're talking about?"

Daniel shrugs and looks at me. I glance up at the ceiling hoping this won't be as embarrassing of a conversation as I think it will be. I look back down at Grayson and take a deep breath.

I blurt out my response as fast as possible like ripping off a band-aid. "Lynn was my first kiss. That makes this different. Can we please talk about something else now?"

Grayson's mouth hangs open. "Wait, what? How can that be true? You had other girlfriends before Lynn. If Lynn was your first kiss, wouldn't I have known that?"

"I dated a couple other girls before Lynn, but never did more than hold hands with them. You didn't know because I didn't tell you." I feel my face heat up and am glad no one else is nearby to hear this conversation. "It's still embarrassing now, knowing I was the last one of us to be kissed. It was much more embarrassing at the time. I didn't want anyone to know."

"But Lynn knew and Daniel knew?"

"I wasn't going to lie to Lynn to save my pride," I start.

"And Lynn tells me everything," Daniel finishes.

"I hoped that everything didn't mean *everything*. But I guess that was wishful thinking on my part," I say.

"If it makes you feel better, she gave significantly less details about you than her other boyfriends." Daniel gives me an encouraging pat on the arm.

I turn to face Daniel fully.

"Mostly that makes me curious and a little afraid."

"I'm not telling you anything Lynn's told me in confidence. Trust me, you don't want to know." Daniel shudders.

"Back to the issue at hand. Neither of you think Lynn kissing Jet's the same as her kissing Oliver because she wasn't Jet's first kiss?" Grayson sounds like he doesn't believe us.

"Basically, yes." I turn back to Grayson. "Tonight wasn't even their first kiss, so it's completely different."

"They've kissed a lot, though, and tonight they made-out," Grayson waves his hands around to make his point..

"Which means they have a history of kissing with it not meaning anything." Daniel rolls his eyes. "The point is, stop comparing tonight to what happened with Oliver. Their kiss meant something to each of them at the time. I guarantee that kiss meant nothing to Jet or Lynn."

"What about Andrew?" Grayson asks. "Lynn danced with him for most of Homecoming."

"In my opinion, that's because Lynn doesn't want to date right now, and Andrew doesn't flirt with her." Daniel rubs his temples.

"She seems to be flirting with him right now." Grayson looks forlornly at the pool table.

"She's being friendly and teaching him to play pool. You don't own her, and you need to calm down." Daniel snaps his fingers in front of Grayson's face, bringing his attention back to us.

"I'm worried Oliver got in her head earlier about being a player and having a thing for jocks. What if she decides she doesn't want to date jocks anymore? Or that she should at least try dating someone who doesn't play sports? Andrew would be her first pick. He isn't like any of her exes."

"I think you're way overthinking this and getting yourself worked up over nothing." Oliver says. "You need to relax and stop worrying about every guy that interacts with Lynn. You know Lynn doesn't put up with overbearing, controlling, or jealous boyfriends. If you're concerned about things working out with Lynn, maybe first work on dialing back your possessiveness. Then when you're no longer getting jealous every time she's around other guys, try dating her. That'd give her time to be ready to date and give your relationship overall a better chance."

"I'd listen to Oliver," Daniel says before Grayson can argue. "Keep in mind he's the only one who's ever had any sort of long-term relationship. As well as the guy who has dated Lynn the longest."

If only my past experience helped me with Kaylee. Everything is different with her and it makes it feel like I've never dated before. Everything is new and I don't know what I'm doing.

"Fine. I'll try to work on it. Can we talk about something else now?" Grayson crosses his arms.

"How about it taking nearly an hour for Oliver to make a ten-minute trip to Lynn's house?" Daniel asks, turning toward me. "Anything you want to tell us about your car ride with the Queen of Punk?"

"There's nothing to tell. Nothing happened."

Daniel cocks his eyebrow with a disbelieving smirk on his face.

"For real, nothing happened. We talked. We did get to know each other a little bit better, though. I think it has potential." I know I'm blushing which isn't helping my argument.

"What about Lynn's concerns about what's his name?" Daniel waves his hand in the air to indicate the guy whose name he's forgotten.

"James showed up at the dance and was a jerk to Kaylee. I'm confident whatever bad blood there is between the two of them is his fault. Lynn didn't scare her off with whatever interrogation took place before the dance, so I'm not worried about Lynn." I shrug.

"If so, then it won't be long before Lynn gives her seal of approval. Then you can start planning the wedding." Grayson lightly punches my shoulder.

"Hardy har har. You're *so* hilarious. And I don't need Lynn's approval to date anyone. She doesn't get to decide who I date." I cross my arms, irritated that Grayson treats me like I'm *so* much younger than him. We're basically the same age.

"Let's pretend that's true." Grayson rolls his eyes.

"Kaylee isn't in our usual group, so who knows, he might not need Lynn's approval. Kaylee doesn't seem to be afraid of Lynn," Daniel says.

"I don't need her approval anyway." I glare at them. "I hate both of you."

"You love us and you know it." Daniel pulls me into an unwilling hug.

I pull away from him and Grayson claps me on the shoulder. "For real, though, I'm happy for you. At least Homecoming went well for one Ridire brother."

"Looks like they're almost done with their game. Let's go play before Grayson can go back to moping." Daniel gestures to the pool table.

"I'm not moping."

"Sure." Daniel walks off.

CHAPTER 48
LYNN

Homecoming this year is definitely one to remember. I still can't believe Mark slapped me. I did *not* see that coming.

It's probably a good thing Xander and Daniel stepped in before I could retaliate. I don't need to be getting into a fight. I know how to protect myself, but I know how much trouble I'd get in for a fight. Especially a fight on school grounds in sight of half a dozen teachers and coaches.

As far as positives for the night, Andrew kept me from the awkward conversations I didn't want to have. I enjoyed spending the evening with him. It was nice to dance and have fun instead of worrying about boys.

Daniel might be right about staying single for a while. I can enjoy hanging out with friends without worrying about my next relationship.

Teaching Andrew to play pool was fun. He's so bad at it. I think he was even worse than Jessica. Which is saying something, because Jessica was trying to do poorly so Tristan would need to help her.

Andrew didn't seem to care that he was terrible or that I'm way better than him. It was refreshing. He just enjoyed the game.

I think I've finally gotten Andrew to relax around me. I'm glad that I seem to intimidate him less.

On the way home from Josh's, we drop Amelia off before heading home. Sara and Callie talk nonstop. It's a nice break to not have to think about anything.

When we get back to the house, my SUV is parked in the driveway and the guys look to have already gone to their respective houses.

Sara and Callie head straight inside, giggling all the way. Xander shakes his head as he follows them into the house.

"What did you think of your first dance?" I ask Andrew.

"It was fun. I'm glad I went."

"I'm glad you enjoyed it. Sorry you got dragged into all of the drama with Mark." I get out of the SUV.

"It's all good. I mean not that him slapping you was good. I mean, it's no big deal. Not that your problems aren't a big deal. Just I, uh, I didn't mind…"

"You still shouldn't have had to deal with it." I walk closer to Andrew as we head to his car.

"Neither should you."

Maybe, but Mark is my ex and therefore my problem.

"Yeah. I guess…" I rock back on my heels.

"Thanks again for inviting me. I enjoyed it."

"I'm glad. I better go inside and check on the girls." I hook a thumb over my shoulder toward the house.

"Oh, uh yeah. Good night."

"Good night." I lean in and hug Andrew.

He freezes, then slowly puts his arms around me and pats my back awkwardly. I let go of him and hope I didn't cross any boundaries.

I mean, friends hug, but maybe he doesn't see us as friends. Or he might not hug his friends. I don't know.

Andrew's face is bright red when I pull away. He looks super uncomfortable.

Great.

The hug was probably too much. I head into the house without looking back at Andrew. I'm worried I made things awkward and would rather not make it worse.

"Point of order," Daniel says when I walk into the living room.

It's our way of saying it's time to talk. When I said "Mau" earlier, Daniel knew I didn't want to talk. It's from a card game our mom taught us. It's called Mau, and one of the rules is you can't talk. If you need or want to say something, you have to say "Point of order," and everyone has to put their cards down. Then you can talk until someone says, "End point of order," and everyone picks their cards back up.

Since he's saying it, he's ending the suspension of the conversation. A conversation I still don't want to have, but I know we need to have.

"I know. Let me check on the girls and make sure they're all settled in first," I say.

"Do you want me to wait here…?"

I cringe a little at the idea of the girls or one of my brothers eavesdropping on any part of this conversation.

"Not really."

"Guest house?"

"How about the castle?"

After the emotional night, I'd like to hold onto a bit of childhood and not feel like I have to have everything figured out right now.

Daniel nods. "Okay. I'll go wait out there for you. I'm giving you twenty minutes before I come back and hunt you down."

"Please do. I'd rather not be sucked into the vortex of giggles." I head upstairs to where Callie and Sara are in my room.

"Can you believe that Carter drank that nasty stuff to avoid kissing me?" Sara is saying as I open the door. She's sitting in the blue chair going through the bag Kaylee dropped off for her.

"Yeah, but your sister is kind of scary," Callie is kneeling down next to my dresser rummaging through the bottom drawer where my pajamas are. Per usual she's just borrowing my clothes instead of bringing any with her. Between that and keeping her toiletries here, she can always stay over at a moment's notice.

Callie looks up to where Sara is sitting. "I could see him not wanting to risk her wrath. Unlike Colten who didn't even give a reason. He drank the stuff twice to avoid kissing me. I mean, it so doesn't have to be a big deal, but even given the option the second time, knowing how gross the drink was, he still chose to take a second drink over kissing me. It's not like I want to kiss him, either, but I don't not want to kiss him bad enough to take two drinks of that vomitastic concoction."

"Colten probably thinks it'd be weird," I reason. "It could mess with your friendship. Choosing to drink from the chalice of shame doesn't have to be a big deal, either. Daniel drank out of it instead of kissing me, and I don't care."

Sara looks over at me. "I thought that was weird though. Y'all are so close. I mean, aren't you curious about what kissing Daniel would be like?"

I shake my head. "Not one bit. Been there, done that, and got the postcard. I don't need or want to go back."

"But that's when y'all were like ten. You aren't curious what it'd be like to kiss him now that he's all grown up?" Callie asks.

"I'm sure it'd still feel like kissing my brother. It was uncomfortable when we were ten. I'm sure it'd only be more so now that we're older. My point is, someone choosing not to kiss you doesn't make you unattractive or gross."

"But you still got to kiss someone. You kissed Austin and made out with Jet." Callie has hearts in her eyes when she says Jet's name.

Great.

"Yeah, how was that? It looked intense. Are you going to date him now that you and Mark are over?" Sara asks.

"It was fine. Jet and I are just friends." I wave a hand dismissively. "That's not changing, especially not over a kiss. Mark and I are over, but that doesn't mean I want to jump into another relationship. Rebound relationships always end up in heartache for all parties involved." I step change into basketball shorts and a T-shirt.

"But you didn't share a peck with Jet; you full on made-out for like seven minutes. How does that not change anything?" Sara asks.

"Because it was still only kissing. No feelings were involved. Besides, Jet doesn't do relationships. I know better than to get involved with him. You should keep that in mind and steer clear of players. They're only going to leave you broken-hearted after stringing you along." I hope to discourage Callie from the crush she seems to have developed on Jet.

"Yeah, but that doesn't happen to you. You beat the players at their own game," Sara says.

"*If* that was even remotely true, that's not why I date and it's not intentional. It hasn't helped me find a lasting relationship. I'm not who you should be looking up to if you're looking for a happily ever after," I say

Oliver's words from earlier bounce around in my head and I start to wonder if he's right. Maybe I'm a player beating players at their own game.

Ugh. Either way, not a conversation to be having with freshmen.

"Anyways, there're spare toothbrushes in the bathroom as well as other toiletries you might need. Callie can show you where everything is. I'm pulling out the trundle bed and y'all can sleep wherever. I'll probably end up crashing in the guest room, so don't worry about me."

They both nod in acknowledgement and I grab a hoodie before heading out back to the castle. I climb up the ladder to find Daniel and Xander waiting for me.

I can't remember the last time Xander was in the castle. He typically says something about castles being for those still pretending to be Knights when I come up here with the guys. Not that we come up here all that often anymore.

"Why does this feel like an intervention?" I pull myself through the opening.

"Because we're intervening in your life when you clearly don't want us to?" Daniel raises an eyebrow and smirks.

"I was going to say guilty conscience, but that works too." Xander shrugs.

"For real though, we're here because we care about you. And I need to know how much effort I should use to try to dissuade Grayson from hurting Mark," Daniel says.

"Mark's an idiot, but I'm over it. I don't want to waste any more time on him or what he might say or do. I'd rather everyone ignore his existence entirely."

"You sure? I mean, the neanderthals act like they'd love to beat him up for you. Especially Grayson." Xander says Grayson's name in a singsong manner.

"I'm sure. I don't want any of y'all getting in trouble over Mark. He isn't worth it. His behavior tonight just proved that to be true. Unless one of you has a secret time machine I don't know about, that I could use to go back and keep me from dating Mark in the first place, there's nothing to do about it." I'm hoping if I ignore Xander's comment about Grayson I won't have to deal with it right now.

Daniel smiles. "No secret time machine over here."

Xander rolls his eyes at both of us. "There's nothing you want to do, but is there anything you want to talk about? I mean, your ex slapped you basically in front of the whole school."

I shrug. "Honestly I don't know what there really is to say. Mark's a jerk who I shouldn't have dated. That's leading to some annoying consequences, but I can handle those."

"But you've been on edge all week," Daniel argues. "And Wednesday—"

"Wednesday was a long day." I interrupt Daniel. I didn't tell Xander about the panic attack and I don't want to tell him now. It'll only make him think there's a reason to be worried about me.

I sigh before continuing. "I'm tired, but I'm fine. Can we please talk about literally anything else?"

"How did girl time go earlier?" Daniel smirks.

I start to relax now that we're moving on from Mark's drama. We talk about anything and everything late into the night.

CHAPTER 49
OLIVER

Sunday lunch at the Kingston's house is always crowded, but today feels as hectic as the holidays. All of Lynn's aunts and uncles were in town for Homecoming as well as her cousins. Sara, Carter, and Andrew were invited to eat with us after services and were highly encouraged by Mama Kingston to join us. Not to mention, most of Lynn's brothers had a friend or two with them.

Thankfully, Lynn talked her mom into letting the teenagers take their food and eat in the guest house instead of trying to cram into the overfull dining room and kitchen.

"Sorry about the chaos." Lynn sits down.

"Is it always like this?" Carter asks.

"Yes and no," Tristan says. "Usually, all of Lynn's aunts and uncles aren't here so it's not always as bad as this."

"Yeah, and that means all the rugrats aren't here, either," Jet adds.

"On the upside, Mama Kingston let us eat out here, which wouldn't normally be allowed." Daniel elbows Jet.

"Dude, will somebody bless the food already? I'm starving." Colten rolls his eyes.

Xander blesses the food and we all dig in. Talk mostly revolves around Friday night's game.

Daniel didn't tell the rest of us anything other than Lynn didn't want to talk about the dance or Mark. I planned on calling her out on it, because if she was fine, she wouldn't care if we talked about the dance. But with Callie and Colten and all of their friends here plus—Sara, Carter, and Andrew—now isn't the time to bring it up.

"Your mom's a good cook, Colten," Sara says.

"Huh?" Colten answers with his mouth full of food. Callie smacks him on the back of the head.

"She's complimenting your mom's cooking, idiot," Callie says. "But that doesn't mean anyone wants to see it in your mouth. Chew, swallow, then try to talk."

"Did I offend your delicate sensibilities?" Colten shoves Callie.

"I'll show you delicate sensibilities." Callie pushes Colten out of his chair and onto the ground where the two of them begin to wrestle.

Lynn lets them go for a few minutes before squirting them with a water gun I didn't even know she had.

"Hey, dipsticks. Stop fighting and eat your food." Lynn sprays them again.

Colten and Callie finally break apart and scuff each other's hair before joining everyone else back at the table.

"Thank you, Sara, for the compliment. I'll be sure to pass it on to my mom. Is there a certain time you need to be home by today?" Lynn acts like she didn't just break up a fistfight with a water gun.

"Um…" Sara looks like she's still recovering from Colten and Callie's brief scuffle. I guess that sort of thing didn't happen at her house. "I have band practice at three at my neighbor's house, so sometime before then."

"Oh, that's right. You're in a garage band with your sister. I can take you home after lunch, or if y'all are still hanging out, I can take you right before you have practice."

"Right before practice works for me. People sometimes watch our practices, if any of y'all want to come." Sara looks at Callie and Colten and their friends.

I'm pretty sure she isn't meaning to extend the invitation to us, but I'm not going to pass up the opportunity to watch Kaylee sing. It's been months since the Fourth of July Celebration and I know her somewhat better now.

"That sounds cool. I'd love to go," I say.

Sara looks surprised as she turns back to our half of the table. She isn't the only one.

"Oh, okay great. What about everyone else?" Sara looks back at the other end of the table.

Colten and Callie and their friends are headed to the practice field to meet up with some other people to play tag football. Daniel, Jet, Grayson, and Lynn all cry off to do their homework.

"I'd love to go," Tristan chimes in. "I'd rather not have to deal with Princess Merida today. I already received a tongue lashing this morning for getting home so late. Sometimes, I swear the perfect little princess forgets she's my neighbor, not my mom."

Merida moved in at the beginning of the summer, and to say she and Tristan butt heads would be a massive understatement. He already spends a lot of time with us, but ever since she moved in next door to him, he avoids his house like the plague. Except, of course, when things swing to the other extreme and he wants to be at home to annoy her.

But today, his disdain for his neighbor is working in my favor. Hopefully, him being with me at band practice will keep it from being too obvious I'm there for Kaylee. Since I know James is going to be there, I'm glad to have a friend there to back me up if I need it.

"Since y'all are staying for band practice, can you take Sara home? I'd appreciate being able to get started on the AP Physics homework right away since it's due tomorrow," Lynn says.

"Of course," Tristan says.

"If you want help on the Physics homework, Drew already finished it yesterday." Carter pats Andrew on the back.

"Oh, um, sure. If he wouldn't mind." Lynn looks a little uncomfortable.

This Mark thing must be messing with her if she's putting her homework off until the last minute.

"I, uh, would love to help." Andrew blushes so hard his cheeks are entering fire-engine territory.

I don't know if he's embarrassed because he doesn't like being the center of attention or if he has a thing for Lynn.

We finish up eating, and Callie and Colten immediately leave to go play football. Sara gets her stuff together, and Carter catches a ride with me to Kaylee's house.

Tristan takes his own car because 'he doesn't want to be in the way if I need alone time with Kaylee after band practice.' I think he's being ridiculous, but I know any protest on my part that Kaylee doesn't see me like that will fall on deaf ears.

Kaylee's house is only a five-minute drive away, but it feels longer. Carter and Sara seem to be interrogating me the whole way there about school, my interests, my taste in music. Sara starts to ask about my family as I park in front of her house.

I'm thankful for the reprieve from questioning and glad I didn't have to answer any questions about my family.

My father's a successful accountant and my mother's a high-powered lawyer. I'd rather not talk about them prioritizing work over me. I'm not sure how long it'd take them to notice if Grayson and I didn't come home. But I know from a few times of crashing at Lynn's, it'd take being gone for more than a couple of nights.

I shake my head to clear any thoughts of my parents as I get out of the car.

"I'm going to head up to my room to change for practice," Sara says to Kaylee as they pass each other in the doorway of their house.

Kaylee stops in her tracks on her porch when she locks eyes with me.

"Uh, what're you doing here?" she asks.

She's wearing an electric blue fitted tank top, a leather skirt, and combat boots. Something about the skirt makes her legs look like they go on forever. She's even more breathtaking today than she was all dolled up for the dance yesterday.

"Sara invited us to come watch band practice," Tristan says before I can get my head together enough to have a reply.

I'm glad he saved me from making a fool of myself as I can't seem to take my eyes off Kaylee.

"Oh, okay. Cool." Kaylee starts walking. "Let's go ahead and head next door. Sara can catch up when she's ready."

"I'll wait and walk over with her." Carter sits on the porch.

We follow Kaylee through a gate that leads into the backyard of the neighboring house and over to what looks like a giant shed. When she opens the door, I'm surprised at what I find. It looks like a small recording studio with a sound booth and rehearsal space.

I sort of assumed they practiced in the garage or something. I was not expecting this. I get so distracted looking at the space, I don't notice what—or more accurately, *who*—is in the middle of the space.

James is standing there with some girl wrapped around him. They're in the middle of what appears to be an intense make-out session, and they don't even notice when we walk in.

James is a real piece of work. I can't believe he gave Kaylee crap about going to a dance with someone when he went and is now making out with some other girl the next day.

"Hey, jackwagon, it's time for practice. Stop sucking face with your groupie so we can get started," a guy, who I assume is Connor, says from behind us.

James and the girl separate at Connor's words. I recognize the girl as Nicole from the dance team.

She's tall and curvy. She has brown hair, which is messed up right now, brown eyes, and chocolate-brown skin. She's wearing a tube top and one of the shortest skirts I've ever seen. She has stilettos on, which seem a bit full on if she's here to listen to the band play.

Nicole is pretty mainstream and stays within the status quo. Basically, I'm not sure she could be further from Kaylee in every aspect. If I had to guess, that'd be James's point. I'm starting to think coming to band practice was a bad idea.

CHAPTER 50
KAYLEE

I can't believe Sara brought Oliver and Tristan with her to band practice. That would've been embarrassing and uncomfortable on a normal day, but after dancing all night with Oliver and talking to him for so long in the car after the dance, I'm feeling all kinds of awkward.

It gets better, because of course, today of all days, James has one of his groupies here, and she seems to be having a hard time getting entirely separated from James as she tries to fix her top and skirt. I'm not sure why she bothers. There's barely enough material there to cover the main bits, no matter how much she tugs on it.

She does seem embarrassed, which is more than I can say for a lot of the girls James usually brings to practice since we broke up.

"Oh, Oliver and Tristan, hi. I wasn't expecting to see you here." Nicole finally manages to fully disengage from James as she walks over to us.

I'm between her and the guys, but she doesn't even bother to acknowledge me. I guess she was only embarrassed because the Knights caught her making out with James. So much for hoping she had some decency.

"Yeah, we're here with Kaylee. Once I found out she was the lead singer in a band, I had to come see her rock out." Oliver smiles at me.

He makes eye contact with Nicole briefly before his gaze comes back to me. I'm not sure if he's trying to sell it to James that last night was a date, or what's going through his head. Either way, I have to give him credit for not even glancing down at the girl and all the skin she has on display.

Tristan, on the other hand, seems to be devouring her with his eyes.

"I'm surprised to see you here, Nicole. I thought you were dating Mackie." Tristan continues to check her out.

"I go out with Mackie from time to time, but not exclusively." Nicole eyes Tristan up and down like we didn't just walk in on her making-out with James.

I guess more power to her owning who she wants to be, but could she be that person somewhere else?

"What are they doing here?" James looks Oliver and Tristan over. "We don't do open rehearsals."

Before I can say or do anything, Connor walks over to James and grabs his arm, dragging him over to the back corner of the rehearsal space. I can't hear exactly what they're saying, but it's clear by his tone that Connor isn't happy with James's antics.

I'm not sure why Connor seems to have a problem now. He's never said anything before when James brings his never-ending line of groupies to practice. Either way, I have bigger problems than puzzling out Connor's motives. I turn back around to face Oliver and notice Nicole sitting on the couch with Tristan. More like Tristan's sitting on the couch and Nicole's about halfway on his lap.

"If you'd rather us not be here, we can leave. Sara invited us and it sounded fun. We could probably get Nicole to leave, too, so she wouldn't bother you." Oliver looks all kinds of uncomfortable.

I guess he doesn't do drama, or maybe he has an issue with PDA, who knows.

"Um, no, it's fine. If you want to stay, you can. I get it if you want to leave after that display and everything with James yesterday. I'm pretty sure he's gearing up to be worse today." I'm not sure how to act around Oliver right now. My body remembers all too well what it felt like being held by him as we danced and it's messing with my head.

"I'd like to stay and listen to you sing, if that's all right." Oliver smiles hesitantly.

"Yeah, that sounds okay." I chew on my bottom lip.

"I know you don't need my help with James, but maybe me being here could be a buffer for you from his bad behavior...?" Oliver suggests. His body sways closer to me.

"I don't want to talk about James." I may not be sure of what's going on with Oliver, but I know I don't want to waste anymore time or headspace on James.

"Okay. Do you, um, have plans after band practice?" Oliver asks

If I'm not mistaken, it looks like he's blushing. Does that mean he's asking me out?

Do I want him to ask me out? I don't know.

I mean, I don't need him to protect me from James, but that doesn't mean I can't spend time with him. Plus, it might help me get information to help Drew win over Lynn. Yeah, because that's the only reason I want to spend more time with him.

"Uh, it's cool if you do. I was just curious." Oliver shifts his weight from foot to foot.

Crap.

I forgot to respond.

"Um, no. I mean, no plans. Sorry, I kind of zoned out there for a minute."

"It's fine. Would you want to go get something to eat afterwards, then?"

"Sure." I'm entirely unsure of what to do.

I'm not confident this is a date or that I'd want it to be. Thankfully, Sara and Carter walk in before an awkward silence can descend between Oliver and me.

Sara takes a quick glance around the room before loudly saying, "So, are we having band practice or what?"

Connor shoots James a look before walking over to where his bass is.

"Y'all are welcome to sit on the couches or whatever while we practice." Connor starts the bass line of one of our original songs before anyone can respond.

Sara gets set up behind the drums, and I walk over to my mic. The second time Connor repeats the bass line, we join in with him.

During the first couple of songs, I feel hyperaware of Oliver being here and watching me sing, especially since James seems intent on standing closer to me than usual and way closer than necessary. Slowly, I get more focused on our music and practice and block out everything else, getting lost in the music. So much so, I don't realize, until Connor calls an end to rehearsal, that at some point Nicole and Tristan left.

Carter is sitting on the couch, playing on his phone, but Oliver's looking at me. The way he's looking at me, I get the feeling he hasn't taken his eyes off of me this whole time, and I'm not sure how I feel about that.

What does he think of our band and music?

Lynn apparently liking heavy metal doesn't mean he does. Not to mention, James has been all up in my space for the last couple of hours.

Wait.

Why am I worrying about this? I'm befriending him to help Drew. It doesn't matter what he thinks about the band or James's behavior. I'm not interested in a relationship with him, so it doesn't matter if he's interested in one with me.

I shake off my weird thoughts and walk over to the couch, ignoring James entirely. Instead of facing Oliver directly, I go to Carter and snatch his phone out of his hand.

"Hey, dipstick. Practice is over."

"What? I can't hear you. I think I'm deaf." Carter cups his hand around his ear.

"No one made you be here. If you don't want to hear us rehearse, don't come."

"But then, how could I tease you about them?" Carter gets up and heads outside after a nod in Connor's direction.

Thankfully, Connor seems to have distracted James with something, so he isn't dogging my steps and being a bigger pain in the rear than he already has been.

"Here's an idea: you could not." I follow Carter out the door.

I see Sara and Oliver behind us, but I don't want to deal with anything right now, not with James present.

"Where's the fun in that?" Carter grabs his phone back from me and we both start laughing.

My laughter abruptly stops when I realize Mary's car is in the driveway. She's home and would've seen Oliver's SUV.

Great.

I can't leave Sara home alone with Mary, especially if she's been on a bender. I don't want her in the house at all.

"Hey, Oliver, would it be okay if Sara came to eat with us?"

"Uh—" Oliver starts and blushes before Sara cuts him off.

"I'm so not crashing your date. I'll be fine at home. I'm not a baby." Sara puts her hands on her hips.

"No one said it's a date. And I know you aren't a baby, but you know this isn't about you." I shoot her a look.

I don't need her arguing with me about this and letting Oliver in on more of my sucky life. She glares back at me, clearly deciding this is a hill she's willing to die on.

"It's cool if Sara comes," Oliver says, interrupting our standoff. "Carter, you're welcome to come, too. We can all go to Luigi's."

Luigi's Pizza Palace is the pizza place in town that has a built-in arcade.

"Sweet. I'm in," Carter says before Sara or I can argue.

We ride in one vehicle, after Carter's insistence that it's better for the environment. I'm not sure when he became such an eco-warrior, but I'm assuming it was in the last five minutes. When we get to Luigi's, Oliver drops us off at the front before going to park his car.

"You wanna tell me why you're afraid of going on a date with Oliver?" Carter asks as soon as the guy in question has pulled away from the curb.

"I'm not afraid of going on a date with Oliver. I don't want Sara alone with Mary, especially after she's been gone for so long." I'm not afraid of a date with Oliver.

If that was even what he wanted. He didn't say it was and seemed to have no problem with Sara and Carter tagging along. Maybe Carter's blowing things out of proportion just to rile me up.

"Oh, so you have no problem with Drew picking Sara and me up to go play video games at his house until curfew?" Carter challenges.

"Of course, I wouldn't have a problem with it, but Oliver's expecting you to be here. It'd be rude to bail." I'm not as confident as I'd like to be at the prospect of spending one-on-one time with Oliver.

"I'm pretty sure Oliver would see us bailing as a miracle, not a breach in etiquette," Carter says.

"Okay, but Drew is hanging out with Lynn. You can't drag him away from that to play video games with you and Sara." I try to come up with a reason they need to stay that doesn't count as me chickening out.

"And I wouldn't, but he texted me when they finished studying and he was headed home, which was a while ago. I'm only pulling him away from being at home alone." Carter takes away my last defense.

I open my mouth to say something, but before I can, Carter cuts me off.

"Drew's already here to pick us up. Unless I should tell him to come in because you're still hung up on James hurting you?"

I know he's baiting me, but I can't do anything about it.

"I'm fine. Go play video games, and I'll text you when it's safe to bring Sara back to the house."

Sara rolls her eyes at my last statement. Carter walks to the parking lot with Sara, leaving me alone to explain to Oliver where they went.

Yippee.

CHAPTER 51
ANDREW

Andrew

$y=x^{2/3}-\sqrt{1-x^2}$

$y=x^{2/3}+\sqrt{1-x^2}$

Studying with Lynn, Daniel, and Xander was nice. They're all smart and clearly care about school. They goofed around while we worked but still managed to stay focused. We got a lot done. It's nice to study with other people. Carter and Kaylee aren't in many of the classes I have, and neither of them are big on studying. In the past when we've 'studied' together, there was always more video-game-playing than studying.

Lynn said she mixed her homework up and already finished her Physics homework, so we finished our stuff for AP Government instead, that isn't due until next Friday.

Being around only the three of them is way less intimidating, and I feel like I get to see yet another side to Lynn.

When I pack up to leave, I shoot Carter a text. He texts back, asking for me to stop by Luigi's to pick him and Sara up.

I park and text him that I'm there. I contemplate texting Lynn telling her I enjoyed hanging out at her house. I'm still staring at my phone weighing my options when Carter and Sara climb into my car.

"I'm all for this plan to get Kaylee and Oliver together, thus keeping her away from James for good. But I was promised pizza and we're driving away from pizza," Sara says, shutting her car door.

Carter twists around in his seat to face Sara. "I'll get you pizza from Pizza Hut, Cornlet." Carter scruffs the top of Sara's hair

"Ew. Pizza Hut is gross, and don't call me that." Sara swats his hand away.

"All pizza is gross. Would you rather I call you baby corn?" Carter turns around and sits properly in his seat.

"That's weird that you'd refer to me as a baby while being so immature." Sara crosses her arms.

They continue to bicker as I drive aimlessly around town waiting for them to figure out where they want to eat. Carter is basically like Kaylee's unofficial brother. He fights with Kaylee and Sara, and he does things to rile them up. It feels like all they do is fight with each other, but they're super close. Even though I've been friends with Carter and Kaylee since junior high, sometimes I still feel like an outsider.

They grew up together and have known each other their entire lives. They're both band nerds. They aren't part of the popular crowd, but they're well known and outgoing. They're so at ease with where they are in the social hierarchy and with who they are as people.

Most people only recognize me as their friend and don't even know my name. It has never bothered me because I don't like talking to new people. Maybe it'd be nice to make some other friends, though. Being friends with Lynn would be a good start, and she could help me be more sociable and outgoing.

After we eat dinner, we play video games and talk about nothing in particular. Out of nowhere, Sara pauses the game without saying anything. I glance over at her, and she's pointedly not looking at either of us.

"There's something I need to tell you." Sara sets her controller down.

We give her our full attention and she finally looks up at us.

"Lynn slept with Daniel last night."

"What?" Carter sprays soda from his mouth.

I can barely form thoughts, much less speak sentences.

"I mean not like *slept with,* slept with. I mean maybe, but I don't know that for sure."

"How about we start from the beginning of whatever you saw or overheard?" Carter grabs a handful of napkins to clean up his mess.

"Lynn gave Callie and me her room and said she was going to sleep in the guest room. Then Sunday morning, I guess Lynn overslept, and Callie went to go get her and I went with her. Lynn wasn't in the guest room." Sara plays with a loose thread in her jeans.

"Callie said she might be in the castle, which is the treehouse in their backyard. So we climbed up to check and Lynn was up there. She was still asleep and cuddled up with Daniel. They were sharing a blanket and everything."

I'm not sure how to feel. It's not like it's any of my business what Lynn does or who she does it with. Her and Daniel are super close, I just didn't think they were close like that.

Sara's eyes are alight with excitement as she continues, "Callie woke them up, saying they needed to get a move on so they wouldn't be late for Bible class. I guess both of their phones died so their alarms didn't go off. They came with us back to the house to get ready, and Callie acted like it wasn't a big deal.

"But I mean, they were out there all night together and alone. I felt like you should know because I don't want you getting hurt, Drew." Sara looks like she feels bad for me but might be more concerned about what she got to witness than my feelings.

"Hold on. I have a few questions." Carter holds up a hand.

I'm still processing and not sure what to think yet.

"First, did Lynn and Daniel act guilty or like they'd been caught doing something they weren't supposed to?"

"No. Lynn seemed a little irritated about being late for church, but that's it." Sara looks confused as to why that would matter.

"Okay, what were they wearing?"

Sara scratches the back of her head.

"Um, Lynn wore basketball shorts and a hoodie, and Daniel wore jeans and a T-shirt."

Carter continues his questioning. "So, Lynn and Daniel, who are very involved in church, didn't act like they'd done anything wrong and they were both entirely clothed?"

"I mean yes, but they were sleeping together." Sara waves her hands around to make her point.

"They've been friends their entire lives. Daniel would rather drink from the chalice of shame than kiss Lynn." Carter points out. "I think you're turning nothing into a big deal. Her mom won't let her go places where there might be drinking. I don't think she'd let Lynn have an illicit affair with her neighbor in her house."

"But they weren't technically in the house," Sara argues.

Carter raises one eyebrow in a 'really?' gesture. Sara looks disappointed, like Carter has ruined the gossip she thought she had.

"What do you think, Drew?" she asks.

I clear my throat. "I think you're overreacting. I'm sure it isn't anything to worry about. Besides, Lynn and I are just friends and barely that. Who she wants to spend her time with is her business. But from studying with Lynn, Daniel, and Xander earlier, I'd guess Lynn sees Daniel as more of a brother. She seems to treat Daniel and Xander the same."

"I mean, if we're going to worry about one of the Knights being a problem, I'd be more worried about Jet. Did you see them when they came out of that closet?" Carter fans himself.

And here I thought Carter might be trying to make me feel better.

Sara and Carter continue their conversation about the night before like I'm not even here.

I stay quiet as I reflect back on the game of Spin the Bottle from last night. I was so nervous because Carter made me participate, but I didn't want my first kiss to be with some random girl for a game. I'm nervous enough about kissing as it is.

But then, watching Lynn kiss that freshman had made me more nervous. He's a freshman and yet, he looked like he knew more about kissing than I do.

Then there was the bottle flip and Seven Minutes in Heaven.

I think those might have been the longest seven minutes of my life. I had tried to not stare at the closed door and be totally obvious, but I know I kept glancing at it and checking the time on my phone.

I refused to look at Carter even though I could feel his eyes boring into the side of my head. Then when the torturous waiting was finally over, Kasey jerked the door open, and it felt like my heart dropped out of my chest.

Jet and Lynn were all over each other. I didn't even know kissing could be that involved. I felt like an inexperienced little kid.

Playing pool together was nice. I might not have known what I was doing, but Lynn didn't make me feel stupid and seemed to enjoy teaching me.

I definitely didn't mind her being in my space as she showed me how to line up a shot.

It wasn't conducive to learning because her closeness and strawberry scent were seriously distracting.

So…friends. I could figure out how to be friends, if it meant being closer to Lynn. And being friends with Lynn would mean getting used to seeing her up close with other guys. I needed to accept that.

I realize that while I was zoned out, Carter and Sara have been arguing over whether Lynn and Jet are a thing or not.

"Guys, drop it. It doesn't matter, anyway." I wave my hands between the two of them.

"Why not?" Carter looks at me.

"Because if we're being realistic, Lynn is only ever going to see me as a friend. If she doesn't start dating Jet, it'll be someone else. If I'm going to be friends with her, I need to accept that and get used to it."

"So, have you moved on from your crush after seeing her and Jet all over each other?" Sara leans toward me.

"More like I know it isn't going to turn into anything, but I'm enjoying being friends with Lynn. But who knows—maybe after being friends with her for long enough, I'll move on from my hopeless crush." I shrug.

Carter looks like he wants to say something. But he takes a long look at my face before unpausing the game and letting the conversation drop.

After we tire of the game we've been playing, I ask Carter how he convinced Kaylee to go on a date with Oliver. Especially since Kaylee gets super protective of Sara whenever Mary's home and awake. Having her out of sight isn't something she normally likes, even if she's only with Carter and me.

"Basically, you dared her into going on a date and then made me be your getaway driver?" I say.

"Pretty much. But I mean, it worked." Carter shrugs.

"Yeah, but I'm sure it made her uncomfortable."

"Anyone with eyes can see that Oliver is interested in her. He stayed through the crap James pulled at the dance and at band practice today. He danced all night with Kaylee for Homecoming, and the next day asked her on a date. She needed to get over herself and give him a chance."

"But you forced her out of her comfort zone. And regardless of what she says, I don't think she's over James. She's got to be upset that he'd bring another girl to a dance when he's never gone to one before. Then he had that other girl at band practice, and Oliver and Tristan were there to witness it." I set my controller down.

"She needed the push out of her comfort zone. It'll be good for her and help her to put James behind her and out of her head."

"Yeah, but Andrew has a point that might've been too much too fast. Not to mention, we ditched her and didn't give her an option," Sara chimes in.

"I can't go back and change what has already been done. How about we skip the next part of this conversation and y'all tell me what you want me to do?" Carter rolls his eyes at us.

"What if we got her a baking care-package thing?" Sara bounces with excitement.

"Like get all the supplies and stuff for her to make fancy cupcakes?" Carter asks.

"Exactly. We could go to United and get all the stuff she'd need to make several types of cupcakes with varying decorations." Excitement builds in Sara as she speaks.

"Yeah Kaylee is a stress baker," I say. "Even if everything goes perfectly with Oliver, it's still new. Plus, there's all the junk with James. I'm sure Kaylee would love the opportunity to bake her anxieties away, especially after the weekend she's had."

"Drew's on my side. That settles it. Let's go shopping!" Sara jumps up and gets ready to leave.

After shopping and taking Sara home, I drive Carter to his apartment.

"So…" Carter starts.

"So what?" I want him to hurry up and get to the point.

"Are you okay with Lynn dating other guys and potentially having a front-row seat to it?"

"I think so." I shrug. "It might not exactly be fun, but I'll have to get used to it if I want to be friends with her. Unlike you and Kaylee, I've never pretended I had a chance with Lynn. I know she's way out of my league and has too many good-looking, athletic, outgoing guys vying for her attention for her to even think about noticing me. I'm enjoying getting to know her better and becoming her friend, but I don't see anything more than friendship growing between us."

Even if my heart hasn't fully gotten that message, my brain knows that's the truth.

"So, you want to become her friend in order to get over her?"

"No. I need to get over her because it's not ever going to work between us." I pause hoping splitting up what I'm saying will get Carter to see that the two things don't have to be connected. "On a separate unrelated topic, we're becoming friends, and I'm enjoying her friendship. It might be nice to have friends aside from you and Kaylee. I'd appreciate you and Kaylee dropping this crusade to get me with Lynn."

"If that's what you want…?" Carter looks unsure.

"It's what I want."

"All right, I'll try to get Kaylee to back off." Carter gets out of my car and heads up to his apartment.

CHAPTER 52
OLIVER

Okay, so it isn't a *date*, but Kaylee did agree to dinner. Even if she did invite her little sister and another guy to go with us.

But maybe that was more about not wanting to leave her sister at home alone. Which is kind of weird since she's fourteen, but maybe Kaylee is protective of Sara.

Maybe this is better, anyway. It's a smaller group than yesterday, but not one-on-one. It'll give us a chance to get to know each other better without any pressure.

Yeah, this is a good thing. I get out of the SUV and head inside Luigi's. Kaylee's hair is easy to find, and I spot the booth she's in quickly. When I get there, she's sitting by herself. I slide into the other side of the booth, not sure where the others are or where I'm supposed to sit.

"Uh, hey." I don't know what else to say.

"Hey, Carter and Sara bailed to go play video games at Drew's house. So, it's just the two of us, if that's okay." Kaylee toys with a napkin.

"Um, yeah, that's great. I mean, that's cool. I'm sorry they bailed on you?" *Ugh, why am I so awkward?*

Kaylee smiles. "It's all good. I'm pretty sure you weren't planning on inviting them in the first place."

"Not exactly, no," I say honestly.

Thankfully before I can get more awkward the waitress shows up to take our order. After the waitress leaves, an awkward silence descends.

"You were great earlier, by the way. It was cool to get to watch you be in your element," I finally say to break the ice.

"Oh, uh, thanks. We don't usually have people watch our practices."

"Oh, Sara didn't act like it was a big deal when she invited everyone at lunch." I shrug.

"She invited everyone to come watch us practice?" Kaylee's eyes get as big as saucers.

"Uh, yeah. I assumed she told you."

"Yeah, not so much, but it's all good." Kaylee looks stiff and like it's not all good.

"It was cool to see you up close and when you were focused on the music and not on performing." Maybe talking about the band will get her to relax.

She nods. "Yeah, maybe you should come to a show so you can see me perform. I mean, watch us perform."

"Uh…" I'm not sure if I should tell her I already saw her perform.

I feel awkward about it now, but won't it be weirder if she finds out later? I should tell her.

Is it hot in here? I'm starting to feel hot.

"Never mind…" She shakes her head. "That was a stupid idea. Don't feel like you need to come see a show or anything. I'm sorry if I made you uncomfortable by assuming it was something you wanted to do."

"Oh, um, no that's not. I mean, I'd love to. Um, what I'm trying to say is, I've already seen you perform." *Did I just say that?*

"You have? When?" Kaylee leans forward.

"Um…" I can feel my face heating up. "At the Fourth of July Celebration this past summer. Back when you had purple hair."

"Oh, really? What did you think?"

"I thought your music was great. Y'all did fantastic covers, and I was impressed by your originals. I love the vocals in 'Reaper' and the lyrics for 'Remains.' Your stage presence is so magnetic. You're magic on stage and command everyone's attention. Your passion for your music shows through your voice and performance. Not to mention, you did a lot of covers of my favorite band."

Oh, my goodness.

I can't believe I said all that.

Based on the size of Kaylee's eyes, my word vomit is freaking her out.

"Oh, um…" Kaylee tucks her hair behind her ear and looks down at the table.

With her hair all the way out of her face, I can now see that her cheeks are pink like she's embarrassed. What does she have to be embarrassed about? Unless she's embarrassed for me because I'm that uncool.

"Thank you," she finally says. "I've, um, never had anyone compliment me like that before. You remember the song names from one show?"

"Uh, not exactly." I shift in my seat. "I've been kind of listening to y'all's music on YouTube since the summer."

I'm not sure if that makes it better or if it makes me more of a stalker.

"So, you're like a legit fan of Outnumber by Hysteria?" Kaylee glances around not looking directly at me. I'm worried she's getting ready to bolt away from me.

"Yeah. Y'all put out good music."

"That's cool. I've never talked to anyone that was a fan of our music. Not that there are many, and most of those are James's groupies." Kaylee fiddles with her napkin.

"If I'm anyone's groupie, it'd be yours."

Oh crap.

Did I let those words leave my mouth? I need a gag.

"I'm flattered. I've never had a groupie before. Although it sounds like you're more a fan of the music than a groupie. Considering my general opinion on groupies, that's a good thing." Kaylee looks away seemingly lost in her own thoughts.

Then she shakes her head and refocuses on me. "While on the topic of groupies, I'm sorry for the whole thing with Nicole and James's behavior at rehearsal. I'd like to say that doesn't usually happen, but James is a jerk, and nothing that happened today was out of the ordinary."

"Why would you need to apologize? James is the one being a prick and trying to use meaningless hookups to prove to you he doesn't care about you. Even if it broadcasts how the opposite is true. He doesn't deserve to be around you, much less deserve you apologizing for his bad behavior." I put my hand over her to cover her fidgeting. Hopefully, it's comforting and not overstepping her boundaries.

"I don't know. I didn't know how you'd feel about him getting all in my space." Kaylee stops fidgeting and keeps her hand in mine.

"I didn't exactly enjoy watching him invade your personal space after trying to make you feel like crap, but you've made it pretty clear you can handle yourself." I rub my thumb soothingly over her hand.

"What is going on here?" Kaylee gestures between us and completely throwing me off guard.

"What…what do you mean?"

"I mean, you know all about my band and music, you keep complimenting me, you sound ready to defend me from James but at the same time, you also know that I don't need your help. Like, are you a fan of the band turned friend?"

"You want the honest truth?" I'm not sure I can tell her that without combusting.

"Yes, even if you don't think I can handle it, especially then."

"I'm pretty sure you can handle anything. The complete truth is I saw you perform in July, and you captured my attention. I like your music and have been listening to it. This past week, I've started to get to know you outside of your stage persona. I may not know you well, but what I know I like. I'm okay with being a fan turned friend, if that's what you want."

"What do you want?" Kaylee uses her free hand to play with the ends of her hair.

"I want to keep hanging out with you and continue to get to know you better."

"So, you want to become better friends?"

I take a deep breath and will my nerve to hold. I've dug this hole this far; I may as well see if the effort was worth it.

"If that's what you want, that's fine. But I'd like to take you on a date." I take her hand fully in mine and link our fingers together.

"Another one? I thought this was a date?"

"I wasn't sure about that since you invited your sister and Carter along."

"It feels pretty date-like to me." Kaylee smiles flirtatiously.

"It feels pretty date-like to me, too."

Our food arrives and we spend the rest of the evening talking about less serious topics as we get to know each other better. After we finish eating, we spend a while playing games in the arcade together.

It's relaxing and fun. I enjoy getting to spend time with Kaylee and still feel a little giddy that this is a date. I like having her in my space and getting to be in her space.

When we get back to Kaylee's house, I put the SUV in park. I unbuckle my seatbelt.

"Um, what are you doing?" Kaylee asks.

"Walking you to your door...?"

Has no other guy she has ever gone out with walked her to her door before saying good night?

"Oh, um, that's not necessary. I'm good on my own. We can say goodbye here."

"But—" Before I can get another word of my protest out, Kaylee kisses me.

She *kisses* me.

My brain shorts out for a moment and I sit there with Kaylee's mouth on mine.

Then I get a hold of myself and kiss her back. I cup her cheek with my hand, and her hand settles on my chest. I slowly move my mouth over hers. Kaylee kisses me back softly and sweetly, and I get lost in her kiss.

Then suddenly, Kaylee pulls away.

"I had a good time. Good night, Oliver." Kaylee slips out of the SUV and up into her house.

I'm too stunned by her kiss to do anything other than watch her go.

I don't know how long I sit there staring at the door Kaylee disappeared through before headlights shine behind me. I see Sara get out of Andrew's car and go into her house, carrying several grocery bags.

I drive home full of hope and call Tristan to let him know how things went. Tristan picks up on the first ring.

"Did you get my text?"

"No, I didn't. I just left Kaylee's house and haven't looked at my phone. Why?"

"Because Nicole told me something you need to know."

CHAPTER 53
KAYLEE

I went on a date with a jock. Not just any jock—but one of the Knights, the most popular group at our school. More surprisingly, I enjoyed it.

Oliver has a similar taste in music, he's laid-back, he has a self-deprecating sense of humor, and he's fairly cute. Plus, he listened to what I said.

He paid real attention and seemed interested in anything and everything I had to say. He kept his eyes on me for the entirety of our date.

Not in a creepy way, but like, his eyes didn't wander. Even with our waitress flirting her butt off and trying to get her cleavage as close to Oliver's face as possible.

He was polite to her, but that was it. Honestly, it seemed like he was so focused on me he didn't see her or her advances.

He's so the opposite of James that it makes my head spin. It feels too good to be true.

Sara walks in the door a few minutes after me, and that's when I realize I've been pacing the kitchen and cleaning it while I try to dissect the evening's event.

She has her arms full of grocery bags that she sets on the dining room table. Sara normally only goes to the store to buy junk food, so the fact that she has bags and bags of stuff makes me curious as to what's going on.

"What's all this?" I gesture to the mountain of bags.

"A peace offering from me and the boys. I know you weren't happy with me inviting the guys to band practice, or Carter and me abandoning you at the restaurant. So, to make amends, we bought you this."

It's bags of baking supplies.

More specifically, the supplies to make mine, Sara, Carter, and Drew's favorite cupcakes. Maple bacon brown sugar, pink lemonade, white chocolate truffle, and hot cocoa respectively.

They got me the items for the chocolate chip cookie cupcake recipe I've been wanting to try. This is exactly what I need, to lose myself in baking until my anxiety dissipates. I pull Sara into a bone-crushing hug.

"Thank you. I didn't even know I needed this."

"We knew. You always take care of me and anticipate my needs. I wanted to be able to do that for you for once. Especially since it's partially my fault you're anxious. I shouldn't have pushed Oliver on you."

"Don't worry about it. Tonight wasn't what I'd expected." I let go of her. "Anyway, enough about boys. How about you wash your hands and we can have some sister time baking and staying up too late?"

I'm extra glad Mary's already passed out in her room now. We have the whole house to ourselves, and she won't wake up until after we've left for school tomorrow. I get Sara started on lining baking pans while I get the first batch of batter ready.

As the first batch goes into the oven, I get a text from Oliver.

"What's that smile for?" Sara asks.

I lift my hand to my face to refute her statement or maybe to hide my smile.

"I'm enjoying spending time with my sister." I hope to distract her.

"Uh huh. Are we pretending I didn't hear your phone go off and see your face light up like a Christmas tree when you looked at it?" she asks.

"Yes, we are," I insist as I type out a reply to Oliver's text.

Sara sighs dramatically. "Fine. If you don't want to talk about it, we don't have to. But I'll say I've never seen you look that way when James texts you. Even when things with y'all were good. Oliver seems to like you, and he could be good for you."

After that statement, she thankfully drops the conversation and doesn't bring it back up even though I continue to text Oliver while we bake.

I send Sara to bed when it's time to decorate the cupcakes. On impulse, I snap a picture of one of the cupcakes and send it to Oliver when I finish them.

I realize we've been texting for hours when I finally tell him good night. As I lie down to go to sleep, I relax and enjoy that my anxiety has completely gone away.

The next day, I wake up feeling more rested than I have in a long while. I check my phone and see a *good morning* text from Oliver that makes me smile. Then I look closer at my phone and realize morning band practice started five minutes ago.

Crap.

I jump out of bed and go to wake Sara up. I guess I forgot to set my alarm last night.

"Sara, get up. We're supposed to be at band already."

"I'm up. We might as well take our time. Mr. Gregory will be just as mad if we're late as he'd be if we aren't there at all."

I'm frantically getting my stuff together when her words register and I realize she's right. As long as I'm there in time for Government, it'll be fine.

We can go in through the band hall, and I can take a cupcake to each band director and apologize for missing today.

I get ready at a much slower pace and load the cupcakes up. I set aside a small batch for the boys that I leave at the house where Mary won't find them.

The rest of the cupcakes will smooth over mine and Sara's absence this morning with the rest of the band. At least we're mostly missing watching Friday night's performance so my absence won't have much of an effect on rehearsal.

We get to school with five minutes left in first period. After I put my van in park, I decide to text Oliver back.

Kaylee: Morning. Meet me outside the band hall before second period for something sweet

Without waiting to see if Oliver responds, I hurry into the band hall. Everyone is excited about the cupcakes, which I set on a table. Sara and I head to Mr. Gregory's office to talk to him about our absence. He tells me not to let it happen again and sends us on our way.

I still have about ten cupcakes left over even after the band descended on them. I head out of the band hall and freeze in the hallway when I see Oliver leaning against the wall opposite the band hall doors.

He looks cool and collected, the exact opposite of how I feel. His T-shirt stretches across his muscular chest made more evident by his crossed arms. I remember what it was like to be in his arms at the dance and feel my body flood with heat. *What would it be like to be that close to him without the pretense of a dance?* To be close to him in a warm embrace.

Sara bumps my shoulder as she heads to her class. That knocks me out of my stupor, and I walk across the hall.

"Hi." My voice comes out all breathy and I mentally kick myself.

"Hey. You said you had something for me?"

"Oh yeah. Would you like a cupcake? There's maple bacon brown sugar, pink lemonade, white chocolate truffle, hot cocoa, and chocolate chip cookie." I try to focus on the cupcakes instead of how awkward I'm feeling.

James and I never actually dated, and any other guy I went on a date with was usually a one-off, so I've never had to interact with them at school. This is new territory for me, and I don't know how to act. I don't know what Oliver is expecting.

Does he think we're together now? Does he want to go on another date? I know he said he did, but what if he changed his mind? Does he think we're better off as friends? Are we even friends?

"Mmm, that's delicious." Oliver licks frosting off his lips. Of course he picked the maple bacon.

His groan mixed with watching him devour my favorite cupcake has me thinking back to last night. I wonder what his lips taste like covered in frosting.

When I briefly kissed him in my driveway, I only wanted to distract him from trying to walk me to my door in case Mary was still up.

I wasn't expecting his lips to feel so warm or to feel fluttery when I kissed him. His lips had moved over mine gently, and I didn't want to break the kiss and run inside.

But I did because I knew Sara and the guys were on the way to my house and didn't want them to catch me making out with Oliver.

"You're a great baker." Oliver pulls me back to the present.

"Oh, um, thank you." I can feel myself blushing and wish I could make myself stop.

I don't want Oliver to know how he affects me. If he knows I like him, he might decide to use that against me.

Crap.

I like Oliver. I guess there's no denying it now. I need to keep my distance and keep my heart locked up so there's no repeat of the James nonsense.

"So, uh, can I walk you to class?" he asks.

I look up to see Oliver blushing and not quite looking at me.

Either he's a good actor or maybe he likes me, too.

"Sure. That sounds nice." I stop by my locker before heading to Government.

Oliver asks me a couple of questions about baking, and I talk most of the way to class.

CHAPTER 54
LYNN

Since Daniel stayed the night last night, I'm actually at school early. I hate mornings and getting up, but Daniel has always been an early bird. He has no problem dragging my grumpy butt out of bed like an excited puppy first thing in the morning.

We spend first period working on homework in the library. With all of the Homecoming nonsense last week, I was worried about getting behind, but between studying with Daniel and Xander and working with Andrew, I've managed to stay ahead of everything.

For English today, we have a substitute and are allowed to work on our projects and sit in groups. Without needing to discuss it, Carter, Andrew, Xander, and I push all of our desks together.

I'm glad because I'm still feeling off from this weekend and don't feel up to spending the whole class worried about Mrs. Green thinking I'm not pulling my weight.

"Andrew, sorry again for dragging you into all of my drama this weekend," I say once everyone else is busy working or visiting.

"Oh, uh, it's fine. I mean, what are friends for?" Andrew's cheeks turn a bit pink.

"Friends shouldn't put you in the line of fire. I'm sorry for the stuff Mark said about you." I place my hand on top of his in a hopefully comforting gesture.

"You aren't responsible for what Mark says or does. Could you stop apologizing for him being a jerk?" Xander butts in.

"But he wouldn't have said anything to Andrew if he hadn't been with me." I turn to face Xander.

Xander rolls his eyes.

"Mark is a jerk and is going to continue to be a jerk regardless of what you do. You aren't responsible for any of his behavior or any of the nonsense that comes from his mouth. Most of what comes out of his mouth is a load of bull, anyway."

I'm starting to get irritated with Xander, even if I should've expected him to get over-protective after yesterday. "Can you butt out? I wasn't talking to you."

"Like I said, it's fine." Andrew takes my attention off of my brother. "Xander's right about it not being your fault. Mark chose to be a jerk. And I wanted to dance with you. You didn't do anything wrong." Andrew squeezes my hand before withdrawing his.

"If anything, dancing with you has increased Drew's popularity." Carter nudges Andrew's shoulder with his.

Andrew shoots him a look I can't decipher.

"What? It's true. How many girls have tried to talk to you this morning?" Carter asks.

Andrew's face flushes and he mutters something I can't quite hear as he looks down at his desk.

"Oh, it's *so* not irrelevant. You usually have no one but Kaylee and me seeking your company. Today, you had three different girls in band come talk to you," Carter says emphatically.

"Can we please talk about anything else?" Andrew says without lifting his head up.

"When do y'all want to come over to work on our projects next?" I let the subject drop.

Maybe Xander is right and I need to let all of Mark's behavior go. He's being a jerk, and it's not like he has a reason to keep bothering Andrew.

From what Carter says, it isn't bothering Andrew that I used him as a shield from Mark and that seems to have actually helped him. If being around me has helped Andrew's reputation with the other band kids, then people can't all be thinking like Mark.

I guess that means Xander and Daniel are right that it's all Mark and because he's a jerk. I wish I could go back in time and not date Mark in the first place. He wasn't worth my time when we dated and is worth even less now. With all of Mark's behavior, I'm done caring about his feelings. But I'm still concerned about my friends being caught in any backlash from him.

The bell rings, and I head to Pre-Cal with Xander. Andrew said he needed to talk to Carter about something and followed him toward his next class.

We're almost to Pre-Cal when Mark steps in front of me.

"Lynn, I want to apologize for Saturday. I didn't mean—" Mark starts to say.

"You didn't mean to what?" I interrupt. "You didn't mean to insult me? You didn't mean to pick on my friend? Or you didn't mean to slap me?"

I keep my voice calm even if it gets more forceful with each question. I feel Xander step closer to me and am glad he's here to keep me calm.

"I didn't mean to do any of those things. I got so jealous seeing you dance with all of those guys. I care about you. It's only been a week since I told you I love you. It's hard for me to see you with someone else. I'm so sorry I lost my head and lashed out at you. I want to be with you."

I take a deep breath to keep from going off on Mark the way I want to.

Xander rolls his eyes. "You don't care about her. You only care about you, and you don't like being told you can't have something. Now, can you move out of the way? We have a class to get to."

Mark is clearly taken aback that Xander said anything to him, let alone that he stood up to him.

"This is between me and your sister. Mind your own busi—"

I cut Mark off with a wave of my hand before he could finish.

"Do *not* talk to my brother like that. This stopped being between us a while ago. I'd say it stopped being between us when we broke up and there was no longer an *us*. But I'm sure anyone you asked would agree, it definitely stopped being between us when you slept with Whitney Saturday. So why don't you stop harassing me and go hang around your new girlfriend?"

Mark visibly pales and his eyes go wide. He clearly thought I'd have no idea about him and Whitney.

"Whitney isn't my girlfriend. She doesn't mean anything to me. I was wasted, and she was there and willing," Mark tries to argue.

I roll my eyes. "That makes it worse, but still not my problem."

I walk around Mark. He grabs my arm to try to keep me there.

"If I were you, I'd let go of my arm right now. I'm fairly confident your coaches don't want you assaulting me on campus again."

"I still love you." Mark releases my arm.

I walk away with Xander and don't stop until I make it to my desk in Pre-Cal. Thankfully, Xander lets me walk the whole way in silence.

I can't believe Mark thought he could say all of that horrible stuff to me, slap me, sleep with someone else, and then get me back. I broke up with him in the first place.

Why would all this bad behavior make me want him back?

I'm so glad that Nicole told Tristan about Whitney and Mark Saturday at the after-party. It helped me let go of any lingering guilt over ending things with Mark and helped me to see he was a controlling jerk who lashed out when he didn't get his way.

Even if that led to a conversation that I didn't exactly want to have with Xander and Daniel. With Whitney doing things with Mark that the guys knew I wouldn't have done, it brought into question whether Mark pressured me or tried anything while we were together.

I didn't want to tell them about him pressuring me to do more than kiss, but after Tristan's revelation there wasn't much I could do to get out of the conversation. Thankfully, Oliver and Tristan accepted my dismissal of the topic when I told them I handled Mark on my own.

I asked them not to talk to Jet or Grayson about it. If they asked about anything, point them my way and leave it alone. I'm hoping neither of them connect the dots on their own. They're both already hot heads and mad at Mark over the slap.

The last thing I want is them getting into a fight with Mark, especially on school grounds. I don't want them to get suspended from school or the team because I dated a jerk. After agreeing to not tell Grayson and Jet, Oliver and Tristan got off the phone.

That left me with only Daniel and Xander to face. After all of my avoidance over everything with Mark, I knew they weren't going to let me get away with a quick dismissal of the topic.

I told them about the things Mark said while we were together and how I had to continually stop his hands from wandering where they shouldn't when we kissed. He made me feel uncomfortable and second guess what I was doing or what I was wearing. Mark made it seem like it was my fault he had these expectations I didn't want to meet. It made me feel vulnerable and small. Honestly, thinking and talking about it still makes me feel that way.

I got through telling them everything before I started crying. I'm glad Xander and Daniel know now, and it doesn't feel like a secret weighing me down. It's good to have their support and validation. It made me realize how worried I was about other people agreeing with Mark.

Once I got my emotions back under control, Daniel and Xander were ready to go to war for me. But I don't want a war; I want Mark to leave me alone. Besides, I don't need them to fight my battles for me.

Now with Mark handled, I start thinking about the other reasons I don't want Grayson to know about Mark trying to push my boundaries. For one, to be completely honest, it was awkward to tell Daniel and Xander, and I tell them everything. For another, I've been starting to think Daniel may have been right about Grayson.

There have definitely been a few signs this past week that he might be interested in being more than friends. I'm not sure how I feel about that yet, but I don't want him going caveman on Mark because he has a thing for me.

I like that the guys know I can take care of myself and that they don't get overprotective of me. I'm not sure Grayson would act like he remembers that I can take care of myself if he knew Mark even hinted at wanting to do more than kiss.

After his behavior this weekend, I'm past caring about Mark's feelings. But I do care about Grayson, and picking a fight with Mark is only going to get him hurt by affecting the team.

Oliver walks in with Kaylee to Pre-Cal and sits next to her. I'm glad things seem to be going well for them. I shake away the worries over everything with Mark and try to focus on the positive things of the last couple of weeks: Kaylee and Oliver becoming closer, Andrew and Carter joining our friend group, Xander hanging out more with the Knights.

By lunch, word has spread of the scene Mark caused, and there are rumors about him being benched or suspended from a game or two for slapping me at the Homecoming dance. From what I've heard the coaches are counting that as having a fight on school grounds, since it took place in the school gym.

I haven't heard anything about anyone thinking I'm dating Andrew, so that's good. I don't want him to become a target for Mark's ridiculous drama. With all that's happened this morning, I'm more than ready to have a break from people staring at me or asking about Mark.

"Want to get food, then hang out at the guest house for lunch?" I ask toward the end of class. I don't ask anyone in particular since our corner of the room is just the Knights and Xander.

"Wanting to hide from the masses after all the drama this morning?" Xander raises his eyebrows.

"Basically." I turn to Kaylee and Andrew who are sitting with us and invite them since I don't want them to feel excluded. "Y'all are welcome to come too." As much as I don't want to be around other people right now, Andrew and his friends seem cool.

"Sounds good. Is it cool if I text Carter to join us?" Kaylee pulls her phone out.

"Yeah, of course." I smile warmly.

CHAPTER 55
OLIVER

Lynn invited Kaylee, Andrew, and Carter to lunch. I'm not sure why.

She was probably just being polite since they were sitting with us in class. Or maybe she wanted to avoid us cornering her and trying to ask about everything with Mark. It's possible she could be trying to help me out with Kaylee. Or it could be that she's on a weird quest to befriend them.

Regardless, I'm nervous about lunch. I want to check in with Lynn about the Mark stuff even though I'm sure that's going to go over like a lead balloon.

I'm nervous about being around Kaylee with all of our friends there. She let me walk her to class, but I'm still not sure where I stand with her.

I text Daniel to let him know I want to talk to Lynn alone. He tells her he'll get her food for her so she can head straight to the house. Daniel takes the rest of the guys with him.

"I'm assuming you want me to ride with you?" Lynn asks as we head to the parking lot.

"Yeah, I guess subtlety isn't my strong suit."

"More like we've known each other our whole lives and I know when the three of y'all are up to something."

"Fair."

"So, what is it that you wanted to talk to me about?" Lynn sounds wary.

I take a deep breath and then release it. "First, I'd like to apologize for what I said on the way to Homecoming. I wasn't trying to insult you or say you were doing anything wrong. I only wanted you to see things from Kaylee's perspective. I know you and the guys aren't looking for a long-term relationship in high school. There isn't anything wrong with that, and I'm sorry if I made you feel like you were doing the wrong thing because you haven't found a guy you want to commit to long term yet. Forgive me?"

"There's nothing to forgive. You were speaking what was on your mind. I overreacted because of all the crap with Mark." Lynn looks relieved.

"Speaking of Mark, what did he say when you broke up with him?" I ask as we get in the SUV I share with Grayson.

"What do you mean?" Lynn's look of relief vanishes with her question.

Now she looks wary.

"I mean, he told me he was sorry and didn't mean what he said. When it got brought up Saturday, you and Daniel both brushed off the topic. If it was nothing, it wouldn't still be bothering you days later. I let it go Saturday because Grayson was in the car and I figured you wouldn't want to discuss it with him around. Yesterday, y'all dismissed it again, but it seemed like you wanted to talk to Daniel and Xander first."

Lynn doesn't say anything as we leave the parking lot. I know the best thing to do is to wait her out, not continue to ask her questions. She'll talk when she's ready.

The drive is silent. By the time I pull into her driveway, I've given up on her saying anything.

If she isn't ready to talk about it, that's her decision. Even if I'm dying to know and part of me wants to interrogate Mark to find out what he did.

As we're walking into the guest house, Lynn finally speaks.

"When we were together, Mark tried to push my boundaries. Any time we were together and alone, he'd try to go farther than kissing. I never allowed it, but he was constantly trying to talk me into it."

"Why didn't you tell any of us?"

"Because I didn't need your help. I had it handled. I don't live in a tower, and I don't need Knights fighting my battles for me. I don't need or want any of you in the middle of my relationships."

"But since you broke up and he's been a jerk, you still never brought it up."

"Yeah. Umm, about that..." Lynn looks uncomfortable and very unlike herself as she tucks a lock of her hair behind her ear.

"You already know Mark didn't like that all my close friends are guys. The night he told me he loved me... Well, before that, he tried pushing things further again. In hindsight, I think he told me he loved me because he thought it'd make me change my mind and say yes. When I stuck with my no and broke up with him, he didn't take it well. He said a lot of hateful things. Among them, he said no girl could have as many ex-boyfriends as I had and never done more than kiss."

Lynn starts pacing around the room, straightening random things. Then she continues, "He said if that were true, I'd have a reputation for being a frost queen or a frigid prude. I argued saying I'd never done more than kiss any of my exes and have always been upfront about my boundaries. He got hung up on the word exes and said that must mean I was doing things with the other Knights. He, umm, said that'd explain why none of us have lasting relationships or hook up with anyone. He made it sound like that's what a lot of the school thought."

"He said that?" I ask.

"Yeah. That we're all friends with benefits." Lynn won't look in my direction as she talks. "I didn't bring it up because I wasn't ready to deal with it. I didn't want it to put y'all on the war path with Mark. For one he isn't worth it, and for two I thought that'd only make it look more like what he's saying was right." Lynn glances my way briefly before going back to pacing.

"Lynn," I say gently. "We're your best friends and always have your back. Us standing up for you doesn't mean we're more than friends; it means we're good friends. All of us would do the same for any of the

Knights. It isn't because you're a girl. We know you can take care of yourself. But I hope you know we always have your back and you don't have to handle things on your own. Even if you only want a listening ear and moral support." I walk over to her and wrap her in a hug.

Lynn's admission makes me feel like a crappy friend. Not only did I not know what was going on with Mark, but I reinforced what he said with my words on Saturday. It looks like her anxiety is worse with everything going on. I'm not sure how I didn't notice it before.

Not that I'm supposed to know she has issues with anxiety, but Daniel and Xander fretting over her so much in junior high tipped me off to something being wrong. Then I overheard a conversation with her mom about her having panic attacks. I've never said anything because Lynn obviously doesn't want anyone else to know.

"I know that. I guess I got in my own head about everything. I know if the situation was reversed, I'd want to know about someone being hateful to any of y'all." Lynn hugs me back hard enough to knock the air from my lungs. I hug her closer to me and take a breath.

"And you still don't want us to kick his butt?"

Lynn shakes her head. "No, he's getting himself in enough trouble on his own. I heard he's suspended from at least one game due to the dance, and Whitney heard what he said to me in the hallway this morning."

"I know he approached you and you told him off, but why would Whitney hearing the specifics matter?" I squeeze her tight once more before letting her go.

"The dumb jerk said they weren't together and that she didn't mean anything to him. Between slapping me and insulting her, I'm pretty sure the entire school is mad at him."

"That's the least he deserves."

"Yeah. Now enough about me. I want to hear about how band practice went yesterday." Lynn wiggles her eyebrows toward the end of her sentence.

I give her the details of everything with Kaylee as we set up the round table at the guest house. I finish when everyone else gets there with the food.

Lynn gives me an encouraging smile when Kaylee walks in. Lynn's drama with Mark has been a good distraction for how nervous I am to be around Kaylee after our date. It doesn't help to have so many of our friends here.

Lynn seems to be in matchmaker mode, setting it up for Kaylee to sit next to me. We talk about nothing in particular as we eat our lunch. Lynn does ask Kaylee about her band and seems to be making a real effort to befriend her.

I appreciate it but am a little worried her being overly friendly might scare Kaylee off. Thankfully when we're done eating, Daniel suggests a game of Horse in the backyard, distracting Lynn. Andrew mutters something about not knowing how to shoot a basketball, and Lynn offers to teach him. Kaylee declines, and I stay inside with her as everyone else heads outside.

"Don't you want to go with them?" Kaylee asks when the door shuts.

"If you want to. Otherwise, I'd rather be in here with you."

"Oh, okay." Kaylee glances around the now empty room.

"Thanks again for the cupcake this morning."

"It's not a big deal." Kaylee tucks a piece of hair behind her ear.

"No one has ever baked anything for me before. I mean, um, given me something they baked. I didn't mean you made it for me." I can feel my face heating and know I'm making a fool of myself.

"I bake a lot, so like I said, it's not a big deal."

"It was still nice of you."

After an awkward beat, I begin to talk about school because it seems like a safer topic.

We continue to talk about nothing of substance for a little while.

"So about last night…" Kaylee starts before trailing off.

I'm not sure where she's going with that and I don't want to open my mouth and mess things up. Not that I know what to say anyway.

"It was nice…" she says.

I can hear the "but" in her voice.

I'm worried she's going to shut me out and I'll lose any chance I might have with her. Which is the only reason I can think of for blurting out my next question after I've already decided to keep my mouth shut.

"When would you like to go out again?"

"Uh, I don't know." Kaylee seems thrown off by my question.

"Are you free tonight for dinner?" If I'm going to push my luck, I may as well go all in.

"I have marching band practice tonight and other band practice tomorrow night."

"Would it be okay if I came to band practice tomorrow?" In part, I'd love to watch Kaylee in her element singing, but I don't like her having to put up with James by herself.

"Do you actually want to?"

"Of course. You're a good singer."

Kaylee blushes, I take that as permission to come, and we move on to less tense topics.

The next couple of weeks, we fall into a comfortable pattern. I walk with her to class. We sit next to each other in the classes we have together. I watch her band practices. We eat lunch together off campus a few times.

Due to our busy schedules, we don't have a chance to go on an actual date until tonight.

I'm glad this is our bye week for football and I get to spend the evening with Kaylee instead of dealing with the tension on the field. Mark was suspended from football for three weeks due to his actions at the Homecoming dance.

Josh Wicks is our second-string quarterback, and he did great during our away game last week. That has made Mark moodier during practice this week. I wish they wouldn't let him practice since he can't play, but Coach Noble is allowing it.

Mark's anger is making him play like crap at practice, which isn't making his mood any better. Maybe Coach doesn't think Mark can skip practicing with the team for three weeks and then be ready to play again when his suspension is lifted. I shake all thoughts of Mark and football out of my head as I ring the doorbell at Kaylee's house.

CHAPTER 56
DANIEL

"How did you end up hanging out with me on the first Friday night in a while that we don't have a football game? Don't you have friends or adoring girls waiting for your attention?" Xander asks when I walk into his room.

"I'm waiting on Lynn to get back from her run. The other Knights are out with their girl of the moment. Well, except for Grayson. I think he's at home moping." I sit in the chair next to his bed.

"And all the girls vying for your attention?" Xander wiggles his eyebrows with his question.

"Brittany started to get clingy, and we weren't even together. I figured tonight was better spent hanging here than giving her the wrong idea, and I don't feel in the mood to find someone new tonight." I lean back resting my head on the back of the chair.

"So, I'm the consolation prize?" Xander smirks mischievously.

"I mean, obviously. Why else would I willingly hang out with a theater nerd?" I roll my eyes.

"I know. I don't even play sports."

I gasp dramatically. "Whatever could we have to talk about if you don't play sports or make out with girls?"

"Because you're clearly a dumb jock who doesn't have enough brain cells to talk about anything else."

"Clearly."

This has become somewhat of a running joke with us because of what everyone assumes about us. Anyone who sees us hanging out is always surprised. It's like they forget he's Lynn's brother and I grew up with him, too.

"So, Lynn has been running a lot lately..." I trail off.

"I guess." Xander shrugs.

"I kind of hoped with Whitney actively turning the school against Mark it'd help. Mark is too focused on Whitney being a gossipy witch to even think about giving Lynn any grief. The rumor mill seems way more interested in the dynamic between the football captain and the cheer captain than any drama Mark tried to stir up about Lynn. I figured that all becoming a non-issue would help Lynn settle down."

"Other than the frequent runs to the park, she isn't acting anxious. And she always runs a lot following a breakup and likes joining pickup games at the park."

"So, you aren't worried?"

"No, I think you're worried because you're overly protective of her." Xander raises his eyebrows.

"Maybe. But she and Mark broke up three weeks ago, and she's still single and running all the time. Normally, her avoidance only lasts a week." I look at the ceiling like it might have the answers.

"Yeah, but you guys have been busy with girls. Maybe she's avoiding spending one-on-one time with Grayson."

"You think she's avoiding Grayson?" That snaps me back to attention and I look at Xander.

"I don't know. I'm spit-balling. You're the one who's around them all the time. How are things going when y'all are all together?" Xander spins in his desk chair.

"Grayson has definitely been flirting with Lynn, and she isn't shutting him down. She hasn't initiated anything, though." I shrug.

"And he isn't allowed to because of your rules. What do you call it again?" Xander stops spinning to look at me.

"The Secret Creed, because it's an offshoot of the Knight's Creed we made when we were little."

"You know if Lynn ever finds out about that, she's going to be pissed at all of you." Xander cocks an eyebrow.

"Yeah, I know. You've been saying that for years."

"And you've been ignoring me for years." Xander rolls his eyes.

"Because only the Knights know about it, and we all have a vested interest in her never finding out." A secret is easy to keep when everyone involved knows bodily harm would ensue should they ever open their mouths.

"Don't look at me when it blows up in your faces." Xander holds his hands up like he doesn't even want to touch the idea.

"Yeah, yeah." I wave my hand, dismissing his objection.

"Well, as much as I enjoy your company, I have plans tonight, so I'm about to head out." Xander grabs his wallet and keys from his desk.

"Finally ask Amelia on a date?"

"Amelia and I are just friends, and you do enough dating for the both of us." Xander rolls his eyes again.

"Y'all are just friends for now. You may not have ever dated before, but that can change when you find the right girl." I get up from his chair and follow him out of his room.

"Yeah, whatever. Anyway, the cast and crew are going bowling. You're welcome to come with us." Xander jingles his keys.

"I think I'll hang out here so I can check in with Lynn when she gets back from her run."

"All right, good luck with that."

I'm in the Knights' room working on my homework when Lynn gets back from her run. I wanted to give her space if she needed it, but I don't want to go home. My parents are out for dinner with some of my dad's work associates, and I don't want to be in that big empty house alone.

Lynn walks into the room. "Hey, can I talk to you about something?"

Her hair is up in a towel still from her shower, and she looks nervous.

"You can talk to me about anything at any time. You know that."

"What do you think about Grayson?" Lynn toys with the towel on her head.

"He's a good ball player and a good friend." I want her to say why she's asking instead of making it easy on her.

"You know that's not what I meant." Lynn rolls her eyes.

"Do I?"

"Ugh. Fine." Lynn throws up her hands. "I want to know what you think about all of the extra attention and all of the flirting. Do you think he means anything by it?"

"If you're asking if I think he has a thing for you, then yeah, it seems fairly obvious." If he was any more obvious, he'd have to take out a billboard.

"What do you think I should do about it?" Lynn wraps her arms around herself.

"What do you want to do about it?" I lean back in my chair.

"I don't know."

"Well, do you want to go out with him?"

"I don't *not* want to go out with him…" Lynn leans against the doorframe.

"So, you're unsure of what you want to do?"

"If I knew, would I be here bugging you about it?" She looks exasperated.

"Yes."

"Shut up." Lynn pushes off the door frame and shoves my chair to send me spinning.

"How about you tell me what you're thinking, and then I'll try to give you advice? If I know more about what you want, I can give you better advice."

"I don't know." Lynn plops down on the bunk bed closest to me. "I mean, obviously I like him because we've been friends our whole lives. I enjoy spending time with him, and he's not horrible to look at."

"A rave review by all accounts." I roll my eyes.

"Would you rather me be completely honest about my thoughts on his appearance?" Lynn pulls the towel off her head and starts drying her hair.

"Absolutely not. I know way too much about most of the guys at our school as it is. I'm pretty sure I'm in danger of losing my man card from hearing you wax poetic about your various crushes and exes over the years."

"I'm not that bad."

I raise my eyebrows at Lynn.

"Okay maybe I am, but I'm not any worse than you are. And I talk about things other than their appearance." Lynn pops me with her towel.

"Like their kissing skills?" I wiggle my eyebrows.

"Shut up." Lynn pushes my shoulder. "Anyway, we're getting off topic."

"So, it sounds like you wouldn't be opposed to dating Grayson."

"I'm worried about what could go wrong. Like even though Mark seems to be public enemy number one, I'm worried if I started dating Grayson, it might give Mark more ammunition and credibility." Lynn goes back to drying her hair.

"I don't think you need to worry about Mark. I'm sure he's going to be too busy dealing with everything going on with Whitney to try starting more trouble with you. I think Mark has taken up enough of your headspace this school year and you shouldn't make any decisions based on how he may or may not react."

"Do you think Grayson's going to ask me out?" Lynn shakes the towel out and hangs it up in the bathroom attached to the Knight room.

"I don't know that he will. I think that if you want to go out with him, then you should ask him out. But I'm not sure if you're ready for another relationship. I mean, you seem to be running and going to the park a lot. If you're still feeling weird over all the crap with Mark, then maybe you should take some time to focus on you."

"You don't have hardly any time between girls. Heck, sometimes you make out with two different girls on the same day." Lynn comes back with a brush and starts brushing her hair out.

"Kissing and relationships aren't the same thing, and I'm not letting any girl mess with my head. You've been single without even flirting with someone for three weeks. I'm pretty sure that's a record for you."

"I'm not letting Mark mess with my head. I'm ready to date, but I'm not sure about dating Grayson. And besides, there's nothing wrong with staying single. Maybe I should wait. I could wait until basketball season." Lynn's rapid fire talking isn't filling me with confidence.

"If that's your way of considering dating someone else on the team, please don't. If you're saying you're going to stay single for an entire month until basketball, I want to know why." Staying single and focusing on herself would be good for Lynn, but anxiously refusing to date isn't the same thing.

"If it's basketball season, Mark won't have a reason or way to take it out on Grayson, and it won't mess up your season. Why don't you want me dating anyone on the basketball team? It's never been an issue before." Lynn puts her brush back up.

"Well, I guess as long as it isn't Knox, it wouldn't be too bad."

"What are you talking about? What's wrong with Aiden?" Lynn plops back on the bed.

"Nothing's wrong with him. I just don't know that I could handle you dating and dumping another captain of the basketball team during basketball season."

"Why is that?" Lynn toys with her hair.

"Last year when you broke up with Mason Renaker, we had to run suicides every captain's practice. And he almost always found a reason the Knights needed to stay late. He'd say we were sloppy during practice or that we gave him attitude. Then he'd have us run lines until we were ready to puke or pass out. It majorly sucked."

"At least y'all were in good shape. I mean, y'all won the regional tournament." Lynn smirks.

"I'd love to repeat the wins this year, but I'll pass on being tortured because you broke our captain's heart. Again."

"I have no interest in dating Aiden, so you have nothing to worry about." Lynn rolls her eyes like I'm being ridiculous.

"Because of what I said, or because you aren't ready to start dating and said that so I'd leave you alone about Mark?"

"Because he's a lovable goofball, but I don't like him that way. I'd appreciate you dropping the Mark thing, because it isn't an issue and I'm tired of hearing about it. I'm ready for another relationship. I'm not sure about trying to have one with Grayson." Lynn's confidence slips away when she mentions Grayson's name.

"If you're hesitant, maybe hang out with him one-on-one and see how it goes. If it goes well, then consider going on a date."

"How am I supposed to hang out with him one-on-one without any of the Knights crashing? If I ask him to hang out just the two of us, he's going to think it's a date, anyway."

"Simple—I go with y'all and then have a reason to bail. Everyone else is busy tonight, anyway. Oliver is on his date with Kaylee. Jet and Tristan are with their girl of the moment."

Lynn looks a little uncomfortable at the mention of their girls who won't last long. I wonder if she might be thinking about what Oliver said during Homecoming and how similar she is to us in how she treats the opposite gender. Lynn gives her head a slight shake.

"Okay. I guess it couldn't hurt to try. You need a convincing reason to bail, though. I don't want him thinking it's a setup."

"I don't think he'll care why I'm leaving as long as I am, but I'll come up with something. Do you want me to text him so he has less reason to be suspicious?" I pull my phone out.

"Yeah, sounds good."

CHAPTER 57
KAYLEE

"Are you ready for your big date tonight?" Carter asks as we leave school on Friday. I'm dropping him and Sara off at his apartment before going home to get ready for the night.

"It's *a* date. It's not a big deal."

"Yeah, but it's your first official date with Oliver," Carter unhelpfully points out.

Honestly, I'm a bit nervous about tonight. But as I've barely admitted that to myself, there's no way I'd tell anyone else. If Carter knew, I'd never hear the end of it.

The last two weeks have been nice. Oliver clearly has no qualms about being seen with me in public, which is a nice change of pace. He's been at every band practice we've had, so James has somewhat behaved. James is still getting into my space every chance he can get, but he watches what he says in front of Oliver. I blocked James's number so he can't text or call me anymore.

"We've gone on a date before," I point out and refocus on the conversation at hand.

"Yeah, but this one is planned and you said yes. We didn't have to make ourselves scarce so you'd have to spend time alone with him," Sara says.

"Okay so this is different from the last date. That doesn't make it a big deal."

"It so does, but if you don't want to talk about it, I'll leave it alone… for now." Carter smiles evilly.

"We can totally drop it, but I want all the details afterwards. Especially since you still haven't given us the details of your first date," Sara adds.

"What details?" I throw my hands up. "We talked. We ate pizza. I had a nice time and he drove me home. Those are the details."

"Those are *not* the details. You aren't sharing the details. Like, is Oliver a good kisser?" Sara asks.

Carter raises his hand. "I'd like it to be known that I have no interest in hearing about how Oliver kisses."

I scoff. "Why do you assume I'd know how he kisses? And regardless, I'm not telling you those kinds of details about anyone ever."

"Are you saying you haven't kissed him yet?" Sara's eyes widen in disbelief. "But you've been dating for two weeks! How have you not kissed yet? If I dated someone like Oliver, I'd want to kiss him all the time."

"Thanks for the overshare, Sara," Carter says sarcastically. He turns to me. "But, Kaylee, you haven't kissed Oliver?"

"Firstly, Sara, that whole tirade is exactly why I'm worried about you dating. Secondly, we aren't dating. Thirdly, I thought you'd already said you didn't want those details, Carter."

"What do you mean, you aren't dating? He walks you to class, you sit together in class, you eat lunch together, he comes and watches your band practices. If that's not dating, maybe your standards are too high," Sara says.

"You're going on dates. You're dating." Carter acts like him saying so makes it a fact.

"My standards aren't too high. I think a conversation needs to take place between two people where they agree that they're dating before they're actually dating," I defend myself.

I'm mostly focusing on the dating thing because I want them distracted from asking about Oliver and me kissing. We've only kissed one time, and I was mostly trying to distract him so he wouldn't walk me to the door.

The more I can keep him away from Mary, the better.

I didn't tell them about that kiss then, and I don't want to talk about it now. I know I surprised Oliver at the time, so I've been waiting for him to make the next move in that regard. He hasn't kissed me yet, and I'm not sure why. But I don't want to think about it and definitely don't want to talk about it.

"Maybe tonight you can bring it up so you're officially dating," Sara says.

"We'll see." There's no way I'm starting that conversation, but I don't want to argue about it with Sara.

Thankfully, we're at Carter's, and they can't keep badgering me about it.

"I'm sure we will. Text me when you're home, and Drew and I will drop Sara off." Carter clearly knows I'm not agreeing with Sara.

"I'm not a small child you know," Sara says, petulantly, like a small child.

"Sure, but Mary has been on a bender this week, and I don't think either of us should be at the house alone with her," I point out.

"Whatever." Sara gets out of the van.

I make sure they make it inside the apartment before heading to the house to get ready for my date. I had offered to drive, but Oliver insisted on driving. That was when he told me the date he has planned is a surprise. I've tried to get information out of him this week, but all he has told me is to dress casual and that it'd probably be warm where we're going.

I decide to wear my black leather skirt, a blue crop top, and my favorite Doc Martens. As I head out the door, I grab my leather jacket in case I need it.

"Hey." I take in Oliver's appearance at the door.

He's wearing a black tee that clings to his muscles without looking a size too small like James's usually do. He has on dark jeans and a pair of black Vans.

"Hey. You look beautiful."

"Oh, um, you don't look too bad yourself." My face feels warm, and I'm hoping my blush isn't too obvious.

"Thanks. Are you ready to go?"

"Yeah. You still haven't told me where we're going."

"Nope, and like I've been saying, you'll find out when we get there." Oliver opens the SUV door for me.

I love that Oliver has a tall vehicle I don't have to crawl into.

"Can I get a hint?"

"Your outfit will blend in even though your beauty stands out." Oliver winks.

He holds his phone out. "Do you want to DJ?"

"You'd trust me with your phone?"

"Yeah, I mean you don't strike me as the type to send fake text messages to stir up drama or sign me up for emailing lists that are going to harass me until the end of time."

I decide to go ahead and take his phone so we can get on the road.

"Those are two very specific examples," I say when Oliver gets back in on his side of the SUV.

"The first happened to Grayson when a girl got ahold of his phone without his knowledge. The second is a prank Jet and Grayson pulled on Daniel."

"So, you aren't worried I'll go through your phone while I'm DJing?"

"If you want to, that's up to you. There's nothing interesting on there, and anything that could hint at where we're going has already been deleted. If you're looking for clues as to our destination, you'll be out of luck." Oliver pulls out of the driveway.

"You aren't worried I'll look through your messages or see that you're talking to another girl?"

"Nope. You're the only girl I'm interested in. The only other girls I text are Lynn and Callie, but Lynn's just a friend and Callie's like my little sister." Oliver shrugs.

"I'm not going to look through your phone, by the way. That's a major invasion of privacy."

"I'm not worried about it either way." Oliver gives me a charming smile. It makes me want to swoon, which is ridiculous, so I shake that thought away.

The ways Oliver is different from James could fill up a book, from the way he treats me, both in public and in private, to how he treats my friends.

I still don't want to jump into a relationship, but I'd rather be with Oliver than James. Not that James was ever an option, but still.

I pester Oliver a bit, trying to figure out where we're going, but he doesn't give me any type of hint. I give up—since I'll know soon enough anyway—and look through the songs he has saved to his music library instead. It's mostly rock and metal with a few pop songs in the mix.

"Based on your phone, you're either into heavier music or very committed to the ruse," I say slightly teasing him.

"You can believe what you want, but I'm not even sure why someone would pretend to love music they don't want to listen to. To go to the effort of fabricating evidence of music taste seems extra ridiculous."

"You look like—"

"Like I'd listen to nothing but Top 40s junk?"

"Yeah…" I should probably stop assuming things about Oliver because he's an attractive, popular jock.

So I say instead, "Since we've left town, I'm assuming we're either going into the metroplex or you're bringing me to the country to dispose of my body."

"I'm still not giving you a hint about where we're going, but I promise I've no intention of letting you out of my sight, much less leaving you in a ditch somewhere."

"Well, as long as murder isn't on the agenda, I can relax," I say with a touch of sarcasm.

We lapse into silence and listen to music for the rest of the half-hour drive. Oliver finds a parking space downtown next to a bar called The Ginger Man.

"So how far are we walking to our destination?" I ask.

"We're here."

"What? You're taking me to a bar? I don't have a fake ID. I couldn't get in if I wanted to."

I didn't expect this from one of Lynn's friends who goes to church each week. Oliver seems like such a rule follower.

"You don't need one to get in, and even if you had one, you still wouldn't be able to drink here." Oliver gets out and comes to open my car door for me.

"They let minors into their bar? Is that even legal?"

"Not any minors, but I know the owner. The flip side of that is he and all of the bartenders know me, and since you're coming in with me, they know not to serve us alcohol. Not that I drink anyway, but it stops even the idea from going anywhere when it isn't an option."

I'm surprised with Lynn's mom obviously not approving of them drinking that Oliver knows where a bar is. That he knows the owner of one and frequents it enough that the bartenders know who he is. *Unbelievable.* But the guy at the door greets him by name and lets us in like it's no big deal.

I follow Oliver into the bar and start to wonder when I'm going to wake up because none of this makes sense. The guy working the bar is a couple of inches shorter than me with curly orange hair mostly covered by his flat cap.

"Ollie! I didn't know you were coming tonight!" The bartender reaches over the bar to give Oliver a fist bump.

"Hey, Uncle Zach. I didn't know you'd be working tonight, or I'd have let you know."

Uncle? This guy Zach maybe weighs 140 pounds soaking wet and doesn't even come up to Oliver's shoulders. There's no way they're related.

"More like you'd have reconsidered coming tonight and kept me from meeting this lovely lady." The bartender grins. "Now act like you have manners and introduce us."

Oliver rolls his eyes at the guy's antics.

"Zach, this is my friend, Kaylee. Kaylee, this is the owner of the bar and the official Ginger Man, Zach."

"Nice to meet you." I return the fist-bump Zach offers.

"The pleasure's all mine. Now can you tell me what a pretty girl like you is doing with a dork like Oliver?"

"Um…"

"Can we skip the questions and get something to drink, please?" Oliver gives Zach a pleading look.

"Fine, fine. I'll have to get the information from my favorite niece, then."

"If you must. Can I have a Dr. Pepper?"

"Coming up," Zach nods. "And for the lady?"

"Coke's fine," I say.

Zach gives us our drinks, then Oliver leads me away and out to the back patio. There's a stage out where a band's setting up, a giant open area I assume is for dancing, and various seating options around the outer edge of the area. Everything's enclosed by a privacy fence, so you have to go through the bar to get back here.

"So, your surprise date is at a bar your uncle owns?"

"Well, sort of. The best part is yet to come." Oliver leads me to a table just off the front of the stage.

"Is Zach married to your aunt or something?"

Oliver lets out a short laugh. "No, Zach isn't married."

"Then how is he your uncle? There's no way you're related."

"He's Mama Kingston's best friend, making him a pseudo uncle to Lynn and her brothers. That sort of encompasses the Knights as well with how much time we spent with Lynn's family growing up." Oliver's smile from his laughter still lingers.

"Okay. That makes sense, I guess."

It doesn't really, but it makes more sense than Oliver sharing DNA with the guy. Everything else about it's weird.

"But on to why we're here," he says. "There's an up-and-coming all-female rock band playing tonight. I figured you'd rather see them in concert than go to dinner and a movie."

"Really? That's cool. They're playing here, though? This place looks a lot more folk music than rock and roll." I'd more expect a guy with a banjo to be playing on this stage.

"Yeah, Zach listens to all kinds of music, so he has all types of bands play here."

The band takes the stage and introduces themselves before beginning what is a pretty killer set. This is definitely better than dinner and a movie and the best date I've ever been on.

CHAPTER 58
GRAYSON

Done. I close my laptop after finishing my English essay. I'm pretty sure this is the first time I've finished an essay the day it was assigned. It also means I'm out of homework. I'm usually more of the mindset of "due tomorrow, do tomorrow."

I've become quite studious the last couple of weeks since I've had nothing better to do. I'm actually ahead in all of my classes, which I guess is a good thing.

Oliver has been spending every possible minute with Kaylee. Tristan's revolving door of girls seems to have increased in frequency. Daniel and Lynn seem to constantly be working on something for school with Xander.

I check my phone again and see that Jet has finally texted me back.

> Vaughn: Sorry something came up when I got home

We were supposed to hang out today, but he disappeared right after school and didn't answer his phone. Now that he's deigned to respond four hours later, that's what he sends?

He didn't even bother to give a real reason. His brush-offs have gotten increasingly vague over the last two weeks. Jet keeps blowing me off when we're supposed to hang out. I don't know what's going on with him, but I'm ready to get to the bottom of it. I'm tired of being home alone doing homework.

I guess it's my fault I'm bored. I'd normally be caught up with some girl like the other Knights are. But since I'm waiting around for Lynn, I'm by myself. Anytime I text Lynn, she's doing homework or going on a run. I'm frustrated with not making any real progress with her.

When I decided to wait around for Lynn, I didn't realize I'd be literally waiting around or that I'd be waiting this long. I mean, at least she hasn't started dating someone else. I wish I could just ask her out. Then she'd say yes or no, and either way this waiting would be over.

Instead, I keep flirting with her and trying to drop little hints that we'd be good together. Maybe I need to be less subtle. I mean, telling her outright that we'd make a good couple isn't asking her out. It's stating a fact. Even if it doesn't go over well, at least I wouldn't be at home by myself indefinitely.

Now I don't even have homework to do. It's seven on a Friday night when I don't have a game, and I'm home alone bored out of my mind. Josh is throwing a small party tomorrow because it's bye week, but that doesn't help me tonight. I guess I could go for a run. It'd be better than being here doing nothing.

I decide to get changed and my phone goes off with an incoming text.

Caballero: Hey you busy?

G. Ridire: Just finished what I was doing. What's up?

Caballero: Want to go axe throwing with me and Lynn?

G. Ridire: Yeah when?

Caballero: Now?

G. Ridire: Yeah. I'll head over there

I get my stuff together before heading out to meet them at Lynn's house. It may not be a date, but at least it'll be the three of us instead of all of the Knights. Even if Daniel is more likely to get in my way than be a wingman, at least he'd be the only other person Lynn could pay attention to, and they're strictly platonic and almost familial.

When I walk across the street, Lynn and Daniel are headed out the side door of the house. Daniel seems absorbed by something on his phone.

"Hey." Lynn looks at me, causing Daniel to look up.

"Hey." I give a stupid little wave I immediately regret.

"Hey, so…uh…I hate to be that guy," Daniel starts, "and I know we always put friends first…"

"But you have a better offer than axe throwing with your friends and you want to know if it's cool if you ditch us?" Lynn asks.

"Something like that." Daniel smirks.

"It's fine with me as long as it's fine with Lynn," I say, knowing she's the most sensitive about us blowing off plans for a girl that won't last.

To be fair, we've been friends for sixteen years, and most of our girls don't last sixteen days.

"Yeah, yeah. Go break a heart, and we'll see you tomorrow." Lynn smiles as she shoves Daniel's shoulder. He gives her a huge grin before shoving her back and heading to his house.

"You ready?" Lynn turns to face me.

"Yeah. Do you want me to drive?" I offer.

I feel like it's the gentlemanly thing to do even if this isn't a date. Maybe if I treat it like a date, Lynn will start to see it that way. My hope for that is dashed, though, when Lynn opens her mouth.

"I'd rather drive, if that's okay. I mean, we're already at my house."

"Uh yeah, sure. That's fine."

Lynn pretty much always lets her boyfriends drive on dates. That makes it fairly clear that she sees this as a friend hangout. I have an evening of throwing axes to change her mind.

We talk about nothing in particular on the drive over. Lynn is distracted when we get there so I pay for her as well as myself.

"Hey, you didn't need to do that," Lynn says when she realizes what I did.

"I know I didn't need to, but I wanted to. Can't I do something nice for you if I want to?"

"When you put it that way, I guess." Lynn shrugs. "I'm buying our food, though."

"As long as there are fried pickles." I try to act more friendly so she doesn't get her guard up about my intentions.

I go to our lane and get the axes set up while Lynn goes and gets food. She comes back quickly.

"A meat lovers pizza, fried pickles, and a blue Powerade." Lynn sets everything down.

"All my favorites. Thank you." I smile at her.

She smiles back, and I get lost in the idea of this being a real date. I shake myself out of my daydream and grab a slice of pizza.

Everything goes well all night, and we go back and forth each round on who gets the highest score. We laugh and joke, and in general, have a good time. I see how good things could always be. If only Lynn could see it. We return all our stuff and head out.

"Do you want to go get milkshakes before going home?" I try to make the night last longer and maybe a bit more romantic than axe throwing.

"Sure." Lynn turns to drive toward the Castle Creamery, a locally owned ice cream parlor.

"This has been nice," I say as we slide into a booth with our milkshakes.

"Uh, yeah it has." Lynn starts to look uncomfortable.

If she's already uncomfortable, maybe I shouldn't try to push the date idea right now.

"So, um, is it something you might want to do again?" Lynn asks. She plays with her milkshake straw and doesn't quite look up at me.

"Do you mean axe throwing or hanging out just the two of us?" I'm hoping she's not talking about axe throwing, but I don't want to push my luck, either.

"Hanging out without everybody else." Lynn's eyes briefly flick up to mine before looking back down at her shake.

"Like a date?" Dancing this line of encouraging her without scaring her off or breaking the Secret Creed is harder than I thought.

"Is that something you'd want to do?" Lynn continues to swirl her straw around like it's the most interesting thing she's ever seen. I'm not sure if she's nervous or indifferent.

"Yeah. If it's something you want, I'd lo— I mean, I'd like to go on a date with you." That was close. I know better than to use the L word with Lynn when talking about dating, but it still almost slipped out.

"Okay, but I want to take this slowly. Is that okay with you?" Lynn finally looks up at me and her hesitant smile fills me with warmth.

"We can do whatever makes you most comfortable." I try to tamper down my beaming smile as I gaze into her eyes.

"Okay, so we can go on one date and see how it goes?" Lynn tucks a lock of hair behind her ear.

"Sure. Do you want to go together to Josh's party tomorrow?" I can feel my hopefulness bleeding into my tone and hope Lynn doesn't pick up on it.

"Umm…maybe something more low-key." Lynn shifts in her seat uncomfortably. "I don't want to have to deal with everyone else's opinions right away. Besides, we're already planning on that being a group thing. We could get dinner on Sunday after evening services."

"Sounds good."

While we finish our milkshakes, we talk about sports and other friend stuff. I try to make conversation that is more friendly than flirty, hoping to make her feel more confident about our date on Sunday.

When we get back, we both head to our separate houses. As much as I'd love to walk Lynn to her door and kiss her, I don't think that'd work well for me overall. Lynn already seems unsure, and I don't want to scare her off when she has finally asked me out.

CHAPTER 59
OLIVER

"They were fantastic! Their stage presence was so magnetic!" Kaylee says as Heartbreak Harlequins finish up their set and head offstage.

I enjoyed their music, but I couldn't tell you anything about their stage presence. I spent pretty much their whole show watching Kaylee. She's so beautiful when she's happy and lost in the music.

"Would you like to meet them?" I ask.

"Oh, are they coming back out to do autographs and meet people?" Kaylee's eyes light up with excitement.

"Not exactly. There's a VIP area they're going to after they put all their equipment away. If you want, we can go and say hi."

"There's a VIP area? And you're allowed in it?" Kaylee bounces in her chair.

"Knowing the owner has perks." I take her hand and lead her back inside.

The VIP area is more like an oversized private room. Two of the walls are lined with one-way mirrors so you can see the rest of the bar and the patio. It has lounge furniture and coffee tables instead of bar stools and tables.

Zach meets us and we head into the VIP Lounge.

"So, Kaylee, did you enjoy the set despite your company?"

"Um, yeah, their music was good." Kaylee smiles, giving me a shy glance. "And the company wasn't too bad, either."

"Don't you have a bar to run?" I ask grumpily.

"I'm a good multitasker. I can run a bar and embarrass you at the same time." Uncle Zach grins. "But I can take a hint. I'll leave you alone."

Zach walks off, and we find a couch to sit on.

"This place is cool," Kaylee says after sitting down.

"Yeah, Zach might be a dork, but he does know how to design a space. So…I, uh, wanted to ask you something." I feel more unsure the more words that come out of my mouth.

"It must be some question if you're this nervous. Do you need one of my kidneys or something?" Her tone is playful.

"What? Uh no, I'm good on kidneys. I just haven't asked anyone this before."

"You want to know if I'll go snipe hunting with you?" Kaylee smiles.

Her ridiculousness is easing my nerves.

"No. I want to know if you might want to be my girlfriend?"

"Oh, um." Kaylee's eyes widen and she has a deer-caught-in-headlights expression.

After all my bumbling, I didn't expect my question to be a surprise. If only it was a good surprise, like the band.

"If not, then uh, that's okay." I scratch the back of my head.

"No." I feel myself deflate, and it looks like Kaylee sees it, too. Maybe I should've waited until after meeting the band.

"No. I mean—not *no*," Kaylee hurries to add.

"What?"

"I don't know. What do you mean by *girlfriend*?"

"We…would…be…dating…?" I'm thoroughly confused.

"Okay, but, like, what are you expecting of me? Because I'm not going to turn into some cheerleader or football groupie."

"I don't want to change anything about you. I want to hold your hand, go on dates with you, talk to you, spend time with you."

I take her hand in mine as I continue to speak.

"I want to date you and no one else. I want people to know we're together. I mean, if you wanted to wear my letterman or anything like that, it'd be nice, but it isn't a requirement. I'd love it if you were willing to wear my jersey this coming Friday so the whole school knows you're mine. But you don't have to do anything you don't want to."

"I already have my own letterman to wear. And if I'm wearing your jersey saying I belong to you, how will everyone know you belong to me? That seems a bit one sided." Kaylee squeezes my hand as she talks.

"Well, how do you want to make that known? I'd say I could wear your letterman, but I'm pretty sure I can't get it on, and if I did, it'd probably rip at the seams. I could get Mama Kingston to make me a shirt that says property of Kaylee Cobb and wear it to the party tomorrow."

"You'd seriously do that?" Kaylee's mouth drops open in surprise.

"Yeah. I like you, and I care about you. I'm fine with the world knowing that." I lift her hand and gently kiss her knuckles.

"I thought you said it was something you'd never asked anyone. Haven't you had several girlfriends?"

"I wouldn't say several, and they all asked me. I've never been invested enough in a girl to ask first." I shrug.

Kaylee blushes and shifts so her hair falls partially in front of her face. Then finally, she says, "Okay. Then, yes, I'll be your girlfriend. I'll wear your jersey on Friday, but I'm wearing my own letterman."

"Awesome." I can feel a dopey grin forming on my face. "What about the party tomorrow?"

"I'll go with you, but you don't need to wear a shirt saying you belong to me." Kaylee's nose scrunches. "As a matter of fact, I'd prefer it if you didn't."

We meet the band, and Kaylee talks music with them for a while. They seem to be cut from the same cloth. They're only a few years older than us, and I can see Kaylee being like them in a few years' time.

Watching her in her element is amazing. She's so humble about her own music. When the guitarist asks if she played, she majorly downplays her band. I start talking about how amazing they are, but then Kaylee elbows me and tells me to shut up.

The band laughs, and she blushes before they move on to other topics. I can't help but brag about her. I did refrain from bragging about her being my girlfriend, even though I wanted to.

Zach comes by a few times to embarrass me, but at least he brings free food with him each time. Kaylee's too caught up with the band to pay attention to anything Zach says, anyway.

With Kaylee agreeing to be my girlfriend, tonight's one of the best nights of my life. On the way back to her house, Kaylee plays more of Heartbreak Harlequins' music. The concert tonight was clearly a good idea.

"I had a great time tonight. Thank you for planning all of this for me." Kaylee smiles shyly.

"I'm glad you had a good time. I'm excited to get to call you my girlfriend now." I smile back at her. "Can I walk you to your door tonight?"

A sigh escapes her lips as her eyes flick toward the front door. "I'd rather you didn't. My mom's home, and I don't want to deal with that. We can say goodbye here, though."

It takes me a moment to catch onto what she's saying before I lean in to kiss her.

Her lips are as soft and sweet as I remember. They move over mine skillfully as she runs her fingers through my hair. I get lost in the feeling of her lips on mine, and time ceases to exist.

Kaylee tastes like cinnamon and honey. I weave my hands through her surprisingly soft hair. Everything about her is soft despite her abrasive attitude. I want to be consumed by that softness.

Kaylee eventually pulls back. "So, I should probably head inside before your windows get any more fogged up."

"Uh, yeah," I say with my head still in the clouds.

When I look at the dash, I realize that thirty minutes have gone by. No wonder the windows are fogged up and my lips feel tender.

"Good night. I'll see you tomorrow." Kaylee smiles before getting out of my SUV.

I can't help the goofy grin on my face from seeing her puffy lips and messed-up hair. She looks like she was seriously kissed, and it makes me happy that I'm the one who made her look that way.

"Good night."

I watch to make sure she gets in her house safely before pulling out of her driveway and heading home. Once I'm off her road, I let out a whoop of excitement.

She said yes!

I don't think I've ever been that nervous before in my life, but it was worth it. Kaylee is worth it.

James didn't see her value or treat her the way she deserves, but I'm not going to be like that.

I see how talented she is with her music. I see how much she cares about her sister and how protective she is of Sara. I see the armor she has built around herself to protect against the pain others have inflicted on her. And I see underneath the armor to the beautiful and caring person with a heart of gold.

I know I'm lucky to get to call her mine and I intend to show her how much that means to me. She deserves to be treated like a queen. Maybe the *Queen of Punk* nickname might be more fitting than I first thought.

As much as I love that she's now my girlfriend, I'm even happier to be her boyfriend. I want her to know I'm just as much hers and probably more so since she's held my heart for some time now.

CHAPTER 60
KAYLEE

I overslept this morning after being up half the night, and now I'm running late. Carter and Drew should be here any minute, and I still haven't showered. *Ugh.* I need to get myself together.

I text Sara to tell her to let them in when they get here and text the boys to let them know I'm running late. I hop in the shower and try to focus on getting ready. We have a marching contest today, and Mr. Gregory will tear us a new one if we miss the bus.

I can't believe I slept through my alarm. Mary left early this morning on a weekend trip with one of her friends, so I didn't have to worry about her. You'd think that would've meant I had *actually* gotten some good rest last night. However, I couldn't fall asleep because of Oliver.

Oliver Ridire is my boyfriend. *My boyfriend.* The first actual boyfriend I've had.

Even half asleep and exhausted, I'm still giddy about it this morning. It's weird. I don't think I've ever been giddy before.

I rush through my morning routine while thoughts of last night continue to play through my mind. The whole date was sweet; Oliver clearly put thought into what I would want.

It's like he sees me, the real me. By some miracle, he likes what he sees. He wants to be mine and for me to be his. He likes me the way I am and wants to be my boyfriend.

Oliver doesn't try to change me like James did. He wouldn't tear me down or treat me like I'm trash. James treated me badly for so long, I have a hard time telling myself I deserve better. But I do, and Oliver seems to want to give me better.

Oliver was so nervous last night about asking me to be his girlfriend. Like he was worried about getting shot down. It still amazes me that one of the most popular guys in school would be that anxious about asking someone out. Especially when that someone is *me.*

It blew my mind when he confessed that he'd never asked anyone out before. It could have been cocky or conceited, him saying the girl has always done the asking. But I think he was stating a fact and trying to explain away his nerves.

It made me feel special to be the first girl Oliver cared about enough to ask out. I'm glad I gave him a chance. He's not a stereotypical jock. He's one of the sweetest, most thoughtful guys I know.

He opens doors for me. He walks me to class and offers to carry my stuff. He makes sure I get inside before driving off. He's just so…so…I don't even know what.

Saying he's perfect feels over the top, but I don't have another word for him or the way he treats me. I can't believe I ever thought he might be a stuck-up jerk.

"Kaylee! Come on or we're gonna be late!" Sara yells as she pokes her head in the door. "Grab whatever you need and finish getting ready in the car or bus on the way there." She rolls her eyes as she heads back out the door.

Recognizing she has a point, I don't bother responding and instead throw my makeup bag and hair brush in my band duffel.

I run downstairs with all of my stuff. Sara is waiting for me by the door with Carter and Drew. We rush to my van and throw everything into the back before hopping in. I'm driving, so I'll have to finish getting ready on the band bus. At least I didn't need to wash my hair this morning.

"So…any reason you're running so late today?" Carter asks as soon as we're on the road. He's sitting in the front passenger seat, so it's pretty hard to just ignore him.

"I overslept more than usual. It's not like it's the first time I've been the reason we're cutting it close." I shrug and hope he drops it. I'm not quite ready to talk about everything yesterday, especially with my little sister listening in.

"You're normally better about competition days. That way we can all avoid a lecture from Mr. Gregory in front of the whole band." Carter turns in his seat so he's facing me.

It makes me wish Drew sat shotgun for once. Not that it'd make sense for him to be up here with him being the shortest, but still.

"If you're worried about a lecture, you could've had your mom drop you off at the school instead of my house. Isn't the school closer, anyway?" I ignore his stare as I focus on the road.

"Yeah, but your house was on the way to her first job of the morning. It was easier for her to drop me off here," he explains. "But more importantly, I want to know why you slept so poorly last night."

I glance over and Carter raises his eyebrows at me.

"I had trouble falling asleep last night, okay? It's not the first time and it probably won't be the last. I don't see how that's interesting or important." I shrug like the conversation is no big deal.

"But last night was the first official date you and Oliver went on. Maybe he's got something to do with you not getting any sleep." Carter wiggles his eyebrows at me, and I roll my eyes.

"Nothing happened between me and Oliver. He did not keep me up all night. You can go ahead and flush whatever thoughts you're having down the toilet where they belong."

"I wouldn't say 'nothing.' Unless you're telling me that you sat in his SUV and *talked* for thirty minutes and that's what caused the windows to fog up," Sara unhelpfully adds from the back seat.

I throw a pen from my center console at her.

"Shut up! You shouldn't be spying on me!"

"I wasn't even home to spy on you. I have my ways of knowing things," Sara says cryptically. I'll have to figure out what that's about later.

"It definitely doesn't sound like nothing happened. Why don't you save yourself some time and save us some outrageous suggestions, and tell us about your date?" Carter leans back in his seat like he's got all the time in the world.

Maybe if I keep them distracted until we get to the band bus, they'll drop it. We only have a few minutes until we're at school.

"Or you can try to put it off and we can have the conversation with the whole band listening in, because I've got no intention of dropping it." Carter crosses his arms.

"Fine, but when we get to the school, this conversation is over. Deal?"

"Deal. Now spill." Carter leans in like he's hanging onto my every word.

"Oliver took me to a concert for an indie rock band, Heartbreak Harlequins. After the show, we got to meet them. It was cool to get to talk with them. We ate at the concert and then came home. We talked about random stuff and had a good night together. When he dropped me off, he gave me a good-night kiss." Hopefully, that's enough details to satisfy them.

"And?" Sara asks from the backseat.

"And what?" I'm a smidgen worried about what she's going to ask.

"Is he a good kisser?"

I can feel my face heating and know my body is giving away the answer even if my mouth doesn't.

"That's not any of your business."

"And more importantly, Drew and I have no interest in knowing how Oliver kisses." Carter makes a face like he's going to puke.

"If you throw up in my car, you're cleaning it up," I remind him, hoping it will distract him from our previous conversation, effectively ending it.

"Yeah, yeah. I know the rules. I'm not going to actually throw up. I am curious about one thing though…" Carter trails off.

I know he's baiting me, but I can't stop the words from coming out of my mouth.

"Curious about what?"

"Your date went well, he kissed you, but you didn't say if y'all are officially together yet or not."

I inhale deeply to settle myself.

"This doesn't leave this car and I'm not talking about it today. I'm not ready to." I pause for a steadying breath. "But Oliver asked me to be his girlfriend."

Before I can even completely finish the sentence, Sara is squealing and bouncing around in the backseat.

"I knew it! I knew it! I knew y'all would get together! You're so lucky! He's so hot and dreamy!"

"Because looks are everything." I roll my eyes at her antics.

"Oliver is a good guy, too." Drew says, finally contributes to the conversation. "And if he found an indie rock concert to take you to, then he seems to know what you like and is being thoughtful. He'll be good *for* you and be good *to* you."

"If y'all are dating, why can't we tell anyone else?" Carter asks suspiciously.

I have a feeling he's thinking about all of the nonsense with James and how he never wanted anyone to know about us. I wasn't even supposed to tell Drew and Carter about it, but I don't keep secrets from them. Or I usually don't.

"It's still new, and I don't want to deal with a hundred questions about it today. Oliver invited me to the party at Josh Wick's house tonight, so everyone will find out then. I don't want to deal with everyone else weighing in or having an opinion on our relationship. It's new and I'm still figuring things out."

"Fair enough. I won't bring it up again while we're with the whole band. I make no promises about after the competition, though." A mischievous smirk lights up Carter's face.

"Fine. Let's go before we miss the bus." I throw my van in park and we jump out, rushing so we aren't any later than we already are.

CHAPTER 61
OLIVER

"Is there a reason we're at the very top of the bleachers?" Lynn asks from next to me.

"It's better for pictures of the whole band…" I trail off. I didn't tell Kaylee that I was planning on coming to her marching competition.

Now that we're here, I feel like I should have mentioned it last night. I know she agreed to be my girlfriend, but she didn't invite me to come today. I just heard her talking about it with Carter earlier in the week. It seemed like a good boyfriend thing to do to come and support her. But now I'm hiding in the stands and wondering if it was a good idea after all.

"Fine. I didn't tell her I was coming, and I'm worried about how she'll react."

"If she's your girlfriend and cares about you, she'll be happy." Lynn rolls her eyes.

"But she didn't even tell me about this competition. Won't she think it's weird I just showed up?"

"No, because it's not weird. If she reacts funky, just tell her I was coming to support Andrew and asked you to come with me." Lynn shrugs.

"But that's the opposite of what happened. I dragged you here so I wouldn't be by myself. I'd rather she thinks I'm a stalker than a liar."

"Then there's your answer. Stop stressing about it. She'll think it's adorable, or I can throat-punch her for you. Now can you just shut up and take pictures until you're not anxious anymore?" Lynn crosses her arms.

"You're grouchy."

"Well, I slept bad and then someone called me at the butt crack of dawn to go with them to a marching contest." Lynn leans back on the wall behind us.

"You got to sleep the whole hour drive here." I called her at seven thirty and we left at eight. I get up earlier for school every day.

Lynn pulls out her phone and makes a show of unlocking it and looking at it. "What do you know? It's still the morning."

I give up on talking to Lynn when she pulls her sunglasses out of her bag and rolls her hoodie up behind her head like a pillow. She settles in like she's going to take a nap using her letterman like a blanket against the early morning chill. Considering her ease at sleeping anywhere that isn't a bed, I'll probably have to wake her up when our band is up.

I look at the program which shows that Carson Valley doesn't perform for another hour and a half. If I'd actually talked to Kaylee about this I would've known that we didn't need to leave as early as the band. I thought that might be the case, but didn't want to risk missing their performance. Now I have an hour and a half of watching other bands before they even come out.

It makes me glad I only told Lynn about this and not the other Knights. Lynn might complain because it's the morning, but after her second nap she should be back to her amicable self. The other Knights would have given me grief about showing up uninvited with no information.

Plus, the teasing from having a new girlfriend. I know they support me and are happy for me, but they show that through picking on me. I'm nervous enough without them piling on. With Lynn napping, I'm left to my own devices and get to enjoy the quiet around us. No one else wanted to climb all the steps to be up here at the top.

They announce the first band, and I watch my first marching show. In junior high I was always at the concession stands during halftime with the Knights, and now that we play in high school football, half-time is spent in the locker room. It amazes me how the band manages to play music while marching and making these different shapes and designs. I'm still struggling with the guitar and that's when I'm sitting with music sheets in front of me.

I get absorbed in everything: the music, the band, the people waving flags around. Time slips away and I'm startled when they announce Carson Valley to the field. I gently nudge Lynn awake. I've never understood how she struggles to sleep in her quiet room at night, but she can sleep here with all the noise and chaos around us.

Lynn sits up and shakes her letterman off since it's heated up with the sun coming all the way out. I'm a bit warm in my jeans and T-shirt. I don't know how the bands are surviving in long sleeves.

Looking down at the field, I have no idea where Kaylee is. They all look the same. I finally find the trombones but I'm not sure which one is Kaylee. Andrew is easier to pick out since there's one trombone player that is significantly shorter than the rest. I try to keep him in sight as I take pictures—hopefully, that'll mean Kaylee is in some of them as well.

The first song ends, and I realize I've missed the whole band from being too focused in on the trombones. I zoom out and quickly get a picture of the entire band before they start their next song.

The rest of their performance blurs by and they're marching off the field. I'm bubbling over with excitement and turn to Lynn who is in the process of putting her phone up.

"I videoed it for you. I don't know camera angles or anything. I'm not you. But I figured it'd be better than nothing." Lynn shrugs.

I wrap her in a bone-crushing hug. "Thank you."

I release her and she shrugs again. "You photograph and video all my games. I took one subpar video. It's not a big deal." Lynn is blushing like she always does when we say something about her doing things for us.

She looks down as she packs her bag back up. She pulls out a protein bar for each of us—strawberry for her and blueberry, my favorite, for me. She might complain about being up this early, but she's the one who still managed to make time to pack a snack.

We finish our food. Lynn finger-combs her hair before pulling it up in a hair clip and getting herself unrumpled from her earlier nap. We watch a couple more bands before our band joins the stands.

Lynn nudges my arm. "Come on, let's go see your girl."

I feel like I'm walking over to a firing squad, which is ridiculous. It's not like Kaylee is going to break up with me for coming to support her. She'll probably be happy. It doesn't seem like she has a lot of support at home.

Lynn elbows me. "It's fine. You'll be fine, and I'll be right there offering moral support. Or distracting her friends so you can have a conversation without an audience."

We get to the band. Kaylee has her back toward me, talking to Carter and Andrew. Carter points in my direction and Kaylee turns around.

I was not expecting a deer-in-the-headlights look when she saw me. Maybe my anxiety was justified.

CHAPTER 62
KAYLEE

Our performance was good. I'm sure we'll hear on Monday how it could've been better, but that's Monday's problem. I'm just looking forward to relaxing and eating with my friends before we head home. I've just about decided on the perfect outfit for tonight when Oliver and I will officially be out as a couple.

I'm thankful Carter has kept to his word and didn't bring it up on the bus ride. I'm already a bit worried about how tonight will go. Popular parties aren't exactly my scene to begin with and I'll be walking in on the arm of one of the Knights of the school. It's not the type of spotlight I enjoy.

We have two bands to watch before we get to go eat lunch and come back for our scores. I'm glad this festival announces each class as they go and we don't have to stay until the very end to find out our place.

I'm talking with Drew and Carter about where we're eating lunch when Drew's eyes go wide.

"What?" I swipe my hand across my face like there might be something on it. Something other than sweat and slightly smeared makeup, anyway.

"Can we talk about it now?" Carter vibrates with energy.

"Talk about what?" I have a gut feeling I know what he means. I just don't know why he's bringing it up now.

"Turn around." Carter gestures behind me.

I turn and there is Oliver as if I had summoned him with my thoughts. Clearly, it's not my imagination because not only do my friends obviously see him, he's with Lynn. I don't think I'd ever intentionally manifest her presence anywhere. Especially not here. Not when she looks like her effortlessly, perfectly put-together self while I look awful.

I'm covered in sweat; my makeup is smeared from it and my hair is wet with it. I'm in a band T-shirt, basketball shorts, black band shoes, and knee-high black socks. My shirt is clinging to me due to my sweat. My ponytail is half falling out and my hair is sticking out in every direction. I look like a hot mess and a dweeb all at once.

Lynn is in jeans and a fitted V-neck with her hair pulled up all cute. She has a megawatt smile as she elbows Oliver in my direction. He looks nervous as he walks over to us.

That's when I realize I went from shocked to irritated and now I'm glaring at him. I straighten and smile at him, but it feels forced. I wasn't expecting to see him here. I didn't know he even knew about the competition.

"Hey, Oliver. I didn't know you were going to be here." *Great opener, Kaylee.*

"Uh, yeah. I just heard you guys talking about it this week and thought I'd come check it out." Oliver looks down like he's not sure what to do now that he's here.

"Y'all should come to lunch with us," Carter adds from behind me.

Crap. The entire band is probably watching this interaction.

"Oh, uh." Oliver looks back up to me. "Would that be okay?"

"Of course. Yeah, that'd be great." I go to tuck my hair behind my ear and am reminded that it's partially plastered to my face with sweat. *Great.*

"Lynn, you can come sit over here and Drew can teach you how marching band works." Carter has decided to play matchmaker. At least it means Lynn is with Drew instead of Oliver and we're being left alone for the time being.

Lynn makes herself at home, seated between Carter and Drew like they weren't complete strangers a couple of weeks ago.

"I hope it's okay that I'm here. I just thought supporting you here would be a good boyfriend thing to do." Oliver shrugs and looks embarrassed.

"No. It's great. Really. I'm just surprised, is all. I didn't know you were paying that close attention to what my friends and I talk about." I shyly look down and decide now is as good of a time as any to sit down.

Oliver sits next to me and gently places his fingers under my chin, lifting my face up. "I pay attention to everything about you." Oliver leans over and kisses me.

I'm about to get lost in the kiss when I get thumped in the side.

"No PDA, or Mr. Gregory will have us doing arm circles until our arms fall off. Save it for later." Carter turns back around and acts like he didn't just thump me.

"What are arm circles?" Oliver looks confused.

"It's where you hold your arms at a ninety-degree angle and move them in circles. It's part of our warmup during summer band and Monday night practice. It's also Mr. Gregory's favorite punishment." Oliver's kisses might just be worth it, but I don't think the rest of my section would agree and Mr. Gregory strongly believes in succeeding or failing together.

It's nice to just sit next to Oliver, though. He asks me a continual flow of questions about marching band, and it feels like I have given him a crash course by the time we go to lunch.

Oliver doesn't seem to notice or care that I'm a mess right now. His eyes keep bouncing back between the bands on the field and me. It's like he doesn't want to look away from me, but still wants to see the bands and follow what I'm saying. His arm brushes mine continuously. It makes me want to take his hand in mine, and I wish Mr. Gregory wasn't so strict with PDA.

Lynn and Oliver fit right in with my friends. I don't know what I was expecting since they've always gotten along at school and the few times we've eaten together. But those times have all been on Lynn's turf, with all of her friends and at her house. She seems just as relaxed around all the people she barely knows. She's nice to everyone that comes up to talk to her, but she never leaves Drew and Carter's side.

I sort of expect her to when some of the more popular kids come up to talk to her. They invite her to their table, but she declines, saying she's comfortable where she's at. Maybe that's a good sign for Drew after all. I guess I can learn to tolerate Miss Perfect all the time since she clearly makes Drew so happy. His smile hasn't dimmed since she started talking to him.

I get to hold Oliver's hand under the table while we eat and get my first taste of what being his girlfriend outside of the bubble of us will be like. He's attentive and sweet. He carried my food for me and even pulled my chair out for me. I mean, we're still eating McDonalds, but him being here makes it seem almost romantic.

There's some pointing and whispering. But either Oliver doesn't notice it, or he ignores it. His focus stays entirely on me, only deviating to occasionally respond to something Carter says. Thankfully, Carter mostly minds his own business and keeps to his conversation with Drew and Lynn.

Maybe being with a popular jock isn't as bad as I made it out to be. If it's always like this, I could get used to being the center of Oliver's world.

CHAPTER 63
DANIEL

"Don't you have houses of your own to go to?" Xander asks when Oliver and I don't go home after church. "And aren't they, like, next door?"

"Hardy har har." I roll my eyes. "You're so funny. If you must know, we were gonna hang out and wait for Lynn and Grayson to get back."

"That worried about damage control?" Xander heads up the staircase and we follow behind him.

"I'm hopeful that everything will go well," Oliver says. "I mean, Grayson has been hung up on Lynn for a couple of months, and everything was fine when they went axe throwing by themselves. I know that wasn't a date, but no one else was there and no one was maimed."

"But this is a real date, and they knew that going into it," I add as we get to Xander's room. "I don't know if Grayson will be able to rein himself in and take it slow. I'm worried he'll dump his months of pining on Lynn all at once. I'm hoping if it does seem like a lot, having us here to break up any potential tension will give them a better chance overall."

"Basically, showing Lynn that her friend-group safety net is still here so she can give things a real chance?" Xander shuts his door behind us.

"Something like that," I admit.

"So, do you think they'll be good together?" Xander sits on his bed.

"They've been friends their whole lives, and they fight less than Lynn does with Jet or Tristan. Grayson seems like he's ready to try to have a serious relationship, so I think it could work." Oliver sits in Xander's desk chair.

"I don't know what type of lasting power they'll have, but I don't see any reason it'd end super badly." I plop on the comfy chair at the foot of Xander's bed.

"Sounds like you're already ready to pick up the pieces when it ends." Xander rummages around in his nightstand.

"Eh, I mean it'd be great if they're endgame material. But to be realistic, the longest relationship either of them have had is like a month. It could be because they're meant to be and that's why nothing else has lasted, but I'm reserving judgment on that until they've lasted longer than one date. A date we don't know they've survived yet." I shrug.

"Hey, if I can get the girl, so can Grayson," Oliver says. "I've been crushing on Kaylee for about the same timeframe, and we're officially dating now. She even said she'd wear my extra jersey to school this Friday."

"Yeah, but you're good at relationships and commitment," Xander points out. "I think growing up you took those skills for yourself and that's why none of the other Knights know how to commit." He finally pulls his script out of his nightstand.

"Hey, just because I don't want to be in a committed relationship doesn't mean I'm not capable." I take the proffered script.

"Suuure." Xander rolls his eyes. "Anyway, congratulations on your new relationship, Oliver."

"Thanks. I still can't believe she said yes."

"Of course, she did. You're a great guy. If we're being honest, you're probably the best of the Knights. You definitely are when it comes to relationships." I flip to the first act in the script.

"Yeah, I guess." Oliver blushes.

"Everything with y'all seemed like it was going fairly well at the party last night." Xander refers to Kaylee and Oliver dancing close before blowing off the rest of the party together.

Parties aren't their scene, so they left early. From Oliver's blushing when asked about it earlier, I'm pretty sure there was plenty of kissing when he dropped her off at her house.

"It was great." Oliver smiles and ducks his head to hide his blush.

Sensing he doesn't want to talk about it, I shift gears. "First act, scene one?" I look at Xander.

Xander nods. "Yeah, I'd like to go through it all if we can."

I continue to run lines with Xander while Oliver takes pictures and fiddles with his phone. When he's distracted on his phone for a bit, I snap a quick picture of him. Mama Kingston complains about not getting enough Oliver pictures because he prefers to be behind the lens.

We've run through Xander's entire script for the winter play when my phone goes off.

"Oh, looks like we're about to find out how everything went. Lynn just texted saying they're five minutes out and she's planning on coming in the front door." I read the text off my phone.

From the other side of the door, we hear: "Front door. Mission is a go."

We rush out of the room to see one of the twins running down the stairs. We spend a couple of minutes chasing down and catching Parker. Once we have him caught, he refuses to say where Sean is, so we leave him with Colten to watch for a few minutes.

Xander goes in search of Sean while Oliver and I go to warn Lynn and Grayson. The last time the twins were at the door when Lynn got home from a date, they pantsed the guy and sang that annoying tree song for months.

Needless to say, none of us want them to pants Grayson, and we definitely don't want to hear them singing about Lynn and Grayson sitting in a tree. That'd be awkward no matter what, but more so if they don't stay together.

We open the front door to warn them at what is probably the worst moment, especially if you'd ask Grayson. Their lips have barely met before they're jumping back and looking at Oliver and me by the door. If looks could kill, Grayson would've murdered both of us. Lynn looks surprised and slightly embarrassed.

"Um, sorry. Sean and Parker were headed this way." I feel a bit uncomfortable with this situation.

"Ugh, what's their obsession with crashing the end of my dates?" Lynn complains.

"My guess would be since there was a time they snuck up on you and got to pants someone, they're hoping this is a moment of weakness and they can have repeat 'success.'" Oliver uses air quotes and everything.

"Well, I guess I'll see you at school tomorrow." Grayson clearly gives up on having any more alone time with Lynn.

"See you tomorrow. Good night." Lynn blushes slightly.

"Night." Oliver follows Grayson across the street.

"Want me to head out or do you want to talk about it?" I ask.

She shrugs. "Not much to talk about. It went well. I had a good time. I obviously let him kiss me good night, even if that kiss was shorter than either of us expected. It was too short to know if it was a good kiss, you know? I mean it wasn't awkward or anything."

"Not awkward is a good thing."

"Yeah. I think I'll have to wait to see if there are sparks."

I raise an eyebrow. "So, that sounds like you're planning on another date…?"

"Yeah. I mean, I think so. We didn't exactly talk about it because you know. But I'd be on board with another date. But since I asked him on this one, I'm going to wait and let him ask me on the next one in case we aren't on the same wavelength."

I laugh. "I'm pretty sure the death glare Oliver and I got for interrupting your kiss says you're on the same page. I wouldn't be surprised if he asks you out again tomorrow."

"Maybe." Lynn looks unsure but hopeful.

"Well, if you don't need to do a whole debrief, then I'm going to head home and go to bed."

"Good night, Daniel." Lynn hugs me.

"Good night." I walk next door. I'm glad their date seemed to go well and there's no fallout or issues to deal with yet.

CHAPTER 64
DANIEL

The next morning, Lynn rides with me to school because her mom needs her SUV to take some of her younger brothers to the dentist today. We're halfway to school when my phone starts going off constantly with messages. I wonder what could be going on during first period that'd cause my phone to blow up, but I have to wait a few more minutes to get to school.

Lynn seems to be ignoring any messages she's getting. She's doing her usual zombie morning routine of drinking Dr. Pepper and hating the sunrise. I pull into the parking lot and pull out my phone. I ignore the texts from everyone else and open up the string of texts from Xander.

Xander: You need to check the school's Insta, then show Lynn

Xander: Let me know you got this

Xander: I'm working on getting the admin to take it down, but I'm pretty sure everyone has seen it already

Xander: Lynn needs to see it before she gets here

Xander: Please say you're getting these

Xander: Daniel

Xander: Please answer

Caballero: Dude chill. I just parked. I'll check Insta now

I pull up the school's Instagram page and have no words for the post that was posted then shared to the page's story to maximize the number of people who'd see it. It's a picture that must have been taken last night and then was taken completely out of context.

In the picture, Lynn and Grayson are kissing. The door is open, and Oliver and I are standing behind them and appear to be watching them. The picture looks bad enough on its own, but it's captioned with '#whychoose?' which makes it so much worse.

I was there and know everything was entirely innocent, and yet, I'm having a hard time not believing the narrative that's being weaved. This is bad and going to be even worse when Lynn sees it. Not to mention, Grayson and Jet are liable to lose it on whoever did this, if they can find them.

"Um, Lynn? I want to start by saying no one who knows you would believe the nonsense that's being implied, but you need to look at this post." I hold my phone up for her to see.

I then watch as Lynn goes from zombie to shocked to defeated. It hurts to see her start to close in on herself as she seems to let this cyber-bully win. I send a quick SOS text to the Knights and to Xander and let them know where we are.

"Hey, it's obviously bullcrap. You don't need to worry about it." I don't even sound convincing to my own ears.

"Really? Because that picture looks pretty convincing to me. It's even worse when you keep swiping."

I look back at the post and realize there are more photos than just the initial picture.

The second photo is of Jet and Lynn making out after the Home-coming dance during Seven Minutes in Heaven from Spin the Bottle.

The third photo is of Lynn and Tristan making out at some football game freshman year.

The fourth picture shows Lynn sleeping on my shoulder on the way home from a basketball game last year.

The fifth picture is of Oliver giving Lynn a piggyback ride at one of the festivals this summer.

The sixth picture is of me hugging Lynn at the Homecoming carnival when she's wearing Grayson's letterman.

The seventh is a group picture we took at the lake this summer where we're all standing in our swimsuits and Lynn is lying across our arms.

The pit of dread in my stomach gets bigger with each photo. This looks bad. Before I can come up with anything else to say to try to make this better, there's a knock at my window.

The other Knights are there and are livid. I get out of my truck. When Lynn makes no move to get out on her side, I walk over there and open her door. The rest of the Knights follow.

"Come on. It doesn't matter what pictures were posted or what rumors are flying. You haven't let bullcrap rumors get to you before and you aren't going to start now." Oliver leans over my left shoulder.

"Yeah, we know the truth and anyone with half a brain knows that post is nonsense. It'll blow over," Tristan adds.

"And when we find out who did it, we'll make sure they can never do anything like this again." Jet has an edge to his voice that promises pain.

"Regardless of what happens today, we'll get through it together, like everything else life has thrown our way." Grayson is aggravatedly pacing.

"I don't know that this is an issue we should face all together." Lynn's voice lacks all emotion.

"What are you saying?" Grayson stops and stares dumbstruck at Lynn.

"I'm saying whoever this is, they're implying that I have a harem and you all are a part of it. It may be better overall and especially for y'all to have some distance from me." Lynn's shoulders slump.

She's still staring out the windshield and has made no move to get out of the truck.

"That's not happening." Jet sounds somehow angrier. He steps up next to me and effectively shoves me out of the way.

He unbuckles Lynn's seatbelt and grabs her hips, turning her to face toward him. He grips her chin in his hands and makes her look at him as he speaks. "We're with you every step of the way."

"Yeah, we aren't abandoning you," Oliver says.

"You're stuck with us." Grayson steps in close to Jet and Lynn.

"You couldn't get rid of us if you tried." Tristan smirks

"You're my family. A misleading post on the internet doesn't change that." I make eye contact with Lynn over Jet's shoulder.

"Last time I checked, my sister was a thick-skinned, brave, hard-core boss who doesn't let anyone push her around or tear her down. So, let's go show them that a few pictures and words aren't going to get to you." Xander reaches his arm through Grayson and Jet to offer his hand to Lynn.

"Okay." Lynn's finally kicked into motion by Xander's words. She takes his hand and steps out of the truck.

"I got the post taken down. Now you need to ignore the rumors and drama for the nonsense they are and this'll blow over. You're the toughest person I know, and you're definitely tougher than this." Xander pulls Lynn to him for a brief hug.

"I'm still not sure about us all walking in together." Lynn looks around at all of the Knights.

"We don't have anything to hide, and that post is stupid. Hiding is only going to add fuel to the fire. We face this head on, and we face it together." I walk on Lynn's side opposite Xander.

"Okay." Lynn nods her head and looks like a little more life is coming back inside her.

The bell releasing first period rings as we walk in the door. The hallways flood with students who are not so subtly pointing and whispering.

We hold our heads high and ignore them as we walk through the hall like we own it. We all get our stuff switched out at our lockers, then head to English with Lynn. Andrew and Carter greet her and Xander like it's any other day, and I see some of the tension leave Lynn's shoulders.

Kaylee, who was walking with them, falls into step with us as we turn away from the English classroom. We get halfway down the hall before some blond guy in black skinny jeans and a too-tight V-neck steps out directly in front of us. He looks like an emo-rocker wannabe, and I'm not in the mood for whatever he has planned. I'm already over today, and the smirk on his face says he's only coming to stir up trouble.

"What do you want, James?" Kaylee says from somewhere to my left, clearly aggravated.

I guess this is the guy in Kaylee's band who has been causing problems for her and Oliver. I'm sure he didn't take it well that they're officially together.

"Oh, I wanted to catch the Ridire brothers before class. I was wondering if they both prefer to date skanks or if it's something that happens to them because they don't know better," James says casually as if he's discussing the weather not attacking Kaylee and Lynn.

"Kaylee and Lynn aren't skanks. Those pictures are taken wildly out of context. You should mind your own business," Oliver bites out, angrier than I think I've ever seen him.

"I could be wrong about Lynn. I don't know her. But I know Kaylee puts out, or she does for me, anyway." James shrugs.

Kaylee shoves him as she storms past him down the hall.

"That may as well be an admission of guilt. Sorry to burst your bubble. You may be a white Knight, but Kaylee's no princess. She's more of a witch who clearly caught you under her spell. Best of luck to you." James shrugs again then saunters away.

To be continued in *Tutoring Her Knight.*

Thank you so much for taking the time to read my book! I hope you enjoyed it! If you'd like more of these characters I created, sign up for my newsletter to receive bonus scenes that include the Homecoming dance from Grayson's POV, the game of Spin the Bottle, and more. Get on the list at:

Kaitynorrissbooks.com/newsletter

For additional bonus content like the lyric sheets for Outnumbered by Hysteria's songs, the characters' class schedules, and *Her Knight in Shining Football Pads* coloring pages, visit my website here:

Kaitynorrissbooks.com/bonuscontent

If you loved this book and want to help get it into the hands of more readers, please leave a review. Reviews are the lifeblood of indie authors, and I love and appreciate each one!

You can find me on Instagram and Facebook. I'd love to hear from you!

tinyurl.com/KaityFacebook
tinyurl.com/KaityInstagram

ACKNOWLEDGMENTS

Thank you to Elizabeth Stevens, Judy Corry, Kerry Evelyn, and Anabelle Raven for inspiring me to write, believing in me and my book, and encouraging me along the way. Izzie, I don't think this book would've existed without your insistence that I could be more than just a beta reader with good ideas. Kerry, thank you for all of the advice and help along the way. You made this journey a lot less bumpy than it would've been otherwise. Carla, thank you for reading my book and helping me bring out the story I wanted to tell.

To Kaylah, thank you for a beautiful character art that brings Kaylee and Oliver to life. Your graphics are truly priceless works.

To Jozy, Kaylah, and Zach, thank you for the hours you spent listening to me talk about these characters and helping figure out just what they were going to do. I'm glad y'all love these characters as much as I do. Thank you for your friendship; I love the time we get to spend together.

To my beta readers, thank you for making time in your lives to read my story and help me make this book the best it could be. Carla, Jane, Shanna, Andrea, Violet, and Katelyn your input was invaluable.

To all of the amazing teachers I had growing up, thank you for helping me become the person I am today. Many of you taught me way more than the curriculum. Thank you for how much you pour into every child you teach. A specific thank you to those who made a difference and allowed me to pay tribute to them through my book: Mrs. Barnes, Mr. Gregory, Mr. Rhone, Ms. Yaya, Coach Burross, Mrs. Kreuger, Mr. Box, Coach Coker, Mrs. Young, Mrs. McCauley, Ms. Harder, Mrs. Gibson, Coach Taylor, and Mrs. Heuring. A special thank you to Mrs. King who taught me to read: thank you for taking your time to help me overcome my struggles and discover a love for reading. This book would not have been possible without you.

To Precy, thank you for polishing my book and making it shine. It was a pleasure working with you. I appreciate all of your input and time you invested in my book.

To Granny and Grandaddy, thank you for always being there for me through the ups and downs. I wouldn't be who I am today without your continual love and support.

To Riker, thank you for believing in me and supporting my dream of becoming an author. Thank you for finding a way to make my ideas work and fit into our life, or sometimes how to fit our life around my writing. Thank you for making this book a reality and encouraging me along the way.

And to God, enough could never be said about how You've watched over me my entire life. Thank You for these ideas and the characters that live in my head. I'm so thankful I get to bring them to life and set them loose in the world.

And to everyone who reads and reviews my debut novel, thank you from the bottom of my heart.

ABOUT THE AUTHOR

Kaity Norriss was born and raised in Texas where she lives with her amazing husband and their goofy dog. She loves heartwarming stories about characters going through real life struggles. When she's not writing, Kaity is a camp nurse by summer and school nurse by school year. Kaity loves reading, superheroes, heavy metal music, and owning a ridiculous number of Converse.

To find out more and sign up for her newsletter, visit Kaity at Kaitynorrissbooks.com/newsletter

Facebook: tinyurl.com/KaityFacebook
Instagram: tinyurl.com/KaityInstagram
Goodreads: tinyurl.com/KaityGoodreads
Amazon: tinyurl.com/KaityAmazon
Bookbub: Tinyurl.com/KaityBookbub

www.ingramcontent.com/pod-product-compliance
Lightning Source LLC
La Vergne TN
LVHW041104080826
845145LV00007B/1688

9781966907008